THE MAN IN THE WALL

ALDHILL MYSTERIES
BOOK 1

KJ LYTTLETON

MIRAMUS BOOKS

Copyright © 2024 by KJ Lyttleton

All rights reserved.

No part of this book may be reproduced in any form or by any electronic or mechanical means, including information storage and retrieval systems, without written permission from the author, except for the use of brief quotations in a book review.

Cover art by Alex Milway.

ISBN: 9798303728288

A NOTE FOR AMERICAN READERS

The Man In The Wall is written in UK English. For you, that will mean an awful lot of extra vowels, for which I apologise. You might also notice some different past participles as well as some stray Ls scattered about the place. In many cases, there will be an S where you would prefer a Z. I hope you can forgive all this.

If in doubt, please assume it's a UK spelling, not a typo. (That's my story and I'm sticking to it.)

PROLOGUE

THE MAN IN THE WALL

He wakes just as the dust begins to settle, although the air is still thick with it. How long has he been in there? He isn't sure. There is scarcely any light, even after his eyes become accustomed to the dark. Not that he could look around even if he wanted to; his head is wedged to the left and he can't move it. In fact, he realises, panic rising within him, he can't move any part of his body.

Why?

He can't quite place himself. Where is he? His head feels woozy and confused, and he can't recall how he got here, in this dark and dusty space, caged in on all sides. He tries once again to move, sliding his head along the wall, scraping his cheek, but he only succeeds in dislodging some more building rubble onto his face. Its direction of fall helps him orientate himself, gravity doing its thing. He is upside down.

The feeling of panic rises in him again and for a third time he tries to move.

'Help,' he calls, the sound coming out as a feeble croak, full of dirt and terror.

Shortly after, he loses consciousness again.

The next time he wakes, he has the sense that it is dark. Somehow it is even gloomier in his prison of dust and sand, but that isn't why he knows it is night. It is a feeling, a sense that the world is quieter. Few cars pass and the birds are silent. As he listens, he begins to hear other noises, night-time noises. The soft tread of mice somewhere near his head, perhaps even a rat or two, and, in the near distance, a fox chattering a shrill, obsequious greeting to a lover or relative.

His face feels colder, as though a cool night breeze is reaching him even down here.

His tomb.

The thought comes to him with a shudder. He wants to wriggle and scream, but neither his body nor his mouth will obey him. Parched. His throat is dry, shrouded in a sheet of cement. He knows the taste from years of working on site. Years of eating sandwiches covered in grime.

He knew it would come for him, eventually. Or rather, he feared it would. He doesn't get to have the happily ever after. And yet, a part of him thinks, why not? Why should he be forced to give up some kind of offering to the universe? People far worse than him have been able to live long and prosperous lives, suffering nothing more than a melanoma from all their sun worshipping. And they are easily removed, easily forgotten.

But it seems his crimes warrant worse than a dodgy mole. The universe has decided. He is to be trapped like Winnie the Pooh visiting Rabbit, grown too big to fit through the hole. He is to be stuck like bread in a toaster, every inch of him held in place by walls on either side.

He read those books to his daughter when she was small – Winnie the Pooh – and then to his son when he arrived years later (their little bundle of joy, beloved by all, his daughter's pet, his wife's sunshine, his own reflection). They loved those stories, the foolish Pooh, the grumpy Eeyore, the tireless Tigger. He thinks of them now, his family, and feels a sob escape.

Tears puddle in his eyes and drip onto his forehead. He imagines they have left tracks in the grey dust that covers his face. His eyes sting. He sniffs and feels more crud enter his airways. His breath is hard to come by. It is enough to stop his sobs and send him into anger. How could this have happened? And that's when he feels the jolt of a memory returning.

Someone pushed him.

He awakes with his heart pounding. He has dreamed he is trapped between two walls, wedged down a cavity like a ragdoll stuck behind the radiator.

He hears a sound and realises it is coming from him. He is howling quietly like a child with a grazed knee.

It wasn't a dream.

His face feels full of blood, and every time his heart beats, his face throbs.

He finds himself laughing, although he isn't sure when it started. The laughter is almost worse than the tears, choking him with detritus that makes him cough and splutter, and, with a small rainstorm of pebbles and sand, he senses his body has moved slightly, dislodging a little to travel even closer to the bottom of the cavity.

What will happen if he reaches the floor of the building?

He can't think about it. He has no movement in his arms or legs; he can only move his face a little, still stuck, looking over towards his left. He is having trouble breathing. If he falls to the floor, he will simply have to kiss the dirt until help arrives.

Help.

Yes, help will arrive, won't it? He just has to hold on until the morning. He tries to take another breath, but his lungs struggle to fill. His family will find him; they know he is here.

He closes his eyes. Sleep comes almost immediately.

MONDAY

ONE

The young woman walked up to the receptionist in the lobby at Virtua Services.

'I'm so sorry to trouble you,' she said, 'but I'm meant to be starting work today, and I'm not sure where to go.'

The receptionist, name-badged as Jessica, smiled brightly behind an expensive-looking tablet secured by a metal arm to the desk.

'Not a problem. Let's get you sorted, shall we? What's your name?'

'Scarlett. Scarlett Stevens. I should be on the system – hopefully.'

The young woman's face lit up with a friendliness that most found hard to resist. Not that Jessica needed encouragement: she too radiated good cheer, and she continued smiling as she typed on her tiny wireless keyboard.

Scarlett Stevens glanced around. The reception was impressive by any standards, but for Aldhill-on-Sea, a faded seaside town on the East Sussex coast, it was positively palatial. From the outside, the Virtua Services building remained the same poorly imagined blot on the landscape it had always been, looming over the genteel Victorian townhouses and quaint Tudor shops with pebble-dashed resentment. But, a decade ago the architects had swept into the interior, retrofitting a monument to minimalism, sweeping away walls and floors, and glazing meeting rooms into privacy-shunning goldfish bowls.

Now, the reception rose all the way to the roof four floors above where vast skylights flooded sunshine into the previously gloomy building. The open-plan workspaces ran around three sides, with opaque glass walkways skirting along each edge, while two diagonal bridges met in the middle to form a platform that seemed to float across the space. Underfoot, giant white floor tiles gleamed like a Hollywood smile and pots of gardenias on the desk sent out wafts of heavenly scent.

Jessica was still smiling, which helped Scarlett Stevens relax. She liked Jessica. Jessica was the sort of person who would have been incredibly popular at school, but for all the right reasons.

'You're meant to be on the third floor, Scarlett. I'll just print off a badge for you and you can head up.'

'Great, thanks!' said Scarlett.

She took her pass, buzzed through a security gate and headed for the lift.

Once she was safely in the metal box, the woman claiming to be Scarlett Stevens took a breath. She caught her reflection, pink cheeks, eyes twinkling. The young woman staring back looked nothing like Scarlett Stevens, who was short and alluring with a wide jaw and a spray tan, not tall and pale like the person in the mirror. The young woman, real name Philippa McGinty – Phil – had to admit she enjoyed the thrill of faking it. This was probably just as well, given her chosen career. As the *Aldhill Observer*'s most junior writer, Phil had already got her foot on a ladder that rewarded tricksters, cynics and sticky beaks. But she was an editorial assistant, not an investigative reporter; going undercover definitely wasn't in her job description.

Still, easier to beg forgiveness than ask permission and all that.

She took a moment to assess her progress. Scarlett's security pass was step one in the plan to infiltrate Virtua Services, East Sussex's largest private sector employer and the company responsible for most of the public sector outsourcing contracts in the county. Step two involved learning as much as possible, as quickly as possible. That is, before someone noticed she wasn't who she claimed to be. Step three was... Well, she hadn't got that far yet: she hadn't had time for anything more complicated.

Phil's opportunity to become an intern at Virtua Services had arrived earlier that morning, and she was still reeling from how quickly she reacted. She had been eating breakfast and scrolling on her phone when she saw it: a post from an old schoolmate, Scarlett Stevens. Not a friend, really, just an acquaintance who had added her and then become a mild irritant, posting out-of-date memes and easily debunked conspiracy theories along with pouting selfies of her makeup contouring efforts.

This latest update was different, however.

'*Sacking off the new job the beach is were its at. it is TOOOOO hot lol!*'

The late September heatwave was apparently too much

of a temptation for Scarlett. The journalist in Phil wanted to add "[sic]" to the end of the post. The precariously employed worker in her wanted to point out that posting publicly about bunking off work probably wasn't the best life choice.

'Her mum's not the brightest spark either,' said her mother Angela when she showed her. 'I remember when she drove round a roundabout the wrong way during her driving test. Then she panicked and just drove over the top of it. She destroyed the floral display sponsored by Blackbrooks.'

Phil would have left it at that and headed into work, still chuckling about Scarlett's post and the Blackbrooks roundabout, had her mother not continued, 'I think it's a job at Virtua, too. Her aunt got her a week's internship. Hardly a long-term commitment, was it? Silly girl. What a wasted opportunity. In HR as well. Good money in HR. Honestly, give some people a gift horse and they'll punch it straight in the mouth, never mind look at it. Right, I'm off.'

Phil was already back in her bedroom, changing her clothes as the front door shut. She put on the closest thing she had to office attire – some wide-legged, high-waisted black cotton-mix trousers that spilled over grubby white pumps and a slate-coloured t-shirt hidden under a deep red bolero jacket. The jacket was almost smart – if you ignored the big black tassels hanging from each sleeve. She had toyed with cutting them off before concluding that the jacket had been too expensive (by her high-street-loving standards). Anyway, she would probably only last for a few hours before someone realised she was an interloper, and she would hate to ruin her tassels for that.

She hadn't responded to Scarlett's post or left any comment. She didn't want to be associated with it. 'Keep your nose clean and don't let anyone else sneeze on you either,' Angela liked to say. She was full of this kind of cut-rate wisdom. Phil often considered putting together a book of her best axioms and selling it at the front counter of a bookstore as a novelty item for Christmas stockings.

'You could call it *Angela's Little Book of Bullshit*,' suggested Angela.

'I'm sure it would fly off the shelves,' said Phil.

Adam Jenkins, editor of the *Aldhill Observer*, had not been impressed when Phil had requested a week off work at the very last minute. But she assured him she would continue to file copy while she was away. That seemed to him to be too good an opportunity to miss: someone who was willing to work during their week off was exactly the sort of journalist he liked to employ. Not that she had a choice. Sure, some of the senior writers could offload their pieces onto a couple of freelance stringers or office juniors when they went on leave, but lowly minions like Phil were expected to simply write all their pieces beforehand, cramming all the same work into half the time. So Adam Jenkins, editor, may have acted all surprised and cheerful when Phil had offered to meet her deadlines over her holiday, but really there was no other way.

'See if you can find me an exclusive while you're away too,' he said. 'Really make a holiday of it.'

'Oh, I will,' she said. Because, while the real Scarlett Stevens was off sunning herself on the beach, Phil McGinty planned to find out who had killed her father.

In the event, no one seemed to bat an eyelid at her clothes when she landed on floor three. There were plenty of people there in jeans and t-shirts – if anything, she was overdressed

– so she was glad she hadn't taken the scissors to her favourite top.

'Rhonda will meet you here,' explained a good-looking woman in her early thirties whose name Phil didn't catch. 'She is in charge of onboarding new recruits. She shouldn't be too long. You can sit here.'

'Thanks,' said Phil cheerfully, sitting at an empty desk and plonking her bag down by her feet.

She only had the very vaguest notion of what Scarlett's job was supposed to be, but Angela had mentioned human resources, and that was good enough for Phil. Her plan, such as it was, was to try to find out what really happened on the day her father went missing. Beyond that, she wasn't sure what she was doing. She had been putting on her work clothes and heading out of the door before she had really come to terms with her decision to impersonate someone else and con her way into a fake job. Jessica at the front desk had been sliding a temporary pass into a plastic sheath with a red lanyard and sending her towards the lift before she had even begun to process any of her choices.

All she knew was that somebody somewhere must have known something about Clive's death. She was convinced of it. Because the story just didn't add up.

'I've got a meeting with the engineer at the St Agnes site tomorrow,' Clive told them at dinner.

'That's starting again, is it?' said Angela. 'About bloody time.'

The new science block had been underway for what seemed like an eternity, various complications holding the project up before it finally restarted – this time with Clive as site manager.

Except, at the inquest, the engineer swore there had

never been a meeting and Virtua Services insisted the building had not been signed off by their health and safety officer. No one should have been on site. And yet, Clive went there. The next day his body was pulled – impossibly – from the cavity wall of the unfinished building.

'Hello, hello! I'll be with you in a minute,' said a woman, rounding a corner grasping a pile of paper and rushing off towards a meeting room. 'I'm Rhonda,' the woman shouted over her shoulder. Half an hour later, Phil was still waiting for this magical 'minute' to happen. As far as she could tell, all of Rhonda's minutes were already taken. Every so often, she would hare past Phil's desk, breathlessly shouting, 'I'm coming!' or 'I haven't forgotten about you' or 'I'll be there in a sec.' During one of her fly-bys Rhonda paused long enough to log her onto the company computer and Phil took the opportunity to have a look around the shared server. She couldn't access any interesting-looking folders, so she opted to check out the company intranet.

Gloria Reynolds, the company CEO, had shared a letter to all staff about an upcoming external audit, which sounded like the biggest thing to happen to the business in anyone's lifetimes. The boss was keen to stress the absolute necessity of complying with all industry regulations, and although the tone was bright and positive, there was an undercurrent of threat. Nestled among the corporate speechifying was a simple message: any industry fine will be held over your heads. *Do not cock this up.*

She checked the human resources section, trying to familiarise herself with words Scarlett should probably know. She read about corporate governance and the latest HR policy changes. Working from home was being reined in; managing career advancement would now be the purview of the employee and not their line manager; the EDI training was being scaled back.

The human resources department would have dealt with the fallout after Clive died. They also had all the personal information Phil needed. She wanted to identify who had been in charge of the St Agnes school project – and who had worked on it. For some reason, when the coroner came to do her report, Virtua's lawyers were unable to say. Apparently, due to a 'clerical error,' it hadn't been recorded. Departments were hazy on the processes. Not one individual from senior leadership could remember anything at all. 'I don't recall' became a kind of slogan for the suits, all of them apparently suffering from a level of short-term memory loss that would alarm a neurologist.

'Like politicians at a select committee hearing,' said Angela.

Next, Phil tried to make friends with the people at the desks opposite. Both were decidedly chilly. The man was slightly more forthcoming. She managed to get his name – Ed Fielder – and a very terse response about his role in the company: something to do with contractor liaison.

'I used to work in construction,' he explained in a strong East Sussex accent, 'so now they use me to translate the corporate bollocks into words a normal person can understand.'

'When did you stop working on site?' said Phil.

'About seven years back,' said Ed.

The year her father died.

'That must have been quite a change?' she said.

He grunted.

'What made you stop?'

His expression grew irritated, as though she were a child asking, 'Why?' for the tenth time in a row.

'I just felt like it.'

He got up then and walked over to the printer, although nothing seemed to be printing. Phil's curiosity wasn't satisfied. If he was on site seven years ago, he may have known her father. But after Ed returned to his desk with a blank piece of paper, he rather pointedly inserted earbuds to listen to music.

The woman – Emma something – was even less friendly. She only managed a tight hello before pointing at her monitor and saying, 'Do you mind? Sorry, I am actually trying to get on with things.' Fair enough, Phil supposed, but also, *what a miserable bunch!*

Instead, she busied herself writing up a couple of short "news-in-brief" pieces – or NIBs, as they called them – for the *Aldhill Observer*. The Hooe United under 11s had just moved to a new Sunday League and were already picking up wins, and an allotment owner had dug up her main crop potatoes to discover the spectacles she had misplaced earlier that year. It was exciting stuff. The NIBS completed, Phil located the stationery cupboard, relieving it of a couple of orange Bic fine tip pens (her favourite) and a stack of sticky notes.

It was frustrating not to have begun searching yet, to still be waiting around for Rhonda's orbit to finally shrink small enough to collide with Phil's desk. Currently, she could see Rhonda writing notes in a meeting room, so she took the opportunity to explore the building, treading the grey carpet tiles around the U-shaped office. The central area – the space that she had earlier gaped up at floating above the reception two floors below

– was used for breakout pods, a variety of soft banquettes and a few isolation booths for anyone wanting to make a private call. Not that the office was noisy; it had the usual mosquito hum of energy-efficient lighting and the deadened acoustics of a building filled with polystyrene ceiling tiles. It turned out, no matter how much the architects and interior designers had tried, they couldn't ever truly shake off the underlying atmosphere of depressing 1970s office. And so the employees blinked under overhead lighting and spoke in muffled murmurs.

And despite the minimalism, the office was festooned with piles of papers around the office, in-trays overflowing and stacks of folders on a few desks in particular, as though the owners were slowly building a wall out of admin. This was not a paper-free office.

But then the day took a more promising turn: she made friends with the office gossip.

Phil liked her immediately. Dee Dee was a woman with short, gamine hair, swathes of costume jewellery and a whole heap of stories. After a brief introduction – 'I work in customer complaints; somebody needs to put me out of my misery' – she had been keen to bring Phil up to speed on all the important goings-on at Virtua. 'Rhonda's the office dogsbody, but I think she likes it. She was her ladyship's PA for many years and I think the power went to her head.'

Her ladyship, Phil assumed, was Gloria Reynolds, OBE, the Virtua Services CEO. Apparently, she rarely made an appearance on their floor. Phil had seen her many times, however, usually standing next to the mayor and other dignitaries at some local event, smiling as Phil took a photo. She looked like a politician, Phil thought, the first time she saw her; all blue power suits and pearls. She was in her early fifties, but her haircut was at least a decade older. Phil's gran would be embarrassed to have a set wave like that. Perhaps she was trying to cosplay as Margaret Thatcher. 'Lamb dressed as mutton,' Angela pronounced.

Dee Dee had a number of passion projects, including her conviction that rude Emma and grumpy Ed were having an affair, and a fledgling conspiracy theory that Jamie the HR manager was the person behind a series of unpleasant anonymous emails.

Phil's eyes lit up at the mention of both the HR manager and the anonymous emails. She needed to find a way to meet this elusive woman and although the emails weren't relevant to her investigation, the journalist in her smelled a story. That said, she was confused by some of Dee Dee's thinking.

'Why would the HR manager be sending rude emails?'

Dee Dee shrugged and leaned in, waves of strong perfume wafting over Phil's desk permeating everything so that for the rest of the day Phil felt Dee Dee was just over her shoulder.

'I have no idea, babes. Maybe it's just out of spite because they won't let her onto the fourth floor.'

The senior management worked on the fourth floor, and had, according to Dee Dee, 'Cushy glass offices with climate control, and serfs bringing them cups of tea and coffee every half hour.' The middle management was on the third floor, suffering the erratic air con, while those in the more nuts and bolts operational roles – 'the people who actually run the contracts our business is built on'– hunkered down on the second floor, 'Never to be seen or heard by her ladyship the CEO.' First floor was sublet to another company, and the fifth floor – the roof – had a 'half-built outdoor cafe and terrace no one seems to have any intention of finishing.' A builder's office is never done, thought Phil.

'She's desperate to get up to the executive level,' Dee Dee said, still talking about Jamie. 'Andrew – the departed HR director – now he was up on fourth, but when he left, no one thought to offer his little backstabber a desk. I'm not being funny, but it's like they forgot she exists.'

As with so many things, Dee Dee had a theory about this.

'I think they didn't want a young woman up there. No offence, but they're all old codgers, apart from Queen Gloria. Their hearts probably couldn't take it, you know? Or their giant egos, for that matter. They like the ladies on floor three where they belong – or bringing them their lattes.'

'But how would sending emails help Jamie get up to the fourth floor?' asked Phil, still unclear about Dee Dee's logic.

Dee Dee simply shrugged. 'Who knows what goes on in people's minds? I certainly don't. And, I'm not being funny, but she was the only one who could have had some of the information that was shared in the emails, you know?'

It transpired that some of Dee Dee's colleagues had been sent messages of a deeply personal nature. Dee Dee hadn't winkled out all the details from her co-workers, but Phil could see that she wouldn't rest until she had. Phil would have continued pumping her new friend for information, but at that moment Dee Dee's line manager appeared and seemed less than impressed to discover her chatting – presumably an all-too common occurrence.

'I'd better get back,' she said.

'Me too,' said Phil gloomily, wondering how she would fill the time now. 'Maybe I should go and see this unfinished roof garden.'

'Go and sit on the wellbeing bench and then no one can tell you off,' Dee Dee suggested.

The wellbeing bench, Dee Dee explained, was one of the

previous HR director's wheezes. Andrew Templeton-Dunbar was Jamie's predecessor, and he was remembered, it seemed, with a mixture of affection and humour.

'Honestly,' said Dee Dee, 'the man was so woke, but then, Scarlett, he accepted the diversity officer role. Would you believe it? Mary – she's in a wheelchair – she could have done it with her eyes closed. Or Paul, poor sod. Totally overlooked. They were both far more appropriate choices, if you ask me. God knows what Andrew was thinking. It was comical. You couldn't make it up.'

After that segue she returned to the wellbeing bench.

'Anyway, this fella killed himself, and Andrew thought it would be a good idea to have a safe space for people to sit when they were feeling miserable. Problem is, I'd need to sit out there all day long and I'm not sure that would go down well.' She laughed raucously and gave Phil an actually quite hard thud on the arm.

'Who was that, then?' said Phil, the pain in her arm distracting her from the nascent dread in her stomach.

'This poor bugger. Clive McGinty his name was,' said Dee Dee. 'He was trapped in a cavity wall – alive, would you believe? Took a day before anyone found him. Doesn't bear thinking about.'

'No,' said Phil. 'It doesn't.'

But sometimes it felt like it was all she thought about.

'I can't imagine why anyone would do a thing like that,' said Dee Dee.

'Me neither,' said Phil.

But she had a week to work it out.

TWO

First day back and Detective Sergeant Jen Collet already had a murder to deal with.

Was it wrong to feel so happy about a dead body?

She supposed it should be, and yet she couldn't help herself. The sheer relief of having something else to think about sent an electrical pulse of happiness through her. It seemed like a long time since she had experienced that emotion – two weeks at least.

Before Nate.

She shook herself. Now was not the time for that. She had work to do. The body, such as it was, had been found last night and because Jen had only just returned from leave, she hadn't been at the crime scene. Now she was standing around the Incident Room trying to take it all in while her colleagues brought her up to speed.

'The cadaver – male – was found in the early hours on the site of the old Helenswood school campus,' said Detective Inspector Lee Hudson.

Jen's boss Lee was brash as a Saturday night in town, but

Jen had to concede he was a good detective – when he could be bothered.

'It wasn't pleasant,' said Grant Pitman 'There was still flesh on the bones in places.'

The journeyman detective constable, pale and pitted, seemed keen to tell her all about the unpleasantness – in minute detail. Luckily, Jen was equally keen to hear it.

'A security guard spotted him. The body had probably been there for a few weeks – hidden in the rubble.'

Hard to believe given the current unseasonal heatwave, but just a few weeks before, an early autumn storm had rattled the building and the outer bricks had collapsed like fresh bread falling away from the knife. The body had been shaken loose from the cavity wall.

'I'm going to go out on a limb here and assume that's not normal?' said Jen. 'Walls don't just collapse in a storm, right?'

'Too right it's not normal,' agreed Lee. 'It's a complete shit show. There will have to be an inquiry.'

'Lucky there were no kids on site,' observed Jen. 'Bad enough to have your young life extinguished by a falling school without the added trauma of being eye to eye with a rotting corpse as you go down.'

Lee eyed her warily as though this gallows humour might be a precursor to collapsing into tears. But Jen's tears didn't come at the thought of death, the tears only came at the thought of the life not lived. All those unfinished plans, all those silly arguments she could never have again.

'I went to that school,' said DC Nandini Roy, idly leaning back in her chair and half-turning to join Jen's informal briefing. 'I used to pray the school would flood or burn down or something. Anything to get out of double maths.'

'Well, looks like your prayers were answered. Do you want to put in a good word for me to win the lottery?' said Jen. 'I could do with a bit of luck.'

Nandini shifted, suddenly awkward. But who could deny it? Losing the love of your life was pretty unfortunate.

'Wasn't this the school that wasted all that tax-payer money?' said Jen, happy to change the subject back to the case.

'That's right,' said Nandini, picking up her notebook. 'The council were paying a bomb to Virtua Services to manage the buildings, do some upgrades and extend the main building, that kind of thing.'

'Oh, yes!' said Jen, remembering. 'The extension was only half built when the school was merged with the boys' school and handed to an academy trust.'

'Right, but Virtua's contract with the council was a ten-year deal,' said Nandini. 'The council was on the hook for the full term. I remember my parents complaining about it when my sister had to move to the boys' campus. They were being paid tax payers' money to clean and maintain an empty school.'

'Imagine being paid to do naff all for ten years,' said Lee, looking a little put out that no one had offered him such a cushy number.

Jen realised with a shudder that the council would only just be coming to the end of the agreement. 'Nice work if you can get it.'

Grant grunted, his belly flaring out as he continued staring at his phone. Jen was sure he wasn't actually listening. The DC had lost interest in the case as soon as he'd given Jen the grisly details and was now back to looking for a late holiday deal to keep his girlfriend from realising she could do better.

'I bet no one was fired for that cock up, either,' said Nandini.

'What was Krista's verdict on the body?' said Jen.

Earlier, while Jen was still mired in HR mental health check ins, Krista the pathologist had taken the rest of the team through what she had so far, and now Nandini read from her notebook, performing an impression of the woman's clipped English alongside her own parenthetical thoughts.

'*Male, early thirties, broken skull – presumably what killed him* (but also not helped by being shoved down the cavity wall of a building) – *and other breaks – some from childhood, one as an adult, others post mortem* (clumsy sod looking at the list). *Teeth all missing – knocked out with something most likely* (i.e., some sicko didn't want him to be identified). *Corpse in situ for at least five years.* (But she's doing more tests before she gives us a definitive date).'

'Could it have been seven years?' said Jen.

Lee glanced up. 'Jen,' he said, a warning tone in his voice. 'What?'

But she knew what. A body in the wall of a school building; they had both heard that before.

Lee changed the subject. 'There will be a full inquiry into what happened with the building. Forensics, building inspectors, and the council are all over it.'

'So you can look forward to reading the report on their findings in about five years, then,' said Nandini.

'And what about Virtua staff? Any missing employees?' said Jen.

'Petra's taking that on,' said Lee, nodding in the general

direction of the detective chief inspector's office. 'Talking directly to the boss.'

'Of course she is,' said Jen. 'Keeping her safe from the hoi polloi.'

'Gloria something,' said Lee, checking his notes.

'Reynolds,' said Jen.

'That's it. Gloria Reynolds OBE dontcha know.'

She did, as it happened. She remembered very well the day Gloria Reynolds, CEO of Virtua Services got her OBE. It was right after a man was pulled from the cavity wall of one of her buildings.

Lee closed his notebook. 'And Grant's checking missing persons.'

'Is he, though?'

'Nothing so far,' murmured Grant, not looking up from his phone.

'Keep up the good work,' said Jen.

Grant ignored her.

'Victim was wearing a sweatshirt for a local business – Prints To Go,' said Lee. 'It shut down a while back.'

'I remember it,' said Jen. 'We used to have these things, Nandini, called photograph albums where we put print outs of our photos. Imagine that.'

'Cute,' said Nandini. I love hearing about the Old Ways. I just contacted the owner of this ancient relic. He's retired, but he said they never had any employees go missing. Says he'd have noticed.'

'You'd hope so,' said Jen.

'Besides, he only ever employed family members and work experience youths and our corpse is too old for that,' continued Nandini.

'Did you ask him what happened to their branded tops?'

'Yeah, he said he couldn't remember, but his wife might have given them to charity. She's dead now so he couldn't ask...'

Nandini tailed off, embarrassed. Jen noticed the atmosphere shift and gave Nandini a withering stare.

'Really? Wow. I'm not made of glass, you know. You can mention dead partners without worrying I'll melt into a puddle.'

There was a ripple of discomfort, as though every buttock in the room had suddenly become clenched. Jen noticed the young constable, the ridiculously named Dean Martin, looking away and felt a flash of irritation.

'And you know what? So what if I did? Who cares? No one's going to die if I start crying. Jesus.'

She rubbed her hand over her head and the anger melted away as quickly as it had arrived.

'Sorry,' she said. 'Shit.'

Now there was a real danger the tears would come after all. She had been so desperate to get back to work, but now she was here she felt the sudden urge to smash through the wall like a cartoon character and run for the mountains leaving only the outline of her body in the brickwork and a cloud of dust. Make up your mind, brain, she thought.

Nandini gave her a tight, apologetic smile and Lee looked at the wall, as though hoping it might render him invisible. Grant glanced up from his phone.

'Anyone been to Turkey?'

Jen picked a tennis ball off his desk and threw it at him. It bounced on his stomach and trundled under a desk behind him.

'Oi!' he said. 'That's signed by Federer.'

'Listen up, everyone,' said Jen loudly as she looked

around the room. 'Just wanted to check if there was anyone here who didn't know Grant owned a tennis ball signed by Federer?'

'Alright, alright,' said Grant. 'Glad to see your sarcasm hasn't been damaged by the grieving process.'

'You're a dick, Grant,' said Nandini as Grant hefted himself out of his chair to collect his ball.

'When's the press announcement going out?' said Jen. She hadn't heard it on the news this morning.

Sideways glances told her something was going on.

'They're keeping it out of the news for now,' said Lee.

'But we're linking this to the Clive McGinty death, right?'

'No, Jen. We are not.'

'But that's crazy! Two bodies down two cavity walls? Possibly around the same time and we're not going back to look at the original case?'

'What's this?' said Nandini, looking from Lee to Jen. 'What case?'

But Jen was still talking to Lee. 'Why not? Did someone senior's golfing buddy get his knickers in a twist about something?'

'Don't, Jen,' warned Lee.

'Don't what? Do my job?'

'Can I have a word, Jen?'

Jen turned to see the beaky nose and beady eyes of DCI Petra Gull as she leaned out from her office door. She waited a few beats, staring back at those glassy brown irises.

'Ma'am,' she said at last, rising reluctantly from the edge of Grant's desk and making her way towards the boss's office.

'Uh-oh,' murmured Nandini. 'You released the Kraken.'

'You're too young for that reference,' said Jen over her shoulder. 'Do you even know who Laurence Olivier is?'

'It was Liam Neeson,' said Nandini, rolling her eyes.

Jen walked into Petra's office with a pressing sense of her own mortality.

'Welcome back,' said Petra, *almost* managing a flicker of a half smile. Praise indeed, thought Jen.

The DCI had arrived over six months ago but still seemed no closer to warming up or fitting in. It didn't help that she wasn't based in Aldhill for most of the time, popping her head in when she wasn't too busy in Eastbourne. When she was there, her attempts at jovial office camaraderie were painful – as though an alien had been given a manual on making friends that failed to explain any of the fundamentals, such as how to smile. When Petra cracked up her face she resembled a ventriloquist's doll invading your nightmares.

'And how are we feeling? OK?' Petra's voice rose to such a pitch that Jen barely resisted the urge to jiggle a finger in her ear hole.

'All good thanks, boss,' said Jen. 'How can I help?'

She was keen to move things along to avoid any more whistle-pitched condescension.

'Clive McGinty,' said Petra, with evident relief that the touchy-feely part of their conversation was over.

Jen could guess what was coming next.

'I'd like you to stay clear of that case at this stage. Lee already knows, but I just wanted to bring it to your attention. As I say, at this stage, until we know more, it would be advisable just to...'

'Exclude a similar case from our investigation?'

'Well,' began Petra, smiling and opening her hands out

like a vicar offering prayers up to God, 'no, I wouldn't put it that way. Just… be a bit cautious about jumping to conclusions that might be wrong.'

'Or might embarrass someone important?' said Jen. 'Ma'am, it's two bodies in two school buildings run by the same outsource building management firm.'

'Clive McGinty killed himself. There was a full inquiry, as I believe you are well aware. You were involved in that case?'

'Yes, I was a DC, and I don't think he killed himself. I never did.'

'And that is where you and the coroner differ. And unfortunately for you, the coroner has the last word.'

Petra had a strained smile on her face. Like a parent pretending to admire a child's painting. Presumably, she was trying to calm Jen down, but it simply made her want to throw something. She took a breath.

'And what about getting a story in the papers?' she said. 'To see if we can drum up some information about our John Doe.'

'I think for the time being we should stick to good old-fashioned policing work.'

'I thought that involved looking for witnesses and comparing similar cases?' said Jen, unable to help herself.

Petra gave her a rictus smile again. 'I know you've been under a lot of stress recently, so if you think this is going to be too much for you, just shout and we'll move you over to something more… appropriate for you.'

'No, I think I'll be able to manage. So, just avoid comparing this death to a similar one and don't appeal to the public for any help? Got it,' said Jen. She was trying for breezy and professional, but landing on tense and irritated.

'Jen.'

A flash of exasperation crossed Petra's face, but Jen didn't wait to hear her reply. She grabbed the door handle and opened it, pointing towards the exit. 'I'll get back to some old-fashioned police work then, shall I, ma'am?'

She walked out.

Still, when Petra joined them in the incident room, Jen did her best to look obedient while the DCI went back over the main lines of inquiry.

'Let's see what we can find out about our John Doe shall we? Teeth records aren't looking hopeful, since he had none...' Jen knew this was not meant to raise a smile, since Petra Gull knew neither the shape, cadence, nor point of a joke. 'But we've got a branded top that suggests he may have worked for a local photography firm. Nandini, I believe you are already investigating that?'

'Yes, ma'am,' said Nandini. 'Dead end, I'm afraid. He never worked there. Although there's a chance he may have got it in a charity shop. I've started ringing round a few, but none of them could remember anything. It's all old people working in those places, isn't it? The person who sold it to him is probably long dead. Besides, who's going to remember a blue top? The Prints To Go logo is hardly that memorable. They should have got my cousin Ajay to design it for them. He'd have made something actually, you know... good.'

'Wouldn't your cousin have been about twelve at the time?' said Grant, looking genuinely confused.

Petra's face displayed a flutter of irritation before she swiftly wrestled it back under control. Normally Jen would be impatient with Nandini's unrelated segues and Grant's bovine stupidity, but she was quite enjoying watching her boss try to keep a lid on her irritation. Pressing Petra's buttons had become an office sport of sorts, with the team taking turns to test her edges, trying to work her out. And there were times when Jen thought she might have finally reached a genuine moment with Petra, only for the chief inspector to stop suddenly and say, 'Well, I think that went well,' as though she had completed her conversation and was now hoping for a good review on the customer service survey that Jen would shortly receive via email. *Five out of five, would chat again.*

Perhaps she was a bot. That might explain things. She wouldn't put it past the Superintendent to bring in the latest technology; he was always banging on about it, despite the fact that the closest thing he ever got to a gadget was when he bought a refillable cartridge for his fountain pen. A week later, ink all over the table, he returned to disposables.

Whatever was going on with Petra, she hoped one of them cracked the code soon, because Jen disliked not getting on with her DCI. She had respected and admired her previous boss, a quietly spoken Welshman who was serious without being officious and fun without making a fool of anyone, and so Petra's arrival had been a shock. It had never occurred to Jen that they would choose someone so impossible to admire. But here they were.

Still, while the DCI was an irritant, she was at least hardworking, which was more than could be said for the detective inspector. Lee seemed more than happy to take credit for Jen's hard work. If she was on a case, he tended to leave her to it. Not that she was complaining, it meant that she could follow her nose wherever it led. And right now, she had a feeling that the local homeless charities might be a good place to start.

'Nandini, did you try Haven for the Homeless?'

'Waiting for them to ring me back,' said Nandini.

'Course you are,' said Jen, feeling a mixture of pride and irrelevance.

Of *course* Nandini was already on the case. She was efficient that way –which only served to make Grant look like an indolent fool by comparison. In truth, he was a pretty solid cop who knew when to suck up to the boss (his allegiance to DI Lee Hudson was legendary), and could be handy in a tight spot.

'Karina's speaking to some of the old timers who might remember.'

As manager of the local arm of Haven for the Homeless, Karina Moore was a regular contact, especially if the police were asked to move on any rough sleepers. Homelessness was a problem here at the seaside, or at least more of a visible problem, which is really all a lot of people cared about, and so police were often asked to move people sheltering in doorways. But Jen took heart in the many local volunteers who made it their business to help people out, and she was convinced it was something that made Aldhill stand out compared to some of the more affluent Sussex seaside towns. Karina was one of the good ones.

'Great,' said Jen, smiling at Nandini. This youngster was already outstripping her.

Petra droned on and Jen thought of Nate, and how if he was at home right now, she would ring him and tell him that Nandini Roy was cleverer than her and less tired than her, and that maybe it was time to think about getting herself promoted after all, or time to retire and get a job in security.

'So,' said Petra. 'I think that went well.'

THREE

Rhonda appeared eventually, still breathless.

'Sorry. I know you've been waiting for me,' she said to Phil. 'Thanks for your patience.'

The woman's pale face was bright red, her frazzled brown hair in total disarray. She seemed to have a stain of something on her blouse (which was half untucked from her suit trousers). Phil had been watching her run back and forth all morning and her overwhelming impression, aside from how busy and harassed she was, was that Rhonda Whitford was a very short woman – probably under five feet. When Phil was sitting down, Rhonda was at her eye level.

Here was a woman, Phil decided, who had never passed a day without feeling overwhelmed, yet who took on anything and everything handed to her. Phil imagined she had never said no to anyone in her life and that she had never been given the credit she was due for keeping the ship afloat. Rhonda was the office's general dog's body. 'Chief-cook-and-bottle-washer,' Angela would call her. She seemed to be running the entire third floor – and without any status whatsoever. People would ask her to do everything, from fixing a jammed photocopier, to advice on how to do their jobs properly.

'Rhonda, how do I make this PowerPoint less ugly?' someone would ask, and Rhonda would spend the next half-hour teaching them.

'Rhonda, I need to book a meeting room,' someone else would say, and Rhonda would get onto the system and find a free slot.

'Rhonda, have you seen the new Telligence supply request?'

'Could you help me with this brief?'

'I need handouts for tomorrow's presentation.'

'The men's toilet on the second floor is blocked again.'

Somehow Rhonda was one of those A-list workers who nevertheless had a Z-list status within the herd. Phil found it irritating on Rhonda's behalf. She didn't like to see someone so capable being treated like this. But she also suspected Rhonda wouldn't have it any other way. After all, if she had been in a true position of power, she wouldn't have been able to interfere with the nitty gritty. And changing an ink toner and summoning building maintenance were things that seemed to give her joy.

She liked people like Rhonda; they were capable, clever and dependable. They also knew everything that was going on. Rhonda was likely to prove vital to discovering more about her father. But for the time being she needed to build up a bit of trust – do a good job. She focused on the matter at hand and listened attentively as Rhonda began introducing her to the company.

'Onboarding' seemed to involve filling in a large number of forms, which felt like a job for HR.

'Normally it is,' said Rhonda, 'But Jamie asked me to take care of it today. She's very busy. We're being audited, you see. That's why we're so glad you're with us, Scarlett.'

Phil did as best she could on behalf of Scarlett. She had created a rich backstory for the girl on the way into work, but now, faced with so many questions (so many opportunities to slip up further down the line by forgetting a detail), she decided to keep it simple: Scarlett was fighting fit, not an allergy in sight, with 20:20 vision and no special requirements. That done, there was an awful lot of reading about fire exits and lifting boxes and health and safety. It seemed all a bit much considering she was only there for one week's internship, but Rhonda liked to do everything by the book.

'We can't have you injuring yourself in the workplace. Not on my watch,' she said. 'Jamie will have kittens.'

Phil dutifully read through everything she was handed and even managed to answer the little quiz at the end that Rhonda set her. Rhonda was delighted with her score.

'Twenty out of twenty! Someone's been paying attention.'

She was beaming as though Phil's success reflected well on her.

'Couldn't have done it without you,' said Phil.

Rhonda flushed a deeper crimson and Phil decided she was sweetened up enough.

'Do you want me to file my forms away for you? I'm good at filing. It's one of my core skills.'

'Oh...' said Rhonda, hesitating. 'Perhaps later. I can show you the HR area. But while we're waiting for Jamie to sort you out, you're going to be helping out the investigations team.'

Phil's ears pricked up at that: *investigations team*.

'Not as exciting as it sounds, unfortunately,' said Rhonda. 'And, I say "team", but it's mostly just Mick in-house. The investigators rarely come to the office – they're always out and about doing their... well, I hesitate to say investigating, but I suppose it is.'

There followed a brief lecture about how Virtua Services held a lot of local contracts to maintain council buildings and facilities, but they also worked for utilities, including an energy firm, digging up roads for the engineers to access the pipes below.

'But sometimes a rival firm or third party contractors might do the work and often they mess it up, causing damage to the pipes. If it's on land that Virtua manages, we send them a bill for the work, along with evidence that they are at fault. The investigations team collects evidence and then puts together a report along with a bill for fixing it. They do the same with us if we break something.'

'Wouldn't it be easier if you just stopped charging each other and called it quits?' said Phil. She was thinking about the cost of employing a team of staff on both sides simply to cancel out each other's fines.

'Who knows what goes through the minds of these great men?' said Rhonda. 'I've long ago given up trying to understand.'

'I guess it keeps us all in jobs,' laughed Phil.

'You're not wrong, Scarlett. Probably best not to over-think it. Your job will be to update the database. A lot of our investigators haven't got to grips with modern tech, so they need you to put together the digital document, and then, once that's all done, we can get the bills sent out. You also need to log the findings coming in the other side. Check through the document, see if it all looks legit. It's fairly mindless stuff. Although you do need to keep an eye out for anything that looks a bit suspicious.'

Phil's ears pricked up again. *Suspicious?*

'I'm all over it,' she said.

Turned out 'suspicious' was overselling it.

Phil spent an hour putting together the case files and the only suspicious thing she encountered through any of it was the name of the wrong company on one of the incoming files. She had put that one into the query folder on the computer and handed the rest over to Rhonda.

'You might try going a bit slower,' said Rhonda when she saw how much Phil had achieved. 'I don't want to give Mick too much of a backlog to deal with. Maybe let's try to keep the pacing to a more realistic level.'

It had never occurred to Phil to purposefully work inefficiently for fear of making colleagues look bad, but she nodded her head and said, 'Right, you are, boss.'

'Let me see if he's got any more for you to do,' said Rhonda.

'I can ask him if you like?' Phil offered, keen to meet another person.

Rhonda looked reluctant. 'No, I think we'll save Mick for now. He can be a bit... funny... with new people. Let me warm him up first.

Apparently, Mick was like an old car. Or leftovers.

Phil watched Rhonda leave and sighed. This was her holiday! What was she thinking? Outside the early autumn sunshine continued blazing. It was into the thirties. She could be swimming in the sea or joining Scarlett and her buddies as they drank rosé and abandoned their chip wrappers on the beach. She could be enjoying the sun's last hurrah before the wind-whipped gloom of a seaside winter descended and everyone huddled indoors in the dark.

She purchased a sad-looking sandwich and a bag of crushed crisps from an Australian who appeared armed with a crate filled with sweating plastic boxes from Arnie's Sarnies. Phil had seen the Australian before around town, a handsome, muscled surfer type, pulling the crate on a trailer attached to his bicycle.

By 11.45am, with nothing better to do, she decided to make a start on the sweaty sandwich. Sitting at her desk chewing warm lettuce, she thought of her dad and smiled. Clive used to eat the most revolting sandwiches known to mankind. He would take them to whatever building site he was working on and leave them out in the sun (or rain) all morning, where they presumably nurtured a whole smorgasbord of bacteria. It didn't trouble him in the slightest. Neither did the inevitable coating of building rubble and cement. He would be tucking in at lunchtime no matter how warm and crunchy that chicken or bacon had got. If anything got him, it should have been food poisoning.

God, she missed him.

He wasn't her real father – not in the strictest sense. For starters, he was black and she was white, which slightly gave the game away. Not that they ever bothered to explain that to people. *Let them wonder.* Besides, the whims of genetics meant he *could* have been her real dad. She certainly felt he was, because the day a six-year-old Phil (still called Philippa at that time) met Clive the builder, they had looked into each other's eyes and seen kindred spirits. That was the day he became her best mate, her guardian and her true dad, and she became his little shadow, his buddy and his angel. And that was that.

If Angela had ever grown tired of her new fella and decided it was time to kick him to the kerb, Phil would have refused to give him up. Luckily, Angela hadn't grown tired of Clive, and the three of them were a happy family unit, soon made even happier by the arrival of Phil's little brother, Lucas. When Angela and Clive got married they asked Phil what she wanted for her bridesmaid gift. She said 'adoption'. So Clive had become not just her step-father, but her legal father, his name on her birth certificate. It had been the proudest day of her life.

Phil finished the sandwich and was about to open the crisps when a thought came to her. She grabbed her things and headed to the lift.

FOUR

Andrew Templeton-Dunbar. It sounded posh, he knew, but actually he had been a grammar school kid from a fairly middle-middle-class house. The double barrel seemed to be some kind of affectation from a recent ancestor: perhaps some bride with romantic notions about her bloodline, feeling too attached to the Templeton name to let it go. Or maybe a father-of-the-bride, distraught at the end of his lineage on the marriage of his only child, had persuaded his son-in-law to take an additional surname.

Whatever happened, Andrew was stuck with the mouthful now. He had toyed with changing it, but it had proven itself useful over the years. When he had started at university, he was the first in his family to go, but his fellow students, private school boys to a man, assumed he was one of them. How he had ended up in an all-boys hall he could never fathom, but the name made things easier, even if he couldn't quite master the other boys' constant banter and their tone of charming condescension towards anyone working in the service industry.

From there, the surname had most likely got him a few interviews. That and the good degree from a good university, he liked to think. His chosen profession – Human Resources – was all about diversity and inclusion, but he could tell from the matey way the HR director at his first interview greeted him that he was getting special treatment. He'd read about this phenomenon: people hire people who remind them of themselves, and in doing so, they often get the worst possible recruits.

But not in this case.

Andrew's boss may have selected him because he seemed like a chip off the old block – he may have hoped Andrew would help them lift this year's Sussex Commerce Charity Golf Cup – but what he got was a man who was good at his job and deeply committed to rooting out attitudes like his. And Andrew kept his head down at first, of course; he wasn't senior enough to make any kind of difference, but he did what he could when he could, taking care not to speak over his female colleagues, ensuring he didn't ask the only black man in the building to speak on behalf of every visible minority.

Yes, yes, he knew he didn't deserve a pat on the back for doing the bare minimum; he knew the bar was set incredibly low. But sometimes, he did like to give himself a bit of credit for making an effort.

He was a good man, wasn't he?

He had been a good man.

Then he got a role at Virtua Services, the biggest outsourcing firm in Sussex, with its eye on large government contracts. His wife Jacqueline had been relieved to leave London, even if Andrew worried it was the end of his career opportunities. But it wasn't long before a position came up for a diversity lead, and his boss had suggested he go for it. Andrew blanched at taking a role designed to broaden their diversity quota, but then it occurred to him: think what he could achieve if he took it.

He could make a real difference!

And so, with some reservations, he had entered his resume, hoping he would lose out to any better candidate. His boss had given him the role in a heartbeat, of course. After all, neither Justin, the only person of colour, nor Mary, who had MS and regularly used a wheelchair, were qualified enough.

'The best man won, fella,' his boss assured him.

Of course, Andrew hesitated before accepting the offer. What right-thinking person wouldn't? It had been a tricky decision. Perhaps the best man (or woman) hadn't necessarily won; perhaps his life experiences weren't the right foundation for understanding the many nuances and challenges of increasing diversity and improving inclusion. But what choice did he have, really? Eventually, he had to concede that he was the only one who would get the job of the three of them. The alternative was to decline and hope that they would bring in someone more suited, but he knew that was highly unlikely. His boss would just employ another doppelgänger who reminded him of himself. And so, thanks to the small-mindedness of his leader and the structure of the company, Andrew genuinely believed he was the best person for the job at that point. He consoled himself with the knowledge that he could at least begin to change the culture from the inside.

And he *had* made a difference.

He made sweeping policies designed to build equity in the workplace and level the playing field. Mary got a parking space right by the entrance. So did any pregnant employees (Facebook COO Sheryl Sandberg gave him that idea in her wonderful book, *Lean In*). He made sure everyone did unconscious bias training. He renamed maternity and paternity leave 'Parental Leave' and didn't discriminate on who took it. He brought in flexible and hybrid working, job sharing and twenty-four-hour office access. He lit up the building in the pride flag colours during Pride Month and made a point never to speak on any all-male panel. After attending a training day that explained how a 'C' grade from a child in precarious circumstances was a bigger achievement than an 'A*' from a privileged child, he changed the employment requirements to allow candidates from any university – and even those without a degree. *Why not?!*

After all, what was he if not the product of luck? He had scraped through the 11+ and gained a place at grammar school, while his cousin – clever, funny, Danielle – had suffered a paralysing attack of nerves and found herself unable to pick up her pencil. She had done fine at her secondary modern, but she never had the opportunities he got, and she soon dropped out of school and married the first boy who asked. He looked at her now, about to become a great-grandmother, working at a supermarket, and wondered what she might have been.

Which is why, as he stared at himself in the bathroom mirror, he knew he was fortunate. Not that he didn't have talent. He knew he was intelligent and thoughtful; humble enough to learn, but inspiring enough to lead. He could have taken on a bigger role, maybe as global HR lead of a large multi-national. Chief people officer for a global FMCG that needed pulling out of the dark ages. He would have brought a lot to a company like that. But he enjoyed making a difference in a *smaller* way, and besides, he had never had any calls from the headhunters, even after he contacted a few to let them know he was available.

Andrew didn't mind. He had forged a happy life here in Aldhill.

When his boss had retired, he was the natural successor. But then the chief operating officer had a stroke in a board meeting, and Andrew was asked to take on a dual role as an interim measure (one which continued until his own retirement). And with those dual roles came true power. Finally, he could make a real difference! For starters, he made a point of hiring a woman as the next diversity lead.

Jamie was young and energetic. She had a reasonable degree from a top university, and she went to private school ('Oh well, you can't have everything,' he told himself.) That she was a niece of Gloria Reynolds, the Virtua CEO, was by-the-by. No one had forced him to select her; she had been by far the best candidate.

Justin had moved on shortly after Andrew was promoted (to the sad detriment of their diversity quota) and Mary was working increasingly from home, which the company fully supported, but was less than ideal for a senior leader. So Jamie had arrived, full of fresh ideas and lots of reverse mentoring for the leadership team, and Andrew had enjoyed working with her.

At the beginning, at least.

After a while, he began to suspect she was very good at talking about her brilliant ideas, but not so good at making them happen. He'd read about that too – people who interview well because they're so charismatic, often end up being incapable of knuckling down and doing the hard graft. At least that was Andrew's interpretation – the article was worded more carefully than that.

She was funny and attractive and everyone liked being around her (especially Rhonda, Andrew noticed, wondering if he should add celebrating "Bi-Visibility Day" to Rhonda's to-do list – she might appreciate it), but Jamie couldn't seem to stick the landing. Rhonda and Mary took on a lot of the grunt work, which meant Andrew still looked like an effective boss, but he began to wonder if perhaps he had made the wrong choice in selecting her as his successor.

Oh well. All that was academic now.

He frowned as he shifted in his armchair. He was stuck on a particularly fiendish clue in *The Times* cryptic crossword. On the mantelpiece, the clock moved towards 1pm. He'd been at it for hours! Such a nuisance – it would ruin his ranking. When he entered the correct answers later to his online account, he would fill it in slowly as penance and leave a comment on the crossword forum confessing it had taken longer than usual. Perhaps twenty minutes instead of the usual ten. That sounded reasonable.

After he had completed the crossword, he would take the dog for another walk and listen to his audiobook. A 'Heinz 57 variety' Jacqueline called her, but he preferred to think of her as of mixed heritage. Then he'd check his emails, send a few out (he liked to keep in touch with people wherever possible) and then fall asleep in his armchair – the calming tones of Barack Obama reading his memoir were incredibly soporific – before reheating yesterday's dinner.

Jacqueline, his wife, still had a part-time job, and she sat on a number of committees, so he often found himself preparing his own meals (as he had at lunchtime today – a rather good ham sandwich with some of the late lettuce that was still growing in the garden) and making do with reheated leftovers from whatever Jacqueline had made the day before. He didn't mind. She was a busy woman – had juggled a career and raising a family – and he admired her for it. If she seemed a little exasperated to have him underfoot quite so much, he put it down to a period of transition they were both going through. Yes, it had been quite a few years now, but he had worked throughout their marriage, and it was going to take a while for everything to settle into a new routine.

He filled in "Abyssinians" for 12 down. He couldn't parse it, but it fitted, so that was good enough. Today, he would have to accept failure.

Just like he had with Jamie.

Just like he had with the St Agnes school incident.

He shook his head. Jamie had been his mistake and that had been bad enough, but St Agnes was the thing that kept him up at night. When early retirement had come knocking, he had accepted it with unexpected relief. Anything to get away from Jamie and his failure. Anything to find a way to forget about what had happened at St Agnes. Failure was not a stepping stone to something better. It was early retirement. It was a frustrated wife. It was endless cryptic crosswords and solitary dog walks.

It was a cuckoo in the nest and a dead employee.

But what could he do? He was a company man. When it came to Clive McGinty, he did as he was told.

He threw down *The Times,* admitting defeat, and laid his glasses on top. Then he groaned with the effort as he rose from his chair and headed out to the hall to collect the dog's lead.

FIVE

Mick looked up as Rhonda approached.

'I've got a whole stack of files for you here, Mick. The new intern's done amazing work on her first day. Looks like you're pretty much all caught up now.'

Rhonda plonked the folders down on his desk.

'All the digital versions are ready to be emailed out with the billing whenever you've got a moment.'

Mick had expected those to keep the new girl busy most of the week, but now he would have to spend the afternoon writing emails and requesting bills from the accounts department. This was irritating; he had planned to finish a bit early today. Not that he was by nature a shirker – he wasn't, he would tell anyone who asked that he had worked diligently all his life – but lately he had begun wondering if there wasn't something more... *worthwhile* he could be doing.

Somehow, the thought of spending the afternoon sorting through case files and billing building companies struck him as pointless – not when the sun was shining and he could be down at the bookies or having a cooling pint outside the front of the Prince Albert listening to the gulls cackling overhead.

He didn't appreciate Rhonda getting involved in his workflow either. *Why is this woman telling me what to do?!* He had been at the company for a long time now – longer than her – and he knew very well how to do his job.

At least he *had*.

Back in the day, he would wait for a fault report call to come in and then he'd head to the scene of the crime to gather evidence for his case file. He lived in an ever-changing sea of cardboard folders – buff and grey and red and blue – all of them colour-coded for their different levels of seriousness and different departments, all of them fastidiously put together and organised.

But at some point technology had overtaken him. Mick wasn't quite sure how or when it had happened. He had started out fairly au fait with it all, and he could type, just about, with two fingers hunting and pecking. He knew how to check his email, so long as someone set the account up for him first, and he could attach photographs after he'd transferred them over from his camera to his computer. But things started to shift and Mick was all at sea. Not straight away, of course; slowly, by increments. He had paddled in the shallows at first, grappling with *Word* and *Excel*, even making a little headway with *PowerPoint*, working out how to use his phone for the photographs. In recent years, he started finding himself wading into deeper waters: he was asked to use some new software that would allow him to create a professional-looking case file and do all the billing requests for Accounts too. IT had paid a lot for it and it included all kinds of extras like 'project status' and 'comments' from co-workers. It also had something called a CRM, which Mick had been unable to fathom (and frankly, didn't want to).

The whole thing seemed over-engineered while also being impossible to navigate. Mick had complained about it to his granddaughter and she said, 'Sounds like it's got shit UX,' which might as well have been Japanese for all Mick understood it. He understood the sentiment, however, and so he responded, 'Yes, it has,' and felt glad a young person had validated his frustrations.

'If it's too hard for you to understand, grandad,' she continued, 'you should refuse to use it. It's not fit for purpose.'

That's what they were like, young people. They had a sense of who they were and what they were worth. Unfortunately, Mick didn't have her confidence. He wasn't convinced an attitude like that would go down well with IT or his managers. So, he opted for a different route: he simply started finding ways to get out of doing the inputting. He claimed the software was broken and raised a ticket with IT to get it looked at. He began to create paper copies of everything claiming the system kept losing files and it was safer to have a paper backup. He made use of the tech-savvy young interns. And, most of all, he relied on Rhonda to do his job for him.

None of it was consciously done, of course. Mick wasn't the sort of person who would knowingly slack off work and let someone else carry the load. Not at first, anyway. He may now be questioning the point of it all, but up until recently it had been a gut feeling rather than an articulate thought. He wasn't the sort for analysis or self-reflection. If you had asked him before, he would say the software truly was broken, the system really did keep deleting files. But in recent weeks he had begun to suspect that perhaps it was *him* who was broken and his memory that was doing the deleting. Hand on heart, he couldn't honestly say if he remembered to save his progress. Perhaps that's where his work kept vanishing to?

And letting Rhonda do his work? Well, who was he to stop her if she wanted to help him out every now and then?

When he was in the navy he had been an eager beaver like Rhonda (albeit less inclined to rush around as though his backside had caught fire). He had made it to chief petty officer, but then something changed. There he stayed, unwilling or unable to advance. He admired the commissioned officers, but only in the vaguest sense, and, when the time came, he decided to retire rather than pursue any further career.

But what to do next? It hadn't been easy identifying a path he could take. He was past forty and rudderless. He spent a decade and a half doing odd jobs here and there, helping out mates on building sites, delivering movie cameras and other equipment in a big white van. And then his passion for the bookies got the better of him and he discovered a pressing need for more money than his navy pension and casual work afforded. With money so tight, around the time when he should have been winding down, he had to start contemplating a role at a local supermarket, or acquiring a used Hyundai and becoming a cab driver. But then he bumped into his old captain.

'Leave it with me,' the Captain told him.

Mick knew he was a man who had always appreciated a hardworking NCO, especially one with native intelligence and deference to rank – and now he had business interests that needed the same skills. That's how Mick ended up moving to Aldhill and running the investigations team. He had no experience of office work, and no qualifications that would get him such a cushy job at his age, but he wasn't about to admit that – to himself or anyone else. If Mick felt nervous walking up to the smiling young girl at reception (long before Jessica's time, but they all seemed baked from the same mould), he wouldn't have been able to recognise it as anything more than mild first-day jitters, the sort everyone experiences going into an unknown situation.

He hid his lack of experience behind quiet, careful words and an understanding of how to pull rank when needed. He was good at not barrelling into a situation: he knew how to watch and learn, and he wasn't afraid to ask questions of his subordinates. Soon he had picked up the basics, and he was confident no one could question his right to be there. These days, he wasn't so sure he was getting away with it.

He glanced up and realised Rhonda was still with him, her finger on his desk, twisting right to left. She blew the hair from her eyes, still a little out of breath from carrying all his files over.

'If you like, I can ask the intern to run you through what she's done, so you can check it's all been inputted correctly,' she said with studied casualness. Mick saw straight through it.

'No, you're alright, thanks Rhonda.' She was offering to get the intern to teach him how to do his job! *This dreadful woman.* She needed to learn to mind her own business.

'Right,' said Rhonda, clearly aware of his stiff tone. 'I'll be off then. Maybe I'll send her over to say hello though, since you'll be working together again, no doubt.'

He knew what she meant by that. Making pointed remarks about his use of intern labour. But what did they expect? They employed him to do a job, and he diligently learned how to do it – was good at it, too. But now? Now he was just expected to be some sort of tech slave or whatever. His irritation began rising. All those years in the navy and he had always been cool as a cucumber, but lately he had been having emotions. It was an alien world to him and that made him angry. He glared at the files again, as though his fury might send them up in smoke.

'What's the new intern like?' he messaged to Ed Fielder, the only person he could stand on floor three (the only one without a stick up their arse who knew the value of a night spent enjoying a few pints in whichever local boozer hadn't gentrified yet).

'Nosey cow,' came the reply. 'Talker.'

It figured. The execs were always banging on about the 'soft skills.' He'd rather shoot staples into his eyeballs than attend one more seminar about emotional intelligence.

He thought again resentfully of what he could be doing instead. He could be eating an ice cream on the beach. He'd been considering taking on an allotment or a beach hut, something to get him outdoors. But all the damn DFLs – Down From Londoners – had colonised them all. You couldn't get a strip of green or a shabby old shed for love nor money down here these days.

He should write a complaint, he thought. Maybe send an email to the local council about this recent influx. Or he could type a letter to the local paper. He'd fired off a few angry emails late at night recently. Perhaps he could compose a note to his MP. She loved turning a dewy eye to the wonder of the British armed forces. Who knows, maybe she could organise a small plot of land for a constituent ex-serviceman.

He looked over at Rhonda, who was chatting to Emma, occasionally glancing his way. His leg jiggled as he mentally composed indignant emails to his local representatives, imagining what he'd like to do to his work colleagues, especially Rhonda and the super-efficient newbie. He had seen her – the new girl – wandering around the office, chatting to people, making herself useful. She was probably after his job. Younger, keener, cheaper, and more able. He should go over there and give her a piece of his mind. He would have loved nothing more than to tell Rhonda and Jamie and all the management to stuff their job up their arses and head off into the sunset in search of that elusive allotment.

But then he remembered the betting accounts, and the loans he had taken out that were accruing interest by the day, and the overdraft and the credit cards. It had started with a flutter and ended with a pile of debt. And what would he tell his daughter – finally talking to him again after so many years – or his granddaughter, who he loved more than he could fathom, and who had moved in with him while she was doing her degree in Brighton? And anyway, he wasn't even into gardening.

He picked up the first folder on the pile, woke his computer, and began slowly typing in the account number.

SIX

Phil stood and stared at her father's memorial bench. The roof terrace was a half-beautiful space, still packed with the last of the late summer wildflowers and some flirty grasses that swished and waved in the slight breeze. The other half resembled a building site. Orange plastic safety barriers – most of them toppled over – surrounded a section of roofing felt for no apparent reason. A pile of bricks and rubble was being colonised by grass and moss, while cream metal raised beds – unmade and unfilled – had been stacked in one corner, one of them still in its cardboard box, disintegrated in patches, chewed by slugs and weakened by rain.

The plaque on the bench read, 'Clive's Bench'. A sign nearby, painted in jaunty lettering, encouraged sitting, and asked, "What is this life if, full of care, we have no time to sit and stare?" A slight misquote Phil was prepared to allow, given the context.

What would Clive think about this? He'd think it was boring. Much better to have a slide in his honour. A bouncy castle. A crazy golf course. Something slightly naff that improved exponentially after a beer or two.

A karaoke machine.

For Clive, sitting and staring was a waste of life. He'd be up and at 'em. He'd be building something or making something or improving something. He'd be dancing, or trying on a new costume for the next big parade in town. If there was any stopping and staring going on, he'd want it to be happening in his direction. He was a one-man tourist destination; he was worth seeing.

There was, claimed Virtua's leadership team, no reason for Clive to be at the St Agnes school building site. Clive was an experienced builder. He had more health and safety qualifications than Phil had tasted hot vegetables – (which, he pointed out, wouldn't be hard). He just wouldn't have gone into a building that hadn't been signed off. What's more, no right-thinking engineer would have agreed to meet him there either. And so, as far as Virtua was concerned, Angela could talk all she liked about how Clive had told her he had a meeting with the engineer that day: Virtua and the engineering firm insisted no such appointment existed.

And eventually, inevitably, the coroner came to the question of Clive's mental health. Phil and Angela listened in horror as she outlined a theory that Clive may have thrown himself off the scaffold balcony on purpose.

'He'd have done a better job of it than that,' said Angela. Offended on Clive's behalf. And anyway, he wasn't depressed. Life was sweet. He was managing a new project. He had a family that loved him. He never suffered from depression.

Somehow, the more they insisted, the more it sounded like they were kidding themselves. Phil could hear the hollow ring to it. Isn't this what everyone always does? They rave about their husbands on Facebook and then announce their divorces the next day. Perfect couples turn out to be cheating; nice guys are secret sociopaths; smiling family photos hide the truth about abusive parents. Trying to claim you were happy and normal – that someone in your family was happy and normal – just made you sound deluded. And Clive hadn't had an easy life. His brother had died of a drug overdose. His early life had been difficult.

In the end, the coroner recorded accidental death, criticising Clive's decision to enter the building before the health and safety officer had signed it off and without an engineer present, 'Or even the most basic of health and safety checks', and included a suggestion that Clive may not have been in a heightened emotional state since he had lied to his family about his reason for going.

And that was that.

The coroner had put away her iPad, stood up, and left the room, probably already thinking about what she might have for dinner that evening. Phil and Angela just stared into space until one of the officials politely encouraged them towards the exit.

'Someone did this,' said Angela. 'Someone sent him there to die on purpose.' Her hands were shaking. The room smelled of carpet and body odour. They were turfed out into the street without ceremony and spent the next five minutes trying to order a cab home. For Phil, it had been worse than the day he died.

In her darker moments, Phil wondered if they had been mistaken – if their confidence in his good mental health had been misplaced. Eventually, there were times when even Angela started to doubt her recollection. Perhaps he was leading a double life, dealing with demons neither of them knew about. Perhaps he was, in truth, deeply unhappy. Maybe he lived under a constant cloud and they were all just too wrapped up in themselves to notice.

But no. Surely not. No.

Somehow Phil felt she would have noticed. She would have seen him sitting and staring. She would have noticed him gazing into the middle distance, lost in his thoughts. Or, if he hid it better than that, still she would have spotted the strained smile, seen how the creases didn't travel to his eyes, noticed the flash of pain at the end of laughter.

Wouldn't she?

She knew it was an idiotic argument. People killed themselves every day to the utter surprise of their friends and family. And perhaps Phil would have been willing to concede to it, if it weren't for one thing. He didn't leave a note.

It just wasn't like him. He was a tidy man with a tidy mind. Yes, he brought laughter and fun to their lives, but it was always organised – always thought through. He would have sorted things out. He would have arranged his affairs first. He would have done the laundry, left his clothes in a tidy pile, not flung over the bed ready to change into when he returned covered in sweat and dirt from the day's work.

He was that sort of person.

The heat on the roof was suddenly oppressive, sun hitting paving slabs and roofing felt. Phil stood and stared at the sea beyond, turquoise and still, and wondered what on earth she was doing here. Over on a far wall, a baby seagull, fat and mournful, still in its mottled grey plumage, seemed to ask the same question, regarding her with reproachful eyes.

And so, with a last squint out into the beautiful blue day, Phil returned to floor three.

In the lift, she changed her mind and pressed the button for the fourth floor. Why not see how the other half live? Natural light flooded the level thanks to the many skylights that had been added by the architects during their big redesign – along with the wide expanses of glass that ran all the way to Jessica far below in reception. Large plants, leaves crisp at the edges from the dry climate-controlled air, had been placed in heavy concrete pots at intervals along the pathways in an attempt to bring the outdoors in. Yet somehow, in spite of the design changes and the foliage, the space still carried the unmistakable aura of grey carpet. It was an approximation of luxury that just missed the mark every step of the way. The windows were still the same drab aluminium glazing (the white paint peeling away in places to reveal the truth); the lifts clunked and shook like they'd been stolen from a multi-storey carpark; and where the new glass walls had brought in light, the low ceilings still felt oppressive. You can take polystyrene tiles from a building, but you can't suck the scent of depression out of the brickwork, thought Phil.

The floor felt strangely empty. Where were all the executives? She trod the nylon carpet to the nearest glass box and listened for the sound of voices. She couldn't see in, unfortunately – opaque decals baffled the view – and there were no shadows or sounds that might suggest humans at work.

She was about to turn and leave when she caught a noise emanating from a large room further along the corridor. Judging from the size, this was their boardroom. A meeting was in progress. Phil padded over and glanced around, checking for errant secretaries or other stray workers before moving as close to one glass wall as she dared. She stayed near one of the plants, hoping any outline visible from inside would pass as shrub rather than human.

The thing about glass offices, she thought, is that they aren't particularly good at stopping sound. Phil could hear the voices, albeit muffled, through the glazed wall. Right now, there was a woman speaking.

'As you can appreciate,' she was saying, 'it's vital we get this all ironed out asap. By which I mean it is vital that we are not found to be at fault in any capacity. In the meantime, I know I can rely on all of your discretion. Thank you.'

Without warning, the doors of the boardroom opened. One of the attendees held the door ready for the speaker to exit and Phil realised she was about to be exposed. She ran as silently and as quickly as she could, lunging forwards like an alarmed ostrich, trying to land softly while also covering as much ground as possible. In that moment, she was aware of the way the floor seemed to thunder under her feet. As she approached the end of the corridor, she slowed to a pantomime tiptoe just as a woman emerged from the office, followed by a group of slightly dazed-looking executives. Phil tapped the button for the lift and prayed for invisibility.

The woman who had exited first looked at her and frowned. Phil registered her power-blue trouser suit and her helmet of steel grey hair. She had seen Gloria Reynolds OBE before, of course. This was a woman who would show up for the opening of an envelope. Phil had taken Gloria's photograph with the mayor and various other local dignitaries at everything from Queer on the Pier, to the local Chamber of Commerce AGM. She had been surprised to see her at the Pride event, actually, given Gloria's status as a lay preacher for a church not known for its tolerance, but the woman was an absolute sucker for a photo op.

Phil continued tapping the lift button and turned to look back over her shoulder. Gloria stopped, her stride interrupted by the sight of an interloper on the fourth floor.

'Got off on the wrong floor; it's my first day, sorry,' Phil said, smiling, hoping she would come across as embarrassed and idiotic rather than snoopy and weird.

'I know you, don't I?' Gloria said

It hadn't occurred to Phil that Gloria might recognise her. Stupid of her. Now she thought about it. Phil didn't meet Gloria at the inquest, but there was every chance that Gloria had seen her there. And then, years later, she may well have been paying attention to the young person taking her photograph at all those events and asking for a quote for the local paper.

'I get that a lot,' Phil said. 'I must have one of those faces.'

Gloria frowned, but then presumably remembered she had more pressing matters to deal with, and gave a faint nod of her head as Phil escaped into the lift and returned to the safety of the third floor.

The personnel list was her main target, Phil decided. She just needed to gain access to the human resources files. Back at her desk, she took out a pilfered Bic and notebook, wrote, 'get files,' and circled it repeatedly as though the emphatic action might act as some kind of spell.

Before Phil arrived at Virtua, she had believed that blaming their missing paperwork on a 'clerical error' was a load of rubbish. Now she had spent a morning turning handwritten notes into digital files, she could well imagine how paperwork might have gone astray. In fact, it was a miracle anything got done at all if this was the level of organisation within the business. Still, strange that no one at the company and none of the contractors working for them seemed able to recall heading up such a large project.

In fact, Phil considered it more than strange. ('Odder than a sock convention,' – another saying from Angela's *Little Book of Bullshit*.) And Virtua had received a mild rebuke from the coroner, but no more. Phil had sat, surprised at the toothlessness of the coroner's words, feeling despair creeping up her spine and into her throat. She had wanted to stand up and yell, but Angela's hand on her hand – slowly gripping her tighter and tighter as the day wore on – had been a kind of ball and chain. And so she merely sat there and listened and vowed to get justice.

She took her time doing a few more investigations reports. All around, people were suffering from the usual afternoon energy slump thanks to the Australian's sandwiches. Phil spotted more than one person on social media, mainly Facebook and LinkedIn. Presumably, those on LinkedIn were looking for new jobs, or perhaps they just enjoyed hearing who'd won an 'Employee of the Month' award and reading 'inspirational' viral posts of dubious veracity.

Given everyone's apparent lack of interest, she risked checking the *Aldhill Observer* website. When Phil became editorial assistant, she quickly realised her role was mainly admin and the most boring news-in-briefs. It wasn't quite the investigative whirlwind she had imagined, and she had to accept she had based her fantasy on a world that no longer existed. She would have done better getting into online influencer circles. She could have built a following and then tried to start a pressure campaign to get the truth about her father. But for someone in her twenties, she was surprisingly old school – always had been – and, anyway, she didn't have the financial security to drop out of her career now.

Luckily, she was not a person who let a job description get in the way of ambition: she quietly took over the paper's neglected website, resurrecting its news offering and updating the layout. Adam Jenkins, editor, had disapproved of the enterprise, mostly because he didn't really understand the internet and didn't trust it either, but once the website started gaining traffic – and ad revenue – he took a keener interest. Soon he was commanding Phil to write clickbait pieces to draw in curious locals keen to discover the 'Five pubs in Rye no one knows about.' And it wasn't long before Phil felt he had let the power go to his head. He was in danger of ruining any reputation the paper had in pursuit of clicks.

'Stop moaning, McGinty. Just write the damn copy or I'll find a more obedient Mac monkey,' he told her, only half joking.

And so she wrote increasingly low-hanging fruit pieces and felt a little resentful every time she ate a banana.

'Ah Scarlett, there you are,' said Rhonda.

Phil jumped and hit X on the browser window. She turned smiling to Rhonda who was standing next to a woman.

'Scarlett, this is Jamie, our head of HR.'

SEVEN

'Try speaking to Doug Graves,' Karina from Haven For The Homeless suggested when Jen got through to her. 'He sorts the deliveries and he was working here back then.'

'*Doug Graves.* Bloody hell.' Grant shook his head in wonder. 'Like the punchline to a joke. His parents must have hated him, poor bugger.'

Nandini, Grant and Dean Martin, the constable doing a stint with them had a good laugh too, which was a bit rich coming from a lad called Dean Martin, in Jen's opinion.

'What's his brother called?' said Grant. 'Phil?'

'Rob?' suggested Nandini, cackling.

Jen wasn't laughing. Neither was Lee. They'd heard all the jokes before.

They'd heard the name before.

When Doug's name came up, Lee had shot Jen a warning look. That's when Jen understood: they weren't going to mention the strange coincidence that Douglas Graves's name had just come up in connection with another body in another wall in another school.

Graves was the in-house health and safety officer at Virtua Services. He had written up the report on the St Agnes's school building site after Clive died. Before he was the health and safety officer, he was a builder with a criminal record for GBH. He was terse beyond the point of rudeness, but he had taken his job as HSO seriously.

Clive's family believed he was meeting the engineer, but Doug said no engineer in their right mind would be on site without a health and safety sign-off. 'Too scared of risk,' he said, as though that were a bad thing.

There was speculation that maybe Clive had gone to do some work there and had fallen off the scaffolding and into the cavity wall by accident. But engineers weren't the only ones concerned with risk: Clive should never have been on site without the health and safety report either. What's more, if he had been working on site, he would have had a labourer with him. That was just standard practice.

Petra had already made it clear that there was some political reason why Clive's death had become *the case that should not be named*. Jen assumed someone further up the food chain had had a quiet word, and the Super, a man known for being mostly upright and honest, but only when it suited him, had done his duty and stepped in to stop them from digging around too much. Anything for a quiet life – and anything to maintain the reputation of the local force.

Still, it wouldn't last. Jen knew that. If there was a connection, they would find it, and eventually the Super would step up. He always did... When there was no other option.

'What was it Oscar Wilde said?' said Jen through a mouthful of ready salted. 'To lose one man down a wall cavity may be regarded as a misfortune; to lose a second looks decidedly dodgy.'

'Something like that,' agreed Nandini.

Jen and Nandini were finishing their crisps in the car.

Normally, Jen didn't approve of eating crisps in the car, but they had been forced to grab a meal deal in town on the way to their meeting and it was either the car or the bench that usually housed the local drug addicts, all of whom were less than keen on the police. Jen couldn't quite imagine asking Spud and Mads to budge up. So they sat outside Haven for the Homeless and judged each other's poor taste in crisp flavours.

There had already been a spirited discussion about the relative merits of Jen's ready salted: 'Classic,' said Jen; 'cardboard with salt,' snorted Nandini, and Nandini's prawn cocktail: 'A sea-based party for the tastebuds,' claimed Nandini; 'An abomination,' insisted Jen. Now they returned to the case.

'I mean, what kind of idiot signs a ten-year contract without a break clause?' said Jen. 'At least this might make the public more aware of the whole fiasco.'

'Yeah, good that this poor bloke didn't die for nothing, eh?' said Nandini. 'Although I wouldn't be surprised if it turned out the council had signed a waiver saying they took responsibility for all corpses found on school grounds.'

'Probably,' agreed Jen with a puff of laughter.

'So tell me what happened to the first fella. I was still in school when it happened.'

'Wow,' said Jen. 'That's just given me a bleak sense of my own mortality.'

'Obviously, I heard the school ground gossip version. Is it true he was pulled out alive and babbling?'

Jen grimaced, feeling suddenly squeamish. It wasn't like her. Had she been as bloodthirsty as this once? Before Nate died, had she delighted in the gory details? Or maybe it was just her age – midway through her thirties, with forty staring back at her on the not-too-distant horizon. She had spent years trying to fathom the depths of human depravity, of trying to find a way to get her head around the casual atrocities humans (or, let's face it, mostly men) meted out to their fellow humans. Perhaps that had taken the thrill out of the gore. It should have calloused her sensibilities, but if it had begun to leave her raw and sensitive. And right now, the memory of Clive McGinty in his final days made her want to fall to her knees and weep.

'He was alive, yes,' she said, wishing the school ground rumours had been less accurate. 'He was alive for about a week, but he didn't really... you know... wake up. His poor family... He had two kids and a partner. They all insisted he wasn't suicidal, and I believed them.'

Nandini gave her a look and Jen knew exactly what it meant. Young as she was, even Nandini knew that happy-seeming people killed themselves all the time. They make plans to meet up, they laugh and smile, they walk home and fling themselves off a bridge.

'Yes, yes, I know,' Jen said. 'But in this case, the whole thing just felt wrong... Don't look at me like that... it wasn't some mystical gut feeling. It was the way he died: it didn't make sense. He was a clever bloke, well-known locally – a real character, you know?'

'Mm, I remember him,' said Nandini. 'I met him. He was always dressing up like a pirate, or doing Santa's grotto. I remember being so excited by a brown father Christmas. He told me that St Nicholas was Greek. I said, "But why are you *so* dark?" "Just got back off my holidays," he said. I believed him! Seemed a perfectly reasonable answer to me.'

Jen laughed and wiped away a stray tear she hadn't noticed shedding.

'It was such a stupid way to do yourself in, and he wasn't stupid,' she said. 'He could tie knots like a pirate – he could have made a noose. He could've topped himself or chosen a hundred and one other ways to die. I just don't believe he would've made such a hash of it.'

'It was properly stupid,' agreed Nandini. 'Right, let's go.'

Jen watched as she tipped the last of her prawn cocktail into her gaping maw, crumbs scattering into her lap, which she proceeded to brush into the gap between the chairs.

'Those will never come out now.'

'Huh?' said Nandini, opening her door while Jen took a moment to despair about humanity. 'You coming or what, then?'

Nandini was still brushing off the prawn crisp dust when they found Doug – just as grumpy as Jen remembered him. He was standing in a small warehouse. The sort of neat, rectangular structure with brick sides and a once tiled, now corrugated, roof that Victorians might have kept pigs in before traders from the 1950s turned it into a storeroom for a few old cars or a winter's worth of market garden produce.

Now it was mostly full of bags, which were mostly full of clothes. The smell of mouldering, damp sweatshirts and tracksuit bottoms filled Jen's nostrils, alongside the earthy scent of a concrete floor trodden on by years of muddy boots. In one corner, a cluster of sofas created a space where Aldhill's homeless could sit and relax under the heat of a halogen lamp; behind it, a door led to the toilet and the tiny kitchenette.

Jen doubted Doug ever sat on the sofa since he himself never relaxed, unless squatting briefly to smoke a roll-up cigarette counted. He was wiry, with skin the leathery darkness of a white man left out in the sun. Years on building sites had kept him lean and strong, and Jen imagined that no amount of showering could shift the last of the cement dust and type one aggregate from his pores. Quite what had induced him to take up a voluntary position as the warehouse manager of a homeless charity was anyone's guess. Guilty conscience, perhaps? Or was that just Jen's cynicism? Maybe he had experienced some kind of epiphany; maybe he'd been overwhelmed by the desire to help some of the most vulnerable in society.

Perhaps he'd found God.

'Jesus H Christ. Smells like a badger's arsehole,' he said.

Perhaps not.

He was staring into a bag full of donations, gripping the handles and squinting down at it with a look of unadorned disgust.

'The crap people give away. Was the tip closed or something, love?' He shouted into the bag, as though the culprit was living inside.

'So, do you remember the tops?' said Jen. This was the third time she had tried to get a straight answer from the man. He kept getting distracted by the donations, flitting from one bag to the next with the urgency of a spaniel seeking cluster bombs. He glanced up, his eyes refocusing.

'We got a job lot of 'em.' He had traces of the older Sussex accent – plenty of country burr mixed with the more modern London twang.

'And do you remember any of the people who got given a Prints To Go top?'

'Could've been anyone by the time we'd handed them all out. Loads of 'em were wandering around in them. Looked like a bloody staff common room in the shelter for a while.'

'Right,' said Jen, feeling her heart sink a little. 'But we know the tops were brand new when they were handed out. The owner mentioned it. But the one this man was wearing was faded from a lot of wear. It had holes in it. 'Was there someone who wore theirs more than anyone else?'

'Maybe.' Doug shrugged.

'...And can you tell me anything about him?' said Jen, when she realised Doug wasn't planning to say more. 'His name?'

He shrugged again. 'One bloke was always down the seafront hanging out. He was only here for a few years – if that. Months, maybe.'

'What happened to him?' said Nandini, pressing the flat of her middle nail to her thumb. Jen could sense her impatience.

'Dunno. Assumed he'd gone back home.'

'What was his name?' said Jen.

'Dunno. It would have been years back'

'Any ideas on the year or month you last saw him?'

Doug seemed to think for a moment and Jen and Nandini waited patiently while he continued scurrying about sorting bags, hefting them from one area to another based on their contents, muttering occasionally, or pulling something out to admire.

'Doug,' prompted Jen.

He looked up as though he'd forgotten they were there.

'Dunno... Longer'n five years, because it wasn't at this location – was in the old place. I remember handing 'em out.'

'Prints To Go went out of business seven years ago, so maybe around then?'

'Maybe.'

'And before you gave him the top, how long had you known him?'

'Can't have been long. Like I say, we thought he'd gone home.'

'Why?' Jen said. So many of the homeless men were vulnerable; a missing one would surely be more likely to have come to harm than have hopped on a train home?

Doug shrugged. 'He wasn't in a bad way, y'know?'

'Apart from the homelessness?' said Nandini, a snort of dry sarcasm cut short by a sudden glance from Jen that said, 'Don't piss him off.'

Nandini might be a good detective, but she didn't do well with people. Jen had been the same once too – still was at times – but now she could tell when someone was looking for any reason to stop speaking. Sure enough, Doug's shoulders tensed, but he carried on.

'He didn't do drugs; he must've had somewhere to stay; he was doing ok.'

Jen knew what he meant. Most of the homeless people in the area had access to sheltered accommodation, either in apartments or dormitory-style space. The few who preferred to sleep rough tended to stay by the beach, tents dotted from one Victorian pavilion to the next (until the council blocked off the entrances, that is), or else in shop doorways in the town centre. Wherever they slept, one of the local homeless charities would have known about it, since they made it their business to connect with every homeless person in the area.

If Doug thought their man had somewhere to stay, that was because the Haven team had never seen him out on the streets. He confirmed as much and briefly speculated on the reasons.

'P'raps he had some bird who took him in. I dunno.'

'Right,' said Jen.

Something about Doug's manner was bothering her. It wasn't just that she found him unlikeable – although she did – it felt like he was hiding something. From her past, brief dealings with him, she knew he was always this cagey around police officers. She'd met plenty like him in the years since. But under that lack of interest and distraction, there was a layer of tension. She had never seen such a hyperactive man seem so still, as though every muscle in his body was simulating Doug's normal level of activity while readying itself to flee.

'And do you happen to remember anything about a woman or where he might potentially have stayed?'

'Nah. Like I said, we just thought he'd got fed up and gone back home to someone. Probably found a sister to pester for money.'

'Did he mention home to you at all?'

'He was from the North,' said Doug, briefly (and for the first time) looking directly at Jen, before he was back burrowing into his donation bags. Eventually, he glanced over again, as if to check they were still there. 'He had an accent. Manchester or Yorkshire or something like that. I didn't really know the bloke.'

'Yes, you mentioned that already.' Jen felt more of her patience ebb away. A glance at Nandini suggested she was suffering the same struggle. 'Seven years. You'd only just started working for Haven for the Homeless, right? Around the same time, Clive McGinty was found in the St Agnes cavity wall.'

Doug shrugged and Jen took a moment to consider her next words.

'Our Prints To Go man... his body was found in the wall of the old Helenswood school. Funny that there were two bodies in two schools being worked on by Virtua Construction.' She felt the air change as Doug's already tense body tensed even more. His jawbone jutted from his cheek as she continued. 'That's the same company you worked for, wasn't it, Doug?'

If she'd hoped to provoke a response, she was disappointed. Doug shrugged and continued his work.

'Quite a coincidence that you knew both of the men,' she pressed.

For a moment, she saw a flash of anger in his eyes.

'I didn't know Clive, and I barely remember this dead fella of yours. So unless you're arresting me, I need to get back to work.'

'No, no,' said Jen mildly. 'Just an observation. Would you mind helping us with an E-FIT?'

'I told you I barely remember him. I'm rubbish with faces and my eyesight's gone,' he said. 'So no.'

'Do you know anyone else who might remember him?' she said. 'Someone else who worked here at the time?'

'No, they're all dead or gone,' he said.

Jen took a beat to assess him. Was he lying? Probably. But that didn't mean much: people like Doug lied to the police as a kind of hobby. They were about to leave when Jen thought she'd give it one last shot. She kept her tone casual.

'You know, I've always wondered what made you give up your job as an HSO to work for a homeless charity.'

Doug plucked out some old t-shirts and chucked them into a box marked 'rags' and Jen realised he was going to let her continue wondering.

'Just fancied a change, did you?' she said.

Was there a job in the world, Jen wondered, where you had to witness more grown adults shrugging? It was a shame there wasn't some kind of PhD you could take in the great art of the shrug. Her thesis would be on the 'The fifteen different types of "off you" that can be conveyed to the police through the movement of the shoulders.'

Of course, the problem for Doug was that by shrugging all he had done was raise her suspicion further. As he flitted from bag to bag – his nose currently in a blue IKEA sack filled with pink children's shoes – he avoided both their gazes. Was it guilt about their last encounter? Or did he have something illegal going on that he was hoping they wouldn't be able to winkle from him if he avoided their gaze?

Still, there was nothing to be done about it all now. She couldn't exactly arrest him for shrugging. It looked like this John Doe wasn't going to get any justice today – or at all at this rate. Their investigation was running out of steam before it even began.

'Well, that's the end of that, then,' said Nandini, giving a weary sigh. They were back in the office discussing the state of the case after today's dead end. In Jen's opinion, Nandini hadn't yet earned the right to weary sighs, but the kid was probably right.

'Seems like it,' she said.

'Do you think Doug had something to do with it? Did he really not know Clive?'

'In answer to your first question, I'm not discounting it at this stage. I admit I never liked the guy – something about him always put me on edge. And in answer to your second...' She thought for a moment or two. 'I can't remember. Let's check his statements at the time and see what he said.'

Nandini nodded. 'Yes, sarge.' She turned back to her computer.

Jen tapped her pencil on her knee, thinking. 'But don't let the boss know you're reading old case files. It'll make him jumpy.'

'Speak of the devil,' muttered Nandini. Jen looked over to see Lee walking towards them, holding a scrap of paper between two fingers like a man brandishing a fiver at a strip club.

'SOCOs have found something in the cavity,' he said, putting the scrap of paper on Jen's desk and tapping it with two fingers. Jen looked down at the smudged dark scrawl from Lee's rollerball. It just read, 'It's your lucky day.'

EIGHT

It turned out the friendly woman who had greeted Phil was actually head of HR and administration.

In fact, Jamie Pilcher *was* human resources.

'We outsource a lot to an HR agency,' she explained. 'They deal with the contracts, and the insurance and all the more admin-y stuff. I'm here to transform and strengthen the organisational culture, leadership development as well as managing the supply chain throughout the organisation. And while we're recruiting a customer services director, I'm overseeing that function as well.'

Phil tried to think of an appropriately business-like response.

'Wow!' she said.

'Our training manager Mary mostly works remotely from home and is only part time anyway due to her disability.'

This felt like a random thing to mention, especially for an HR person. Phil couldn't shake the sense that Jamie was implying that Mary was a shirker. Ironic, really, since Phil was willing to bet Jamie offloaded as much of her work as she could.

Maybe that was why she was so bright and cheerful.

Phil found herself strangely in awe of this attractive woman with an expensive haircut and relaxed-looking trouser suit. She was living her best life. Paid to manage a team that barely existed, outsourcing all her work to agencies, and armed with a loyal office dogsbody, willing to make her look good in the form of Rhonda.

And boy, did she need it. They were standing in Jamie's work area and the first thing that struck Phil was the utter chaos. Everywhere she looked, there were stacks of papers and files. And beyond that, there was a general feeling of grubbiness. Coffee cups and food wrappers; a smashed iPhone; a snapped nail file; a makeup bag – contents spewing out from the open zip. It was like a teenager's bedroom, totally at odds with Jamie's pristine appearance.

Despite being within the open plan layout, Jamie's area had privacy of sorts, thanks to a wall of filing cabinets, some screens, and the effective annexation of a nearby breakout area. What had been a soft citrus-green banquette where two people could perch for an informal meeting was now a place to dump more files.

Not that Jamie was prepared to take the blame for the mess.

'I'm afraid I'm still trying to regain some semblance of order after my predecessor left,' she explained.

'Oh, right,' said Phil. 'When was that?'

'I think it's about a year or so now,' said Jamie, without a hint of shame. 'It's been a pretty major job. He was old school, you know? Paper not digital. It's just that generation before – you know what they're like. Not that age matters, of course. Our older people bring a wealth of knowledge and experience.'

'Oh, that sounds like a complete nightmare,' said Phil, obliging her with the response she clearly sought. 'So what are you having to do about it?'

From Jamie's long and garbled reply, Phil concluded that the answer was, 'Not much.' There was a lot of chat about 'optimising workflow,' and 'streamlining functionality,' and not a lot of actual action.

Phil's fingers twitched. How she would love to get stuck into this chaos to truffle out the secrets surely buried in there somewhere. She smiled her sunniest smile.

'I'd be happy to help you,' she said. 'I've finished all the investigations reports and I'm a pro at filing.'

Phil had barely filed anything in her life, but how hard could it really be? Besides, by the time anyone noticed she had only the faintest grasp of the alpha-numeric system, or that she would inevitably resort to saying chunks of the alphabet out loud any time she needed to know what order the letters came in, Scarlett Stevens would be long gone.

'Wow! Finished investigations already?' Jamie said, flashing her perfect orthodontistry. 'In that case, let's give you something else to do.'

Phil hadn't expected it to be that easy. Jamie might as well have said, 'You can do my job for me, if you like?' And Phil did like it. She liked it very much. This was her ticket into the inner sanctum of Virtua Services. Things were coming together nicely.

'Sure! Sounds great,' she said. 'I'll do whatever.'

. . .

Famous last words, thought Phil, balefully surveying her new workspace. It turned out her offer to do 'whatever' had doomed her to an afternoon spent in a windowless room surrounded by boxes.

When Jamie had led her there, Phil thought it was a joke. It was literally a cupboard, albeit one big enough for a desk and wall-to-wall shelving units. The only natural light came in the form of a small panel of metal-meshed glass in the fire door, and the little squares of sun that bled through an air vent. A single LED strip light supplied the kind of migraine-inducing white haze that manufacturers promised would keep seasonal affective disorder at bay, but in reality made you feel like you were being questioned by the security services of a hostile nation. In the centre, a single brown veneer desk sat at a jaunty angle, suggesting it was there purely to act as additional storage and would not support even the mildest feng shui assessment. It was accompanied by a black swivel chair, and yet the two seemed only distantly related: the chair had such high arm rests there was no hope of ever scooching it far enough under the desk to reach a satisfactory working position. Phil could only conclude they had been bought independently by two people of vastly different heights, tastes and budgets.

'It's quite simple, really,' explained Jamie. 'I need you to sort through these letters.'

She gestured to a corner stacked with boxes. In fact, the whole room was filled with them, mostly of the pale grey lidded cardboard variety. The majority were housed on matching grey metal shelves that lined the walls, but when that space was filled, some enterprising soul had begun stacking the boxes in piles in front. The overall effect was that of the world's most boring box fort.

'It's a cat's paradise,' murmured Phil.

She found herself thinking of the final scene of *Raiders of the Lost Ark*; the giant warehouse filled with crates of state secrets that were best forgotten. But somehow she suspected the ark of the covenant was unlikely to be inside a grey document box in a second tier outsourcing firm two hours from London. The particular area of chaos Jamie was pointing at constituted a stack of boxes labelled 'Public Correspondence' in green marker pen.

The journalist in Phil approved of green ink being used to denote letters from members of the public. Picking up the nearest one, Jamie plonked it on the desk and lifted the lid to reveal countless crumpled sheets of paper – everything from flowery pink handwritten letters to printed emails on plain A4 addressed to 'Whom It May Concern'.

'Wow!' said Phil.

'I know,' said Jamie. 'People still write letters. Some are forwarded from our clients, some are sent directly to us.' She picked up the top letter. 'As you can see, this letter has a Virtua-headed reply stapled to it. That's what you'll be looking for. This means that the letter has been dealt with. You will need to read each letter and check it has the appropriate reply attached. Anything that has been handled you can put into a pile.'

'Got it,' said Phil.

'Now, if you find a letter that seems like it should have had a reply, but doesn't have one attached, put it in a second pile.'

Phil already had questions, but she waited for Jamie to finish.

'There will be a third pile for letters that didn't get a reply, but which also didn't *need* a reply.'

'Okay,' said Phil,

'And how do I know which letters should have had a reply?' asked Phil, hoping that wasn't a stupid question.

'Good question,' said Jamie. 'If the letter requests a specific reply or has a grievance that clearly needs following up – for example, if Virtua damaged the writer's property in some way – those should have had a reply.'

'Ok, got it,' said Phil.

'Just use your common sense, really,' said Jamie. 'The only letters that don't need a reply are probably from people saying thank you for how their grievance has already been handled.'

'Are you sure you don't want me to tackle that backlog in your office?' said Phil, hoping for a last-minute reprieve. 'I'm happy to get stuck in.'

Stuck into the HR filing cabinets, she meant.

'Oh, that's so sweet,' said Jamie, and Phil half-expected her to pinch her cheeks. 'But this is where you can make the most impact, Scarlett.'

'Is this something to do with the audit?' said Phil, thinking of the message from Gloria on the intranet, and the ominous-sounding executive meeting she'd overheard.

Jamie looked at her watch. 'That's my conference call just starting,' she said. She smiled at Phil. 'Better dial in before they notice.'

Jamie started to head to the door, but hesitated.

'You may find another type of letter in there. Possibly something marked "internal" about... oh, I don't know. Let's say a staff complaint or... just anything that isn't from the public – forms or internal admin.'

She was clearly trying to act casual.

'These should be put into a pile and ignored. They

should have been filed elsewhere, but I don't have complete faith that my predecessor was on top of the filing system.'

'Do you want me to put them in a specific place for you?' Phil said. 'Maybe in a filing cabinet somewhere or...?'

'No, just bring them straight to me without reading them and I'll deal with them. It'll only be boring stuff about parking spaces, most likely. No need to inflict that on you!'

Talk about pique a person's curiosity, thought Phil. She might as well have said, 'Don't look in the box marked "exciting secrets".' Phil couldn't think of anyone who wouldn't be tempted to read a letter they had been told not to. It was basic reverse psychology. She was amazed Jamie had even mentioned it. There must have been a hundred better ways of giving her the instructions to ignore the internal letters without making them sound so enticing.

'Right you are,' she said, dutifully, and took the first letter off the pile in an industrious manner that screamed, 'You can trust me, I'm extremely efficient and reliable and I won't look at internal documents.'

Jamie smiled, apparently reassured, and headed out, leaving Phil in her airless box.

If Phil had hoped that doing this job would lead to uncovering some exciting stories of corporate neglect, she was sorely disappointed. It took less than an hour to establish the bulk of the letters were gripes from members of the public who didn't appreciate Virtua's vans being parked near their driveways. One man was upset that his view from a favourite window was blocked. Even the genuine complaints were for extremely dull things – a hit and run on a garden gnome or a misjudged kerbside delivery.

Many were handwritten notes that Phil had trouble deciphering. The hardest ones in the tiny floral cursive she associated with older generations. But she eventually developed an eye for it, and, by the end of the first hour, she was adept at unravelling even the shakiest lettering. But the challenge didn't occupy her mind for long. She began to look back on her time working in the investigations team with genuine fondness and even the dullest editorial assignments developed a rosy glow. She would rather be attending a school play or doing three hundred words on Mr Thompson's funny-looking carrots than sitting in this stark box staring at grievances about a dented dustbin or an inelegantly filled hole in the pavement. Soon she was ready to run screaming from the room, begging forgiveness and promising never to impersonate an intern again.

After she read one particularly mind-numbing missive, in which Tina Drover, aged seventy-five shared a rambling conspiracy theory that a Virtua van parked further down the road was trying to catch her naked in the bath (a letter which did at least raise a number of chuckles to begin with, but then spoiled it by rambling on for another six sides of A4), she felt her gaze drift around the room as though searching for something to save her. As she stared at the wall of mushroom-coloured box files, she wondered at her own lack of curiosity. After all, she was an investigative journalist and boxes of files were their bread and butter. This was how all the good stories were uncovered back in the day, wasn't it? Rummaging through old documents (maybe with a handy anonymous whistleblower in a dark carpark thrown in for good measure).

She realised she had briefly become so swept up with behaving like Scarlett that she forgot that she was Phil – the sort of person who would snoop at every given opportunity. And what about Jamie's request that she ignore anything internal, thus implying that there were some important documents missing? How had that slipped her mind so quickly? Perhaps her brain was starved of oxygen. Maybe her blood sugar was low. Keen to make up for her failure, she pushed her uncomfortable black chair away from her ugly brown desk and rose to survey the shelves.

Picking a box at random, she slid it forward off the shelf and peered under the lid hopefully. She couldn't see much in the gloom, but it looked like a collection of something interminably dull, like progress reports (or something else office-y that Phil didn't understand). Still, she had to try, so she grabbed a file off the top and spent a disappointed minute reading what she soon identified as closed investigation cases from Mick and his team.

Did they really need to keep these?

What possible benefit to the world could there be in holding a paper trail of the claims other outsourcing firms made against Virtua? It really would be so much easier if all of those companies just agreed to some kind of truce. They were simply passing money back and forth, employing teams of people to end up at evens.

After the fifth box, which turned out to be just as boring or pointless as all the others, she decided it was probably time to accept her fate and return to the letter sorting. Better the devil you know, she told herself.

'At least in there, there might be some more conspiracy theories about Peeping Toms,' she said out loud as she shut the file she was holding.

A couple of milliseconds passed as the synapses in her brain shot a message to her conscious mind. She flipped the file open again. Inside was a single letter. The date was the same day as her father's death: 21st October. Same year too.

There didn't seem to be anything fishy about it. It was simply a bog standard complaint letter. The only odd thing was that it was in one of Mick's Investigations folders and not swimming around with all the other customer complaints. It didn't seem like there had been any damage to the property and there was nothing to suggest Mick had actually investigated it. So why was it here?

She re-read the letter, hoping something would jump out. Mrs Kaye Cooke of 33 Nicholswood Drive, had written to say that a Virtua van had blocked her driveway, making it impossible for her to get out when she had been trying to make a trip to shop at Iceland. She didn't ask for any compensation beyond an apology.

So why was it in this box?

Phil took out her phone to snap a photograph.

'Still here?' said a voice.

Phil barely managed not to drop her phone. Rhonda was standing in the doorway, lit from behind like some angelic saviour come to deliver her from admin. Phil grinned, hoping Rhonda wouldn't realise she had caught her having a rummage. She needn't have worried – the office manager didn't seem to have noticed anything odd.

'It's home time,' said Rhonda. 'No need to stay beyond your allotted hours.'

Phil closed the file and smiled breezily.

'That sounds like a great idea. It would be nice to see daylight again.'

'Yes, she has got you in a bit of a cave, hasn't she?' said Rhonda.

'I feel like I've had an insight into what it would be like to be a naked mole rat,' said Phil, then immediately regretted her choice of metaphor. Would Scarlett know what a naked mole rat was?

Rhonda hesitated a moment, perhaps unsure how to respond to a sentence that contained the words 'naked', 'mole' and 'rat.'

'I expect you'd be glad to go back to the investigations team again,' she said.

'Yes, who knew I'd be missing that so quickly?' Phil said. She laughed – glad to be back on safer ground.

She closed the file casually and chucked it back in the box. Rhonda waited at the door while Phil grabbed her things, then held the door open for Phil as she left. She's making sure I leave, thought Phil. Had she noticed the folder?

'Bye then, Scarlett,' said Rhonda. 'See you tomorrow.'

And Phil felt Rhonda's eyes on her back all the way to the lift.

Phil didn't head straight home from Virtua. Instead, she made her way to the Tesco carpark and wandered the perimeter, staring up at the rowan and alder trees that had been planted in little diamonds of mud throughout the concrete space. She had been doing that a lot lately. Today, however, she was venturing further, making her way into the housing estate attached to the rear of the car park. There, she took a moment to reflect on what had brought her to this rather bleak pocket of Aldhill.

Poo.

Dog poo, to be precise.

So here she was, after a long day spent faking her way into an unpaid internship to investigate her father's death, wandering the streets looking for dog poo.

There were a few things that exercised the *Aldhill Observer* readers more than dogs' mess. In fact, Phil was pretty confident that turds represented *the* most pressing concern for the local residents. Forget potholes or teenagers putting their feet on the train seats. The constant slalom run of dog mess on the slopes of Aldhill-on-Sea pavements was the thing that sent the residents writing letters and emails. It was easy to roll your eyes and laugh, and for a while Phil did, but then an email arrived that made Phil stop and think. It was from a man named Simon Barker.

Sir,

To many people, I'm sure this seems like a frivolous topic. But the simple fact is that nothing ever seems to be done about it. Dogs' mess is a scourge on our society; the offenders (by which I mean the owners, not the dogs), are litterers of the most heinous kind. And the very worst are those who take the trouble to bag up the offending article before, perhaps fatigued by the exertion of bending down to scrape up the dog's left behinds, hanging the bag from the nearest tree.

This unappealing craze has taken over one estate in particular: the tree outside my house now bears the foulest fruit.

What could possibly possess someone to do this is beyond me. Who could be the perpetrator of such reckless and irrational crime? What kind of person takes the trouble to pick up the mess only to abandon it? What monster would decorate a tree with baubles of black bags?

Quite aside from the appalling nature of the crime, I have to confess I am fascinated. I would love to ask one of these poo bearers what compels them to litter in such a strange way. Why not simply take the bag to the nearest bin – which is, after all, just a few feet from where they are hanging the bags – probably no more than twenty seconds' walk away?

Is it some strange ritual? Do they have some kind of superstitious belief? What goes through the mind of a person who would do this? Much as I would like the littering to stop. I would, above all, like to know WHY.

Yours in desperate curiosity,
  Simon Barker

He was right, of course. Aside from the humour of the letter, and the comedy of his indignation, he was right.

Who on *earth* was leaving poo hanging on a tree?

Once she had read the note, she started to notice the stuff everywhere, especially in the Tesco carpark next to where Simon Barker lived. She had taken to delaying her exit after a shop and popping by at different hours, hoping to chance on someone in the act. It had become a strange kind of obsession

'Have you thought about acquiring a sensible hobby?' asked Angela. 'Knitting is back, I hear.'

And today she would be meeting a fellow obsessive: the letter writer himself.

'Looks normal enough,' she muttered as she stared up at Simon Barker's house. It was a compact, white-doored new build on a small estate. What could be more average?

She knocked and braced herself. She needn't have

worried. Mr Barker (*'Call me Simon'*), was every bit as funny and charming as she had hoped. He was in his late sixties and wearing the sensible clothes and comfortable shoes you'd expect from a keen allotment gardener. The house surprised her, however.

'We bought the show home,' Simon explained, catching her eyeing up the cluster of generic wall art on the staircase. 'Some of it is a bit shiny and silver for our liking, but it saves spending money on doing it up. Of course, now we've got it, we'll have to keep hold of it until it falls apart.'

He cared about the environment, he explained, and couldn't in good conscience get rid of a perfectly serviceable door knob just because he wasn't keen on brushed chrome. His wife Debbie was even more eco-conscious, apparently.

'She still works three days a week doing the books for a couple of local charities. Just don't get her started on Astro-turf or single-use plastics.'

Their eco-worrying (as Simon called it) meant living with some feature walls that were not entirely to their taste.

'The wallpaper is a bit busy in here, I'm afraid,' he said, leading her into their front room, 'but it's got a good view of the rowan.'

They stood and stared out the window at the tree over on a small patch of green. Oakwood estate had once been a broadleaf woodland, and to celebrate that the developers had named all of the streets after the trees they had felled when they built it. To prevent the locals and the council from complaining too much, and to replace the ancient oaks and venerable beeches, the developers had dutifully planted a few weedy saplings that they then neglected to water. Simon and a couple of other residents had come to the trees' aid.

'We've adopted one each and we make sure ours is watered properly and looked after.'

One particular sapling – a sorry-looking rowan tree – seemed to catch the eye of the dog poo bag fiend.

'That's my tree,' said Simon.

They stared at it.

It was bowing under the weight of what Simon email had referred to as 'poo baubles.'

'Debbie says it looks like a lost pagan ritual to encourage a good harvest,' said Simon. 'The worst thing is, they're not even degradable bags.' He stared out at the laden tree mournfully. 'All that single use plastic on the planet for the rest of eternity... swaying in the breeze.'

'Haunting,' said Phil.

'I remove them usually,' said Simon, turning to her, his natural cheerfulness returning in an instant, 'but I left these in your honour.'

'Well, I don't know what to say,' said Phil. 'Thank you, I guess? I don't think anyone ever left poo hanging from a tree for me before.'

'You clearly haven't met the right person,' said Simon with a cheerful wink.

'I'll have to start aiming higher,' said Phil.

'Just like our Phantom Poo Thrower,' said Simon. 'Honestly, I'm amazed by how high he gets some of them. I think we might be seeking a giant. Anyway, I hope you can catch him. I feel like I've been staring out of this window for hours at a time and have never managed to spot the culprit.'

'I'm sorry, can we just go back,' said Phil. 'What did you call this person?'

'Oh, he goes by many names here on the estate. "Father Shitmas" – always leaving presents under the tree – "the Poo

Fairy," – you never know, it could be a woman, although she'd have to be taller than you to reach some of the branches, the "Turd Tosser" (possibly a bit too vulgar) and, my personal favourite, and a homage to the *Two Ronnies* (who you are no doubt too young to remember), The Phantom Poo Thrower.'

Phil stared at him with a mixture of admiration and horror, while also wondering which one would work best for the paper. Simon carried on with his theorising.

'It's my suspicion that whoever is doing this is doing it very early in the morning, or very late at night. I have stood sentry for nearly an entire day and never caught the Faecal Fiend – that one is my wife's – but the next morning there was a new present hanging from the lower branch.'

'Sounds like I need to organise a stakeout,' said Phil. 'I can come tomorrow?'

After all, why not spend this week off as an intern by day and Poo Fairy hunter by night?

Simon was delighted at this idea. 'I can join you if you like?'

'Oh, no, I wouldn't dream of it,' said Phil. 'It gets freezing as soon as the sun goes down. No, I'll sit out in the car, and maybe you could bring me a cup of tea before you go to bed?'

'I'll bring you a slice of cake too if you like?' said Simon.

'Sounds perfect.'

Phil was glad when she finally got home. Angela had cooked up a batch of spaghetti bolognaise, the hidden vegetables pulverised in the blender, so Phil, a woman in her twenties, wouldn't see them – even if she was now grown up enough to know about them.

'How was your day?' said Angela, and Phil told her about the news in briefs and the hunt for the Faecal Fiend.

'I like Phantom Poo Thrower,' decided Angela after some consideration, 'but I'm not sure it will work for younger readers.'

Phil didn't mention the day of impersonating Scarlett Stevens. Not that her mother would have particularly disapproved – she loved a bit of disruption – it was just that it was a lot to tell a person.

'I'm so proud of how you're using your expensive education,' said Angela when the Fiend's tale was told (through mouthfuls of spaghetti). She stroked her daughter's hair with a gentle irony, 'You've grown into such a valuable member of society.'

'Tracking down Father Shitmas *is* worthwhile!' protested Phil.

'If you say so, Philby,' said Angela, patting her on the head before rising to collect her mug of tea and book. 'I'm off to my bed.'

'Night,' Phil said. She was ready to drop herself, but she took a couple more minutes to process the day, washing the dishes before making herself a cinnamon and liquorice tea.

Phil had been seventeen when Clive died, convinced something had happened to him that the inquest hadn't got to, but unsure how to begin getting to the truth. Until, one night, she poked her head round the door and discovered her mother half-watching, half-sleeping through a special investigation on TV. The programme was doing an exposé on fire safety equipment in schools. Phil came in and watched as the reporters revealed corruption and incompetence in the outsourcing firm responsible for the building. These were the people who could get her the answers, she realised. It took three emails and a letter before eventually a reply arrived by post:

'While we understand that this is an important and deeply personal story, we already have our reporting underway for the coming year.'

And because they had done a similar story about building safety standards, the letter continued,

'It is unlikely we will revisit the subject so soon.'

So it was up to her, then.

Phil could have opted to join the police, of course, but becoming a police officer didn't occur to her, and not just because she was from Roosevelt Court – one of the high rise council blocks on the estate, where people weren't known for their love of the local constabulary. As far as she was concerned, the police must have been in on her father's death. How else to explain their apathy? Angela had tried going to them when Clive was still lying in the hospital, his neural pathways damaged beyond repair, his body shattered and misshapen.

'I want to report a crime,' she said. 'Criminal neglect. Corporate manslaughter.'

She had been politely patronised out of the building by a detective who seemed to be struggling to hide his amusement.

'Try writing to your MP,' he suggested, tie covered in burger sauce, a piece of bread roll still caught on the side of his face, undiscovered by his exploring tongue, untouched by his paper napkin.

The MP had been, Angela said when she returned from a local surgery, 'about as useful as a chocolate condom.' And that had pretty much been that. Clive had died shortly afterwards, complications from his injuries conspiring to bring about his downfall, a massive heart attack taking him in an instant.

Phil, Angela and Lucas were lost to grief and mourning.

They all responded in their own ways. Angela had cried for a long time, had briefly toyed with religion before discarding it as unhelpful – 'If there is a god, he's changed his phone number and diverted all calls to voicemail' – and eventually, slowly rebuilt her life, still full of laughter, but much of it hollower than it was before. Lucas remained trapped in his misery, unable to find a way back to the little boy he had been before his father's death. Phil had buried as much of her emotion as possible, finding solace in a sudden interest in schoolwork so she could get into a university, while still hunting down parties like a tracker pursuing prey.

She finished her drink and headed for the bathroom, hoping to sneak in before Lucas could begin his nightly ritual of hogging the shower.

Even now, Phil couldn't believe the coroner had been satisfied with accidental death as a conclusion. There were too many things that made no sense. If the project was, as Virtua admitted, beginning to cost them money thanks to the delays (for which, read: eat into their profits), why had their in-house health and safety officer not done the report so they could get on and finish the work? And why did Virtua have no recollection of anything and no paperwork to support their version of events? After seeing the amount of paper the company still used – deep into the digital age – she couldn't believe that not a single scrap of anything useful was waved in the coroner's face.

And whenever Phil began to wonder if perhaps there

truly was nothing to it, that her dad had simply lied and then killed himself, she remembered Angela's words that day.

'He'd have done a better job of it than that.'

Maybe that was what was driving her need to track down Simon's Poo Bag nemesis: it was so illogical, just as it had been illogical for someone to send Clive into the St Agnes science block that day. Who throws poo into trees? Who on earth would want to endanger Clive? Clive, who was such a loved member of the community that strangers still approached her to tell her how much he'd meant to them.

And now she had a chance to track them down – these agents of irrationality – and find out what possessed them, what motivated them. If she could explain this world, perhaps she would find it easier to live in it without her dad.

'I've caught your need for answers,' she told Simon when she left.

'Ah, then I think you'll be disappointed,' Simon replied. 'I think you'll discover our friend the Tesco Turd Tosser – oh, that's a good one, write that one down – has absolutely no rhyme nor reason for his behaviour. It is totally irrational.'

'Well, I'm prepared to risk it,' said Phil. 'Because since you wrote that letter, it feels like there's a huge gap in my life that can only be filled by speaking to a person who hangs poo in a tree.'

Simon had laughed uproariously. 'Well then. Perhaps I'll get that cake now to celebrate you joining me in the stupidest obsession known to man.'

TUESDAY

NINE

Andrew had been proud to have a female CEO.

He thought of her now as he polished his shoes. It was a job he usually saved for quiet Sunday afternoons, but he had awoken already feeling at a loose end and so he thought he might take stock, perhaps get rid of a few pairs. After all, how many brown leather business shoes did a retired man really need? He really should have got to it sooner.

Gloria Reynolds OBE, a woman of many talents, non-executive director for three respected businesses, including one multinational, *and* regular lay preacher at her Anglican church. Truly someone to admire. Of course, Andrew had no problem at all being led by a woman and he was glad of any opportunity to prove it. If she asked him to do something, he took satisfaction in saying, 'No problem,' or, 'I'd be delighted,' especially in front of others. He was glad of the example he was setting: you've got to change a culture from the top down; you've got to lead by example; you've got to walk the walk.

He flipped over a leather brogue and polished the section

of leather in the arch between the heel and the sole. It was a habit he had learned from his father, a navy man who took pride in his appearance. Andrew had followed his father into the navy before he joined the corporate world. There, the sailors spent many hours bulling their toe caps, but no one ever polished the sole. He'd been surprised. Perhaps it was just his father's foible. He moved onto buffing the tops, sweeping brush over shoe like a violin bow.

Gloria was a hard taskmaster (mistress? Person?), but when it came to day-to-day business, she mostly stayed hands-off, letting Andrew have his head, so that he was able to bring about many of his most cherished changes in a short space of time. She had paid attention to his business transformation plans – his bold ideas for a top-down and bottom-up culture shift – but only in the polite way Princess Anne might enquire about a stockman's cattle at the Oxford Farming Conference. She had more pressing things to think about.

Apart from the St Agnes school project, that is.

Work on the school building had begun a few years previously, but had been put on hold when the incoming headteacher discovered a hole in the finances that took a while to plug. When work was scheduled to recommence, she had taken an unexpectedly keen interest. He had wondered why.

'I've got a nephew at the school,' she explained. 'I'd like to make sure it's the best it can be, you know, for him.'

That was a surprise. From what he had gleaned, her niece was the only child of her only sibling. And, since the niece wasn't married, he wasn't sure where this nephew had come from. Still, he didn't query it. It was one of her longer speeches about her personal life and Andrew felt honoured she had confided in him.

'What's his name?' he asked, hoping to continue the chat.

'Trevor,' she said and then blinked.

'Trevor?' said Andrew cheerfully. 'You don't hear that name very often these days, do you? Good to see it's coming back into fashion.'

'I've got a conference call,' she replied.

Gloria asked him to personally make sure they had their best men working on the project ('people,' he had mentally corrected her).

When the roster of building contractors came in, she had idly picked it up from his desk and said, 'I assume these are the best? I have no idea who any of them are.' And she laughed in a breathy exhalation, like she was trying to fog a window. 'But I've heard that Clive McGinty is very good. Why isn't he on the list?'

'Nothing but the best for Trevor, eh?' he said with a cheerful smile.

She stared at him blankly for a moment and then replied faintly, 'Yes, that's right.'

Normally, he wouldn't dream of interfering. He had written a post on LinkedIn entitled: 'If you don't trust your people to do a good job, you're the one who should be fired,' (which had over eighteen hundred views and twenty comments, a personal record). But he mentioned that the boss wanted, 'The best,' to Ed Fielder, the manager in charge of head count on the project.

'I've heard that Clive McGinty is very good,' he said.

'Yes, Clive is good,' agreed Ed. 'I'll find out if he's available.'

'Well, if he isn't, perhaps you could shift things around. Gloria is very keen to have him in particular.'

Ed, slightly put out at having this unusual oversight – and hardly the most cheerful person at the best of times – reeled off a list of other names, asking if they passed muster, but Clive was the only name Andrew remembered now.

Because Clive was the only person who had died on that building site, toppling into the unfinished wall where he was later discovered on a day so awful Andrew still had nightmares about it. And Andrew knew that his had been the hand that pushed him.

TEN

The bungalow at 33 Nicholswood Drive hunched near the top of the hill. Even in her distracted state, Phil took a moment to admire the sea view. The sun was already gearing up for another unseasonably warm adventure across the sky and for a moment, Phil hoped to bleach away the Scarlett so she could continue being Phil a little longer. She parked the car at the top of the hill and wandered down towards Mrs Cooke's bungalow, watching a couple of clouds pootling gently along the shoreline in the distance. Phil may have been born and raised at the seaside, but she never failed to take a breath when she saw the water. She couldn't imagine ever taking something so changeable and glorious for granted. And today the sea was looking glorious, all showy sparkles and emerald glitter.

You big show off, Phil thought.

Not that this sea view made much difference to the inhabitants on this side of the road; the houses all faced northwest. The gardens with their southeast aspect, might have got the occasional glimpse of blue so long as no one had too many tall shrubs in front of the patio, but it was their main view that had brought Phil here today, because this side of the road had a panoramic display of the fields of St Agnes's secondary school.

To Phil's eyes a bungalow was all wrong. Say what you liked about the council block she had grown up in (and she often did), but she had sweeping vistas on all sides – the sea to the south and the great woodlands to the north – and they rarely closed the curtains. As a child she had pretended she was riding a giant eagle right into the clouds, and to this day she found extreme satisfaction in peering down at the world from her lofty tower. She couldn't imagine hunkering down in a cul-de-sac. From her vantage point, the bungalows looked like squat beetles ripe for squishing.

Phil had planned just to take a look at the building. It was early and experience had taught her that retirees often took their time getting up. But she spotted movement at the front window and an elderly woman peeked out at her from between two slats of the plastic blinds, so she smiled and approached the door to ring the bell.

What sounded like a thousand little dogs began yapping frantically. By the time the owner reached the front door – during which time the dogs had been repeatedly, but ineffectually berated – Phil had made out just three small creatures through the frosted glass, along with a woman who clattered a buffet of locks and opened the door. Eventually, Phil found herself greeting a cheerful woman with close-cropped white hair and photochromic glasses. The dogs made figures of eight around the woman's legs looking extremely indignant that anyone might come to their house, while also sneezing and wagging their tails in evident delight at Phil's arrival.

'Don't mind them,' said the woman.

'Mrs Cooke?' said Phil.

'Yes?' said the woman. 'Are you collecting for the RNLI because I've already given this month and I'm only on a state pension, so...'

Phil had been planning to lie. She was going to tell Mrs Cook that she was from Virtua's customer complaints department doing a survey to see if people were happy with the service they have received. But then she looked at the woman's round, warm eyes and realised she couldn't do it. The *Aldhill Observer* had done so many pieces over the years about scammers taking advantage of the elderly on the doorstep that Phil didn't want to be one of them.

'Hello, sorry to bother you,' she said, handing over her card. 'My name's Philippa McGinty and I'm from the local paper.'

Mrs Cooke grappled with her reading glasses for a moment before scrutinising Phil's card.

'I'm doing a story about the increasing problem of company vehicles being parked across people's drives and a contact at Virtua Services said you might be a good person to talk to.'

Well, it wasn't entirely a lie, even if the contact at Virtua was called Scarlett Stevens and just happened to be standing on Mrs Cooke's doorstop, having her ankles licked by a couple of Yorkshire terriers. Phil could see immediately she had made a mistake. Mrs Cooke's previously friendly demeanour changed in an instant, her face shutting down like a laptop. When she replied, her tone was cold and, Phil thought, a little afraid.

'I have no idea what you're talking about,' she said, handing Phil back her card. 'Goodbye.'

Shutting the door took longer than Mrs Cooke would

have liked because she had to coax the dogs back indoors. While she was desperately trying to get recall on Poppy and Patsy and Treacle, Phil was making a last-ditch effort to win the old lady round.

'It won't take a moment. I just wanted a quick quote about how inconvenienced you were. Something short and simple and maybe a photo?'

Mrs Cooke was having none of it. Eventually, with a few final ankle licks, the dogs returned to their mistress and Phil found herself once again staring at the frosted glass of the front door.

Without thinking, Phil found herself bending down to call through the letterbox.

'Mrs Cooke, did you see a Virtua Services van parked in front of your house on the day Clive McGinty went missing?'

'Go away!' said Mrs Cooke. 'I'll call the police.'

Phil, feeling like an elder abuser, stood upright. 'Sorry. I'm going. I didn't mean to frighten you.' She pushed the business card through the letterbox, careful her fingers weren't chewed off by an infuriated lapdog. 'If you change your mind, just give me a call.'

On her way down the front path Phil noticed the very nice-looking caravan next to a very nice-looking Honda – not new, but in excellent condition. She took a moment to marvel at the things people chose to spend their money on – certainly nothing else about Mrs Cooke's lifestyle seemed to suggest she had the money for top-of-the-range touring caravans. She took one last glance back up the path towards the bungalow and spotted the plastic blinds in the front room swinging back into place.

. . .

'Do you fancy getting lunch?' said a voice.

Phil looked up from her pile of letters.

'It's a lovely day,' continued Rhonda, 'and I had a falling out with the sandwich boy, so I don't think I can face another one of his soggy creations.'

'Did he scrimp on the fillings?' said Phil.

'Something like that,' agreed Rhonda. 'I'm sure Arnie's Sarnies was better before he joined.'

Rhonda led Phil to a little café Phil had never noticed before, tucked in between two nondescript office buildings. It didn't look very promising from the outside and Phil thought wistfully of Beachy Shed, her favourite local coffee-and-lunch spot, where you could get a fish finger bun for five quid. But, in the end, she was pleasantly surprised. The tiny little space had a full array of sandwich offerings – from avocado to German salami and Jarlsberg – and she was able to custom make herself her ideal creation.

'Mild cheddar,' she said to the man behind the counter.

'Very adventurous,' said Rhonda, raising an eyebrow. The sarcasm was warranted, she couldn't deny it: she had the eating habits of a toddler.

'Listen,' she said. 'It's not as bad as it used to be. Just be grateful I didn't ask for tomato ketchup.'

'Oh God,' said Rhonda, before ordering prawn and avocado – a combination that made Phil's stomach turn.

The beach was relatively busy. Although all the schools were back and the holidaymakers were mostly gone, the late heatwave had brought out local sun worshippers. Phil had a sudden moment of dread: what if Scarlett was here today? What if she came over and said, 'Hi Phil,' or introduced herself to Rhonda? It was unlikely: Scarlett would be further up the beach near all the cool cafés and cocktail huts. Nevertheless, Phil couldn't help scanning the beach to make sure. Anyway, she told herself, it's not Scarlett you need to worry about. She was a born and bred Aldhill local; it was a small town; she couldn't remember a time when she had left the house and not bumped into someone she knew. All it would take would be for someone to spot her and come barrelling over for a chat.

Bit late to think of that now. She reached into her bag and pulled out her sunglasses, as though a pair of shaded lenses would render her invisible.

They found a spot on the pebbles by the adventure playground and enjoyed the sea view while they ate, keeping close watch on the circling herring gulls overhead.

'So tell me about yourself, Rhonda,' she said. 'How did you end up here?'

Rhonda snorted. 'You wouldn't believe me if I told you,' she said.

Phil assessed her for a moment, a thought forming. She made her prediction: 'You followed a man here, didn't you?'

Rhonda's sour face told her the answer.

'I thought he was the right one,' Rhonda said. 'Turned out he was *a right one*, if you get my drift. Drinker. Gambler. He spent all his time here on the slot machines like a little boy. I'd walk to the beach to meet him and he'd be surrounded by beer cans and bags of coins. At some point, I finally saw the light and kicked him out. I think he's over in Brighton now. Useless so-and-so. Honestly, I really do know how to pick them.'

Phil got the impression Rhonda was holding back on her language for her sake.

'Better luck next time?' Phil said, and Rhonda snorted again.

'I'm done with all that, more trouble than it's worth.'

'But you decided to stay here?' said Phil.

'By then I already had a job at Virtua. And I like it here. I haven't really looked back.'

'Well, I expect you haven't had the time to look back,' said Phil, trying to bring the conversation around to office politics.

'That's true,' snorted Rhonda.

'You're always so busy,' said Phil.

'Yes, I do sometimes wonder if I'm the only one doing anything at all, present company excluded. It's a lovely day, isn't it? They said it's going to continue all week.'

From her swift change of subject, Phil got the sense that Rhonda wasn't given to indulging in a good moan. She was about to pipe down in case she offended her when the office manager continued.

'You getting those reports done in an afternoon yesterday was a real eye-opener. The boys in investigations usually take all week to get that much achieved. Makes you wonder what they're doing the rest of the time.'

'What about the others?' said Phil. 'It seems like you're doing some people's jobs for them.'

Rhonda shrugged. 'I just help out occasionally,' she said in a closed tone. 'Look at those wally seagulls fighting over that bread.'

Phil left it there. She didn't want to get on Rhonda's wrong side; it was clear she wasn't about to get stuck into Jamie or any of her colleagues. A shame, thought Phil. She enjoyed a good moan. But there was no point forcing it, and so they chatted about other things until, towards the end, Rhonda appeared to have a change of heart and returned to the subject.

'Jamie means well. She's a lovely woman, but I think the job might have overwhelmed her. She used to have a boss above her and a whole team, but then Andrew... that's the previous head of HR... retired early, and a lot of the older, more experienced team members were made part-time or redundant. We use an outsourced HR firm for a lot of it, but still... I don't think Jamie really knew what had hit her.'

'That sounds tough,' said Phil, who honestly didn't feel that bad for Jamie. She got to keep her job when others around didn't, yet barely got into a sweat about anything – and she appeared to have a willing slave in Rhonda.

She thought about Jamie's boss. Retired early. It sounded like a euphemism for 'taken out back and shot.'

'What was the previous manager like?' she enquired, trying to make it sound like a perfectly innocent question.

'Andrew? Oh, you know,' said Rhonda in a tone that suggested she didn't like to speak ill of the dead (or recently retired, at least). 'He had his foibles, but he had a good heart, I think. He was always good to me – very supportive – but, like I say, he definitely had his foibles.'

Well, now she was intrigued. 'How do you mean?'

'Oh... I don't know,' said Rhonda, blinking with one eye as she gazed towards the sky. She just wasn't that sort of woman – no blabbing for Rhonda – and so Phil had to content herself with filling in the blanks alone. But where to start? Was he a boor? A bully? A pervert? A layabout? There were too many options. Eventually, in the silence, Rhonda spoke again.

'He had lots of very interesting ideas and he was a passionate leader. We all liked him. It's just that he ruffled a few feathers when he got a particular promotion and I'm not sure it was done in the most, let's say, sensitive way.'

Ok, that narrowed it all down a bit. So he had trampled some egos on his way up the ladder.

'Is that why he retired early?' Phil asked.

'What?' Rhonda looked confused for a moment and then shook her head. 'No, that was a while afterwards. No one's really sure why he retired early. It wasn't really that early – he was at least sixty – but the senior leaders tend to hang around here – some are well into their seventies – so it felt unusual. The company was going through some restructuring, so perhaps it made sense – they could cut some costs, get someone a bit younger–'

'And cheaper,' said Phil.

'Yes,' agreed Rhonda without breaking stride. 'And to be honest, he was never quite himself after…'

Rhonda stopped herself short and pressed her lips together, the living embodiment of the phrase, "button your lips".

'After what?' said Phil.

'You may have read about it,' said Rhonda. 'Or perhaps you were too young to be reading the news.'

Rhonda took a breath and suddenly Phil knew what she was going to say next.

'A man… one of our builders… died on a building site about six years ago.'

Seven, thought Phil and suddenly became aware she was digging her nails into her leg.

'And although it wasn't Andrew's fault, I think he always felt like it was a terrible failure. It ruined the company's safety record. It was all very sad.'

She sighed, and Phil tried to collect herself. She had to say something, but she couldn't trust her voice not to break. She could feel her lips turning down involuntarily, the muscles jerking as she fought against them, so that she thought she must resemble the saddest of the sad-face emojis.

'That's terrible,' she managed at last, and gave a cough to clear her throat and regain control over her expression. She took a bite of her sandwich.

'Yes,' agreed Rhonda, 'but like I said, he wasn't to blame.'

Phil chewed, using the bread to buy time. Being there, right in that moment, was suddenly one of the hardest things she'd ever done. She wanted to rise up from the pebbles and run home as fast as she could. *He wasn't to blame.* Then who was? Why was it so hard just to get a simple answer? She took another bite and swallowed slowly.

'What happened?' she said at last. She was grateful that they were sitting on the beach, staring out to sea: it made it easier to turn her face away. She collected up a handful of rocks and began balancing one on top of the other, squinting in the sunlight.

'It was just one of those sad accidents that happen from time-to-time unfortunately,' said Rhonda. 'It was ruled death by misadventure. No one's fault – just bad luck.'

Mention again that it was an accident – that it was no one's fault – thought Phil. Every sentence Rhonda uttered felt like some sort of disclaimer: Virtua Services accept no liability for the following statements.

'How horrible,' was all she managed to say.

'Anyway,' said Rhonda, giving a tight smile, 'let's not dwell on that on such a beautiful day.'

Phil took that as an invitation to spend a little time in quiet contemplation, but while Rhonda admired the beauty of the beach, Phil felt like her insides were boiling. She shut her eyes, pretending she was worshipping the sun, and took a few deep breaths, calming herself to revert to cheerful Scarlett the helpful intern again.

Phil opened her eyes. Out at sea a man wobbled carefully upright on his paddle board. The water was relatively flat, but he was inexperienced, and he took his time to slowly stand, gaining height by increments, every inch a triumph over gravity and motion. Seeing his small battle with physics cheered her a little and eventually she felt able to carry on pretending to be Scarlett.

'I expect Dee Dee's told you about the emails?' said Rhonda, breaking into Phil's daydream. 'I saw you talking to her.'

Phil had decided not to mention Dee Dee or the emails directly, and now Rhonda had brought it up, she wasn't sure how to reply.

'She mentioned them, yes.' She was trying not to sound too eager, hoping to get Rhonda to do as much of the talking as possible.

'Well, she's wrong about who sent them, in case you're wondering. Yes, I've heard her theory, but there's no way Jamie could have sent them.'

'Oh, really?' said Phil.

'I mean, the whole idea is preposterous. Dee Dee doesn't know what she's talking about,' said Rhonda. 'And anyway, I was with her – Jamie, that is – when one of the emails was sent. We were in a meeting the entire morning, so I know it wasn't her. And, before you say it, she definitely didn't use her phone or anything. I would have noticed. I always do.'

Rhonda took a neat bite of her sandwich and stared thoughtfully out to sea. 'So, it's definitely not her.'

Phil watched Rhonda chomping and decided to risk sounding nosey.

'Have you had one?'

Rhonda swallowed before responding.

'When I got out of that meeting with Jamie, there it was on my computer waiting for me.'

Phil pulled a face, 'Creepy. What did it say? You must have been really spooked?'

'It wasn't very pleasant, no.'

Out at sea the man on the paddle board, defeated by gravity, had resorted to kneeling.

'And you've got no idea who it could've been?' said Phil.

'I have my suspicions,' said Rhonda, 'but unlike Dee Dee, I don't throw out accusations willy-nilly without a bit of evidence.'

'How would you go about getting evidence?'

'I honestly have no idea,' side Rhonda. 'But all I know is, whoever it was has access to secrets they shouldn't have access to.'

'Maybe it was Gloria Reynolds,' said Phil, and Rhonda snorted a laugh.

'She never puts anything in writing,' said Rhonda.

'You were her personal assistant, weren't you? What was that like?'

'Executive assistants they are now. I'd be better paid than I am now if I'd stayed. But it was a lot of work. You do a lot of running around after people.'

'Doesn't sound much different to what you do now,' Phil observed.

Rhonda laughed. 'No, I suppose not. But what I do now feels less stressful, if you can believe it. Gloria could be quite unpredictable.'

On the walk back, Phil decided to risk mentioning the emails again.

'Isn't it a bit scary knowing there's someone out there who knows private information?' she ventured. 'I'd be terrified.'

'Well, try not to worry,' said Rhonda. 'IT are on the case.'

Rhonda explained that IT had discovered the IP address of the email and were in talks with the ISP to get the address of the sender.

'It all sounds like gobbledegook to me,' said Rhonda, 'but apparently it means they're on the trail. But the emails aren't being sent from the building, that's for sure.'

So IT were busy playing detectives, which was all well and good, but staff were being harassed, which made Phil wonder why they hadn't got the police involved.

'I think they're hoping to avoid any controversy. Hoping to handle it all internally,' explained Rhonda.

Let me guess, thought Phil. They don't want to get investigated for a considerable data privacy failure within the company. Especially not with the audit right round the corner.

She didn't say that out loud, however. She didn't want to come across as weirdly knowledgeable about General Data Protection Regulation. It didn't seem like the kind of thing Scarlett would have had an opinion on.

'If you want to be offered a permanent job here,' said Rhonda, 'I suggest you stay out of Dee Dee's way as much as possible. She's trouble, that woman. She will only drag you into her mess. She's had two verbal warnings, and a written warning over the last few years.'

'Noted,' said Phil, immediately resolving to speak to Dee Dee as much as possible, and to extract the full story on the warnings.

Out at sea, the man kneeling on his paddleboard hit a ripple and tumbled into the water.

'And I wouldn't mention the emails to anyone else if I were you,' said Rhonda.

Although her tone still sounded light, there was a studied air to it that gave Phil the distinct impression she was being threatened.

'Double noted,' she said, immediately resolving to find out who sent the emails.

ELEVEN

When Jen was twelve she had visited Aldhill on a family holiday. Her parents weren't given to extravagances and holidays were basically non-existent. But, for whatever reason (perhaps they'd won some money on the Premium Bonds), they booked a weekend in a holiday park near-ish the sea front (once you'd walked down the hill and crossed the main road). Jen and her siblings had had a great time, hardly able to believe their luck at a weekend spent throwing stones in the ocean, scoffing down chips and ice cream and, for one happy hour (at the pursed-lipped disapproval of their mother), feeding their pocket money into the penny drops and claw grabbers at the amusement arcades.

Years later, when Jen had moved to Aldhill as an adult, she had taken Nate on a date that included a spending spree in Luckyland. The easy abandon with which he handed over his pennies to the various machines should probably have raised some red flags, but Jen watched the spendthrift she would someday marry with unalloyed pleasure: here was a man who knew how to have fun. Luckily, the red flags were unnecessary: in normal life, Nate was sensible enough with his earnings; he just knew how to let his hair down. Turned out Jen needed a man like that.

'What's money for if it's not for buying nice things?' he said once, and she found she was utterly thunderstruck. This thought had genuinely never occurred to her.

What was it for?

She had no answer. In her family, it was either something you hoarded or something you desperately tried to earn more of before the bailiffs came. (Not that they ever did, but her mother kept everyone in fear that they *might*.) That it could be earned specifically to spend on something nice was utterly mind-boggling.

Today, when she arrived at Luckyland with Nandini, she scanned across the rows of penny falls and claw cranes – the lights from the air hockey and games machines throwing out bright strobes of colour. Somewhere Zoltar in a polyester turban was promising to reveal more of his secrets. An ache in Jen's throat, scorched and tight, grew so strong she knew it would take her a moment to regain her voice. Swallowing, she continued her search, hoping to glimpse Nate's black curls, to hear his gravelly laugh as he won 1op.

Ridiculous woman.

These moments should be lessening, shouldn't they? She should be moving past all that towards some kind of sad but accepting state of widowhood, not scanning every crowd for her dead husband. But she couldn't seem to stop.

Yes, he was dead – but where *was* he?

She had never believed in heaven, but that didn't answer her question. He can't be nowhere at all, she thought. When his heart stopped beating, and he breathed his last breath, where did he go? All those neurons that stopped firing, those little electrical impulses, they must have gone somewhere. To the worms? Into compost and humus. But where else? Into the ether? Along telephone wires, into every space where he had once been? She touched one of the pinball machines – hoping to feel the electrical pulse from where his fingertips had once pressed buttons with childish delight – and shook her head.

What a fool.

Of course he wasn't here. She was an idiot. She swallowed again, trying to shift the painful lump that had formed, and smiled as the manager, a pale-faced man called Ryan Sharman, approached.

'He's only about twelve,' muttered Jen, her throat still dry from emotion.

'That's only because you're ancient, sarge,' said Nandini.

And Jen wondered if it would be a breach of HR regulations to kick her in the shin.

Ryan Sharman, it seemed, was extremely obliging. So obliging, in fact, that he obliged them to come and sit in the back room while they spoke where they would 'be more comfortable'. Presumably, the sight of two detectives was going to be upsetting for the patrons, which currently numbered one person: a bald man in his fifties wearing a faded red t-shirt, a pair of flimsy tracksuit bottoms and sliders with grubby white socks.

As Jen and Nandini made their way to the back room, Jen appraised the patron's chosen machine. She didn't fancy his chances of winning: the two pennies in the trays didn't look precarious enough to topple for another few hours yet. Still, she reasoned, some fool had to get the coins piled sufficiently high so that one lucky gambler could win a quid later in the day.

Now she knew who that fool was.

'No, sorry, I don't remember anyone by that description,' said Ryan.

They were now squashed into what Ryan claimed was his office, but looked more like a looted stationery cupboard. Jen was on the only chair (one of those moulded plastic seats which seemed designed, Jen always thought, for the buttocks to spill out through the gaping hole at the rear), while Ryan perched awkwardly on the laminate corner of his desk. Nandini lingered near the doorway as though ready to take flight, perhaps afraid that the polyester lining on Ryan's suit might spontaneously combust in the cramped space.

Jen thought he looked like a bad drawing of an estate agent, all sharp stick-like angles and that terrible, ill-fitting suit. She wondered if he'd got the shiny grey suit from a charity shop. She hadn't seen iridescence like that since the early nineties. He sniffed violently for the second time and rubbed his nose; an action that seemed born more of habit than necessity.

'The CCTV would have been recorded over by now. It loops every forty-eight hours,' said Ryan.

Why is he wearing a suit anyway? Surely this was a polo-shirt and smart trousers kind of management position? Ryan looked like he was hoping to get a job as a trader on the London stock exchange in Thatcher's Britain.

'He might have been homeless?' she said, wondering why she was bothering. Ryan's mum was still probably cutting his sandwiches into triangles when their victim was visiting Luckyland. 'Perhaps he came in for a bit of warmth and shelter occasionally. He might have stuck in someone's mind. Have you got anyone who worked here back then?'

'We don't let the homeless in here,' sniffed Ryan.

Jen thought of the man in the sliders and flimsy tracksuit bottoms and smiled to herself. Did Ryan think he was running a high-end casino in the Square Mile?

'Everyone who works here only started a few years ago, max,' Ryan continued.

The joys of the seaside, sighed Jen inwardly. The transience of the labour force always made things harder; all teenagers doing summer jobs before they start their A-levels. She wondered if Ryan had started his yet.

'So, you don't remember anyone in a Prints To Go top?' she said. 'Would have been about six or seven years ago, maybe? We're still waiting on exact confirmation.'

'I was at school then, so I'm afraid I can't help.'

Oh, the confidence of youth. To tell her that no homeless people came in while also admitting you were still basically a foetus when their John Doe walked the streets. The image of the fool at the penny drops popped into Jen's mind. The grubby red t-shirt, those flimsy coin-filled tracksuit bottoms appearing in her mind's eye like a persistent pop-up ad.

'Do you have any regulars?' she asked.

'What kind of bloody nickname is Babycakes?' hissed Nandini on their way towards the giant man-baby currently failing to win a prize on the claw grabber.

Those thin joggers Babycakes was wearing provided Jen with too much information about his crotch region as he waddled from a claw grabber to one of the penny drops. At a glance, she knew which side he dressed on, and also, thanks to a second bulge in his pocket (and the unmistakable jangling sound), that he was loaded up with coins. The coins weighed down one side of his tracksuit so that Jen expected them to fall down at any time. His smooth head and loping gait would have given him the appearance of a giant baby had it not been for the three-day stubble and the scab by his lip.

'An apt one?' replied Jen, eying the stains on Babycakes's red t-shirt with suspicion. 'I'm pretty sure that's apple puree on his top.... At least I hope that's all it is.'

'Hello sir,' she continued smoothly as they reached him. He was shuffling over to a new spot, clearly hoping to find more luck at a different machine. They followed him as he moved. 'I'm Detective Sergeant Jen Collet and this is Detective Constable Nandini Roy from Aldhill Police. Ryan, the manager, thought you might be able to help us. Would you mind?'

Babycakes didn't even glance at them as he fed a two pence piece into the slot, tongue sticking out as though the process required a high level of technical skill. Jen glanced over. Nandini, ever-impatient, looked ready to press the man's cheek onto the glass casing and handcuff him.

'We're trying to identify someone who used to come here regularly,' continued Jen. She shot Nandini a warning look, but Nandini was glaring at Babycakes, chin jutting out, this close to losing patience. 'He would have been wearing a blue Prints To Go top.'

They all watched the coin landing in the machine and, as the paddle approached it, Jen found herself weirdly invested in the outcome. Balanced on the edge of the coin pile was a roll of Luckyland tickets. Such treasure! But as the metal swept forwards, the coin was subsumed amongst the rest and the roll of tickets didn't even wobble.

Shame.

Unbowed, Babycakes reached into his tracksuit bottoms

and pulled out a handful of cash, eyeing the pile like Jen's great-auntie choosing a biscuit from a selection box. He spoke without looking up.

'Pennywise.'

Nandini tilted her head. 'What was that?'

'Pennywise.'

'Pennywise what?'

Babycakes shrugged.

'That's what we called him.'

I gathered that, dipshit. That's what Jen wanted to say, but she swallowed down the sarcasm and simply said, 'No surname?'

Babycakes shrugged again as Jen sent up a silent prayer for patience to whichever god might be listening. Babycakes lifted a plastic bag and Jen realised it was stuffed with Luckyland tickets and a few more handfuls of coins. Bitter experience from her time spent gambling in Luckyland with Nate had taught her that even with that roll of winning tickets, he would come away with not much more than a handful of gummy sweets and (possibly) a very small cuddly toy.

'He didn't work here,' said Babycakes.

He'd selected a coin by now and was shuffling around, hungrily seeking a new slot.

'Was he a regular then?' said Jen as Babycakes shrugged yet again.

'Used to see him sometimes.'

It seemed there weren't any gods in today, which would explain why Jen could feel the very last of her patience ebbing away to be replaced by a hot rush of anger. Why must it always be like trying to get blood from a stone? Why couldn't this man, who clearly had something to tell them, look them in the eye and give a whole paragraph on his friend's full name, job and last known address? It was like trying to get a toddler to admit where he'd hidden the peanut butter sandwich.

Perhaps that was the key to it: treat him like a child.

Worth a try.

'Babycakes, I've had it up to *here* this week with surly men who can't seem to string a sentence together, who need to be coaxed into telling me the most basic information. So I'm going to give you to the count of three to tell me everything you know, and if you're still staring at that bloody machine and muttering, or if you shrug one more time, I'm going to get angry. Ok? One... Two...'

'What the hell?' said Nandini as they left Luckyland. She was grinning from ear to ear and Jen, striding next to her, was trying to smother her own grin. 'What were you planning to do when you got to three? Put him over your knee and smack his bum?'

'Christ, don't put that image into my head,' said Jen. 'The truth is, I have absolutely no idea. I think I would have tried two-and-a-half first.'

Nandini cackled as Jen felt tears of laughter prick her eyes. 'Then two-and-three-quarters.'

After they had regained control of themselves they took stock of what they had learned from a more obliging Babycakes (real name Tim Noakes). Sure, Jen conceded, he had still maintained eye contact only with the coin dropper, but he had at least offered up as much useful information as he could as quickly as he could muster (still not fast enough for Jen's liking, but it was better than the protracted misery of their first moments together.)

First, they had discovered that Pennywise's real name may or may not have been Danny or Benny 'Or Jimmy or summink like that.' Second, they learned that Danny or Benny or Jimmy spent a lot of time with Babycakes and although he did sometimes work, it was mostly casual labour jobs. He may have taken the odd job on a building site, but Babycakes couldn't suggest any of his employers beyond 'the usual lot.' Which, when pressed, turned out to mean, 'I dunno. Any of the local companies who build stuff.'

'Virtua Services, maybe?' suggested Jen.

Babycakes shrugged. 'Maybe.'

Babycakes thought that Danny or Benny or Jimmy must have fallen foul of money lenders or similar, since he'd simply stopped turning up one day. Pennywise was normally pretty regular at coming into the arcade, but Babycakes hadn't thought to raise any alarms or report it.

'Wasn't my business,' he said when Jen asked.

'And can you remember when you last saw him?'

There was no exact date, but Babycakes remembered the man had gone missing the same year the Aldhill Bonfire Society had paraded a Guy Fawkes that looked like, quote: 'that dead bloke from the school wall' through the town. He remembered because it was the last time he had been to the bonfire night – the same year he won his biggest ever jackpot.

'I thought of Pennywise and wished he'd been here to see it,' he explained.

'The bonfire?' said Nandini.

'The jackpot.'

'That's easy, then,' said Jen as they reached the car. 'It was seven years ago, right after Clive died. They dressed a Guy up as a pirate and burned it in his honour, although I can never quite work out whether things are tributes or effigies when it comes to bonfire night.'

'So, middle of October?'

'Yup.'

It had amazed Jen how much of a big deal Guy Fawkes' night was in East Sussex. Rather than clashing over the fifth of November, a lot of towns in the county held their festivities on different weekends so that all the drumming groups and bonfire societies could attend them all. Lewes, the biggest and best-known had dibs on Bonfire Night itself on the fifth; Aldhill was a few weeks before.

'So our John Doe died the same time and the same way,' said Nandini.

'Yep,' said Jen. She knew what Nandini's tone implied.

'And he used to work on building sites, just like Clive.'

Jen opened the car door.

'Looks like even DCI Petra Gull won't be able to claim that's a coincidence.'

TWELVE

After lunch Phil went in search of caffeine. The kitchenette stank of reheated leftover food and some kind of weapons-grade kitchen cleaner, but it had a decent array of tea bags and a selection of coffee pods. She spent some time reading the various packets before selecting a medium roast black coffee. She loaded up the machine and set it to work, going slowly so that she could delay the return to her cell. She was idly sipping her coffee, leaning on the worktop to read the health and safety posters around the walls when Dee Dee appeared.

'I see they've still got you cooped up in the box, babes? Oh my god, Mick and his team had to work in there for months on end. Can you imagine? All crammed in like sardines in the dark. They finally found him a space in the office near a window and got the others hot-desking. I'm not joking, when the poor sod came out he was completely grey – all pale and sun-deprived, you know, like one of those creatures that lives underground.'

Naked mole rat, thought Phil, but didn't say it out loud

this time. 'I'm not surprised, she said. 'I can feel all of the vitamin D leaving my body.'

'And you know what they've got you doing, don't you?' said Dee Dee, leaning in conspiratorially, her bosom seeming to join them in their confab, her tongue poking the inside of her cheek as her eyebrows raised. The classic face of someone about to impart a juicy secret.

Phil raised an eyebrow and leaned in as well.

'They've got you hiding evidence, babes,' Dee Dee said. 'They are due an audit from an external agency and they are absolutely bricking it. I said to Jan (she works in biz dev, ever-so nice, bit thick), I said: "You know what they've got her doing, don't you? They've got her hiding evidence," I said, "They don't want to get caught out not replying to letters," I said. "They're going to come a cropper if they don't sort it out," I said. They work for a lot of council and utility services you see, babe, and they have to abide by particular regulations.'

She began reeling off a list: responding appropriately; engaging in a timely manner; handling complaints sensitively and responsibly.

'But they got rid of so many staff that a lot of these letters get ignored. Mick is meant to look into some of the damage ones, but he has a pile of paperwork on his desk that he never seems to touch (it's a mystery what he does all day, babes, no one knows). It's my job to deal with some of the more mundane complaints: the old ladies who have had the electricity cut off by a clumsy digger; all the people who have their drives damaged by a reversing truck. All that kind of crap, and I do a good job there, no matter what anyone might tell you. (I expect you're bored stiff reading them all, sorry about that.) But so many of the letters fall through the cracks.'

Here she pointed a self-satisfied finger in Phil's direction. 'And you're only looking at the hard copy letters that are sent, babes. I'm not joking, the emails are a whole other nightmare. People have been working all hours to get those processed.'

'Ugh. It sounds like you're really rushed off your feet,' said Phil. So rushed off her feet, in fact, that she could only spend three-quarters of her day chatting to her fellow co-workers. Dee Dee carried on as though Phil hadn't spoken, still full of things she wanted to get off her chest.

'Thankfully – as I said to Jan – "Thank God, Jan" I said. "They've finally got some basic automated responses set up," I said. "And about bloody time too," I said. Can you believe it's taken so long? And IT has promised they're going to sort out one of those bot things that pretends to be a human, but I'll believe that when I see it, babes. No offence, but IT are a bunch of time wasters if you ask me. They just sit around all day eating custard creams and being sarcastic. I can't stand them personally. Although I shouldn't complain. If they ever do get off their arses and build a bot, babes, that'll be bye-bye Dee Dee. I'm not even joking. I can't see them keeping me on if the computer can do my job for me. The powers that be'll take any opportunity to sack us all if it saves them a few quid.'

This was the kind of conversation Phil lived for. She was in her element. She he spent the next ten minutes commiserating with Dee Dee and encouraging her to vent her spleen even more. Eventually, when Dee Dee was finally losing steam, Phil asked, 'So, what happens to all the unanswered letters I'm sorting, then? Are you going to have to try to answer them all before the audit, or...?'

The answer that came was exactly the one Phil had been expecting.

'I expect Jamie will put them into a black sack and chuck them in a bin somewhere far away from here. Not that I blame her, babes. I wish her well.'

'But you think she's the person sending all the emails, don't you?' Phil said, raising an amused eyebrow. 'I'd be fuming.'

Dee Dee didn't miss a beat. Without a moment of embarrassment or shame, she replied, 'God no. I never thought it was her babes. No way.'

Phil had to applaud the boldness of this lie. She wanted to jab her with an elbow and exclaim, 'Oooh, you big fibber,' but she remained silent as Dee Dee continued. 'But whoever it is has been getting information from her somehow.'

'What do you mean?' said Phil.

'Well, the stuff this person knew about me must have come from my HR file – or from someone working in HR. But I don't think it's her.'

'Why not?' said Phil.

Dee Dee craned her neck backwards, looking along the room in each direction, checking for eavesdroppers. She spoke through closed teeth. 'They're asking for money now.'

'What?!' cried Phil in amazement.

Dee Dee nodded grimly. 'Yep. Jan's came through last night. They want five hundred quid or they're going to tell the world that Jan had a nervous breakdown the March before last. Don't tell anyone I told you that, will you? Jan doesn't like people to know.'

Phil was willing to bet the whole office already knew. Dee Dee carried on.

'So, there we have it. A request for money in return for

keeping their mouth shut about Jan's little secret. But the joke's on them because I don't care who knows what's in my HR file. I'll tell anyone who asks.'

Phil thought of those warnings Rhonda had mentioned – rather indiscreetly, come to think of it – and was thrilled the mystery was going to be resolved so soon. But Dee Dee's face changed, and she said loudly, 'I'll see what I can do about that for you, babes. And if you need any more advice about dealing with complaints, just give me a shout, yeah?'

And with that she strode off. Phil poked her head around the side of the kitchenette divider and spotted Dee Dee's manager looking decidedly unimpressed. Time to return to my cave, Phil thought with a sigh.

'I've got a weird question,' said Phil.

She was on her way down to the car when she took out her phone and, without really thinking, called her ex-boyfriend Dean Martin.

'Doesn't sound like you,' said Dean.

'Ok, ok, even weirder than usual.'

'I find that hard to believe. Surprise me.'

'If a company disposes of a load of letters from the public that they were meant to reply to, is that breaking the law?'

Dean paused. 'Ok, you did it. You surprised me.'

It took another few minutes for Phil to slowly explain the question. 'It's just a hypothetical,' she said. 'It's not as though I know anyone currently sorting through piles of correspondence that they believe is going to be destroyed.'

By now Dean was not only confused he was also suspicious.

'Oh, forget it,' said Phil, 'Let's change the subject.'

'No, no, you've asked now. Let's try to come up with an answer. If a company was destroying letters, it's presumably some sort of compliance issue. If they're getting rid of them ahead of an independent audit, it's fraud and you should probably report it to their governing body.'

'That's what I thought,' said Phil.

'Of course you did,' said Dean. 'It's hardly rocket science is it? So why are you really calling?'

'Just to hear your voice,' said Phil. She shouldn't say things like that to him, shouldn't flirt with him; it wasn't fair. She was the one who had broken up with him, after all. But it was true; she did just want to hear his voice. He had a lovely voice, a kind voice, full of laughs and all her happy teenage memories of their childhood together as young sweethearts. It wasn't his fault she'd fallen apart after Clive died. She'd broken Dean's heart, first by dumping him and then by getting off with everyone from Bertha Mayfield, a local swimming instructor, to a beautiful foreign student visiting from South Korea whose gender Phil couldn't entirely determine even after the snog.

'I call BS,' said Dean. 'You're ringing me because you want to confess something. Come on, admit it.'

That was true too: he knew her too well.

'Never,' said Phil.

'Jesus, Phil. I'm not your priest. If you're in danger, you need to tell me now, but if you're just up to something and want to get it off your chest, I don't want to know about it.'

This was a personality fault of hers, she thought. She'd always been a blagger, always been happy to bluff her way into a situation; she probably should have been a confidence trickster since serial fibbing came easily, but she was a blabberer too. She liked to share things with her friends; she could only lie for so long before she felt the urge to say, 'Only kidding,' and laugh. She liked to be open and honest with people – for the most part – so the fibbing was usually only temporary, only enough to get her out of a parking ticket or into a club.

It was a relief in a way – discovering she wasn't a total sociopath. She couldn't have spent her life like one of those charlatans who pretend to be a doctor or a pilot; fantasists who take over people's lives and inhabit new identities like a hermit crab switching shells. She liked humans too much to constantly undermine their trust. She could sweet-talk her way into a corporate building, but she wouldn't last longer than a week pretending to be Scarlett: she already felt bad for Rhonda who had enough on her plate. She might even feel guilty about Jamie if she spent enough time with her, despite Jamie's own questionable psychological foibles. And the thought of Dee Dee discovering her lies pained her.

'Oh you know me, Dean, always hustling,' she said. 'How's the coppering coming along?' The change of subject was a relief to both of them, and although Dean's sigh let her know he was onto her, he answered.

'It's ok. I did my stint with the SOCOs.'

He proceeded to tell her all about his time learning about crime scenes, how he'd spent the week peering at more brain matter than he'd ideally like. And Phil enjoyed shouting at him to, 'Stop speaking now,' while continuing to ask him questions.

'Anyway, I'm playing detectives this week,' he finished.

'Have you decided what you'll go for yet?' she asked.

'Not yet,' he replied. 'It's too hard to choose. There are things I love about being there in the thick of it all as a uniformed officer, responding to calls first, being able to help people, but I like seeing things through too, finding out who did it.'

Dean had all the qualities you need to be a good police officer: calm in a crisis, unflappable, intelligent, willing to do the right thing. Whatever specialism he chose, the force would be the better for having him. She heard him take a breath.

'Look...' His tone changed and suddenly he sounded strained and sad. 'I need to go.'

Phil, unsure whether to take this sudden awkwardness personally, tried to sound breezy.

'Places to be, people to save, right?'

'Bye Phil.'

She said goodbye and wondered if he had already started hanging up before she finished speaking. He's just busy, she chided herself. He's got other things to do besides chat to his ex like nothing's happened.

For a long time after they'd got together, her classmates would look at her in surprise and say, 'You're with Dean? What... really?' Phil began to suspect she was some kind of moose, but really she was above average in that department, albeit in a slightly scruffy and lanky way. It was just that Dean looked like a wholesome underwear model, the sort of corn-fed pretty boy Americans liked to cast as the dimpled lead in teen dramas. It would be hard to imagine anyone other than an American movie prom queen standing by his side.

Phil had been hard as nails, good for a laugh, brash and opinionated; she was barely seen as a sexual being by the other boys until Dean started dating her. She hadn't 'blossomed' as a teenager, like something out of a movie, hadn't taken off her glasses and revealed a beauty hidden behind the lenses. She had never succumbed to the lure of drawing in huge lips and eyebrows with thick pencils. She didn't wear teeny tiny skirts and tight, tight tops. Although she'd had a few boyfriends in those early innocent days of secondary school, she hadn't been with anyone seriously. But now, handsome Dean, the class dreamboat – and the nicest boy in school – was interested, and Phil felt her stock rising the longer the relationship continued.

And he was so lovely, just a proper sweetheart. What's more, he *liked* her. He laughed at her jokes, and enjoyed arguing with her about the important things in life (music, films and TV shows). He even liked her friends. Dean was – and she could admit it now it was too late – the perfect man.

But it hadn't been enough to keep them together.

She had broken his heart, Dean. That's certainly the impression he had given her when she told him it was over. He had cried a lot. But she wasn't so sure. Could someone so beautiful be brought so low by little old Pip McGinty? She couldn't imagine it. Didn't want to imagine it, more like. Because she had rejected a perfect man and every now and then she wondered if she would regret it for the rest of her life.

She climbed into the car she shared with Angela (and which her mother had reluctantly parted with for the evening for the purposes of what Angela called, 'The saddest stakeout of all time') and headed off to see a man about a dog poo.

Phil awoke with a start.

She had been in the car since 11.00pm, the time at which Simon had slapped his knee and announced, 'I must away to my chamber, I'm afraid,' before rising from his armchair to follow in the footsteps of his wife, Debbie, who had gone to bed a good hour before, apologising profusely to Phil for abandoning her so early and insisting she was too tired to keep her eyes open. Phil had noticed Debbie clutching a book she had nearly finished and didn't blame her in the slightest for abandoning her husband to sit in their garish front room with a stranger from the local paper.

So Phil had retired to her own chamber – that is, a Ford Fiesta with shards of crisps in the footwell, a gaffer-taped-on side mirror and the persistent smell of damp carpet. The moss growing on the guttering around the roof of the car was Angela's most prized possession ('It's my carbon offset') which is why Phil no longer picked off the little clumps of minuscule rainforest to admire their beauty and fortitude, since Angela had been deeply distressed at the last moss cull.

It had been warm enough to begin with, but the temperature soon dropped and Phil had shivered for a while before grabbing her big down-filled coat from the boot and snuggling under it to wait out the night. Now the clock said 12.30pm, which meant she had barely been out there an hour and half. *Useless.* Clearly she wasn't accustomed to a proper office job. The effort of pretending to be an intern called Scarlett while also filing news stories was taking its toll. Or perhaps the warmth and comfort of the puffa had convinced her subconscious she was back in the womb. Either way, she had missed something important because there was a man lingering near the rowan tree holding what looked like a barrel on a lead in one hand and a plastic bag in the other.

The barrel turned and sniffed the grass before sprinkling the area with the scantest dribble of urine. There was no streetlight on Simon's stretch of road and his outdoor light didn't quite reach where the man stood, but the dog was darkish – brown or red, not black – and despite one slightly cocked leg, the peeing technique suggested a female. But Phil was more interested in the man who was sliding a bag over his hand, raising it in the air like a surgical glove. From where she was sitting, she could see him pull the bag back over his hand, deftly trapping the poo.

She grabbed her camera, a proper Nikon digital SLR with a good zoom lens, and began to snap photos. The glomping sound of the shutter seemed so loud in the dark quiet of the Acorn estate that she felt strangely nervous. Her heart was pounding. What if he saw her? She was all alone and vulnerable. The thought brought her back to reality.

Get a grip, Philippa.

She wasn't exactly exposing a drugs cartel, was she? Peering through the viewfinder at the dark figure, she could see a tall white man with grey hair and an anorak. She couldn't see his face, but he seemed like a normal old man. She wasn't sure whether to be surprised or disappointed. Of course, she had hardly expected a criminal mastermind, but she thought he might look a little more feral. Or maybe she really had expected a phantom or fairy or something. He was just a normal, run of the mill, sensibly jacketed old man.

She held her breath as he raised the knotted bag higher.

He was going to put it in the tree!

She laughed inwardly at how worked worked up she was getting. She took photos as he began to hang the bag and then deftly switched to video to get footage of the deed being done. There he was, in the grainy glow of the distant streetlights, under a waning moon, hanging a turd like he was trimming the tree for Christmas. It was just bizarre. She carried on filming and tried to grab her phone from the cup holder without ruining her framing. She had forgotten to ring Simon! She had solemnly promised to ring him if Father Shitmas came to call, but thanks to the unscheduled nap she hadn't been ready when the mystery man arrived. Still dazed, she fumbled the phone, dropping it in the footwell. Holding up the camera, she reached down into the footwell, swearing softly as she clawed around her feet.

Grasping the phone at last, she looked up to check her framing. The tree was still in shot, albeit slightly off centre, but the man himself was nowhere to be seen. Scrabbling for the door handle, she jumped from the car and ran to the tree.

He was gone.

She spent a quarter of an hour running up and down the various side streets and alleyways round the tiny estate in the hope of finding the phantom. This was followed by a full tour of the Tesco carpark, something she would have preferred to avoid at this time of night. The empty space felt desolate and eerie, but at least the rats hanging around the recycling bins ignored her, confident this was their time not hers.

Her man was nowhere to be found.

'Well, that's a bit of a setback, but at least you proved he exists,' consoled Simon when she roused him. They sat in his lounge staring out mournfully at the newly bedecked tree. Simon had cleared it before she arrived in preparation for gathering evidence, and now the lone bag swung forlornly in the night breeze.

'I feel like I've let you down,' she said. She dunked a Hobnob in her tea and bit it glumly.

'You got evidence! I think that's a very good start. It's better than I've ever managed.'

He was disappointed, she could tell. He was just being polite. The photos, grainy and hurried, didn't help much with identifying the culprit.

'I'm just surprised he arrived so early. I've kept vigil until 1am on numerous occasions and never caught him. I wonder what happened to make him change his routine.'

'Well, I guess I'll have to try again tomorrow, won't I?' said Phil, taking another biscuit and dunking it. Little shards of oaty goodness floated gently down into the murky water, waiting to be retrieved when she drained the cup later.

'I wonder if Woodward and Bernstein ever felt like this when they were investigating Watergate,' she said.

Phil needed to get her act together.

She had fallen asleep and missed the Faecal Fiend. She let out a groan of embarrassment as she drove home. Bad enough that she'd failed in her stakeout, but the simple truth was, she realised (with a shock of self-loathing that caused her to bang her hands on the steering wheel), she wasn't getting anywhere with her investigation into Clive's death either.

What had she been thinking? Did she imagine that the truth would just drop into her lap? That she would just find the answers at the bottom of a cardboard box? The thought made her bark out a resentful laugh. She only had three more days in which to discover the truth of her father's death, and that meant taking a few risks. It meant not dutifully doing tasks set by Jamie and Rhonda as the clock ticked. She didn't want to let down Rhonda or Mick – she didn't want to let down Jamie either for that matter – but the time for being employee-of-the-week was over. There was no way she was going to see any kind of success unless she took matters into her own hands.

She had been joking when she mentioned the Watergate journalists to Simon, but in the cold light of day she was sure they would have achieved more by now. There was something important she was missing, she could feel it. And the answer surely lay in Jamie's quagmire of files.

Phil pulled over, trying to think. The files had to hold the answers. Even now, she wasn't sure what she was searching for. But she could start by trying to look for evidence of who had been overseeing the project. That would tell her something. She thought of the piles of folders on Jamie's desk, and the walls of filing cabinets surrounding it like fortifications. She sat for another minute, staring into the middle distance as she made a decision, before swinging the car into a U-turn and headed towards the Virtua building.

The car park sat in darkness as Phil pulled into a space. She was hoping to evade the security guard who took over from Jessica the receptionist for the night shift. She was lucky: he wasn't on sentry duty at the front. She imagined him sitting at a bank of CCTV cameras in some cupboard-sized surveillance room, probably eating a sausage roll or something. A stereotype she had created in her own mind, having never seen a surveillance room at Virtua (or a security guard with a sausage roll, for that matter).

She buzzed her security pass at the front door and entered, her footsteps echoing on the white tiles as she made her way to the stairs, which felt very far away suddenly. She tried to look purposeful, walking with a straight back and staring ahead as though it was perfectly normal for her to be at work after midnight. A fluttering erupted in her stomach as she passed the reception desk: she was really doing this; she was breaking into Virtua and stealing a load of files. And suddenly, she felt less like Bernstein and more like the Watergate criminals.

Oh lord, she was getting grandiose.

One poxy Sussex company infiltration and a failed stakeout of a creative litterer and she started thinking she was Bob Woodward meeting Deep Throat in an underground car park. She could just hear Angela now: 'Don't get a big head, your brain will fall out.' This wasn't Watergate. She wasn't about to unmask some global conspiracy. A man had died at a building site and no one had done anything about it. That was it.

Big whoop.

But screw that attitude, she thought, punching the lift button with sudden resentment. It didn't matter that it was just a tiny, unimportant story in the scheme of things. Her father had died before he should have. Her brother was an emotional black hole who was incapable of having a proper relationship with anyone. It might be unimportant to the world at large, but it was important to her. And it was important to her family.

She would make damn sure Clive's death was important to Virtua Services too. They had sent a wreath for his funeral. *That was it!* Some of his work colleagues had come along to the service, but no one from senior management turned up. The respect was left to the Virtua contractors, who had appeared still covered in building rubble and plaster from a morning of work, clasping their hands together and bowing their heads as if in prayer, before they headed back to their building site to, presumably, eat a crunchy, food-poison friendly sandwich in Clive's honour.

Phil arrived at the third floor and felt her confidence falter. She stepped out as though the floor might fall away under her feet, and fought the urge to tiptoe. Instead, she trod softly, placing her feet with precision, until she arrived at the glass door that separated the lifts from the open plan office space. She peered through, craning her neck round to check if the coast was clear.

No one there.

This was all proving surprisingly straightforward. She opened the glass door with a *swoosh*. LED ceiling strips made pools of icy light at random intervals, with Jamie's desk under a spotlight, surrounded by darkness and shining like a beacon all on its own. Hardly the ideal set up for someone hoping to go unnoticed, thought Phil. She would have turned off the lights, but that might draw more attention, and so she stood under the glow and considered what she would do if anyone came in.

(Conclusion: hide.)

Thanks to Jamie's efforts to create her own space with low privacy screens and the wall of filing cabinets, hers was the most isolated part of the office (apart from Phil's windowless cave). Still, it was still more exposed than Phil would like; she felt vulnerable on all sides, including the side next to a giant window. She imagined a sniper training a rifle on her, waiting for the order to squeeze the trigger. Would she get buried as Scarlett Stevens? Would she be doomed to haunt floor three, sending shivers up the spines of her ex-colleagues any time they entered the kitchenette?

She pulled her thoughts back to reality and stood at Jamie's desk trying to orientate herself. If I had a load of incriminating files relating to a workplace death, where would I file them? she asked herself. She stood for a second longer as though hoping to spot a file marked "Workplace Deaths: Top Secret" before beginning to systematically open and close first Jamie's desk drawers (mostly just a collection of top quality pilfered stationery and some protein balls) and then the filing cabinets. They were locked, of course – HR data privacy and all that – but the keys were in Jamie's top drawer, because of course they were. Phil was endlessly amazed by how lax people were with things like this. It was as if no one believed data theft could happen to them. As though the sight of a row of boring grey metal boxes filled with paper would be enough of a disincentive to snoop. After all, filing cabinets were boring. Who could possibly want to rifle through them all?

Nosey journalists, that's who.

Phil began flicking through the various files, hoping something would jump out. During university she had done a project on the early days of PFI when outsource firms like Virtua Services negotiated contracts with local councils on such favourable terms that your eyes would pop to read them. She knew these sorts of firms took on government contracts and buried their tax liabilities in a fleet of shell companies seemingly run by lowly secretaries in the Philippines. But when it came to the ins and outs of the HR paperwork, she wasn't knowledgeable enough.

The office was still and silent so that even the sound of Phil rifling through filing cabinets felt deafening, the buzz of electric lights like a herd of malfunctioning fridge freezers. She could feel her heart beating harder the longer she stayed, exposed under the bleaching LEDs.

She slid open another drawer and walked her fingers across the labels. Near the back was an unlabelled drop file. She pulled it towards her and, with her head turned sideways, read the first page. It was a collection of health records. She took it out and cupped it in her hands like a prayer book, scanning each page before placing it down on the top of the open drawer.

Towards the back she found something: a report detailing the mental health support offered to staff in the wake of Clive McGinty's death. All teams, including contractors, had all been 'reached out to' to invite them to talk to a professional about their experiences. All staff members had been given a session with a counsellor. The health and safety officer Doug Graves was singled out as someone who needed additional support. Doug had spoken to a counsellor a number of times and there was a note that HR would need to, 'Connect with him regularly after a recent mental health episode.'

Doug Graves?

She knew who he was, of course. Who could forget a name like that? He was the person who insisted at the inquest that her father had no business being at the school that day because the site had not been signed off as safe. Why had he needed to speak to someone after Clive had died? He certainly didn't seem particularly cut up about his death at the inquest. If anything, Phil remembered him being irritated at having to be there.

A man named Andrew Templeton-Dunbar had written a further note saying, 'Douglas's wellbeing has been monitored throughout the inquest. We have reached out to him regularly to ensure he continues to thrive in this challenging time. As a representative of Virtua Services, we want Douglas to feel supported.'

Phil supposed this was meant to sound considerate, but actually it came off as slightly creepy: as though Virtua

Services and Andrew Templeton-Dunbar were keeping a close watch on Doug Graves. There was a further note. Doug Graves had, according to this, been briefly hospitalised for an overdose of painkillers. Shortly afterwards, he was signed off sick. Then, shortly after that, there was a note about voluntary redundancy. Just a few weeks after Clive died, Doug Graves had tried to kill himself. A few months after that, he had been offered – and had taken – redundancy.

Phil took a photo of the pages and slipped them back into the cabinet. The folder made a soft thunk as it landed back in its drop file and she closed the drawer slowly. Then she returned to a file filing cabinet she had opened earlier. There they were: the personnel files. She located Doug Graves's file and checked for his exit interview. He hadn't said much in his final conversation with Andrew. He was acknowledged as struggling with his wellbeing and had opted to take up a role at a local homeless charity. He was moving on through his own choice, but was given £30,000 redundancy pay out. Phil stared at Doug and Andrew's signatures and tried to fathom if any of it meant anything. Was it a message for her to decode? Did it mean anything at all? Or was it simply the inner workings of a career gone sideways, a man toppled by a tragic accident who was already leaning towards depression?

Abruptly a different thought came – as though her subconscious was sending up a distraction, a lifeboat for her despair. *Don't think about that horrible stuff, think about this instead.* Phil bit her bottom lip, making a choice. Dee Dee Dabrowski's file was lifted from its sheath and Phil began scanning for that juicy bit of gossip Dee Dee herself had so far failed to serve up. She read with satisfaction. Dee Dee had repeatedly called in sick with 'food poisoning', despite being seen in the pub the night before on all three occasions. You think she'd have learned her lesson the first time, Phil marvelled, in awe of Dee Dee's brass neck. How she wasn't fired was anyone's guess. Perhaps she had some gossip on one of the senior managers. The thought made her smile: if anyone did, it would be Dee Dee.

There were Dee Dee's two written warnings too. She had paid compensation to a complainant's letter that was deemed 'excessive' and 'not in-line with company policy,' What did excessive mean here? The mind boggled. Perhaps Dee Dee would spill the beans if Phil could find a way to ask her.

Next, she checked Jamie's file and stared in unexpected delight. Jamie had been given a verbal warning. This was too perfect. She had got it back when she was an HR manager, for 'tardiness,' and 'unexplained absences during the working day', suggesting she had form when it came to swanning off without notice. The warning was issued by Andrew Templeton-Dunbar, her predecessor. The one, she remembered, who had once taken a diversity lead position ahead of a disabled woman and Paul. Dee Dee hadn't explained why Paul was a better choice, but Phil assumed there was a good reason.

She checked a few more people. Mick had been reprimanded for having alcohol in the office just before Christmas, which felt a little harsh to Phil, but then again she worked in publishing where the editor frequently got drunk at lunch and didn't return to the office for the rest of the day. Rhonda's file was clean (of course), although there was a note about her boyfriend turning up at the office (presumably he of the bags full of coins) and causing a bit of a scene. The note was more about keeping vigilant and checking in with Rhonda for her own protection than anything else. She had been invited to have a mental health session with a specialist (declined) and had been given a leaflet about coercive control (accepted).

Phil was about to try to locate Andrew's file when she heard the lift ping.

Phil looked up. Frozen in horror, she listened as the glass door made the sucking sound as it opened. Footsteps approached.

Shit!

She ducked down under the privacy screens.

She was crouching beside the desk now. The footsteps drew closer. Cautiously, she risked a peek. There was nobody there. It already felt as though she had been crouching down by the desk for an age. She could hear her body making small noises, her breath passing over her lips, the barely audible squeaking of her knee joints, everything reduced to the microscopic until she almost believed she could hear her fingernails growing and the slick sound of her mouth making saliva.

'Who's there?' said a voice.

Rhonda.

Phil almost felt a bubble of hysteria hiccup out. It was only Rhonda!

Oh god, it was Rhonda.

Somehow this was both the best news in the world – it wasn't a psychotic murderer come to suck the marrow from her bones – and the very worst: it was Rhonda, the woman she most needed onside.

'It's me,' said Phil. She was unsure where the reply had come from. Her subconscious seemed to have taken over. She had said it in a funny voice too. She sounded... drunk.

She really hoped her subconscious knew what it was doing.

Rhonda poked her head around the screen and in that moment Phil realised Rhonda had been as terrified as she had been. Phil found herself falling backwards onto the floor, her legs spreadeagled as she sat like a weeping drunk on the kitchen lino.

'I'm so sorry,' she said.

'What are you doing here?' said Rhonda. She looked faintly appalled, like she was about to get involved in something she would rather not. She glanced at the doorway briefly. Was she looking for security, or wishing she could make a quick exit to get away from this drunk girl on the floor?

Phil started to cry.

'Rhonda, you're my only hope,' she said pitifully. 'I've done a really stupid thing.'

She gave a few seconds to the charade, covering her face and heaving her shoulders, giving her eyes a quick poke in the hope of bringing on some moisture. Would it be wrong to think about her dad to get the real tears to come? On balance, she decided it was all in pursuit of justice for him, and therefore acceptable.

'What's the matter, honey?' said Rhonda, bending down, her thighs straining against her cotton trousers. She was very flexible, Phil noticed, bending down towards Phil with ease before squatting down to join her on the floor.

'Good hamstrings,' said Phil.

'What?' said Rhonda, confused.

'I said you've got good hamstrings.' Her voice was a pure mix of blubbering and booze. She needed to get the balance right. Too drunk would appear indefensible in the eyes of a company woman like Rhonda, too blubbery would make her seem unhinged. She'd be sent home on mental health grounds on full pay. Not that she was getting paid. Presumably Scarlett's bank account would be receiving the daily stipend given to interns at Virtua.

'Thank you,' said Rhonda. 'Now what's this stupid thing that you've done?'

'You're going to hate me.'

'Ooh, I'm sure I won't. Come on, you can tell Rhonda.'

Rhonda gave her a prod in the arm and Phil resisted the urge to rub where her finger had dented the muscle.

'I lied,' Phil wailed. 'I lied on my application. On the forms you made me fill in. I panicked.'

'I see,' said Rhonda.

Rhonda stiffened at the confession and Phil wondered if she'd got the balance right. This was not something the Rhondas of this world could shrug off. Rhonda shifted her weight and slid down onto her thigh, resting both legs on the floor and leaning her weight onto one hand.

'What did you lie about?' she said.

Phil had no idea. But, again, her mouth seemed to do the talking for her.

'I said I'd got nine GCSEs, but actually I only have eight.' She let her body lean into the misery, feeling her bottom lip tremble. She began to believe that she really was drunk on the floor of her workplace, racked with remorse. 'And I only got a four in further maths, not a seven.'

Rhonda barked out a laugh. Not that she was the sort of person who would usually find falsifying a job application humorous, but perhaps the ridiculous spectacle Phil had put on – seemingly coming to her place of work in the dead of night, drunk, in a bid to scrub out the weak advanced maths score, made it too much even for Rhonda to resist. Phil had done what she set out to: she had managed to distract Rhonda from the very real sight of her breaking into the office and rifling through her boss's files.

'I was hoping to find the form on Jamie's desk, so I could correct it,' continued Phil, her voice taking on a slight slur. She was aiming to convey a "misguided but harmless bridesmaid in the toilets halfway through a wedding" level of drunk. But she needed to avoid the "dangerous and overemotional bridesmaid in the toilets at the *end* of a wedding" level of drunk. She needed to be pitiful but easily cheered, not a red-faced vision of sobbing and snot and ripped hemlines.

Or maybe she just went to the wrong sort of weddings.

The gibbous moon was shining through the large window near Jamie's desk, its opal light bathing them in a glow that made it seem like a stage set. It felt about as real as that to Phil now. What had she got herself into? She couldn't imagine how she would ever return to normal life again. Perhaps she would have to pretend to be Scarlett for the rest of her life: filing investigations reports and drinking milky coffee from the machine, eating Lachlan-the-sandwich-man's flaccid lunches and gossiping with Dee Dee.

Aldhill was not a big town, everyone knew everyone – or knew someone who did. She would almost certainly bump into Rhonda again one day, and then what would she do? Confess the whole thing? She could see the inevitable farce unfolding in her mind's eye. She'd be in a pub somewhere, enjoying a night out with friends, or maybe trying to interview a local dignitary about a controversial planning decision, and Rhonda would appear, calling her by the wrong name and looking at her with the nervous, wrong-footed smile of someone about to discover a terrible betrayal.

She was being dramatic again. Perhaps it was the moon's stage lighting, or maybe she really did feel drunk and emotional, the make-believe seeping into her being and turning her maudlin. The truth was, she didn't like letting people down.

'Well,' said Rhonda. Giving her thigh a pat to emphasise the change of tone. 'It's not the end of the world, is it? But I hope you've learned your lesson. Lying never got anyone anywhere in life.'

Phil wanted to make some pointed comment about politicians, or estate agents or large corporations who weaselled out of blame for the death of an employee, but instead she hung her head in shame and looked truly sorry. She *was* truly sorry. She didn't feel good about lying to Rhonda, and this was her opportunity to express it, albeit in slurred tones.

'I'm really sorry, Rhonda. You've been so nice to me and given me a brilliant opportunity. I hope you'll forgive me... and maybe not tell anyone about this?'

'Hmm, well,' said Rhonda, although Phil could already tell she had softened at her heartfelt apology. She looked disapproving for a moment longer and then a decision seemed to be made. She laboured to her feet, grabbing the edge of Jamie's desk to return to standing.

The desk was mired in chaos, piles of paper everywhere, but Rhonda ignored it all and made her way instead to her own computer, which awoke as she shook the mouse. Rhonda's need to instantly commence work clearly trumping any environmental concerns, despite the rallying calls to 'think of the environment' from the posters all around the building (put up by Rhonda, who was their office green rep).

'I've already inputted all your info on the database,' she explained. 'We're trying to go paperless and if I leave it on Jamie's desk... well.'

She didn't continue. Even here in the dead of night with an apparently drunk intern who would only be around for a couple more days, she maintained her discretion. Phil admired her for it.

'I'm surprised the security guard let you in,' said Rhonda once she had updated Scarlett's record (a change that pained Phil, who had been a class swot and an able mathematician).

'The entrance was empty when I walked through,' said Phil and then felt bad for the security guard when Rhonda replied, 'I shall have to have a word with Duncan, by the sounds of it. He's probably been kipping in the cleaning cupboard again. He's about four hundred.'

'Oh, I imagined he might be peering at me behind a wall of CCTV monitors.'

'That would be nice. You'd think we might have a bit of security here, given Virtua owns a security firm.'

'Does it?' said Phil. This was news to her.

'Inference Technology Solutions,' said Rhonda.

'The tech support company?'

It was another big local firm. Why hadn't she connected the two businesses before? Then again, she knew from earlier digging that Virtua was registered to some offshore address in the Philippines, so unravelling the various company connections was hardly straightforward. Still, her investigative ego took a hit.

Rhonda stood, and Phil followed. It seemed she was being escorted out of the building. Rhonda continued as she punched the button for the lift.

'They do CCTV as well. We could be packed to the

rafters with cameras, but the top brass don't seem keen for some reason. Makes you wonder what they get up to.'

'Yes,' said Phil.

Makes me wonder what you get up to, too, she thought – coming into the office at night to work. But she didn't say it – she couldn't afford to get on Rhonda's bad side. The person caught drunk on the floor of her temporary office doesn't get to ask the questions.

Rhonda seemed to read her mind, however. 'I often come here at night to work,' she said. 'I've got a bugger of a brain. Can't seem to switch off. Everything's always whirring around. So I started thinking, sod it, may as well get up and do the jobs that are on my conscience, give me a head start for the morning... Oh look, there's Duncan.' She waved at the security guard. 'You alright Duncan?'

She enunciated slowly, patronising – a children's entertainer addressing the birthday boy. Duncan was old, white hair in shaggy disarray. He shuffled along, raising a hand to wave back as he made his way to Jessica's reception desk.

'You not got that young fella of yours with you tonight then?' he said with a wink.

Rhonda said under her breath: 'No, thanks to the court injunction,' but then gave him a nod and a smile, like he had just said something funny and clever. 'Not tonight, Duncan,' she hollered, before turning back to Phil. 'I think he's going senile.' She held Phil's gaze and said, 'I won't mention what happened here tonight. Let's draw a line under it. Have a lie-in tomorrow. Come in after ten. You'll be good for nothing otherwise. I'll get home in a bit and get some more kip before I have to get up again. Just need to do a couple of things first.'

Towards the end of her speech, Rhonda's body language stiffened slightly and Phil took that as her cue to leave. She thanked her profusely for her help, giving Rhonda a soulful look that hopefully conveyed the right level of drunken remorse and gratitude, then she headed out into the night and made a beeline for Roosevelt Court and bed.

It wasn't until she got in that she checked her *Aldhill Observer* email account. The most recent email had been sent just a minute ago. Subject header: *I know your secret.* She opened it: '*I know the truth about you. Your secret is safe with me... for now. WATCH. THIS. SPACE.*'

WEDNESDAY

THIRTEEN

'It's a coincidence, Jen,' said DCI Petra Gull.

DI Lee Hudson, standing next to Petra's desk, looking down at Jen in her seat, nodding his head vigorously, made Jen feel positively mutinous. They had kept her waiting until this morning for this conversation.

'Ma'am, with all due respect,' she managed, the stock phrase sounding hollow even to her ears, 'there are too many similarities. They both worked for the same building firm…'

'Let me stop you there,' said Petra, lifting a bony hand. 'Virtua – and its many off-shoots – is one of the area's biggest employers.

Like she's quoting a press release, thought Jen.

'And, needless to say, if you're going to take that route, we could start claiming that every death in the region is connected, since everyone works there, worked there, or knows someone who does.'

'But the wall cavities!' said Jen. 'Two bodies, two schools, two builders, one building company.'

She genuinely couldn't believe what she was hearing. If

Petra didn't have a straight face emoji where her sense of humour should be, Jen might have suspected this was all a big windup. 'The fact it was two schools!'

'The building for our victim was unsafe,' said Petra, as though that proved something.

Jen squinted, parsing this new information.

'Just had the prelim report,' explained Lee. 'The entire extension to the block had been built with just a handful of wall ties. What's more, they were the wrong ones. Way too small. Was only a matter of time before it fell down'

'And,' continued Petra, 'there is nothing to suggest that was the case for Clive McGinty's wall. If–'

'How would we know?' interrupted Jen. 'Virtua took the whole wall down getting Clive out. For all we know, it was just a handy way to cover up another one of their cock-ups.'

'Are you suggesting,' said Petra, 'that the bodies were put in there as an excuse to pull the walls down without being caught? Because I'm afraid I have to say that is the most far-fetched–'

'No! I'm not saying that,' said Jen.

She was talking loudly now, and Lee shot her a warning look. She had spoken over Petra twice and she knew she was skating on thin ice, but the DCI had got her back up. She could feel indignation coursing through her like hot coffee on a cold day. 'Who in their right mind would put a body in a wall so they could tear it down? No, what I am saying is they – our victim and Clive McGinty – might have known something about the poor building quality, and this was a way to shut them up. We know that the council had been in to inspect the buildings and given them the all-clear, so it certainly wouldn't look good for them–'

Petra shut her eyes as she interrupted, praying for

patience presumably. 'Jen, that is the most ludicrous thing I have ever heard. So now you're saying the council was involved?'

'What?' said Jen, the wind taken out of her sails by this turn of logic. 'No, I am absolutely not saying that. I'm just saying that there is a very good reason why these two people might have been murdered. Or perhaps it was simply someone who knew the sites were somewhere to dispose of a body. Maybe the first one was an accident – an argument gone wrong – and the second one was more thought out.' She ran a hand through her hair. 'I don't know. All I'm saying is, it would be crazy not to explore the possibility that the two deaths are connected in some way. That's all.'

'Jen, the inquest was thorough, and the conclusion was death by misadventure.'

'How would you know it was thorough?' cried Jen, feeling the urge to reach over and shake Petra by her sharp shoulders. 'You weren't even here then. I'm telling you, these two murders are linked and we need to reopen the–'

'And I'm telling you, Jen, that if you continue in this vein, I'm going to have to sign you off sick for a week.' Petra leaned forward as though she were talking to a child. 'Now, you've been under a lot of stress recently, God knows, no one can blame you for feeling emotional right now, and I think it would be better for everyone if you stepped back a little from–'

Jen stood up, catching her chair on the floor so that it fell backwards with a loud thud. Lee stepped forward, putting a hand behind Jen's back and ushering her to the door.

'That sounds like a great idea, Petra. Jen, let's get you out of here.'

He marched her out of the room and Jen turned on him

as he closed the door behind them. But he grabbed her arm and pushed her towards his office before she could begin protesting. I'm going to kill them both, she decided.

'I know you want to kill me, Jen,' said Lee. 'You don't need to tell me. I've looked plenty of murderers in the eye over the years and right now you're the spitting image of a particularly nasty cannibal I once interviewed.'

Jen, who had been furious until that moment, felt all the anger pop like a lanced boil and she blew out her cheeks and smiled.

'Boss,' she said, ready to begin a sensible discussion. Please God, let him see sense, she thought.

'Look, this is out of my hands, but if you ask me, there's nothing wrong with you checking a few things out. Petra's been liaising with the senior brass, but why don't you see who you can speak to at Virtua? Speak to some of the monkeys rather than the organ grinders'

'Got an appointment with HR later,' said Jen. 'Grant and Nandini are checking out the procurement team. They're trying to get a list of anyone who worked on that site.'

'Right, good. So have a word with them. See if they flinch when you mention Clive. Keep digging. Go pester a few people if you can tie it in with the John Doe investigation – knock yourself out – but for God's sake, Jen, don't go storming into the Gull's nest again and making demands. She's only here occasionally. Don't give her more bloody reasons to leave Eastbourne.'

'I know, I know.'

'Yes, you do. And you also know that there were people at the council very keen to get that case put to bed faster than a trafficked Albanian teenager. The boss isn't about to let you get crap all over her nice clean reputation. I dread to think which posh knobs we were inconveniencing with that investigation back in the day. You remember, don't you? Yes, of course you do, so let's be a bit less like a dick in a knocking shop and stop trying to screw everything, yeah?'

'Wow,' said Jen.

She was still trying to work out which of Lee's analogies had offended her the most when she felt herself being once again manhandled towards an exit.

'And now what I want you to do,' said Lee, 'is get your big gob out of here and back home for a nice big glass of rosé or whatever godawful lady juice you drink; wash your hair, have a cry, all that crap; and come back in tomorrow smiling at the boss with no more bollocks about reopening files. Yeah? Good.'

And with that, he closed the door to his office.

FOURTEEN

Phil should have called ahead. It would have been the sensible way to do things. That way she could have made an appointment and planned the right lie, but she had been flying by the seat of her pants all week and she saw no reason to stop now. She was standing in front of a detached Arts and Crafts house with leaded windows and a wide drive. The doorbell – one of those expensive reproduction bells – tinkled as Phil pressed the button. With a large exhale she attempted to relax her facial muscles into one of her broad, friendly smiles. Somewhere in the back of the house a dog barked and she heard a man's voice remonstrating with the creature before a shadow approached the stained glass of the door.

'Hi,' she said, smiling hopefully at the man who appeared at the entrance.

Distinguished – that was how you described men like him, Phil realised. Somewhere in his sixties, but tall and fit, with a thick head of salt and pepper hair and an expensive-looking sweater. Cashmere, probably.

'Hello?' The man's tone was one of polite confusion. He was ready to close the door on her, she could tell. He was probably expecting some sob story about a broken-down car along with a request to borrow a few quid to pay for a cab. Phil found herself uncharacteristically lost for words.

'Er...' she managed eventually.

She was going to spin another yarn. She had vague plans about claiming to be studying for a masters in human resources with a focus on... whatever it was he used to specialise in. But then something in his expression (and in her tiredness) prompted her to simply take a breath and say, 'Hello Mr Templeton-Dunbar, I'm Clive McGinty's daughter.'

His brow knotted.

'Oh, you poor thing. Come in, come in.'

She stepped into the wide entrance hall and a dog rushed in to greet her, barking energetically.

'Betty,' said Andrew. 'Get down.'

'Hello Betty,' said Phil, holding the dog's head and giving her a good fuss around the ears. Betty wagged her tail in appreciation before wandering back off in search of something else to vent her terrier energy upon.

Andrew said, 'Would you like a cup of tea?' He looked at her as though she were a precious creature who might be fatigued from her journey. There was a lightness in the way he held himself, his hands raised like he was conducting a flute solo. She could imagine him performing a soliloquy at the Bexhill amateur dramatic society.

'Yes,' she said. 'That would be lovely.'

FIFTEEN

Andrew switched on the kettle. Poor girl! Turning up on the doorstep like a foundling. Like a little lost lamb. He had half wanted to press his hands to the sides of her shoulders, 'There, there, child, it will be alright.' But, of course, he wouldn't dream of actually doing that. And besides, it wouldn't be true.

'How can I help?' he said when he had delivered a cup of tea and a plate of biscuits to the low table between them. He'd taken her through to the sitting room rather than the little snug he sat in to do his crosswords and now he rather regretted it. She looked out of place on the pristine sofa. Everyone did, truth be told. Jaqueline had bought them to look good, not to sit on. She herself watched TV in bed in the evenings while Andrew tended to stay in his snug for as long as possible before retiring to his own bedroom next to his wife's.

The girl said, 'I don't really know where to begin. I just wanted to talk to you, I suppose.'

He nodded like he understood, but really he wasn't sure what had brought her here – or how she had found him out.

'After your father died, it was my job to handle the people side of things,' he said. Was this what she wanted to hear? He scrutinised her face and saw her eagerness. Perhaps this was what she wanted from him, just more stories from someone who was a witness for her agony. He could do that.

'We have certain protocols in place for workplace accidents. I contacted the contractor liaison manager and asked him to organise a full review, which meant identifying if there were protocols that had misaligned – from a managerial point of view. He liaised with the health and safety officer–'

'Doug Graves?' supplied the girl.

'That's right – and asked him to write a report, which meant ascertaining why Clive had been on site that day and why the accident had occurred... But you know all this already.'

'Please. I'd just like to hear it from you... if you don't mind.'

Andrew nodded and gave a tight smile before continuing.

'While the HSO was trying to create a timeline of the circumstances around your father's death, I was liaising with the contractor to see what pensions your father might be entitled to. If he had been one of our Virtua people, his dependents would have received a contribution from the benevolent fund. But because he joined us via a third party, identifying what his family – you – might be entitled to wasn't so straightforward. While that was ongoing, I connected with the people involved, including the HSO and Clive's usual labourer, to offer mental health support. Not all were Virtua people, but I felt it was only right that we step up to support them as we would our own people.'

'But Doug was the only one who took you up on the offer, is that right?' said Phil.

Andrew shifted in his seat. This sofa really was hard on the backside. Perhaps he should speak to Jaqueline about finding something else.

'I'm afraid I can't really talk about that.'

Quite to his surprise, the girl seemed to grow half a foot. Before Andrew's eyes, she went from a lost child to an angry young woman. It was astonishing – and a little disturbing. He shuffled backwards, his buttocks seeking in vain for a softer part of the seat. Perhaps somewhere a little further away from her.

'I need to know,' she said, her voice shaking a little, her hands emphasising her request. 'Something happened to my father that day, and I believe someone was responsible.'

Doubt crept through Andrew like the breeze rippling through a forest. He was a good man, wasn't he? He was an honourable man. He had always done the right thing, played everything straight down the line, no messing about. He would never give away the mental health details of a man who had tried to kill himself.

And yet, somehow, he found himself nodding.

'I believe you might be right,' he said.

And it was a relief.

SIXTEEN

Phil walked away from the house feeling Andrew's eyes on her back. The sun was shining again – another beautiful late summer's day, well into the thirties. She would have liked to stop to strip off to the camisole under her shirt, but she wanted to escape Andrew's gaze. She knew he would be looking – sad-eyed and a little concerned. Maybe a tinge of suspicion had crept in at her line of questioning. She didn't have the energy for it, so she carried on, the heat making her feel a little dizzy, the stress of the day hitting her like a sudden brick to the temple. A tear formed, but she brushed it away before it could make its bid for freedom.

No time for tears.

Thanks to her late night break in, she already knew Doug had spoken to the counsellor a few times. The photo she had taken of the file didn't tell her much more than that, however. And Andrew couldn't reveal what the conversations were about either, since he didn't know. But one thing he did know: there was something a little strange about Doug's behaviour in the weeks that followed Clive's death.

'I asked to speak to him for a catch up after his second session,' Andrew told her. 'Just to find out how he was getting on... and really, I have to say, if anything, he seemed more angry about it all than depressed or sad. So defensive. I always felt that he wanted to tell me something, though I couldn't say what. I tried to get him to talk more and he clammed up. I let it go.'

He gave a vicarish, watery smile, as though these lambs of god needed his guidance. 'I was only interested in his well-being at the time. Only... well, it has always stayed with me. I wonder to this day whether I should have pressed him further, encouraged him to open up more. I always wondered if there was something he wanted to get off his chest.'

'You think there was something he knew?' said Phil, frowning.

'Oh, I don't know about that,' said Andrew hastily.

He talked for a while about how responsible he felt for Doug, how he felt they had failed him in some way, but Phil wasn't really listening by then. She was finding Andrew's compassion oppressive – like he was trying to smother her with a blanket. And the tone he was using! So full of empathy and yet somehow *empty*. She just wanted to get out of there.

Until Andrew had changed the subject, that is.

'It wasn't the only thing that was odd about your father's death.'

She waited for him to continue. When he didn't, she said, 'How do you mean?'

He turned away, waving his elegant hands to shoo the thought away. 'Oh, I don't know, maybe it's all just nothing.'

'Please. I'd like to know. Anything at all.'

'Well...' he began, steepling his fingers. 'Our CEO, Gloria Reynolds...'

Andrew shifted in his seat uncomfortably like he was wrestling with his loyalties. She waited until he spoke again.

'She paid an unusual interest in the St Agnes school project.'

'How's that? Surely it's her job to pay an interest?'

'In the broader business, absolutely, but it seemed to be just this particular school. We held contracts for four other schools in the local area and she didn't ask a single question about those.'

'So what was special about this one?'

'Well, she claimed to have a nephew at the school called *Trevor*.'

Phil let this sink in a moment. No one has a nephew called Trevor. The last Trevor was probably born sometime in 1983. Trevor wasn't due to come back into fashion until Gen Z had babies and turned an ironic eye towards grandad's birth certificate. From the way that Andrew said the name, she sensed he was of the same opinion.

'But I have never heard her mention a sibling and the only young relative I'm aware of is her husband's sister's daughter,' he said.

Phil puzzled that out for a moment, staring up to her left and repeating Andrew's words.

'So her niece?'

'That's right... Funnily enough, she works at Virtua Services too.'

Phil tried to sound casual.

'Oh, really?'

I employed her, for my sins. She turned out to be quite a disappointment. It wasn't nepotism, let me assure you. No,

Jamie was an exceptional candidate. But that's often the way: people who interview well can turn out to be all sparkle and no substance. Being good at interviews is a different skill to true leadership.'

Jamie was Gloria's niece?

Of course she was, thought Phil. This explained so much. She tried to keep her face bland.

'So Gloria paid this project special attention?' she said 'Because of Trevor?'

'Yes, the elusive nephew.'

'Who possibly doesn't exist?' said Phil and Andrew held out his hands like serving platters as if to say, 'who can possibly tell?'

'I'd recently been asked to take on more of the Operations side of things,' he continued, 'which involved overseeing some of the Procurement function – just while we restructured the business and brought in more senior management. But still, even in that short time, I had never noticed Gloria paying the slightest interest in day-to-day operations like that. She's far more of a big picture person. Business development, acquiring new companies, that sort of thing. She had her eye on a wider role at Virtua's holding company. Working with the top brass. Turning that OBE into a damehood. She's a NED for about four other companies; she doesn't have the time. But – and here's the strangest thing about all this – she asked about the project, and she asked for your father by name.'

Phil had to remind herself to breathe.

'My father?' she managed.

'Yes. She said she wanted "the best people for the job," and said she'd heard Clive McGinty was good. I was astonished. I pride myself on being excellent with names, and I certainly knew everyone in the business, but I had never heard of your father. And, looking back, I can't help thinking how unlikely it was that Gloria would have heard of him... Not unless someone gave her the name for a reason.'

Phil could feel her heart thudding against her ribs, her head pulsing to the same rhythm. But Andrew seemed not to have noticed her distress: he was staring off into the middle distance, as though conjuring up visions of the past that he had long wanted to go over with someone.

'Then Trevor seemed to vanish without a trace.' Phil looked at him and he explained, 'I asked Gloria how Trevor was coping with the shock of... you know... being discovered at his school, and she looked at me like I was quite mad.'

He took a sip of tea. 'Mind you, Doug and Gloria weren't the only ones behaving a little strangely after your father passed.'

Now he was tapping his wedding ring on his cup in sudden contemplation, and Phil wished she could speed him up like a podcast.

'Perhaps it was to be expected – after all a colleague was lost; everyone was not quite themselves. Even Mick spent more time out of his office trying to reassure Dee Dee, who *really* went to pieces. Ed Fielder, our contractor liaison manager, took it badly. He'd only recently started in that role. Perhaps he felt responsible since he had made Clive the site manager?'

Andrew, who had spoken all of this in one long speech, seemed to clam up, like a Hollywood spy realising he'd given away state secrets after being dosed with truth serum.

'Funny how none of these details were mentioned at the inquest,' said Phil accusingly.

'Well,' Andrew said, 'I wasn't invited to speak, otherwise

I certainly would have mentioned it.' He hesitated a moment, and Phil saw an expression flash across his face that she couldn't quite place. Remorse? Fear? Whatever it was, she had the sense there was still something he wasn't telling her, no matter how candid he seemed. 'We put a bench into the roof garden for your father,' he said, evidently keen to change the subject. 'Did you know? It was for anyone struggling with their mental health. I often saw Doug out there. And Mick and Dee Dee used it a few times too. Even Ed.'

'What about you?' she said. 'Did you ever sit on it?'

He seemed – *chose*, Phil thought – not to hear her.

'Anyway, I'm afraid I need to take the dog for a walk, Ms McGinty.... How did you say you found my details again?'

'Oh, don't let me stop you from taking Betty out,' she responded, leaping to her feet as though the idea of the dog having to wait a moment longer was too much to bear. She was suddenly desperate to get away from him. 'Thank you so much for your time, Mr Templeton-Dunbar. I really do appreciate you talking to me.'

And then she had scuttled out as quickly as possible, before he noticed she hadn't answered his question.

She turned the corner and reached the bus stop, whorls of sunlight bouncing off the plastic timetable as she peeled off her jumper with a sigh of relieved air. She paced up and down a few times before sitting down suddenly to cry. Fat tears sprang from her eyes and sugared her eyelashes. A loud sob escaped, but then she wiped her eyes, sniffed loudly and took a huge gulping breath to calm herself again. That had been intense, but work beckoned, and she didn't want to look like a ragdoll with blotches of crimson on her face.

So Gloria had specifically requested that Clive work on the project. What did Gloria Reynolds have to gain from

Phil's father dying? Phil couldn't think of any reason, but there must be something. She hadn't even considered how Jamie might fit into all of this. To Phil, Jamie was just an inept manager who helpfully kept piles of confidential documents lying around the office and had a lax attitude to locks. But maybe she was actually a master criminal, burying evidence under a mountain of paper. Hiding the answers in plain sight. The thought made her laugh.

And what about Doug and his mental health crisis? And Ed and everyone else? Was this a mass cover up? Again, the thought seemed suddenly ridiculous. Maybe this whole enterprise was ridiculous. Was she seeing clues where none existed?

As a child, she had lived in mortal terror of the shadow of a moose on the bathroom wall. Every evening she would sit on the toilet, petrified, praying that the moose, forever gazing off to the right, wouldn't turn and notice her. It didn't seem to register in her five-year-old brain that the moose was just the shadow of the lampshade throwing strange shapes onto the wall. She never even questioned why the shadow creature was evil (which it definitely was), nor what it might want with a child (nor, come to think of it, what it was doing peering out the bathroom window every evening).

Was that what she was doing now? Seeing evil shadow elk where none existed? Was Mick just curious? Did Gloria harbour a secret passion for school refurbishments? Was Doug truly cut up about a colleague's death? Did Mrs Cooke simply not fancy chatting to nosey parkers on her doorstep?

Had her father just killed himself?

Fat tears once again sprang from her eyes, and this time she didn't brush them away.

. . .

Phil yawned. In the confines of her dark store cupboard, she could easily have grabbed a little power nap. Of course, she hardly slept a wink after she got in. First the failed stakeout, then the failed Virtua expedition, and finally the mysterious email: none of it contributed to peaceful rest. She might not have even bothered going to bed, but there was really nowhere she could pace up and down without waking everyone in the family, and so she had sat propped upright on her pillows for a long time, staring at the mysterious email she'd received, the glow of the screen washing her face with a blue filter.

It was nearly lunchtime. Where had the last few hours gone? Passed by in a blur of cursive handwriting and stock replies. Perhaps she would just rest her head on the desk for a minute. The thought had barely entered her mind when the door opened and natural light flooded into the room. Phil blinked like a kidnap victim being released by her captors.

'I brought Mick to meet you,' said Rhonda before turning on her heels and rushing off.

'Hello Mick!' said Phil, rising from her chair to greet him.

'Yes, I thought I should meet this dynamo that everyone's talking about. It seems you've made quite an impact. I'd better watch out or you'll be after my job.'

Phil laughed, but at the last minute she spotted something in his eye – a tension around the corners – and her heart speeded up a little.

'Oh, no,' she said, waving a hand as though to waft a bad smell. She leaned in cheerfully. 'I don't think I'm cut out for investigations. There seem to be far too many decisions to be made. Like, how do you work out how much to compensate people, for example, and how do you know how much to charge the other companies?'

She hoped the question sounded stupid enough to allay his fears whilst also giving her a small insight into what Dee Dee had done that was so wrong.

Mick said, 'A little bit by luck and a little bit of judgment, I suppose. I've been doing it a long time. You get a feel for these things after a while… with experience.'

'Oh, I'm sure.'

'We usually have a sliding scale, but I'll be honest, I don't get involved in that too much. Although, of course, I have to sign off on some of the ones involving my investigations team.'

'To check they're legit?'

'We've had a few over the years where none of us were anywhere in the vicinity on the day in question.'

'You sound like you were in the police.'

'Ex-navy,' he said.

He was tall and lean and Phil felt herself standing a little to attention, keeping an eye on the exit behind him; wishing Rhonda hadn't closed the door.

'Wow. So, it's just members of the public trying it on?' she said.

'You could say that, yes. Or, to give them the benefit of the doubt, they just mistook someone else's vans for one of ours – maybe one of our competitors or just a company with a similar name.'

'Huh. And does that happen a lot?'

'On the odd occasion,' Mick said with a slight smile, 'but that's what I'm here for. We tend to do more B2B investigations. Other building firms causing trouble. But we're sent out to investigate the more dubious-sounding compensation claims from the public and they're often not quite what they seem.'

'Really?' said Phil. She was running out of appreciative noises. 'And what's the biggest compensation payment you've ever made?'

'Oh, I don't know,' he said, lightly. 'I can't say I keep track.'

I don't believe you, thought Phil.

'Don't you have a limit on the maximum, then? And is there a total budget for the year, or whatever, or is that a stupid question?'

She smiled like she was being a ditz, but Mick eyed her suspiciously.

'It's just, I've been amazed by the disparity in some of the claims,' Phil continued, trying her best to give off the wide-eyed fascination she imagined Marilyn Monroe might employ if she were stuck in a cupboard trying to wring information out of a strangely sinister veteran in his seventies.

'Just one of those things, I suppose... Anyway,' he said, suddenly rapping his knuckles on her desk and smiling lightly. 'Just wanted to say hello, meet the girl of the hour. I'll leave you to it.'

Phil suddenly felt like a prisoner, desperate to cling onto a visitor. 'I expect you're keen to get out of this place.'

'Why's that?' said Mick.

The shift in his tone caught Phil by surprise, and her pulse quickened again.

'No reason... it's just Dee Dee mentioned you used to work in here, so I thought, you know, you might be a little...' she trailed off awkwardly.

'That's right,' Mick broke into a sudden smile and put his hand to his forehead. It was a gesture that felt entirely staged and not a little threatening. The smile didn't reach his eyes. 'Do you know, I had completely forgotten about that?'

'Perhaps you buried the memory,' said Phil. She tried to make her laugh sound as unforced as possible. 'There's still some of your paperwork in here, I think.'

Somehow, she'd said the wrong thing again. Her smile froze as he took a step closer.

'Don't touch any of that,' he said darkly. 'And don't pay any attention to Dee Dee.'

'That's a relief! I've got enough paperwork to sort as it is… and, yes… totally know what you mean about Dee Dee.'

He nodded as though satisfied, then gave the most laboured smile Phil had ever witnessed. Like a psychopath at a parole hearing, she thought.

'Glad that's understood,' he said.

He turned smartly, opened the door and strode away.

Phil took a moment to shake herself out of her confusion. She was willing to bet it wasn't the best first impression either of them had ever made. Clearly, he thought she was after his job (presumably because he believed a career in the Investigations team was the pinnacle of human ambition), but he'd been oddly cagey about the room. Was he territorial? She had half expected him to start wandering the perimeter, rubbing his scent glands on the shelving units. And what was the thing about the boxes of paperwork? Never had one man been so possessive over some seven-year-old photos of broken cables. The more she thought about it, the funnier it got.

And the more she was determined to search through all of his Investigations reports.

But first, she had something to do.

'Ed?' Phil said.

The surly ex-builder she had met on the first day glanced up at her but didn't say hello.

'Who has a Virtua-branded car?' she asked.

'How do you mean?' he said, eventually.

'Like, who gets to have one of the vans with the company branding on?'

'Why? Are you hoping to get one?'

He smirked and Phil resisted the urge to reply that yes, actually, she was looking to get on the career path that ended with a Ford van. Partly because sarcasm wouldn't help here, and partly because she *would* actually quite like a Ford van. He answered her question without waiting for a reply. Clearly, cars were something he was willing to chat about.

'Anyone client-facing. So someone working putting out road signs or fixing a utility.'

'What about someone going into a school?' said Phil, realising how strange this question sounded and hoping he wouldn't notice. But he cocked his head and looked at her, interested for the first time.

'Why?'

Phil smiled. 'Rhonda's got me looking at these complaints letters and there's one about a van parked near a school. Curtain twitcher type, you know.'

She rolled her eyes, and Ed grunted in amusement.

'Well, the old dear might be right, but I've never met any nonces with a company car.'

'But in theory, there might have been someone with a branded van working near a school'

'Given we have contracts with most of the schools round here, and I said anyone client-facing was likely to have a van, I think you already have your answer.'

Alright, Ed, keep your shirt on, thought Phil.

'Thanks so much, Ed. You've been really helpful,' she said.

Phil had arrived back at her cupboard with a renewed sense of purpose. She made a beeline for Mick's old investigations reports, balancing her tea on a shelf while she manhandled the grey boxes down to the floor. If someone from HR spotted her, she'd be shipped off to a health and safety briefing about the correct way to get a box down from above head height (which no doubt discouraged the use of a swivel chair as a footstool).

But her enthusiasm soon waned: there really wasn't anything in the boxes worth seeing. None of the reports were for sites anywhere near her father's death. There was one at Helenswood school a few weeks later. That was the site of the old secondary – the one Phil had attended before it was merged with the boy's school. She flicked through the investigation, but it was nothing special. Just a note about a claim against them by the electric company. Mick had investigated and concluded there was no payment to make and closed the case.

'Kill me now,' she said out loud to herself as she kicked the box.

That was the precise moment that the door opened and Jamie walked in.

'Hi Jamie!' Phil's greeting came out with strangled panic.

'How are you getting on Scarlett?' said Jamie, who either hadn't heard her wishing for an early death or was pretending she hadn't.

'Nearly there,' said Phil. 'I should have all the boxes finished by the end of the day.'

'Great! Go you! Let me know when you're done and I'll get Rhonda to bring some more in.'

Phil swallowed. 'More?'

'This is only the tip of the iceberg, I'm afraid. We have quite a backlog.'

When Phil wished for death earlier, she realised she had been premature. She sent up a silent prayer for a sudden fatal allergy to cardboard.

'Oh wow,' she managed. 'Sounds like I've got my work cut out.'

She could feel Jamie losing interest, already turning a fraction, ready to head off to... wherever it is she went to during the working day. In desperation, Phil scrambled for a way to make her stay.

'Were you around when the man died?'

For a second the question seemed to hang in the air like a bad smell, neither one wishing to acknowledge it, but Phil resisted the urge to change the subject or pretend she hadn't said anything. The question had bubbled up from her subconscious, but now she realised it was exactly what she wanted to know. Eventually, Jamie responded.

'What man?'

'Clive, I think his name was. I've heard a few people mention him.'

Jamie gave Phil a look that Phil couldn't quite parse.

'Not really. I'd just started,' she said.

Phil blinked and felt her mouth go dry. It wasn't that the answer was unexpected, but somehow she felt wrong-footed by it – actually, physically. She shifted her feet to regain her balance and, when she spoke, attempted a casual tone that came out a few semitones too high.

'Would you mind talking me through what happens in that situation?'

Jamie pursed her lips and so Phil said, 'Just so I understand what to do from an HR perspective.'

It was a fair question, but Jamie seemed flustered.

'Oh, well...' began Jamie. She managed a few half-hearted answers, filled with corporate nonsense like 'reached out to the talent matrix,' before glancing at her phone and exclaiming, 'Sorry Scarlett, I've got a meeting on Four in five... In fact,' Phil watched the thought formulating in Jamie's mind and knew what was coming next, 'Can I ask you a favour? Would you mind making me a coffee and bringing it up so I can pop for a wee? Thanks so much, you're a lifesaver.'

'Sure,' said Phil, who recognised a worthy adversary when she saw one. She had managed to shake off unwanted curiosity either out of a reluctance to talk about a bad time for the company, or, (more likely in Phil's mind), because she didn't know the answers to Phil's questions on HR procedure. Either way, it was a win for the HR director.

Well played, Jamie, she thought.

Well played.

She left her box fort and made her way to the kitchenette.

'I know what you're doing,' said Mick.

Phil glanced up in surprise. She had been attempting to coax the coffee machine into action, peering into the top of it like a brain surgeon attempting her first craniotomy.

'I wish I did!'

It took her a moment to realise he wasn't smiling back.

'You're trying to take my job,' he said.

'I'm... sorry what?'

The laugh of surprise exploded from her without warning and she immediately knew it was the wrong reaction.

'You can laugh, but I warn you, I'm not someone you want to annoy. I've seen off worse than you without a second thought.

'OK,' said Phil. 'Listen–'

He interrupted her before she could reassure him.

'I won't hesitate to make sure you go the way of the dodo.'

'I've always wanted to go to Mauritius,' said Phil and then kicked herself. She found it hard to take people seriously when they spoke like a bad soap opera, but waves of malice seemed to be emanating from Mick. *Now is not the time.* Mick took a step forward and Phil realised with a grim certainty that he would not hesitate to hurt her. The thought made her feel suddenly winded, her breath catching as she struggled to take in air. She took a step backwards as he reached out to grab her by the arm.

'I'm watching you,' he said, his voice rumbling like gravel down a cliff.

'Take your hand off me,' she said, her mood for jokes well and truly gone. She pulled away, ignoring the throbs of pain from his fingerprints.

'Ah, Mick, there you are,' said a voice.

Phil looked over at the entrance to the kitchenette to see Rhonda, light beaming in from a window behind her back, giving her a golden aura like an angel from on high.

Mick stepped back but continued to stare at Phil.

'I believe you're wanted in the conference room. Some of the investigations team have arrived for a briefing.'

Mick rearranged his face. 'Right,' he said through clenched teeth, pushing past Rhonda as he went.

Rhonda stepped further into the kitchenette. 'Everything OK?' Her tone was light, as though the past minute had been a figment of Phil's imagination. 'I thought maybe we could have a catch up later, perhaps find something more interesting for you to do tomorrow?'

'Sounds good,' said Phil. She could feel her body start to shake a little and she wasn't sure how much longer she could pretend to chat casually about admin before she began to cry. She rubbed her arm absently.

'You're not the only one...' said Rhonda suddenly.

Phil looked up and saw tears in Rhonda's eyes, her cheeks bright pink as the blood rose to her face.

'He scares me too.'

Then, just like that, Rhonda pasted on a smile, the sort a brave child musters after a painful graze. 'Now then, let's get this coffee machine working, shall we?'

When Phil carried the coffee up to the fourth floor, she was still shaking. Mick had rattled her, and feigning calm while Rhonda showed her how to fix the coffee machine had taken up serious amounts of self-control. She needed a biscuit or something – a bar of chocolate – to restore some energy to her frazzled mind. As she walked carefully out of the lift, it was all she could do to keep the mug from sloshing the hot liquid onto her hand.

She'd forgotten how light it was up here, a world away from her dark cupboard. At first, she wasn't sure which way to turn. But the sound of laughter drew her attention. In a corner towards the far end of the space, Jamie stood, her back against a wall. Phil's eyes widened at the sight of Lachlan, the sandwich man, standing over her, his arm resting on the wall above her head, the other hand touching her cheek.

His studied pose reminded her of the web influencers with their big male arms and their cheesy grins who post thirst trap videos that made Phil cringe so hard her teeth nearly shattered. And what to do now? Should she keep going? Cough politely? Their hiding spot was hardly the best choice. Presumably, in their nook to the right of the conference room and behind a tall plant, they believed themselves invisible. Or perhaps up here on the fourth floor, different rules applied and Jamie wasn't afraid to be caught flirting with the sandwich delivery boy.

Phil was just trying to decide what to do when Jamie, with a final smile, tucked her hair behind one ear and headed off into the conference room. Lachlan stared appreciatively at Jamie's backside as she departed. Phil, who had been hovering in her spot by the lift, also began walking towards the conference room. Lachlan, still grinning, turned and spotted her.

'Ah, it's you,' he said, grin only growing broader. 'How are you getting on, new girl?'

His tone was incredibly flirtatious, and Phil had to admire his shamelessness. Just seconds ago, he had been touching the cheek of another woman, and yet here he was already in pursuit of a new conquest.

'I see she's got you delivering drinks to her already,' he said. 'You want to watch out for that or she'll have you picking up her dry cleaning and polishing her shoes.'

He was dripping with self-conscious sex appeal. Phil wasn't sure she had ever met a man as pleased with himself.

'You seem to know her very well,' she said, raising an eyebrow.

'I make it my business to know everyone,' he said. He leaned in towards her, his tall frame bending to meet her eye-to-eye. Phil felt a strange urge to meet his smirk with one of her own.

'I know you very well too,' he said. 'Things not work out at the paper for you, then?'

Shit.

Phil felt her stomach travel all the way to her bowels for some kind of crisis talks. She tried to control her voice as she gave a casual laugh. 'Just trying out some options before I commit, you know.'

If she could, she would have lengthened her stride and walked away like nothing had happened, but she had over-filled the coffee and had to settle instead for a rather harried retreat, one hand cradled round the lip of the hot mug, feet shuffling in careful little steps.

Behind her, Lachlan chuckled. 'Sure you are.'

She heard him grabbing his crate of sandwiches and glanced over her shoulder to watch him heading towards the lifts. As he pressed the button he winked. Phil looked back towards the conference room and toddled away.

There was no time to recover from the shock of Lachlan's words. Did he know who she was? She was racking her brain, trying to remember if he had ever been to the paper. Of course he must have; after all, she had recognised him. She thought she had just seen him out and about with his sandwich-laden tricycle, but now a vague memory was surfacing. An editorial meeting coinciding with Shazia the sub-editor's last day. Adam Jenkins, editor, in a rare moment of generosity. *Sandwiches all round.* Gales of sarcastic mockery at Adam's idea of a treat.

That was it!

Arnie's Sarnies had catered Shazia's final editorial meeting and, she supposed, Lachlan had pedalled round to their building with his soggy bread-based foodstuffs. Shazia stared at Adam and told him she was 'Totally and utterly... *whelmed* by his gesture,' and the team were reminded once again how much they would miss her.

Oh well, thought Phil. Either I'll be outed by the sandwich delivery man, or I'll spend the rest of what is meant to be my week's holiday delivering coffee to a narcissist. Either way, I lose. She pushed through the glass doors to the conference room and spotted Jamie perched on the edge of the glass table chatting to a colleague. Jamie turned to hail Phil as she approached.

'Ah, there you are, Scarlett. Just pop it down here. You're a *lifesaver*.'

Jamie's raptures appeared to be all for the benefit of the other managers. Presumably, she was keen to show that she had a minion to command and was therefore *important*. A quick glance around the room suggested no one was unduly impressed. They met her loud paroxysms of pleasure with utter indifference – if they even noticed her at all.

Phil recognised a few faces. Not only had she glanced at the company website 'Meet the Team' page on her first day of work, she had also paid particular interest in the company's org chart during the inquest. If her father's death had been caused by negligence, she had every intention of finding out where the buck stopped. In the event, the coroner had been reluctant to name anyone senior as responsible for Clive's death, preferring to solely blame Clive for his carelessness and to insist he should never have been on site in the first place.

Now Phil resisted the urge to eyeball these overpaid executives and demand answers. But boy did she want to take each one by the lapels and shake a confession out of them. She looked over at the leaders she recognised. The finance director and the heads of sales and IT were discussing their winter holiday plans. *What a charmed life they lead.* She thought of Angela, working her bum off for the local authority and living in a council flat.

And what had Jamie done to be denied a place on the fourth floor? She was young and female. Perhaps those two things counted against her. What had Dee Dee said? *'They like the ladies on floor three where they belong – or bringing them their lattes.'*

Phil, having safely delivered the coffee to the table without spilling anything, could find no excuse to linger, although she would love to stay and be a fly on the wall during the meeting. She wanted to see them all in action, to watch how the politics played out amongst the leadership executive. Reluctantly, she turned to go. The atmosphere in the room changed. People stood straighter, voices calmed to a murmur, chairs were dragged out so seats could be taken – and Phil watched as an impeccably dressed silver-haired woman strode in.

Gloria Reynolds, OBE, had arrived.

'Hello everyone, how are we?' said Gloria to murmurs of greeting from her team.

'Good thanks, Gloria,' barked Keith Reed, the CFO, removing his blue spectacles to give them a polish.

Gloria immediately began trying to get her assistant's attention, presumably so she could order a drink to arrive just after the meeting started, disrupting proceedings before they'd barely begun.

Phil thought about Andrew, fidgeting on the hard sofa as he questioned Gloria's interest in the St Agnes school project. Was it really so strange for a boss to pay an interest? Perhaps in this case. Phil hadn't seen her on the fourth floor all week and it seemed from speaking to others that Gloria was hardly a hands-on leader. Dee Dee had called her the Absent Vicar and joked that she was so hands off they'd get more guidance from a cardboard cut-out of a woman pointing.

So what was special about this project? Perhaps Trevor the nephew really did exist.

'Jamie,' she said. 'Do you have any brothers or cousins?'

More than anything, Jamie seemed surprised that Phil was still in the room and, wrong-footed as she was, simply blinked, said 'Er, no,' and then blinked again.

'Just wondered,' said Phil breezily before stepping swiftly towards the door.

'I'm afraid I have to start the meeting with some rather bad news,' said Gloria. 'Or, that is rather sad news, which – it must be said – is also very bad...'

She glanced at Phil, noticing her for the first time. Phil had, naturally, stopped walking as soon as she heard Gloria speak, and now she found herself caught like a rabbit in the headlights, trapped by the gaze of the chief executive and her leadership team.

'Who is this?' said Gloria.

'Thank you, Scarlett, that will be all,' said Jamie, glaring at her. 'Sorry Gloria.'

'Yep, sorry,' said Phil, 'I'm just leaving.' She rushed to the glass door and made her way stiffly along the corridor, into the lift and back to the safety and anonymity of the third floor.

Before Phil reached her cupboard, she got a phone call. She glanced at the screen and had a brief moment of fear, like a child caught stealing sweets. She ducked into one of the central breakout spaces, sitting in a bubble-shaped object that acted both as chair and felted-noise baffle. It provided a privacy of sorts, which, short of returning to her office, was the best she was going to get around here.

'How's the holiday?' said Adam Jenkins, editor.

'Great!' said Phil, hoping he couldn't hear the buzz of office lighting and the sound of a hundred souls slumped and sighing in their chairs.

'Barry's picked up a tip off that something major might have happened.'

'What?' said Phil, ears metaphorically pricking up.

'You tell me,' said Adam. 'Know anyone at Virtua Services?'

'Er,' said Phil.

Was this a trap? Was Adam about to reveal that he was actually standing behind her and knew exactly how she was spending her week off? She did actually glance around, just to be sure.

'Come on,' said Adam. 'You like to tell us how you know everyone, don't you? And everyone knows someone at Virtua Services.'

'Right,' said Phil. 'Presumably, that includes you?'

'Tried them already. They either hate me or they're not in the right meeting rooms. Barry's having the same problem.'

Phil made it her business not to help Barry Brooker with anything in life and she wasn't planning on starting now.

'Well, he must know something,' she said. 'What did this contact tell him?'

'That something major has happened at the old school campus – the girls' school.'

'Right,' said Phil, tentatively. She waited for him to continue.

'That's about as far as it goes. Lots of police vehicles there in the last few days, looks like there's a crime scene tent up. I sent Mick down to take a look and he watched the CSI boilersuits come and go. No one would talk to him, even the gobby coppers who usually spill the beans. Some uniforms moved him away from the gate. Oh, and he spotted some people from the council too.'

'Wow,' said Phil.

'None of our usual contacts are helping us out beyond a few hints.'

Phil didn't know what to say. She felt a creeping dread, her heart seeming to speed up one moment and slow to a halt the next.

'Was there a body?' she said. Was that why the scenes of crime officers were there?

Adam sucked in a breath and she could imagine him, his body raising up a little as he inhaled, his hand swiping his gingery stubble.

'Not as far as we're aware,' he said. 'Look, I know it's a touchy subject for you. But is there anyone you can ask?'

She knew who he meant, of course. He didn't want her to speak to someone at Virtua. He wanted her to ring Dean. And, not for the first time, she really wished she'd never mentioned she knew Dean Martin.

'I'll see what I can do,' she said.

SEVENTEEN

Jen stared at Jamie Pilcher and tried not to feel like a rumpled mess. Until this moment she had considered herself a fairly natty dresser, with her smart tapered leg trouser suits, slim belts and crisp white shirts. But after Nate had died, the personal care had taken a bit of a tumble and although she was still wearing the suits and shirts, there had been a decline in... finesse. Here, standing opposite this early thirties goddess in her white wide-legged crepe trouser suit with its excess of wool and silk, Jen felt decidedly out-dressed.

She suppressed the urge to rub a corner of Jamie's suit fabric between a thumb and forefinger. Jamie, oblivious to Jen's inner battle, ran a gold-ringed hand through gold-tinted hair and said, 'I'm sorry, but as I've said, all the records from that era have been lost.'

The head of HR at Virtua Services had been late, blowing breathlessly into the conference room at fifteen minutes past in a chaos of apologies, clutching a mobile phone in one hand and a steaming skinny latte in the other. And now she was being suspiciously unhelpful.

'I've only just been briefed about the body in the wall,' said Jamie, as though this meant she was exempt from being asked any hard questions about anything.

Jen was surprised. Why only tell the head of HR now? Surely, she would have been told, along with all the other senior leaders?

'Is the information not in an archive somewhere?' said Jen in a more generous tone than she normally used for someone so vague. If only she'd ironed her shirt properly; she couldn't even be sure it was entirely clean. She bet Jamie smelled of dry cleaning and expensive perfume. She inhaled involuntarily, but then shook her head to regain her senses. This was not like her. How had this walking *Vogue* photo-shoot unsettled her so much?

'I'm afraid my predecessor was not good at record keeping,' said Jamie. 'It's taken me months to get the paperwork on our current people digitised, so you can appreciate that the records of casual labourers, probably employed through one of our contractors, has not been a priority. We're focused on making sure everyone has a sense of Purpose, and has completed the full suite of unconscious bias training.'

Sense of Purpose? The 'p' had definitely been capitalised. Jen could hear it. Did Jen have a sense of purpose? Was that her problem? Was she adrift in a sea of utter pointlessness, her North Star actually just a speck of dust on the lens? It felt like she had no sense of anything at all. But she couldn't let herself be derailed by HR-speak. She focused on the only useful thing Jamie had said.

'I met your predecessor, I think? Andrew Templeton...' she clicked her finger, trying to remember. Normally her memory was impeccable, but things had seized up from so many months of sitting on the bathroom floor crying.

'Dunbar,' supplied Jamie. 'He left a while ago under a bit of a cloud. Early retirement.'

She pulled a face and made a sucking noise with her teeth as though he'd tripped and fallen in a hole instead of doing something perfectly normal.

'Oh?' said Jen.

She had hoped Jamie would continue supplying her with very un-HR-like gossip, but Jamie was clearly bored with the conversation. She eyed her gold watch and took a sip of coffee.

'Can we have a list of contract firms or outsourcing agencies that may have worked for you during the last five to ten years? Perhaps they will have records,' said Jen.

'Possibly,' replied Jamie. 'I think most of our people have always been in-house, but we might have a few agencies on the books. Now, as you can imagine, we have quite a lot to prepare for.'

Jamie stared at Jen meaningfully before shifting impatiently. 'Is there anything else I can do for you, or…?'

'I asked your assistant to book us in for half an hour and you were late.'

Jen's straight talking didn't faze Jamie, who was too busy reading a message on her smartwatch.

'That's OK' she said, still looking down.

Jen was about to tell her she hadn't been apologising when Jamie continued:

'Things are so hectic at the moment. It's a bit of a nightmare, to be honest. Anyway! If you need anything else, I'm sure Rhonda can help you. Rhonda Whitford. She knows everything that's going on round here. We've already told her about the… incident. She can let you know about the third parties.'

'Is that your assistant?'

'That's right,' said Jamie, and Jen knew she was lying. She remembered the woman who had shown her into the meeting room had introduced herself as the office manager, not as a PA or junior HR lackey. Still, if Jamie wanted to pretend she had an assistant, that was her business. Chances are, Rhonda was the one doing everything around here anyway. Jen had met her type before: Rhondas were running the world, even if no one noticed them.

'Do you have the contact information for Mr Templeton-Dunbar?' she asked. 'Perhaps he might remember.'

'Oh, I shouldn't think he'll remember anything. He was notoriously disorganised. That's why things are the way they are round here and he was only getting worse as he got older. These dinosaurs were responsible for all the mistakes and now it's up to us to put the company back together. Rhonda has spent months trying to collate everything. We've had to call in extra help. We've got an intern helping us try to restore order as we speak. Speaking of which, I'm afraid I really do have to go. It was great to meet you Jenny. I'm sorry we couldn't be more help.'

She grasped the handle of the glass meeting room door, her rings clanking on the brushed chrome, and swung it towards her before smiling at Jen expectantly, waiting for her to leave. But Jen hadn't finished.

'Just to be clear, you do understand that Virtua is under investigation for serious failures in building standards, not to mention a dead employee?'

Jen watched Jamie's face flush.

'Yes, I'm well aware,' she said, still holding the door for Jen.

'If you know the identity of the man in the cavity wall – a cavity wall that appears to have been improperly built – or if you know who is responsible for the mistakes in the wall construction, then you'll be doing yourselves no favours by keeping it from us.'

Jamie's face dropped. She closed the door again.

'These are some very serious accusations, DS Collin,' she said.

'Collet,' said Jen, but Jamie wasn't listening.

'Virtua will of course be doing everything it can to assist police with their investigation into the Helenswood school incident and we're working together to identify how and why this error could have come about. I assure you that we will be doing everything in our power to get to the bottom of this.'

Jen had the strange sensation that she was talking to a press release. She tried to reply, but Jamie hadn't finished.

'And let's not forget, Jenny, that the building was inspected by the council during the works and no problems were flagged at the time. Perhaps the council needs to be investigated as well.'

She wasn't wrong, thought Jen.

'As I said, Ms Pilcher. If you know anything about the identity of the man found dead in the wall of one of your buildings, please do get in touch and let me know. In the meantime, since you are unable to check your records for me, I will be applying for a warrant. The police are very good at searching through documents. Perhaps we can help clear your admin backlog.'

It's always enjoyable seeing their faces go white, she thought.

'Let me see what I can do,' said Jamie.

'That's very kind of you,' said Jen, brushing past Jamie as she stood holding the door open.

If I'd ironed the shirt, thought Jen, this moment would have been perfect.

She was pressing the button for the ground floor when Phil McGinty walked past. There was a moment where they suffered the same jolt of recognition, startling in unison like drama students practising mirror work. And then the lift shut and Jen was staring at her own frowning reflection in the metal doors.

Of course, Rhonda knew where Andrew Templeton-Dunbar lived, which is how Jen found herself standing on the doorstep of the ex-HR director's door listening to the approaching clap of footsteps on terracotta while a small dog barked on the offbeat. The house was as fancy as the surname, albeit with the kind of middle-class scruffiness you'd expect from a hallway filled with muddy wellingtons and Barbour jackets. Andrew ushered her inside and endeared himself to her immediately with the offer of biscuits and tea; a much warmer greeting than the one his successor had provided back at the Virtua offices.

'But no, thank you,' she said. 'I just have a few questions. It shouldn't take long.'

'Come in, come in,' he urged, sweeping aside the dog's blanket so she could sit on the expensive, ageing sofa. He took a seat in a wingback armchair. 'How can I help?'

'I'm afraid they've found another body,' said Jen.

'Oh,' said Andrew. Jen watched as he turned greyer than a January sky. 'Oh dear. I am so sorry.'

She tried not to read too much into people's reactions when they heard news like this. Innocent people could say the strangest things, and guilty people didn't always give themselves away. But 'I'm so sorry,' struck her as an interesting choice.

'In the same place?' said Andrew. 'Hang on, *another body?*'

As though she might have misspoken.

'Yes.' Jen watched him closely. 'In the wall of the old school at Helenswood. We don't think it was an accident.'

'Christ. Who was he? ...Or she.'

'That's what I'm hoping you can tell me.'

He reached for a biscuit, and Jen noticed his hand was trembling.

'Are you alright, Mr Templeton-Dunbar?'

'Yes, sorry. It's just – please call me Andrew – it's just that we were told the last gentleman – Clive – was... well, was a suicide. But now you're saying there's another one?' His voice rose to such a pitch Jen wondered if he might cry. 'I'm sorry. I don't know why this has hit me so hard. It's just... Please, do go on.' He seemed to make a conscious effort to pull himself together, softly clapping his hands between his legs before looking up at her. 'What can I do?'

'The gentleman seems to be someone who may have worked for Virtua Services, possibly as a casual labourer via an agency.'

'In that case, you can try looking back through all the records,' said Andrew. 'Though we didn't keep files for every agency person who worked for one of our partners; we didn't tend to have that level of detail. But if one of our partners supplied a labourer, they should have the information. Really those recruitment agencies are just glorified payroll providers, however, so I'm not sure how much data they'll still have – especially if it's more than seven years. It's just a way for companies to avoid offering people reliable contracts, as far as I'm concerned. I always argued against it. How can someone really *care* about a company's mission if the company doesn't *care* about *them*? I wrote a piece about it for LinkedIn. I can find it for you if you're interested?'

'No,' said Jen, more abruptly than she'd intended, 'No, thank you. But if I could just go back to what you said about the agencies. Could you tell me who that might be?'

'Possibly PeoplePower or similar. Or sometimes we just employed a smaller local building firm. Jamie can check for you. Or maybe better to speak with Ed Fielder. Our head of procurement left and I believe still hasn't been replaced.'

'I've just come from a meeting with Ms Pilcher,' said Jen. 'She said the files were in some… disarray.'

Andrew chuckled. 'Oh yes,' he said. 'The big "sort out". She started that when she was working for me – decided there was some better system we could be using; wanted everything digitised. A good idea, I thought, and about time. Except she began the endeavour by taking everything out of the cabinets and then couldn't seem to get up the interest to get it all finished. Like a child tidying her bedroom.'

Jen knew how she felt. She'd made the same mistake when she'd cleared out the understairs cupboard. In the end, Nate had saved her from herself by piling it all back into boxes and shutting the door on it.

'And when was this?' she said.

'That must have been about seven years ago now.'

'When Clive died?'

Andrew thought. 'Oh, I suppose so, yes – come to think

of it. She joined us just weeks before he passed and commenced her digitisation project just after. I remember because I was so busy in the weeks that followed. You know, liaising with procurement and our various agencies to get any insights we could into Mr McGinty's suicide – not to mention checking on our people to ensure we had more robust mental health practices in place. Jamie swooped in and took control of a lot of the organisational aspects. I was grateful at the time. She started out brilliantly, but I'm afraid things rather got away from her.'

'So–' began Jen, but Andrew hadn't finished.

'I'm surprised Rhonda hasn't taken it all in hand. Towards the end of my tenure, she regularly did Jamie's job for her – especially once they pushed Mary and some of the team into part-time roles and got an agency to do a lot of the day-to-day stuff. Then Paul left, of course. But I'm sorry, I'm rambling. You don't need to know all this.'

'They've got an intern in, I believe. But in the meantime, Jamie suggested you might remember something.'

'Why on earth would I remember an agency person from... how long ago do you think this poor man died?'

'Seven years.'

'Same as Clive McGinty? How awful. And do you believe they were both killed?'

'We're keeping an open mind at this stage.'

'Between you and me, I always thought the Clive McGinty death was strange.'

'Oh? Why's that?'

'Ach, I don't know. Just that he had such a lovely young family, and he seemed like he had so much to live for... Of course, I realise that mental health can be a silent killer, but it struck me as an odd way to end your life. They say it took him a long time to die...' His gaze was fixed on the window behind Jen's head as though he was picturing the scene. 'How on earth a body can even fit down those cavity walls? I'll never know. They're so narrow! And now you're saying there's another one?'

'I'm afraid so.'

'I mean, I can't believe it. It's just horrific.'

'Yes,' agreed Jen. She was beginning to wonder if he meant to keep asking the same questions. Was he stalling? Or was he just in shock?

'But I don't see how I can help. I hardly ever dealt with contract teams. I tried – many times, in fact – to bring in new policies to welcome our external people more firmly into the Virtua family, but I'm afraid I could never quite get the backing of the rest of the VLT.'

'VLT?'

'Sorry. Virtua Leadership Team. You know what these big companies are like with their TLAs. That's Three Letter Acronyms,' he added, noticing Jen's blank look.

'Right.'

'They just wouldn't embrace the notion that our external teams were just as much a vital part of the business as our internal teams. To my mind, they were often more important, since they were representing us out in the world, if you see what I mean.'

Jen wasn't sure how she'd got herself involved in a debate about the purview of human resources, but here she was. It was like being stuck in a TED Talk.

'So you didn't keep records, and you were unlikely to have met the contractors?' she said, trying to get things back on track.

'Afraid not.'

'He was wearing a blue polo top. You might call it a dark royal blue, but faded from lots of wear, with a Prints To Go logo in gold embroidery.'

Andrew's beatific smile dropped.

'Well now, you know, that does ring a bell.' He wagged a finger, 'Yes...'

Jen waited for him to go on, but he just continued wagging his finger. She sensed he was trying to get his thoughts in order; buying time.

'Can you tell me what you remember?' she prompted.

'That's just the thing. I can't quite place him. A Prints To Go top, you say? Did he work for them?'

'We believe he was given the top by a local homeless shelter.'

'Was he homeless? Oh dear – poor man.'

'Yes, but as I said, we believe he may have had work as a casual labourer with Virtua, or perhaps one of its contractors.'

'Hmm.'

He was steepling his fingers and leaning forward like he might suggest a prayer. Jen tried to move things along.

'I believe I may have once had an altercation with a gentleman who was aggressive in the lobby, harassing the receptionist.'

He pronounced 'harassing' with the emphasis on the first syllable – on the 'ha' instead of on the 'ass' – a pronunciation you didn't hear much of these days. *A man who does everything by the book.*

'I'm afraid I rather lost my cool. We had already escorted him out once – very politely – but this time I was alerted by reception and came down to meet him in the lobby. He got quite belligerent – almost certainly drunk or high, or both –

and since our security was... who knows where... I decided to help him to the door myself. I was very concerned for my colleagues' welfare and safety and I may have used strong and firm language to encourage him not to visit again.'

'Visit? Was he visiting someone? Why was he in the building?'

'I don't recall,' Andrew replied, and immediately Jen knew he was lying.

'It would really help the investigation if you could tell us everything you know,' she said. 'I think we should probably continue this conversation down at the station.'

'I'm not sure what else I can tell you,' Andrew said.

They were in an interview room. Nandini had joined them and Jen had read Andrew his rights for this voluntary interview.

'Why didn't you call the police?' said Jen.

Andrew spread his hands and gave an apologetic shrug. 'I really didn't think about it. It felt like the situation had been dealt with. We never saw the chap again.'

'Until his body turned up in the wall cavity of one of your buildings.'

Andrew stiffened.

'I'm not sure what you're implying, detective.'

'That you had an argument with the deceased shortly before the last known sighting of him.'

'If you think I have the wherewithal to stuff two innocent souls down two cavity walls, in school buildings – schools for Christ's sake – I'm afraid you are mistaken.'

Jen raised her hands, 'Mr Templeton-Dun–'

Andrew spoke over her. 'But if you really want to solve this, you might consider why Gloria Reynolds was so interested in the St Agnes school project and why she mentioned Clive by name as someone who should work on it.'

'I'm sorry, what?' said Jen, thrown off balance. 'Why didn't you mention this at the time of the coroner's investigation?'

The question seemed to take the wind out of his anger. 'Oh, well, I didn't think much about it at the time – not really. But, it has played on my mind ever since. And sitting at home, with just the dog and the cryptic for company, one's mind tends to start looking back, and what one finds is that the boss's niece has turned the building into the Circumlocution Office. That's Dickens,' he added in a tone Jen would have found patronising had she not been jotting the word down to google later.

'Then there's the health and safety report,' he said.

'What about it?' said Jen.

Andrew looked stricken, but the expression passed and Jen was once again staring at the calm face of a people leader.

'I should have thought of it sooner, but I honestly didn't realise – what with all the chaos and emotion of the inquest. It's only really coming back to me now.'

Jen knew he was lying. She wondered if he knew it too, or if he had convinced himself that whatever he was about to confess was truly an innocent mistake.

'I believe Doug Graves testified that there hadn't been a health and safety report of the building yet?'

'That's right,' said Jen.

'Which was why Clive was blamed for entering a building without waiting for sign-off?'

'Yes,' agreed Jen. *Where was this heading?*

'But I have been reflecting back on that time, and I distinctly remember Gloria waving the signed off report at me. She was thrilled because it meant work could start.'

'You're absolutely sure?'

'Yes. No doubt about it. She told me the St Agnes school site was safe.'

EIGHTEEN

Dean wasn't answering Phil's calls. It was a novel experience. After she'd seen DS Jen Collet in the office, she had tried to get through to him multiple times to find out what was going on, but he didn't pick up. He didn't respond to her messages, either. Was he avoiding her? It was possible. Highly likely, in fact. She had been neglecting their friendship, ringing him only when she wanted something, being nice to him and then ringing off when she had what she needed. And she was hardly one to judge when it came to screening her calls. She regularly sent him to voicemail; she sometimes took weeks to reply to his messages.

She'd had to message Adam with the bad news: she had nothing for him. She couldn't even risk telling him she'd seen DS Collet in the office, since she'd have to cook up an excuse for being there.

'Something's going on,' he replied. 'Try someone at Virtua.'

And so she did. She wafted casually past Dee Dee's desk, expecting to be grabbed by the arm and given all the gossip.

But Dee Dee had gone home, or gone rogue. Wherever she was, she wasn't at her desk any time Phil swung by. Phil made so many cups of tea that it started to look like she had a problem. Dee Dee's manager eyed her suspiciously the last time she went by.

'She's not here,' he said gruffly.

So she tried Rhonda. But Rhonda wasn't at her desk either. Ed Fielder put his headphones on as she approached, and Phil didn't want to risk pestering him again. Everyone else seemed to drift from her gaze whenever she tried to make eye contact. Was it just midweek ennui, or was the whole office ignoring her for a reason? Michelle, her Hobnob-loving first day friend, was happy to chat as ever, though.

'Has something happened?' Phil said. 'It's just that the office is very quiet.'

'Some of them have been read the riot act about this audit,' said Michelle. 'And the leadership lot have been having a big meeting, which always gives everyone a bit of the heebie-jeebies, you know – we all expect a round of redundancies or something terrible. Plus,' she added. 'It's hump day, isn't it?'

So maybe it was all in Phil's head. That's what she told herself when she made her way home at the end of the day. She didn't head straight to Simon's for her stakeout. She needed to get some provisions from home. She wanted a moment to herself to unwind. Her afternoon had been spent sorting more letters, piling them into bin bags, committing probable fraud. Did this count as her second crime of the week? Scarlett's Letters.

Roosevelt Court was a weird choice of name. Who the hell was Roosevelt to the Aldhill inhabitants? Most didn't know who he was (she had done a survey once for the paper) and they weren't sure how to pronounce it, either. It was weird living somewhere where everyone said their own address differently. Rose-velt, Rooz-velt, Roser-velt, Roozervelt. She'd heard every option until she was no longer sure which one she said herself. When someone asked her where she'd grown up, she tended to avoid telling them. Not because she was ashamed, but because she didn't entirely know. She was a woman without a home. Maybe she was being dramatic. But then again, a life lived without hyperbole was a life half-lived. Oh god... she was turning into her mother.

At home, she changed into warmer clothes. She was planning on spending the night in the car and, despite the warm weather, it would get chilly later in the evening. She rummaged around in the kitchen cupboards for a while until she found what she was looking for: Clive's old thermos flask and a decent sized Tupperware box. She filled the flask with tea and made a few rounds of peanut butter sandwiches to see her through, along with some crisps and chocolate. At some point, she would have to start eating like a grownup. But for now, she was going to stick to her current habits; she would learn to like olives another day.

The house was quiet. Her brother Lucas was off somewhere doing whatever it was Lucas did, and Angela was having a drink after work – something she did more these days. Angela's job consisted of listening to petty grievances from sex offenders unhappy with their social workers and it was grinding her down. As far as Phil could make out, a lot of the complaints amounted to not much more than 'I don't like the way she looks at me.' Angela was adamant that the social workers were all incredibly professional and did not employ the stink-eye no matter how much they disliked someone, but

Phil couldn't imagine how they could get through a meeting without at least pursing their lips a couple of times. She felt like there should be some special exemption for anyone willing to be in the same room as a monster: let them shoot daggers as much as they needed to.

She took a moment to worry about Lucas. She hoped he was being sensible wherever he was. After their dad died, Lucas had spoken less and less. It was hard to know if it was just typical teenage boy stuff, or if he was slowly being overwhelmed by depression. Phil knew the figures on male suicide and she often worried about her little brother. But he didn't speak to her much, and Angela had tried many times to reach him with little success. The school seemed unconcerned because his grades weren't terrible. But both Angela and Phil knew he wasn't himself. His grades were lower than they had been, and he didn't seem to relish learning in the same way. Watching him becoming more withdrawn was heartbreaking. Phil often found Angela sitting in the kitchen in the dark, looking at photos of the four of them on her phone.

'Look how happy Lukey is here,' she would say, showing her a shot of a boy with a big cheesy grin.

The young man who lived with them now was a stranger. He had received counselling for a while, but that had ended recently. And anyway, Lucas came out of each session with the same hangdog expression and the same monosyllabic replies to every question. 'How did it go?' 'Fine.' 'Did she think you were making progress?' Shrug. 'Are you hungry?' 'No.' And then he would slope off back to his room and play video games.

'Give it time,' said the counsellor, Julie. But Julie would say that, wouldn't she?

'She doesn't have a son at home who looks like he's going to throw himself off a cliff any day now.' said Angela.

Angela was a great believer in saying the most extreme thing possible.

'Mum,' chided Phil. 'Don't say that. He's getting professional help. What else can we do?'

But then the professional help came to an end and Lucas walked around like a shadow and Angela sat in the dark in the kitchen mourning her dead husband and her missing son.

Phil borrowed the car again. This time, she was determined to catch the Poo Fairy red handed. She sent Dean another text – this one a mournful, 'Have I done something wrong?' which made her feel needy and pathetic – and then headed out for an evening of watching a rowan tree.

NINETEEN

The glow from Mick's computer screen lit up his face, the rest of him bathed in dark shadows in the gloom of his studio flat. He read the email back. He was satisfied. He felt like it put enough of the fear of god into the recipient without making himself sound like a danger to society. It was a fine line these days – you weren't allowed to say boo to a goose without being accused of triggering some trauma or other.

It's a miracle these kids could even step out of the house, he thought. Mind you, a lot of them didn't, did they? They all met up virtually now, barely felt the breeze on their faces. And they pathologised everything. Concentration was now an ancient skill lost in the mists of time. His granddaughter informed him he only had these opinions because he was 'neurotypical', whatever that meant. If everyone was so special and different, why did they all suffer from the same afflictions? Soon being 'neurotypical' (which Mick translated as: 'normal') would be the abnormal state, not the other way round.

It was all just an excuse for being feckless and unreliable as far as he was concerned.

He checked his list. He had sent almost all the emails he planned to for the evening. He knew for a fact at least two of them would ruffle feathers. Should get him a few extra quid, but really it was sending them that really excited him. Anything else that came out of it was just a bonus. He imagined the recipients seeing a new message in their inbox, opening it up, expecting something nice, perhaps. He would love to be a fly on the wall – watch their faces dropping as they read his letter.

His phone rang and he grabbed it from the desk, paling as he saw the caller ID.

'Yes,' he said. He paled even further when the voice spoke. Still holding the phone to his ear, he closed down his email client and shut his computer down. The light on the monitor blinked into blackness as Mick felt his world come crashing down.

'Right,' he said once, and then fell silent, listening to instructions once again, ever the obedient servant.

He grabbed his keys from the side, put on his coat, whistled for the dog, and headed out into the evening air.

TWENTY

Andrew bent down and put Betty on the lead. It had been too warm today – unseasonably so. He had hidden inside for most of it and now he felt stiff and old. It was late, but he needed to move his body, and the dog needed to stretch her legs. He wanted to think about everything.

Two bodies in two walls.

His legacy.

What had he done? How could he have been so careless?

He thought gloomily back to the time before he had got himself involved in murder. Where had it all gone wrong? He had been a man of promise and ability. He could have been CHRO of some mighty London firm by now, if only he hadn't given up trying. But three years being overlooked at his first company had knocked his confidence. Of course, later he realised it was because he didn't know the right people. Oh, to have been privately educated, he thought.

Instead, he saddled himself with a woman so ruthless that she thought nothing of sacrificing people to get what she wanted. But what did that say about him? He had made a choice, after all. Gloria Reynolds had been keen to get her mess tidied up, but why had he been so eager to help her? Perhaps, he admitted, he had already seen the writing on the wall: Jamie had joined the company; the niece. It would be the work of a moment to make his position redundant and pass the role onto the cheaper, pliable relative. Gloria must have realised Jamie wouldn't even need a desk on the floor with the VLT.

'We want you to be able to bring your whole selves to work,' Andrew had written in an email to the Virtua people when their mental health initiative had been set up. And he had meant it, too. But then Gloria had asked him to get Clive McGinty onto a project, and Andrew had done exactly as she asked. And deep down, he knew her interest in Clive wasn't anything paternalistic (maternalistic? parentalistic?). And not long after that, a troubled member of their contracted workforce had come staggering into the lobby and Andrew had seen red. He wanted the fellow *gone*.

Bring your whole self to work, so long as your 'self' is within the boundaries of acceptable norms. That's what he meant really, he supposed. But that wouldn't have played as well on LinkedIn. He couldn't imagine getting many applause emojis for that admission.

He *had* made a difference though, hadn't he? He had brought in so many policies that made a tangible impact on his people's lives. The pregnancy parking bay. The paternity leave. Would society really judge him cruelly for the two bodies in the wall?

On the lake, a duck quacked indignantly in the dark, and Andrew found himself smiling – first at the comical noise and then at the ridiculousness of the situation. Two bodies! He wiped a hand over his mouth, embarrassed at his sudden mirth. The loss of two of his people was not a laughing matter, and yet it was all he wanted to do. He had been found out! Everyone would know what he had done, and he was going to pay the price for it at last.

The detective had seen right through him, of that he was sure. In the end, under her steady gaze (she looked like she had been crying, he thought), he had decided honesty was the best policy – or at least as close to it as he was prepared to get. Certainly, he wouldn't be getting into the weeds on the Clive McGinty affair, and he had no intention of telling her anything else about his run in with that reprobate who caused mayhem in the foyer. He couldn't regret what he'd done there: the fellow had to pay for scaring his people.

'Gloria was keen for me to check that Clive was involved in the project,' he had told the detective. 'I think it speaks volumes about her style of leadership that she assumed I was in charge of personnel on sites. Still, I did as she asked.'

'Put Clive on the project?'

'I made sure of it. You know, Detective Sergeant, I sometimes wonder if I inadvertently killed the man myself.'

What the detective said next had floored him.

'Perhaps you did, Mr Templeton-Dunbar,' she said. 'And perhaps you killed our other victim, too.'

Andrew wasn't sure what had brought him here. It was the middle of the night, for goodness' sake! He should be tucked up in bed with *The Times Quick Cryptic* book by now, trying not to listen to Jacqueline's increasingly loud snores from the bedroom next door. But here he was, walking the dog, staring up at his old place of work like some sort of jilted lover pining at his girlfriend's bedroom window.

Truth was, he had been doing a lot of night walks since he retired. Sometimes he woke up with a start after a few hours' sleep; other times, he spent the night tossing and turning, never quite dropping off properly. Eventually, he came to accept there would be no getting back to sleep and when that happened, he would clamber out of bed, throwing on a coat, and waking Betty for a stroll.

He sometimes drove down to see the sea, enjoying the navy ripples under starlight. Other times he went through the woodland near his house, past the new estate (he still thought of it as new), stopping by the 24-hour Tesco, Betty waiting patiently outside, to buy an early edition of *The Times* and a red apple. He had seen some things on those night rambles – a side to Aldhill he hadn't known existed.

He would have preferred chocolate to the apple, but he had agreed with Jacqueline it was time to cut out sugar. The year before that, it had been alcohol; the cigarettes had been banished in the 2010s.

Perhaps I should give up caffeine too. It was a sobering thought.

What would there be to live for if he gave up another of life's great pleasures? It didn't bear thinking about. On balance, he decided he would rather have insomnia.

He looked at the building and wondered yet again what had brought him here.

The Virtua Offices.

When he started working at Virtua, the building had been grim. The refurb had made a considerable difference to their working environment, but it hadn't fixed the outside.

You can't polish a turd.

The marketing team had taught him that one. An ugly phrase, he always thought, but nevertheless he returned to it regularly. Perhaps that had been the problem with him: he had tried to polish too many turds and had got himself covered in excrement.

He grimaced at his own metaphor and tried to think about something else.

That's when he saw her. His protégé. The woman responsible for his downfall. The turd he had tried to polish.

Jamie.

What was she doing still at work? In theory the office had twenty-four-hour opening for those who needed to work late or early (after all Virtua offered services that didn't sleep), but these days those having to do any night shifts would usually work from home (one of Andrew's many edicts when he took over as the HR director). Besides, Jamie never needed to work nights; there were junior people for that.

Andrew watched as she emerged from the building in dark jeans and white trainers (he had loosened the dress code, but under her rule things had got even more casual). Was she carrying a black bag? She carted the filled sack over to the large wheelie bins, lifted the lid on one and swung the bag in. Then she rubbed her hands together as though that would remove any dirt she might have picked up, headed over to her car (which, he noted, was parked in one of the priority spaces he had put in for their pregnant and differently abled people), clambered in, and drove off into the night.

A thought went through his mind, not for the first time: I'd like to teach that girl a lesson she never forgot.

He was far more dangerous than people realised. He knew that about himself. For all his talk of equality, he had to check himself a number of times over the years when he felt his thoughts turning dark. Mind you, he wasn't keen on his own sex either. They were often lazy, craven and not willing to make the hard choices for the betterment of the business. To him, it was all about building something *better*. Otherwise why bother at all?

Perhaps he had been too loyal. Sometimes he wanted to rebel against it all, leave his mark, make it clear that he really had wanted to shake things up and make the corporate world a safer, more equitable space for everyone. But maybe he had fixed his gaze on the wrong problems. Maybe he had spent his career polishing turds.

Andrew stood for a moment, still looking at the spot on the horizon where Jamie's car had been. Seemed like a bizarre time to be taking out the rubbish.

'Well, Betty,' he said eventually, 'Let's go and get the paper. And then I suppose we had better get home before your mum notices you're missing.'

Betty looked at him, head cocked at a jaunty angle, trying to decipher his words. She was an obliging creature, always willing to join him on his adventures, and soon the two of them would be wandering back towards the house to get a few more hours' sleep before morning.

'But let's just pop over here first,' he said, leading the dog across the road, towards the Virtua carpark and over to the bins.

TWENTY-ONE

Phil took a sip of tea in the car next to Simon's house and listened as the American podcast host introduced the next section of the show. Or she half-listened. The other fifty percent of her brain was contemplating life as an office lackey. She had checked and the pay was better than her salary at the paper; perhaps she should apply for a permanent position. Maybe she really could take Mick's job. He had a pretty cushy life, outsourcing all his work to interns and eating biscuits. She could work mindlessly all day and then come home on time. She could start cooking healthy meals for the family, take up a few hobbies, get better at photography; maybe do some volunteer work; perhaps even afford the rent to get her own place. Save for a deposit. Imagine that. And she wouldn't need to spend her evenings in a car waiting to interview a man who defiled local trees with his dog's output. She could work her way up to some soulless corporate management position; start wearing trouser-suits and claiming six weeks' holiday pay; live out her days being called Scarlett. It wouldn't take long to get used to. She quite liked the name, as it happened. Better than Philippa, anyway: a bit more racy; a bit less, "jolly hockey sticks".

She pictured herself striding into a meeting room wearing statement jewellery and giving minions jobs to do. She could look pained and start every request with, 'Could you do me a favour?' as though they had a choice.

The sad thing was, she *could* imagine it – could see a whole other life where Philippa McGinty became a corporate nightmare, talking in jargon, sourly offering evidence at a government select committee, giving cliché-laden #inspirational speeches at graduation ceremonies and young leadership events, talking about how she came from humble beginnings in a council house to take over the world of outsourcing.

Yes, she could definitely imagine it. But she could also imagine returning home to her enormous architectural monstrosity on millionaire's row with a sea view and a log fire to cry into a glass of pinot noir while her latest long-suffering partner wheeled a suitcase full of hastily packed clothes into a taxi and drove away from their loveless relationship. The thought rather put a dampener on her passion for corporate careers.

Anyway, who was to say she'd make it to Gloria's level? It was far more likely she'd look back in twenty years and discover she was the new Rhonda, forever doomed to haunt the halls of floor three, poking her nose in where it didn't belong. Yes, Rhonda was the queen of knowing other people's business. Perhaps *she* was the evil emailer, Phil thought with a chuckle. The smile transformed swiftly into a frown. She opened the email she got after her late night at the office.

'I know the truth about you.'

No one in the office had given the slightest impression they knew who she was...

The realisation hit her like a freight train. There *was* someone in the office who knew something about her. What an idiot she had been. Suddenly it seemed obvious. She took out her phone and began forming a reply:

'Hey. I know who you are too. Fancy meeting tomorrow lunchtime?'

She stared at her phone for at least thirty seconds, hitting refresh constantly. No reply. She chucked it onto the seat next to her. A watched phone never texts back (as Angela used to tell her when Phil was mooning over some girl or boy and wondering why they never replied). Instead, she grabbed her flask and poured another tea. She stared out at the rowan. The dramas of the previous two nights were catching up. A sudden yawn overcame her and she gave into it, indulging the experience to the fullest – mouth wide, fists raised, making a satisfied sound, blinking her eyes – before taking another sip of tea.

All this for one man and his dog.

A group of her friends were round at her rich buddy Miles's house right now. She could be there with them enjoying the benefits of his parents' generously stocked booze cupboard (not to mention the wine cellar) and playing Playstation, or attempting billiards. There would almost certainly be a fantastic array of snacks. But here she was, about to spend a night watching a tree.

She probably needed to reassess her priorities.

Phil watched the bag swaying gently in the tree. A black pendulum signalling the arrival of Acorn Drive's most wanted man. Moments before, a tall dark stranger had stood in silhouette and left the bag stranded on a limb. As he strode away, fresh from making his mark, Phil hesitated. She should be following. She should rush up, press her phone towards his face, ask him if he had a quote for the local paper, but she found herself rooted to her seat. This man looked familiar. Tall and lean, old but muscular. She imagined putting a hand on his arm and having a monster turn to glare at her. Or – almost worse, somehow – someone she knew.

What if he was violent? What if he decided to reach out and grab her round the throat? She had a sudden vision of herself hanging from the same tree, another bag of his discarded waste. She shook her head in self-disgust. This was her job. How could she be an investigative journalist if she was afraid to investigate? And yet she remained seated.

'Get a grip, Phil,' she muttered out loud. And eventually, through sheer force of will, she opened her door and stepped out into the night. A few seconds had passed in the time it had taken for her to shake herself out of petrification, and the Faecal Fiend was already making good ground.

Thankfully, before her moment of panic had sent her into a stupor, she had at least managed to snap a couple of photographs, and now she left the camera swinging at her neck and tried to catch up with the man without creating any noise. For now, it was enough that she had stepped out of the car. She wasn't ready to confront him, and so she followed at a safe distance watching as he strode along, pulling the dog's leash impatiently any time the dog stopped to sniff or leave a dribble of urine. Facebook for dogs, that's what Angela called it. 'The pavement's more interesting than the *Aldhill Observer* to our pooch friends.'

'Except the *Observer* doesn't leave you with pee all over your beard,' Clive had replied.

'Come on!'

The voice startled her. It sounded familiar, didn't it? But the voice was hard to identify. Two words wasn't enough. Was that a local accent? Or something a little more Received Pronunciation? She couldn't be sure. She watched as he moved under the streetlights before turning up a dark unlit footpath. Was it so wrong to hesitate to follow a criminal down a dark path in the middle of the night? She knew it wasn't and yet she felt frustrated.

When Phil was at school she had been the only one not afraid to knock on the door of Flat 7, Roosevelt Court. The flat was empty, apparently abandoned, and in such a state of disrepair that even the landlords didn't think it was right to offer it to tenants. Over the course of six months the children built it up into some kind of haunted mansion in their own minds. An old lady had died in there, one claimed. Her ghost could be seen peering through the letter box and calling for help. Sometimes, if you walked past after dark, a hand would reach out and try to grasp you as you passed. By the end of the six months, the kids were in such an ecstasy of terror that none could pass the flat at walking pace, and some would go all the way around to the steps on the other side of the building just to avoid going past that door.

So when Charlie Maxwell offered two pounds' worth of pick n' mix to anyone willing to go up to the door, knock, and then place their hand in the letter box for ten seconds, Phil took up the challenge.

The ten seconds had felt like the longest of her life. The other children counted her down, but their voices were drowned out by the thumping of blood in her ears. She was terrified.

'How did you do it?' asked someone after she had claimed her reward.

'Simple,' lied Phil. 'I'm not a wimp. Plus, ghosts aren't real.'

That night, she dreamed she could feel the cold hand of the old lady grip her hand and drag her under a lake of ice. The water, as it rose around her face, turned to steaming fire and the flames of hell engulfed her. She woke up screaming. It took a moment to register that she had wet the bed.

'I hope the sweets were worth it,' said Clive as he fetched fresh sheets.

Was this worth it, Phil wondered? It would hardly be carved on her tombstone, would it? Here lies Philippa McGinty, who died avenging a rowan tree. Still, she followed the dark figure down the dark path and prayed that when her body was discovered, her colleagues wouldn't plaster the story on the front cover to drive pick-ups.

He was going at quite a lick for an old man and Phil struggled to keep a decent pace without making any noise. Occasionally, he would stop to yank on the dog's lead as it attempted to inspect an interesting scent. Phil would freeze on the spot, but he never looked back. It was like playing the world's worst game of Grandmother's Footsteps.

As they walked further into darkness, she began to lose her nerve once again. Perhaps it was time to call it quits. Maybe she should come back another night with Simon or a friend and ask the bloke for a quote then? But before she had the chance to turn back, he disappeared. She reached the spot she had last seen him. A small path – presumably made by a few errant humans and some of the local wildlife (the urban foxes and badgers made their own rules round here) – veered off the pathway and into the scrub. She heard a crack of twigs and caught a glimpse of her prey. He vanished behind a tree only to reappear further along the track, snatches of his dark coat just about visible through the undergrowth.

What to do? Follow Father Shitmas into the unknown? Or head home to attempt to snatch some sleep in preparation for another day of pointless administration? Phil had just enough time to long for a third option. Maybe a night of dancing at Forbidden Fruit, or a visit to that new bar in town. Perhaps she could meet up with an old flame and have a night of passion she could regret the next day. Anything to make her feel like a twenty-something living her best life, rather than a local reporter with a questionable nose for a news story.

People had better care about this dogs' mess story now, she thought, or she would never hear the end of it back at the office. Her reputation would be in the bin, which is where this man should be placing his dog poo, she thought, irritably. And anyway, why wasn't he placing his dog poo in the bin? It was right there, literally a few metres from where he hung the bags. She thought of Simon, her partner in outrage, and she knew she couldn't let him down. If not for herself, she decided, she must do it for him. They couldn't go to their graves not knowing what motivated this kind of violence on the landscape. They needed to know why.

She took a breath and plunged after him into the bushes.

The track came out on a patch of gravel and concrete. Perhaps an old utilities building had once stood there, or a scout hut long forgotten, barely visible from the road just a hundred yards beyond. Whatever it was, it was now a disused space, grown scruffy as the weeds pushed through cracks in the tarmac. Except it currently wasn't disused. A group of about ten cars were parked up, all of them empty apart from one.

That one car was attracting a lot of attention. A group of people, mostly men, stood around it, peering in through the windows. Phil had a brief innocent moment imagining they were admiring the upholstery of a classic motor, when her brain clicked into gear and she realised what she was seeing.

It was a dogging site.

Brilliant, she thought. Was everything she encountered on this story going to involve dogs?

Without really thinking, she lifted her camera and took a few photos, imagining that she might liven up the story of the Poo Fairy with a bit of scandalous public indecency. But the twist in the tale was nixed before she'd even clicked the shutter; Father Shitmas walked right by them all as though nothing out of the ordinary was happening. He didn't even glance in their direction. The doggers didn't acknowledge him, either. Presumably, they were accustomed to this strange man walking through their outdoor sex party.

What could she do now? She wasn't about to squeeze past them all saying, 'Sorry, sorry, don't mind me, I'm just following this man. You carry on.'

Perhaps she could return to the path and try to find another way to access the road.

But before she had time to decide, he continued off down the track and strode off out of sight. Even if she could find another way to reach him, she would be incredibly exposed under the bright lights on the road. A bit like the woman in that car, she thought, catching an unwanted glimpse of flesh pressed against the side window. She turned on her heel and headed back to the safety of her own car.

'Oh dear, you aren't having much luck, are you?' Simon

said when she retreated back to the streetlit haven of Acorn Drive. It was Simon's polite way of saying, 'Sounds like you messed up again, McGinty,' and Phil didn't need the reminder.

She hadn't mentioned the doggers.

'I think I'm going to head home,' she said with a weary sigh, and Simon tilted his head in a gesture of sympathy.

'Burning the candle at both ends? You get yourself home.'

Before she left, however, they took a moment to stand shoulder to shoulder, peering at the screen of her camera.

'You got some good ones there,' said Simon with a broad smile. He was in his dressing gown and slippers and trying to keep his voice down to avoid waking Debbie. 'I think we might almost be able to identify him.'

He squinted at one particular image, which showed the culprit hanging the bag in the tree, the light from the moon rendering his face almost identifiable.

'I really hope so,' said Phil, 'Or I've literally spent the week chasing shadows.'

She packed away her things. 'I'll get him tomorrow,' she said.

As she made her way back to the car, Phil checked her phone.

An email had come in.

'I'll be in all night,' was all it said, along with an address.

Phil got into the car and contemplated where her evening might go next. Home to bed was the most appealing option. She tapped her steering wheel, made a decision. She reversed and headed the opposite way to home.

TWENTY-TWO

Jen flicked from channel to channel, from streaming service to streaming service, but nothing grabbed her in the way she was hoping. She tried something mindless that involved cakes, but the warm cheerfulness of the cooks made her shout 'Oh for god's sake' at the screen. She switched to a monster movie in which every character was so unbearable she was soon rooting for the creature, hoping it would gut and gobble every last one. But once the monster was being shot at by some flat-haired army general, she lost interest. It would have been more fun with Nate, of course. They could have spent their time picking apart the plot holes, asking if the army general had ever even *seen* a monster movie before. Didn't he know that nuking them never worked?

The day had gone surprisingly badly considering her conversation with Andrew. She had expected this to change everything, but Lee's reaction was less enthusiastic than she'd hoped.

'Hold fire on any arrests for the meantime,' he said.

'What are you talking about?' she asked, rebellion already rising in her belly.

'Petra is very keen for us to cross all the f's on this one. By which I mean, get it the eff right.'

There were times that Jen would like to stop her conversations with Lee just to enquire about the people who had taught English at his school. But in the event, she caught the gist of what he was saying and was too angry about it to call his idioms into question.

'So, no publicity and no arrests? Is that how we're handling this murder investigation? Is it? Oh, and no connecting one murder to another almost identical death. Is that right? And now, even in the face of some pretty compelling evidence, no pursuing any suspects for answers?'

Lee had sighed at that, as though she were an errant child truly trying his boundless patience. If he only knew the things she wanted to say, but didn't.

'We just need to tread carefully, that's all. Look, I agree with you that the two cases have some similarities.'

'Ha!' said Jen, aware that her hollow resentment probably wouldn't win her any friends.

'But look at it from the bosses' point of view. If it turns out we missed a murderer in the Clive McGinty case, it's not going to look good, is it?'

'Apologies for inconveniencing anyone with this,' said Jen, still not keeping her sarcasm in check. 'Would you prefer if I just stopped investigating it altogether?'

Lee shut his eyes and pressed his lips together. 'Has anyone ever told you what an annoying bloody woman you are?' He pointed an accusing finger suddenly. 'And don't go running off to HR saying I called you a "bloody woman." You know as well as I do it's a pure statement of fact. You know no one wants you to stop investigating the murder. All we're asking is that you don't go making a big song and dance about it. Find the evidence, make your case, but until we can be certain there's any reason to believe otherwise, keep Clive McGinty out of it, because if it turns out we were wrong, we sure as hell want to have as much of the case solved as possible before the bloody press and the politicians find out.'

'Lee, surely you can see that Doug at the very least should be invited in for questioning? And Andrew knows something, it's obvious he knew more about the victim than he was telling. Petra's not going to object to that, surely?'

Thinking about it now made her grind her jaw. Petra didn't actually strike her as someone who let politics affect her judgment, so what the hell was going on? She asked Lee, but he brushed off the question.

'Ours is not to reason why,' he said. 'Ours is to do as we're told.'

'Can you just ring her now? Please Lee.' And he had relented in the end. She headed out to Doug's flat in the meantime, but he wasn't there. He wasn't in work either. Had he done a runner? This was why she needed to bring him in, for god's sake. She had waited for Lee to call back all the way to the station, checking her phone at every light like a love-struck teen. But when she got back to the incident room, Nandini told her Lee was out.

'Where the hell does he go? It's like he's got a second job,' Jen said.

'Maybe he's doing a shift at McDonald's to help pay for his divorce. Anyway, listen, we've had no luck so far with tracking down contractors or Virtua staff who worked on Helenswood site.'

'What about people who worked at St Agnes's?' said Jen,

checking first that no one would hear. She had told Nandini to go back and check the names from the Clive McGinty inquest, knowing that there was a risk someone at Virtua would get on the phone to one of her bosses to query it. And Nandini was hardly the most discreet person. She suspected Dean would have better luck. You could probably hear the dimples over the phone, but Lee had sent him off on some errand or other with Grant and so she only had the office terrier to assist her. It's almost like we don't have a murder investigation going on, she thought.

Nandini handed her a notebook, and she managed to make out a few names she recognised from the original inquiry and a few others she hadn't seen before.

'Your handwriting is dreadful,' she said.

'Ed Fielder is some sort of in-house liaison at Virtua these days,' said Nandini, pointing to where she had scrawled his name. 'But he was working on site at St Agnes's. In fact, he's been the most useful at giving us names so far. He actually knew the builders.'

Just an hour later, everything changed again.

'Just had a new list through from Virtua. Apparently Ed Fielder was site manager at Helenswood,' said Nandini.

'You think he might have mentioned that,' said Jen. 'Given how helpful he's been.'

And then, an hour after that, Lee reappeared.

'Boss says we are good to go with the press,' he said. 'She says hold off on arresting anyone until after it's gone public. We'll put it out tomorrow. But definitely have a word with Doug and this Ed person. Petra wants to speak to Gloria Reynolds before you go after Templeton-Dingbat, or whatever his name is.'

'Are they all in the same rotary club or something?'

'But in the meantime, Jen, I think you should go home,' said Lee. 'Before you say something that I'll regret.'

Jen changed channels and put her legs out onto Nate's side of the sofa, wishing he was there to squeeze her feet and tell her the bosses were all jobsworth knobheads. Now the press were being briefed, Lee would be all over the case, making sure his face was seen as much as possible. If it went national – and surely it would – he'd be there looking solemn on camera, standing next to Petra. Jen felt like she had a brief window to get the case resolved before the senior officers descended and buried her in an avalanche of enquiries.

TWENTY-THREE

As soon as Phil walked into the bedsit she realised she had been foolish. The space was tiny: everything on display; the rumpled bed right there next to a sink filled with dirty dishes and a brown sofa covered in crumbs. Somehow the intimacy of the space made her situation feel even more stark: she was alone with a man willing to blackmail people, a man built like one of the lesser Hemsworths.

'Alright?' Lachlan drawled, giving her a sleepy, sexy grin. 'Can I get you a drink?' He gestured to the tiny fridge as though it were a cocktail bar.

'I'm not here for a social visit,' Phil said, wondering if it was too late to share her live location with a friend. What the hell was she thinking? She got her phone out and tried to act casual – just a Gen Z kid addicted to devices – but he reached over and took it from her fingers.

'Can't have you recording this convo,' he said. 'I'll give it back when we're done.' He chucked the phone on the rumpled bed and Phil began considering if she had ever made a poorer set of choices in her life.

'So why are you doing it?' she said.

'Really?' he said with another smile. 'You're asking the sandwich bloke in a bedsit why he's trying to get money from people?'

'Who's in on it with you?'

'Oh, I have my sources. Whether they know it or not is another matter. I tell ya, it's amazing how thick supposedly intelligent people can be. How they haven't put two and two together to realise it's me is a mystery.'

He chuckled and raised his arm to scratch his head, looking up at Phil in a flirty manner, his t-shirt lifting to reveal a line of blond hair on his stomach. Phil felt like she was stuck in some sort of TikTok hellscape.

'So you sleep with Jamie, and she unknowingly tells you everyone's secrets?'

'You worked it out!' Lachlan laughed and clapped his hands together, looking up at the ceiling. 'Not that it was hard. But the real question is,' and suddenly Phil could feel the menace in him, 'what are we going to do about you?'

She shifted slightly and glanced to her left. Could she make it to the latch before he could grab her? 'What do you mean, do *about me*? Am I that terrifying a foe?' She gestured elaborately, using her whole body, waving her arms like a monster, just so she could take a step closer to the exit.

'What I'd like to know,' said Lachlan, 'Is what a journalist is doing working as an intern at a company like Virtua? Writing not work out for ya?' He wagged a finger like he was trying to figure something out. 'And you know what? I looked through the whole paper and I couldn't see anyone called Scarlett. Isn't that bizarre?'

'I'm working undercover,' she said, hoping that would impress him somehow. 'Investigating working practises at local firms... maybe I should switch and write an exposé on a local sandwich guy who blackmails innocent workers. I imagine you're up to the same tricks in every place you visit, right?'

He laughed to himself again. 'You got me.'

'So you might out me, so what? It's my holiday, anyway. If anything, you'd be doing me a favour. I could take a long weekend.'

'Oh, I don't want to out you,' he smiled, moving a step closer. 'Not at all. I've got a much better idea.'

THURSDAY

TWENTY-FOUR

Phil rubbed her eyes as she entered the building and pasted on a smile. Not only had she had an early start, she'd had a late night. After her (frankly weird) meeting with Lachlan, she had returned to Simon's house to sit in her car for another four hours waiting for the Poo Fiend, before eventually giving up and heading home. On the way through the carpark she thought she spotted the Phantom before realising it was Andrew Templeton-Dunbar. What delights does the twenty-four-hour Tesco hold that couldn't wait until morning, she wondered? She watched Betty the dog – a dead ringer for the Poo Fiend's own, it must be said – dutifully trotting by his side, looking up at him through reproachful eyebrows.

Despite her tiredness, Phil was filled with a kind of nervous energy. She had never felt more determined to find the answers she had come here for. Lachlan's plan, outlined slowly in between flirty smiles and irritating smirks, might have been half-baked, but it gave her insights she hadn't been expecting. She just needed to get back to her cupboard full of boxes and pray she had enough time and luck left.

The lift took her upwards as she read back over her notebook, filled with anything and everything she had discovered so far. It felt like a whole heap of nothing, but she couldn't help re-reading it just in case. She tapped a finger at the question mark by 'missing HSO report?'. It was the last thing she had written before she went to bed.

The lift pinged and the doors opened. She walked out and waved at the few people who had been friendly – or nearly friendly – towards her so far. Biscuits Margaret, a man called Nick who had told her at length about his cycling holiday in Yorkshire, and Grumpy Ed Fielder who had thawed by one degree when he caught her saying something sarcastic. Mick was staring as she made her way to her windowless box.

'Alright Mick?' she said, refusing to respond to his weirdness with anything other than weapons-grade friendliness.

'Scarlett,' he said, as though acknowledging her before a duel. She could see him wearing a stetson and spinning a pistol, spitting on the ground.

Inside the cupboard, she headed straight for the boxes she had yet to tackle. Lachlan had given her hope. The person he hadn't managed to blackmail yet was the person who had fed him all his information.

Jamie.

She of the flapping tongue.

What Lachlan had suggested was they work together to uncover evidence of Jamie's own transgression.

'She's got serious generational wealth,' he said, licking his lips like a collie gone rogue. 'And I know for a fact she's been spending her evenings – when she's not with me, of course –

trying to find some documents. Her aunt wanted her to tidy up some lose ends from some dodgy project, but – I don't know if you've noticed this – she's not the full quid. Silly cow can't find the folder. If you can track it down, I reckon the two of us stand to make a pretty tidy profit.'

'What does the folder contain?' said Phil.

'Apparently, some poor bloke died in a wall a few years ago?'

'Yes,' said Phil, stiffening like a starched collar.

'Well, there's a document out there somewhere that shows the building was unsafe and the big knobs must have known about it. She told me the whole thing was just an unlucky accident and had nothing to do with the unsafe wall, but it's not going to look good if it comes out, is it?'

'Why the hell would they keep that?'

'I asked that. Her aunt needed to hold on to it in case her bosses ever tried to pull a fast one. You know what these rich people are like. They're always stabbing each other in the back.'

'Unlike sandwich delivery guys who are upright and honest.'

'Exactly,' he grinned.

So Gloria had kept a document as security against her own bosses, further up the Virtua corporate food chain, but had mislaid it (because apparently carelessness with paperwork was a family trait), and had set Jamie of all people the task of finding it. If only Lachlan had tried to blackmail Jamie sooner in the week. The time Phil could have saved reading investigations reports and complaints letters! Not that she entirely believed him, of course. Why on earth would there still be evidence out there incriminating senior leaders? But he was adamant: Jamie was meant to tidy up the mess and instead she had made it worse. And that was something Phil could believe.

Still, she was impressed he had managed to get that information out of her.

'It's amazing what people tell you when they're naked,' he said, flashing her a wolfish grin. 'I honestly wonder if they realise I'm listening.'

She was also impressed that Jamie hadn't put two and two together and realised he was the blackmailer yet.

'I told you, she's thick – and she's self-absorbed,' said Lachlan. 'The only reason she looks at anyone is to see if she can catch her own reflection in their eyeballs. If you went in tomorrow with pink hair and a beard, she wouldn't notice. Plus, she's never there, is she?'

It wasn't long before the airless cupboard and the endless drab grey boxes made her rub her tired eyes, but this time Phil was determined not to stop until she found something. Her week had been spent trying to find meaning in the endless complaint letters and investigations reports, but now she knew what she was looking for. Somewhere in here was a piece of paper proving this company had been negligent.

Hopefully.

There was a chance the folder was still languishing in one of Jamie's desk piles, or it could still be tucked away inside a drop file in the wall of cabinets, but Phil decided even Jamie would have taken the time to search those. Perhaps she had satisfied herself that the folder no longer existed and had given up the chase. Perhaps she just didn't care enough about her aunt's reputation to keep looking. Presumably she thought that if Scarlett Stevens came across a document like that, she wouldn't look at it twice.

But Phil McGinty certainly would.

Box after box surrendered to her feverish search, but none yielded the evidence she was seeking. Until, that is, she spotted an unmarked, buff-coloured file wedged by the back wall of the top shelf behind a box. She wheeled her chair over and climbed onto it, wobbling as the seat began rotating gently westwards. She took the risk and made a grab for it, jumping straight off as the chair moved backwards away from her. As she swung her arms and landed, an A4 document fluttered to the floor.

She reached for it and felt a jolt of surprise: Lachlan was right. In her hand was a health and safety inspection report written by Doug Graves for St Agnes's school. She scanned the document, her heart racing. Phrases such as 'serious concerns' and 'incorrect brick ties' jumped out at her. The work really hadn't been signed off as safe; quite the opposite. Here it was – proof that the extension walls were in fact dangerous. Had her father known this? He can't have, or he certainly wouldn't have gone there. It was one thing to believe he might have stepped onto a building that hadn't been checked over, but to step onto one that was condemned simply beggared belief. It wasn't possible. Which could only mean one thing: Virtua Services had covered this up. And when the time came to get her father's body from the wall, they had the perfect excuse to pull the extension down before anyone noticed.

Phil scanned through the document again. Here was Ed Fielder's name listed as the site manager overseeing the original extension work. Before the project had been shuttered by lack of funds, Ed had been the person in charge of it all. Phil thought back to their conversation on the first day. He told her he had gone in-house seven years ago. Right when this project was being brought back online. Right when her father was given the job of overseeing the build. Right when Clive had been killed. She had wanted to ask him if he knew Clive and now she realised he may have been the cause of his death.

Phil bit the edge of her thumbnail trying to get her head around what might have happened. Doug and Ed had known all about it, and yet neither of them had spoken up. Ed, presumably, had moved to a job where he couldn't make any more catastrophic mistakes, and Doug had simply denied he had been to the site. Which meant someone at Virtua – someone senior – also knew what was going on. Why else would Doug keep it quiet? Why would he risk his professional reputation if he wasn't being paid to do it by someone further up the food chain?

Abruptly, almost without thinking, she picked up her bag and headed for the door. She needed to speak to Doug. She paced unseeing down the aisle between desks in the open space, heading towards the exit, the HSO report still in her hand.

'Everything alright, Scarlett?' said a voice.

Phil focused her eyes and discovered Jamie standing in front of her, all sleek lines and smooth skin.

'Yes, good!' Phil managed, 'Keeping out of trouble.'

'That's great,' said Jamie. 'Nearly there with the letters?'

The muscles in Jamie's face attempted to form a crinkle of concern, but the botox won out, creating the suggestion of a frown without forming a furrow.

'Getting there, said Phil. 'I'm a dab hand at reading bad handwriting now. Something to add to my CV.'

She winced, wishing she hadn't said that. The last thing she needed was someone looking up Scarlett on LinkedIn.

But Jamie hadn't noticed. She was too busy looking at the HSO report in Phil's hand.

'What have you got there?' Jamie said, pointing at the piece of paper.

Shit.

Phil's first impulse was the hide the sheet behind her back, but she overrode that impulse and simply turned it down towards her leg so Jamie couldn't see what it was.

'Letter,' Phil said. 'For Dee Dee.'

Dee Dee looked up at the sound of her name.

'What's that, babes?' she said.

'Just got a letter here for you,' called Phil. 'It's a recent one. Must have got in with the older letters somehow.'

'Wouldn't surprise me, babe,' said Dee Dee. She gave Jamie a pointed look. 'Things are a right mess round here.'

Jamie glanced at Dee Dee but didn't take the bait.

'I'll get to it after lunch,' said Dee Dee. 'I'm so busy today I can barely breathe. I don't think I've had a single cup of tea all morning.'

Given it was only 9.30, this was hardly the suffering Dee Dee seemed to think it was.

'I'll make you one,' said Phil, popping the piece of paper hastily face down on Dee Dee's in tray before Dee Dee could look at it. She picked up a soft beanie toy from the desk and plonked that on top like a paperweight, as though the sad-faced rabbit would act as a guard against anyone tempted to peek.

'You're a genuine lifesaver. Do you know that babes?' said Dee Dee, 'I'm absolutely gasping here.'

'Count me in,' said Jamie. 'Coffee. Heat the milk this time if it's not too much trouble. There's a frother in the drawer.'

'Why don't I pop out and get you a proper coffee?' said Phil in a flush of inspiration.

'That would be amazing,' said Jamie. 'Flat white, extra hot.'

'Two coffees coming right up,' said Phil.

'I'm happy with a normal builder's tea,' said Dee Dee, leaning out into the aisle.

But Phil was already heading for the door.

The sun was low in the still-pink sky when Phil walked up into the Haven for the Homeless courtyard. A mist clung to the sea – just visible through a gap in the houses. Soon, the warmth of the day would send it fizzling into oblivion. It hadn't been hard to work out which homeless charity Doug had gone to work for. Haven for the Homeless was the obvious place to look. After her night of rifling through the personnel files, she had simply emailed the manager, Karina, who confirmed it straight away.

Doug was squatting down, rolling up a cigarette before his day started. Even crouched down in that position, he seemed to vibrate, all tense muscles and potential energy. Phil remembered him from the inquest, leg twitching, eyes darting about, faded blue prison tattoos snaking up sinewed arms. A man in constant motion.

He hadn't looked at her or her family when he spoke. He simply answered the questions with quick, tight sentences, each answer wrung from him like scum from a cloth. He had not signed the building off as safe. In fact, he hadn't even inspected it at that point. That's what he told them. Phil hadn't believed him. Neither had her mother. And it seemed they were both right.

So why had he lied?

To save Virtua's reputation? To protect Ed? Or, given he was the man who signed the work off, perhaps it was simply to protect himself for missing the errors the first time round.

That was something Phil was determined to ask. When she was a kid, she had been too intimidated to try. No. More than that: she hadn't realised she had a right to answers. Phil simply trusted that the process would reveal the truth and that the coroner would see through all the lies. But she hadn't. And now here he was: the man who had made her father look like a victim of nothing more sinister than a poorly chosen suicide. A man, she now knew, who had himself attempted to take his own life shortly after giving evidence.

'I'm Phil McGinty,' she said. 'Clive's daughter.'

He glanced at her very briefly before standing to light his cigarette.

'Don't look like his daughter,' he said, his voice so quiet he could have been talking to himself.

'I'd like to ask you some questions about him.'

'I'm on a break,' he said, as though being on a break meant he was not obliged to speak to anyone.

'It's 9.30,' she said.

He sucked on his cigarette and looked away, his attention apparently drawn in by the cracks in the concrete.

'I just wanted to know why you told the inquest you hadn't signed the building off as safe?' she said.

'I hadn't.' Not looking at her, puffing out a cloud of smoke.

'Really?' She was trying to approach the conversation cautiously, knowing that he was likely to turn and shut himself in the warehouse before she could ask him everything, but really she wanted to do something extreme: pull out a knife and demand answers; wave a gun at him and threaten to shoot his kneecaps. If only real life was like the movies, she could drag him over to the nearby water butt and hold his head under until he promised to squeal like a piggy.

'Why do you think my dad went there that day, then?' she said. 'You knew him. Is that something you can imagine him doing?'

He took a long drag on the small roll-up, already nearly at an end. Phil needed to get to the point before he headed back inside.

'Do you know what I think? I think you realised the site wasn't safe. I think you told the bosses that Ed Fielder had messed up the wall ties and the next thing you knew, Ed was being taken off the project and you were being leaned on to pretend you hadn't seen anything.' She was making it up as she went along, but it sounded eminently plausible. 'I think you changed the report, which is why Clive went ahead with organising the meeting with the engineer, but when Clive died, you all pretended it had never happened. I think you felt so guilty about it, you tried to kill yourself, and then you left and got a job here. Penance for your sins.'

She watched him closely, the muscles in his jaw twitching as he smoked his cigarette. She felt a surge of anger, suppressed since she had first seen the original HSO report – before that even. Since she was seventeen and the weight of an entire company seemed to fall on them from on high, suppressing the truth of what really happened to Clive.

'Or maybe that's not it,' she said, the fury making her shake. 'Maybe my dad spotted your cock ups. Maybe he knew about the wall ties. Maybe you met my dad at the building site and you pushed him over the edge of the scaffolding and watched as he fell down the cavity and then you left him there to die.'

Karina appeared at the wide entrance.

'Everything alright?' She held onto the door frame, the shutter tracks pressing into her hand. 'Hello Phil. What are you doing here?'

Doug looked at Phil for the first time then, smiling a tight, rueful smile – a smile that said 'you don't know the half of it, my girl' before he exhaled, stubbed his cigarette out in a nearby plant pot and passed Karina, heading wordlessly back inside.

TWENTY-FIVE

Jen was still sitting on the end of her bed wrapped in a towel and staring into the middle distance when Andrew called.

'Hello, Mr Templeton-Du–,' she began.

'Kings Road,' interrupted Andrew.

Jen briefly wondered if he'd read all the research showing how often men speak over women and how that chimed with his touchy-feely HR persona.

'Kings Road?' she said. 'Is that–'

'I remember now. The poor chap in the Prints To Go top. I sent him off in a taxi and the address struck me because it was right across from my old flat – the one I lived in when I moved here after uni.'

This did not surprise Jen. Coincidences like this were common in a small town. She knew not to take it as some sort of sign, even if it felt like one.

'It was 8 Kings Road.'

'8 Kings Road?' said Jen like a bad echo. She couldn't help herself. There may be a lot of coincidences here in Aldhill, but as things went, this one was a doozie, because 8

Kings Road just happened to be the same address as Doug Graves.

'Doug's not here,' Karina said when she emerged from the Haven for the Homeless office (a small, cold room inside the warehouse where Karina shivered in hat and fingerless gloves). 'He took off just a moment ago. He'd forgotten he was meant to be at Brands Hatch with a couple of mates. He's so forgetful.'

She said it with real fondness, and Jen was surprised to discover that there was someone in the world who apparently thought Doug was a good guy.

'He'll be gone all day and then out drinking after,' Karina continued. 'God knows where he'll end up.'

Doug's benders were legendary, apparently.

So Doug would have to wait. She could have gone after him, but she needed a bit more than, 'Apparently, you might have shared an address with the deceased,' to justify a trip to Sevenoaks at this stage. Not when there were still people at Virtua Services who must be able to identify a homeless man called Pennywise. At this stage, Jen was getting tired of not knowing who the poor bloke was. She thought of Babycakes, wondering if he was already heading towards the penny drops. And then the metaphorical penny dropped.

'I've realised why they called him Pennywise,' she said when Nandini answered the phone.

'Because he was a scary clown?' replied Nandini.

'Because he's penny wise, pound foolish.'

Nandini was less impressed with that insight than Jen hoped. In fact, Nandini spoiled the whole thing by demanding what the hell that meant.

'It's 9.45am,' she said, as though 9.45 was 5.00am. 'It's too early for wordplay. I'll see you at Virtua in a bit.'

Then she hung up while Jen was still trying to win her over to the cause. 'Now we just need to work out why they call him Babycakes... Nand? Nandini?'

The news would be reporting on the body in the wall this evening. Jen liked to believe that she had won Petra around, but it was more likely that it was about to leak anyway. People in plastic overalls were all over the Helenswood campus and Jen couldn't see the media being kept in the dark for much longer: the story was too good. Another body in another school wall – this one with a fatal flaw.

The building firm assured them that the Helenswood site had now been made secure – as secure as a falling down building could be at any rate – and the council were making a lot of noise about employing some big shot architect and a procurement expert to begin an independent inquiry. Presumably so that when the news broke they would appear on top of things. She wondered if they were a little bit pleased about the body in the wall. It pushed the problem onto the police and helped to distract from the nine tonnes of masonry that could have fallen onto local children.

She headed down towards her car. It was further down towards the sea front than she'd hoped, but it was nice to get out before the sun got too hot. Wandering past the dog walkers, avoiding the electric cyclists, she kept half an eye out for Andrew Templeton-Dunbar and his little dog.

Could he be the killer? It seemed bizarre to her that the mild-mannered ex-HR director at Virtua Services – a man whose idea of a bold choice was wearing brown shoes with a blue suit – had threatened her murder victim right before he went missing. Jen didn't see him as a violent type, but she wasn't foolish enough to discount a person simply because they wore leather slippers.

She considered the facts. The victim had been in the Virtua building around the time of his disappearance, apparently causing trouble. Andrew had made it clear that his staff – his 'people', as he called them – were his main focus in life, the reason he came to work. Perhaps the sight of them distressed had sent him over the edge, which is what he did with the poor man's body a few days later.

It could have happened, she supposed. He could have booked the victim in for a day's work and met him at the building site, ready for a fight.

But what about Clive?

If the two murders were connected, what possible motive could he have for killing Clive? And they *had* to be connected. There was no doubt in her mind. Or very little, at least. Who could afford to be sure about anything in life? She and Nate were meant to be together forever, after all, she had been sure of that, and then he went and died on her like a thoughtless tosspot, leaving her childless and lonely and careering towards middle age.

Perhaps Andrew had discovered the truth about the wall ties and decided it was better if people didn't discover it. She could imagine the HR boss taking a utilitarian view: two men's lives in return for everyone else's jobs. How much would the company stand to lose if it turned out every building they had worked on in recent months had been built incorrectly?

Or, she thought, warming to her subject, what if someone at the council had been rubber stamping all the work without checking it thoroughly? What if they also had a big incentive to keep it all quiet? After all, someone would have gone over to check the work at some point. Andrew was bound to have friends in high places. Maybe one of his golfing pals had needed him to despatch some pesky contractors, some jobsworths who had paid a little too much attention to the correct way of doing things.

Then again, Jen just wasn't sure murder was in Andrew's list of core abilities. She couldn't imagine anyone endorsing him for that on LinkedIn. Key skills: diversity and inclusion; mental wellbeing; purpose-led leadership; stuffing people down cavity walls. No, if Andrew wanted to dispose of someone, he would find a more civilised way to do it. This was too messy; it lacked dignity. He would delegate the job to a junior staff member; she imagined he was good at delegating.

Speaking of which, there was always Jamie Pilcher, brought into the fold to cover for Auntie Gloria's poor business management? Maybe Jamie had learned about the faulty wall ties and decided to get rid of anyone who had known about them. This actually felt more believable. Jen could picture Jamie committing murder, latte still in hand. Probably in the middle of a conference call on her Airpods. Using a toned leg to kick Clive off the edge of the scaffolding so she didn't break a nail; hoisting the dead body of Pennywise into the boot of her Audi. Then again, Clive McGinty had been pure muscle. Jen couldn't see him being bested by a willowy blonde, even if that willowy blonde did do pilates.

The sun was already beginning its unseasonal warmth. Well, they called it unseasonal and yet Jen felt like there had been a late summer heatwave every year in recent times. It was warmer today, Jen realised, than it was when Clive's body was found. She wondered if he was cold as he hung upside down, slowly dying.

Despite the heat, she shivered.

Whoever killed Clive had been ruthless. Bad enough to take a life, but to walk away without knowing if he was still breathing? Not caring how much he suffered? That seemed especially cruel. Her mind turned to Gloria Reynolds. She of the smart dress suits and the Sunday sermons. Could the CEO-lay preacher square murder with her faith? Jen had met enough dodgy vicars over the years not to discount the woman altogether, but did people with OBEs need to commit murder? Then there was the strength imbalance again. Gloria was angular and slight. Jen imagined she could crack a rib changing a lightbulb. Her string of pearls probably left bruises. Anyway, people like Gloria had lackeys to do their dirty work for them.

Lackeys like Doug Graves. Perhaps Jen was wrong not to go chasing after him. But maybe not – not now another potential lackey had been unearthed. Lee and Petra were meant to have spoken to the senior leaders already, but no one had asked Ed Fielder why he had gone from site manager at Helenswood to in-house liaison. And although at the time Virtua had insisted they didn't know who the previous site manager was, Nandini had already established Ed had worked at St Agnes's. As far as Jen was concerned, he must have presided over the dangerous wall at Helenswood and could easily have been the site manager at St Agnes's, too. Did that wall have the same flaw?

Time to go and ask him.

TWENTY-SIX

Phil felt sweaty and flushed as she walked back towards Virtua Services clutching a tray of paper cups. She had wanted to chase after Doug Graves and wipe that smirk off his stupid face, but Karina had asked her if she was OK and Phil managed to paste on a smile and say:

'Good thanks, how are things with you?'

She was pretty sure this made her a psychopath.

Inside her stomach was turning over like a tumble dryer, but outside she was the same sunny Phil she had always been. Perhaps it was just her way of coping. Whatever it was, it was currently being deployed for good, because getting emotional wasn't going to do her any favours: she needed to collect the evidence. She had been a fool for wandering around the office holding the HSO report like a temporary stop sign. She needed to find a way to retrieve it from Dee Dee's desk before Dee Dee checked her in-tray.

The HSO report was evidence that Doug had committed perjury. He had lied in court. Surely that would be enough to look at Clive's inquest again? And the HSO sought mental health support and shortly afterwards tried to kill himself before he got the job at Haven for the Homeless.

Phil stopped to pull out her phone, which was vibrating in her pocket. The face of a handsome man was on screen. Dean Martin. The boy with the ridiculous name.

'About time! Come on then, spill,' said Phil. 'What have you got for me?'

She was expecting the gossip on what was going on at Virtua.

'I've got to tell you something.'

'Let me guess. They've found out Virtua's been hiding letters?'

'What? No. Have they?' Dean's voice became muffled like he was pulling on a top. 'Listen, I need to speak to you.'

'It's fraud, right? Listen, I can tell you more later, but right now I'm carrying three drinks and I'm meant to be back at Virt... at work.'

She was ready to end the call, but Dean interrupted.

'No, it can't wait. I need you to pay attention for a change, Phil.'

'OK Dean, keep your hair on.'

She wasn't sure why she was always so mean to him. It made her hate herself and the fact that he put up with it made her hate him a little bit too. She realised she should probably speak to some sort of specialist to find out what that was all about.

'Listen, they're going to announce it to the press later today, but I wanted to speak to you first. I shouldn't really do this, but I think you have a right to be warned. Hopefully, someone will make an effort to talk to your mum, but... I don't know if they will.'

'Oh, God. What's happened?'

He puffed out a held breath and Phil realised she felt sick to her stomach.

'There's been another body found,' he said. 'In a wall... in a school wall.'

Phil didn't reply. She was too busy feeling the floor come spiralling towards her. Her vision became tunnelled. She put out her hand to grab the wall and sat down on a raised step in the doorway of a shuttered shop, too distracted to worry about getting her work clothes dirty. She forgot about her phone for a moment until a small voice brought her back to herself.

'Phil?'

'I'm here,' she breathed, bringing the phone back to her ear. 'Tell me.'

'I can only tell you what they're going to announce this morning. That he's a male and they're hoping someone can help identify him. That he was killed with a blow to the head, probably about six or seven years ago. They're going to announce that the building cavity wall was built wrong and when it fell down in the storm, his body fell out. That he was known to frequent the arcades locally and that he may have been a casual labourer on building sites. Probably for Virtua Services. There's now an investigation into Virtua for unsafe building practices.'

It was too much to take in. Another body down another school wall. Unsafe building practices. Her mind was swatting at thoughts like a cat at flies, hitting on some things, missing others. She couldn't organise herself into coherence. Murdered? He was murdered? Dean's voice came through to her like a weak radio transmission.

'Phil, they're going to say there's no evidence the two deaths are linked.'

Suddenly, she was alert.

'What?'

She felt the colour rising in her cheeks, hot swells of emotions forming a mix too complex to separate: anger, sadness, shame, indignation, helplessness.

'This man died before he was put down the wall; your father died after falling down there. They're going to say it's more likely that the murderer heard the news story and copied the idea.'

Phil didn't know where to begin. 'That's utter crap! Two bodies in two school buildings. You'd have to be dense not to see a connection.'

'I get the feeling there's something political going on,' he began, before stopping. 'Listen, Phil, I can't tell you much more, but you know that if you need me, I'll be here and you can ring me whenever. I'll answer if I can and, if not, I'll call you back as soon as I'm free.'

He'd rung off before Phil could finish asking questions. How could this possibly have happened? Now they had someone out there murdering people? She had always believed her father had been killed, but only on her worst days had she been convinced it was part of some giant conspiracy to keep him quiet. She had accused Doug to try to shock him, but really she always found it was more comforting just to believe it had been a mistake, that the murderer panicked and ran away, that he lived his life in constant guilt and sorrow.

But to find out there was another body?

That suggested either her worst instincts were correct and there was some conspiracy at play. Or there was a serial killer out there. How many more walls would contain bodies? She thought of all the school building openings she had been to over the past few years. Maybe a handful – half a dozen, she estimated. Would there be a body in each, placed there like a dead cat to ward off witches?

She reclaimed her abandoned tray of drinks. She had to get back to the office and get that HSO report before Dee Dee did something with it. And then she had to find out anything and everything she could about another dead body in another Virtua wall.

TWENTY-SEVEN

Mick looked up as the new girl arrived back in the office. Her face was flushed like she had been for a run. She'd be good looking if she put some makeup on, he decided. He liked a woman to be well turned out: nails, perfume, nice blouse. You didn't get many like that these days. Even the girls on the reality shows looked scruffy to him. All that grooming did and they still couldn't get a decent hairstyle. Too many clumpy blond locks that fell down their backs like rope. Give him a Marilyn Monroe over one of those grubby-looking girls any day.

Marilyn would not have had a tattoo.

He tried to keep a subtle eye on her – the interloper. He needed to observe without being caught because he didn't want to be accused of staring. Women these days were so touchy about being looked at, as though a man's gaze needed to come with a trigger warning. It was a miracle the human race still continued with all these angry women around shouting about being treated like objects.

His granddaughter had tried to explain it all to him. She'd started giving a big speech. Something about gay men being able to control themselves in the changing rooms. He'd stopped her mid-flow to tell her that he had no problem with homosexuals – had served with plenty in the navy – so long as they kept it to themselves and left him alone. She shouted that he'd missed the point, but he refused to hear any more about it. She would have sulked for the rest of the day, but he'd won her round by giving her a twenty and telling her to get herself something nice.

He wasn't interested in the new girl – not in that way. He just wanted to know what she was up to. The last thing he needed was for her to go trotting off to management, telling tales about how 'Mick doesn't do anything all day. Mick can barely work out how to open the software, let alone use it.'

He had managed to stay under the radar for this long and he wasn't planning on being found out. Not being able to do his job wasn't going to stop him from trying to keep it. In a couple more years, with the side projects he had going, he should have paid off his debts, and he'd have the company pension plus the navy one to see him through. He may be nearing seventy, but so far he'd swerved any hints that it was time for him to sling his hook.

She was heading for Dee Dee's desk like a woman on a mission. Whatever she was doing, it seemed urgent. She put the tray of drinks down so hard the cups wobbled. At the far end of the office, he could see Rhonda also watching the girl. God, he hated that woman. *Rhonda.* Always sticking her nose somewhere it didn't belong, getting a finger in every pie, bossing him about like she ran the place. There wasn't a day that went by that he didn't wish she'd go under a bus. Or worse. He'd happily shove her off a pavement. Or a cliff, for that matter. Rhonda caught him looking at her and gave him a little wave.

He frowned and went back to his work.

TWENTY-EIGHT

Phil lifted the beanbag bear and grabbed the top piece of paper. Even without turning it over, she could tell it wasn't right. The texture of the paper was wrong, the folds weren't the same. This wasn't the health and safety report. She bent down and began sifting through the pages in the in-tray, expecting to find the report a few pages down. Perhaps Dee Dee had added more in the time she'd been away. Perhaps she had already begun sorting them. Dee Dee wasn't at her desk, so Phil couldn't ask. It took her longer than it should have to realise no one was at their desks. Still, she sorted through the pages, panic making her unable to care where everyone else had got to.

By the time she had sorted through every page in the in-tray and every page in the out-tray and every spare piece of paper she could discover on Dee Dee's desk, she had to accept that the report was no longer there.

'Ah, there you are,' came a voice.

Phil looked up and managed a smile. It was Rhonda. Always there when Phil was trying to snoop.

'I was just coming to look for you,' Rhonda continued. 'We've been called in to an all-hands meeting. It's about to start.'

'I was just dropping off Dee Dee's drink,' said Phil, lifting the paper cup out of the cardboard tray and popping it on the desk.

'Well, that can wait,' said Rhonda.

'I've got one for Jamie too,' said Phil, moving towards Rhonda.

'She's in the meeting,' said Rhonda. 'Come on.'

Rhonda's gaze slid from Phil to the far corner of the room. Phil turned to see what she was looking at. Mick was still at his desk, the only human in a sea of empty office furniture.

'Everything alright, Mick?' said Rhonda.

It was a light tone, but there was tension there. Phil remembered what Rhonda had said about being afraid of Mick and she tensed too. Mick made her think of werewolves – that under all that human flesh was a monster waiting to break out and devour them all. But when he stood, still glowering, he said only:

'Yes, just coming now,' in a calm voice and Phil wondered if her nights spent looking for a bogeyman had made her mind play tricks on her. Mick was just a disgruntled pensioner, angry with the world. He might grouse about young people taking his job, but he wasn't about to don a bonnet and eat her grandma.

'After you, ladies,' he said, and Phil felt his eyes on their back the whole way to the lift.

The fourth floor boardroom was packed with humans, the air plump with the kind of expectancy that you could almost reach out and grasp. Instead of the usual chatter you'd expect, the room was filled only with a soft murmur as people speculated out of half-closed mouths, wondering if this was a mass sacking, or an announcement of a company takeover. Maybe it would be good news – a huge new contract to service, or an exciting acquisition – but no one here was banking on it. When Gloria arrived to speak, Phil felt the despondency had reached whatever the opposite of a fever pitch was.

'I'm afraid we have some bad news,' she began, doing nothing to allay anyone's fears. The atmosphere, somehow, grew even more depressed.

'Last week, during the storm – hard to believe we had a storm now isn't it, what with this heatwave? – a wall fell down at the old Helenswood school. On a building we were responsible for building and maintaining.'

Phil was impressed with this start. Not only had Gloria already allowed herself to be waylaid by irrelevant details, she had begun by burying the lede so far down the speech it was going to be awkward to segue into it. Why not simply start with the sad discovery of a dead person? The assembled employees shuffled, clearly intrigued by this news, but, Phil imagined, already doing the mental arithmetic to establish whether their department was now due a bollocking or not.

'The wall had not been built properly and there will now be a full inquiry into where the error occurred. Obviously, we are already co-operating fully with this, and we will be holding our own internal review concurrently to establish precisely what happened.'

Still no mention of the body. Phil was impressed by her ability to swerve the main story. She scanned the room, trying to seek out Ed Fielder. There he was, taller than those around him by a good foot or more. Only Mick could meet him eye to eye. He rubbed his stubble and looked irritated, like he'd rather be anywhere else.

Andrew Templeton-Dunbar had told her that Ed was the man who had made Clive the site manager at St Agnes's. She wondered if Ed had been responsible for hiring whoever built the Helenswood site too. Did he know about Doug's HSO report? He certainly didn't seem troubled at the moment. As Gloria spoke, Phil kept watching him, wondering how he would respond to the Gloria's big reveal.

'And I'm afraid the bad news doesn't end there,' said Gloria.

Give this woman a medal for insensitivity, thought Phil. And it suddenly occurred to her that Gloria had been telling the senior leaders about the dead man on the day she had infiltrated the fourth floor meeting. Phil had assumed she was talking about bad news to do with the audit, but no: she must have been telling them about the body, using the same, 'Well, isn't this inconvenient,' tone she was using now. Which meant Jamie had known for most of the week and yet had carried on as normal, still displaying the same level of detached boredom she had shown since day one of Phil's time here.

Phil sought her out in the crowd and couldn't spot her, which was precisely the moment that Jamie entered, late as usual, her head bowed slightly in a semblance of apology, which she then spoiled by standing behind and to the left of Gloria and checking a chipped nail. Gloria glanced at Jamie before swiftly continuing.

'When the wall came down, unfortunately, a man's body was discovered.'

The sharp intake of breath from her audience seemed to surprise Gloria, as though it hadn't occurred to her that people might be moved by the news, as though she had forgotten how terrible it sounded. She raised her voice slightly above a ripple of murmuring.

'Police have so far been unable to identify the man, although we understand he may have worked in some capacity for Virtua Services in the past.'

This sent up another flutter of sound and fidgeting.

'Police also believe he may have been to the office on one occasion and had an altercation with some of our Virtua employees in the downstairs atrium.'

It was at this moment, as the murmurs rose to a chatter, that Phil noticed the detectives. She'd been so busy keeping an eye on Ed Fielder that she hadn't spotted them lurking to one side near her, tucked in behind the accounts department. She recognised two – DS Jen Collet and DI Lee Hudson – but wasn't sure she knew the third, a young woman of south Asian descent with a scruffy ponytail and an air of swagger. Gloria turned to them.

'Perhaps you would like to take it from here, detective?' she said.

Lee Hudson stepped forward. Phil didn't like him. She'd seen him giving statements a number of times over the years, and she always got the feeling he regarded the press with more than just the usual cordial dislike. He made it seem personal somehow, and it always made her wonder if he was hiding something.

'Thank you, Mrs Reynolds,' he said, his tone surprisingly formal. Even when he was reading statements, he usually emitted a laddish air, but here he seemed strangely diminished. He introduced his team, then continued. 'I'm sure this has come as quite a shock to you all, but I'm afraid we will need to take statements from anyone who was at Virtua

Services around the time of the victim's death. I believe we have a list, and we will be talking to each in turn as the day goes on.'

'I have given the detectives the use of some of our meeting rooms,' said Gloria. 'Please make time for them when you are invited to speak.'

Lee smiled at her and tried to regain the floor, but Gloria hadn't finished.

'In the meantime, I'm sure you will all want to discuss what has happened, which is why Jamie will be facilitating two half-hour interface sessions to explore any concerns or anxieties this news may have surfaced. And, let me assure you, we are not looking at redundancies at this stage. This is a legacy issue with one of our older buildings, and we will not be jumping to any conclusions or pointing any fingers until the inquiry is complete. I don't need to remind you that we still have an audit to prepare for and we will expect you to continue working responsibly.' She turned her head slowly, taking the time to make eye contact with as many people as she could before she snapped abruptly back to business. 'Ed, I believe you are first on the list.'

Phil could feel people's response to this. Having said no one was to blame, Gloria immediately singled out someone everyone would have their eye on as an obvious fall guy. Everyone, that is, apart from Ed, who looked up in surprise at his name and frowned.

Phil did her best to duck out of the room without catching Jen Collet's eye. The last thing she needed was the detective outing her. She was shuffling out in the mash of people when Dee Dee caught her elbow.

'Ed Fielder looked like he was going to have kittens, didn't he?' Dee Dee said. 'I said to Jan, I said, "Jan, look at

Ed's face. It's paler than a Scotsman's backside." Didn't I Jan?'

Dee Dee looked around for Jan for back up and before Phil could ask her about the HSO report, she lost her in the bustle.

TWENTY-NINE

Jen had wanted to interview Ed Fielder down at the station, but Lee insisted that it was better sticking to Virtua's preferred way of doing things. They wanted to keep their staff on site and for Lee and Petra it made sense.

'We need them to cooperate fully,' said Petra. 'Let's get the main interviews done and then you can bring in any potential suspects afterwards. It will keep things a bit calmer and stop the wild speculation these cases tend to attract.'

In other words, Petra was terrified of upsetting the area's largest employer without being confident there was good cause. Jen was finding it hard to suppress her frustration with Lee and Petra – that they had delayed this for so long, preferring to speak to senior leadership discreetly and refusing to release the information to the public until today. As far as Jen was concerned, as soon as the body was found in the Virtua building, anyone who had been working at Virtua during that time should have been first to be interviewed. And yet, so far as she could tell, this was the first time Ed had even heard the news. And so here they were, sitting with Ed in a meeting room, explaining his rights to him while he gazed back at them in surly silence.

'Mr Fielder,' Lee began, which threw Jen for two reasons. First because he tended to leave the talking to Jen unless he thought he could deliver a finishing blow, and second because she had never heard him be so respectful to any suspect. She wondered what he had been like in the interviews with the senior leaders. She had read all the transcripts, but there was no way of knowing if he'd tugged his forelock. 'You were working as a liaison between the contractors, builders and in-house office workers here at Virtua, is that right?'

'Yep,' said Ed with evident impatience.

'And you've been given a description of what we know about the gentleman in the wall. Do you recognise any of the details?'

'Nope.'

Jen leaned forward. 'You never worked with a man who regularly wore a blue polo shirt with a Prints To Go logo on it?'

He tilted his chin down and looked at her like an impatient teen. 'No.'

The conversation continued in this vein for long enough that Jen began to think fondly of her time speaking to Babycakes. If only she could threaten Ed with the 'I'm going to count to three' technique. But somehow she suspected he wouldn't fall for it.

'Tell me,' Jen said towards the end of their conversation. 'Why did you move in-house? Doesn't really seem like your kind of thing.'

He shrugged. Another shrugger, thought Jen with an inward sigh.

'Fancied a change,' he said. 'My back hurt.'

'You were the site manager on the Helenswood build, weren't you.'

'I don't remember.'

'We know that you were, Mr Fielder,' said Lee still maintaining his strange politeness.

'Maybe,' said Ed with the kind of affected boredom Jen would expect from a teenager.

'You worked on the St Agnes build too, didn't you?' she said.

'I can barely remember what happened last week let alone seven years ago,' he said.

'Did a man in a Prints To Go polo shirt ever work with you on those projects?'

Ed just stared at her.

'Did he do the bad work, or did he just see you doing it?' Jen asked.

More silence.

'What about Clive? Did he spot your bad work?'

'What the hell are you talking about?' said Ed. And now he'd move past sullen to angry. 'Clive?'

He shook his head.

'You know what I think?' said Jen. 'I think you were the site manager on both of those projects, and I think people realised you were presiding over shoddy workmanship.'

Ed shook his head again and looked away in disgust.

'And I think,' he said, leaning in with an abruptness that nearly made Jen sit back. 'That you're a nutter and we're done here.'

He got up and walked out.

THIRTY

Phil had expected to spend the afternoon in agony, waiting for the end of the day. She had already begun planning her escape while she was in the lift, plotting to feign illness or remember an important doctor's appointment, but in the end the day had passed in a heartbeat, filled with speculation and gossip and Jamie's facilitated sessions which were little more than an opportunity for even more speculation and gossip. And, of course, for anyone there long enough, it was inevitable that Clive's name would resurface. After all, two bodies in two school walls run by the same company. What were the chances of that happening?

Everyone had a theory. Perhaps Clive had killed him and then topped himself via the same method. Perhaps the dead bloke had seen someone pushing Clive in and had been given the same treatment. Rumours started circulating that he was someone who had gone missing around that time, but no one could remember the poor man's name, until eventually Mary appeared in the building and told them that the man they were thinking of was alive and well and living in Seaford.

Phil hadn't found the HSO report. She'd finally managed to corner Dee Dee who looked at her blankly for a few seconds before remembering what piece of paper she was talking about.

'I haven't touched it, babes. I've been run off my feet all day. I haven't had a chance to do anything with anything.'

'So you didn't maybe move it to a different folder?' Phil said.

'No babes. I'll get to it eventually though, don't worry. Aren't you the diligent one?'

And Phil hadn't attempted to explain again that the letter was missing. Whatever had happened to it, she was satisfied it was nothing to do with Dee Dee.

'Fancy a coffee?' said Dee Dee.

Phil had been about to say no, but Dee Dee was suddenly walking her down the aisle towards the metal divider that signalled the opening to the kitchenette.

'I bet you're glad to be out of that box today?' continued Dee Dee before rounding into the kitchenette and dropping her voice to conspiratorial volume. 'Make the most of it. We'll be back with our noses to the grindstone tomorrow. Got to take these opportunities where we can.' She put her hand to her head in a dramatic gesture of remembering. 'I didn't tell you did I? The blackmailer finally came for me.'

'No!' said Phil, interested in spite of her distraction. What was Lachlan hoping to get out of Dee Dee?

'They're wanting money in return for keeping their mouth shut about my *little secret*. But the joke's on them because I don't care. I'll tell anyone who asks: I was given a written warning for paying too much compensation to some old biddy, ok?' and here she raised a finger and gave an imaginary person in front of her some sass, 'But it wasn't my fault. And anyway, I hope she enjoyed the money and bought herself a nice caravan or whatever.'

Caravan.

Old biddy.

Phil felt a jolt.

Mrs Cooke!

She forced herself to stay calm. To be Scarlett not Phil. She leaned in, aping Dee Dee's gossipy stance.

'Who did you pay the compensation to then?' she said.

'This old dear who had her driveway blocked by one of our Virtua vans. And I'll tell you something else an' all,' Dee Dee continued, leaning in even more. 'Between you, me and the microwave, I've never once in my entire time working here paid someone that much.'

'How much?' said Phil, utterly sucked in.

'Twenty grand,' said Dee Dee. 'Twenty thousand smackers, can you believe it?'

When Phil had seen Dee Dee's HR file with the warning on it, she had assumed the overpayment was something like two hundred pounds when only twenty was justified.

'Twenty grand?' she said. 'That's about fifty times the biggest payments I've seen.'

Proper hush money.

'Tell me about it, babes. I had no idea. I was new, you see. Mind you, she didn't get it for free. Poor sod had to sign a non-disclosure agreement saying she'd never speak of it again, and what have you. Probably signed all her grandchildren over to the company, knowing what this place is like. Wouldn't surprise me at all.'

'Who made her sign the NDA?' said Phil. Surely Doug

or Ed wouldn't have had that much power within the business? Someone higher up had to know. 'Was it Jamie?'

'God no,' said Dee Dee. 'This went all the way to the top.'

At this Dee Dee pursed her lips and pointed up to the sky like she was afraid of being struck by lightning.

'Her majesty,' mouthed Dee Dee.

'Gloria Reynolds?' blurted Phil. Dee Dee gestured to keep her voice down as though saying her name might cause her to appear right there in the kitchenette. 'But that's crazy. What could... she... possibly have to do with a blocked drive?'

'You tell me, babes,' said Dee Dee. 'I wondered if Gloria was in debt and using the old lady to pay back a loan shark or something. Or maybe she just wanted to give an elderly relative a few quid? Who knows? Maybe she knew something she shouldn't? But that seems unlikely – when did you last hear of someone in a bungalow making someone like her majesty Mrs Reynolds quake? And Andrew gave me so much grief for it. Presumably he hadn't got the memo from her holiness about the payment because he found out and went spare. I thought he was going to fire me on the spot. But he took pity, I suppose. I told him it wasn't my fault.'

'Whose fault was it?' said Phil.

'I was new, and I did as I was told,' Dee Dee said. Phil tried to focus. 'And then I got in trouble for it. I said to Jan at the time, "This is a travesty, Jan" I said. I said, "If anyone should get written up it should be him."'

'Who?' said Phil, trying to untangle the threads of Dee Dee's rambling story.

But the customer services rep was on a roll.

'He stood there, bold as brass. Said he had no idea what I was talking about and that he would never have told me to pay so much money. Said there was nothing I could do about it because her majesty, Gloria in excelsis, was on his side, insisting the whole thing hadn't happened. But he was the one who told me to pay the money and he was the one who blocked the poor woman's drive.'

'Who was?' said Phil. She ran a metal roll call. Andrew? Doug? Ed Fielder?

'I shouldn't say...'

For the first time, Phil got the sense that Dee Dee was actually going to keep her mouth shut. A brief battle seemed to play out over the woman's features as she wrestled with her desire to gossip at all costs.

The gossip won.

'Oh sod it. What does it matter? You're leaving tomorrow. Who are you going to tell?'

Luckily, Dee Dee didn't seem to expect an answer, so Phil didn't have to lie.

Dee Dee opened her mouth to reveal all and was interrupted in that moment by her boss summoning her.

'The police are ready for you,' he said, looking at her with the same weary resignation of a long-suffering life partner.

And just like that, it was time to go home.

Except Phil didn't go home.

The dogs barked again as she rang the doorbell and she waited as the same buffet of locks was attended to. Mrs Cooke's face appeared at the door and the dogs sprang towards Phil's legs, yapping with untold glee, seeing her off while also welcoming her in.

Mrs Cooke was less keen.

'I told you to go away,' she said.

Phil felt like a doorstep thug.

'I just want to talk to you, Mrs Cooke,' she said in a pleading tone that she hoped might move Mrs Cooke to pity. No such luck.

'I've got nothing to say,' said Mrs Cooke, who would have closed the door if only she could shepherd the dogs back in.

'I believe you might have witnessed a murder,' said Phil and watched the fear cross Mrs Cooke's face.

'What do you mean?' she said. Whatever she had seen that day, she certainly didn't think it was murder. Not judging by the look of horror and confusion on her face.

'The van that blocked your driveway,' said Phil. 'I think you saw the man who killed my fath – who killed Clive McGinty.'

'Who?' said Mrs Cooke, growing flustered.

She wasn't frail and confused; she wasn't forgetful. Phil could tell. She was simply swamped with too many stimuli in the form of three over-excited dogs, an unwelcome visitor, and now this strange claim about a murder and a man she hadn't heard of. Phil tried to make things more simple.

'The day the van parked on your drive, Mrs Cooke. Did you see a man?'

Mrs Cooke made a little noise, a squeak that conveyed her fears – as well as her desire to be left alone. Phil pressed on, feeling like a villain, but desperate to get the answer.

'Maybe a skinny muscled man with dark slicked back hair and tattoos?'

And at that, Mrs Cooke looked directly at Phil.

'No. That wasn't him.'

'What was he like then?' said Phil.

'I signed something,' said Mrs Cooke. 'I said I wouldn't talk about it to anyone. They'll be after me.'

It was hard to tell if Mrs Cooke was being dramatic or if she really believed she might be in some sort of danger. And Phil couldn't ask because, somehow, Mrs Cooke had managed to wrangle the dogs into the house and shut the door, at which point Phil found herself in the shameful position of calling through the letterbox again.

'What did he look like?' she said. 'Please, Mrs Cooke. Clive McGinty was my dad.'

A man walking his dog on the opposite pavement looked over, and Phil had a sense of just how threatening she appeared, yelling through a bungalow door at an elderly woman. She was about to stand up to leave when Mrs Cooke called out.

'I sent a photo,' she said. 'I sent a photo of the van with the letter.'

And she disappeared into a room and out of sight.

Phil turned at the movement from Simon's front door. He was heading her way, still in his slippers, crouched low, creeping along with lunging strides: a movie star trying to storm a government research facility.

Earlier, she had swerved any questions about how she was.

'I'm going to head straight to the car,' she said, running off to the comfort of her mother's Fiesta.

But now Simon was here, climbing into her passenger seat, proffering a tin of biscuits.

'Is everything alright? You seem a little out of sorts,' he said after watching Phil staring gloomily at her cup of tea. 'You'll get him tonight, I'm sure.'

'Yes, I'm sure I will,' said Phil, attempting a smile.

She could feel Simon observing her with a gimlet eye. 'It's something else, isn't it?' he said.

And now her smile was genuine, rueful. 'What makes you say that?'

'No one gets that downcast about missing out on a litterer, no matter how villainous.'

'Fair point. He's hardly the Zodiac Killer, is he?'

She hoped Simon would lose interest, but he was still staring at her patiently, awaiting a response, and so she had relented. 'I'm working on another thing at the moment. A story about a local man who was discovered down the wall cavity at the St Agnes school years ago.'

'Clive McGinty,' Simon said. 'I remember it well.'

Phil wasn't shocked that he remembered; it had been a big story at the time (hardly surprising: 'Missing man found trapped in school wall' is a gift of a news piece.) It had been covered extensively by the local papers and was picked up by the national press as well.

'They've found another body,' she said.

'I heard it on the news,' he said. 'Terrible business. They're saying there's no connection.' He saw the look on her face. 'But you don't believe them?'

But then Simon said something she wasn't expecting.

'I was there,' he said.

I was there.

'What do you mean?' she said.

'At St Agnes's. The day Clive... you know. I was a teacher. I think I told you that, didn't it? History. Well... it was my school at the time. I was there the day it happened, preparing my classroom for the term ahead, tidying up some books, getting the place presentable for the next generation of reprobates to step through my doors.'

'But you weren't at the inquest.'

'Oh, I didn't go.' He said it in an offhand way, as though it was perfectly reasonable. 'I wasn't invited. I would have gone along anyway, just to see if I was needed, but I was in hospital having an angioplasty. It's why I gave up teaching in the end.'

He tapped thoughtfully on the moulded plastic door and stared out of the front window. 'I always wondered why no one asked. I did get in touch with the police, but they didn't get back to me. I supposed I wasn't needed – although the whole thing struck me as a bit odd. They said it was an accident, but...' He shook his head, leaving the thought unspoken.

'What did you see?'

He turned to her, startled a little at the passion in her voice.

'You knew him,' he said.

Phil felt her ears ringing and her eyes fill with sudden saltwater. All she could manage was a nod, the tears dripping to the floor before she could chase them away with her fingertips.

Simon said, 'I am so sorry.'

Phil nodded again, acknowledging his kindness, before pleading him to speak with one simple, choked out, 'Please.'

Simon took a sad breath and spoke.

'I came out of my classroom and I spotted someone heading towards the science block. I went out and a middle-aged black man raised his hand and said, "Good morning." "Are you starting work?" I asked, and he said, "Not yet – I'm just here to meet the engineer." We chatted for a moment or two longer, discussing what the block would look like once it was finished, and then he said something along the lines of, "I must be off, don't want to miss her." I bade him farewell and watched as he walked up the hill path and onto the gangway that took you onto the scaffolding. That scaffolding gave me nightmares – trying to keep the teenagers off it all year long. Anyway, then I headed back into my classroom. "Take care now," were his last words to me.'

Phil felt a wave of sadness, but she was desperate for the story not to end (desperate for Simon to reveal that Clive had got in the car, driven back home to his family – that the whole thing had just been a terrible nightmare). To her surprise, he continued.

'Five minutes or so after that, I saw a tall white man with dark hair walking towards the building. I assumed it was the engineer and carried on sorting my shelves. It was only a while later I remembered that Clive had said, "I don't want to miss her." But the engineer who met him there was very definitely a man. Shortly afterwards, I left for a weekend away to see my daughter and then we travelled to France for a week. I didn't think about it again until I spotted the story in the paper. I left a message with the police, but no one got back to me and by then I had had the heart attack, so I'm afraid I rather let it slide. I did contact them again afterwards, but they told me the case was closed. Death by misadventure.'

He spoke it in a rolling baritone, enjoying the drama of the words, and for a brief moment Phil had wanted to scream, 'He was my father!' and shake him until his jovial demeanour evaporated into contrition. But it was just Simon being Simon. Even in the short time she had known him, she knew he was one of the good guys. He had not pushed her father into a wall cavity.

The tall white man had.

The tall man who followed her father onto the scaffolding the day he went to meet a female engineer there. And now Phil was going to track him down and make him pay for what he'd done. She knew it was the most childish fantasy, but she couldn't help it. What else had she worked all her life for if it wasn't to find the truth about what had happened to Clive? To punish whoever was responsible.

'Thanks Simon, would you mind letting me just have a moment on my own?' she managed, and he nodded kindly and clambered out of the car, leaving her the tin of biscuits.

Phil took out her phone and sent a text. A minute later, the phone beeped a reply. She looked down and read the message: 'Give me twenty minutes.'

She looked back up at the tree and waited.

Twenty minutes later, Phil's passenger door opened and Dean Martin got in.

'I need you to do me a favour,' Phil said.

'Not again,' he said.

'There was an eyewitness who saw my dad with another man on the day he died. A tall white man followed him onto the site.'

'What?' said Dean, flummoxed.

'My dad thought he was meeting a woman – the engineer – just like we told you lot at the inquest.'

It didn't matter that Dean was still in school with her when Clive died. In this moment, he was as bad as all the rest.

'But a man arrived. And because you didn't follow up on the eyewitness, dad's murderer is still out there. I need you to find out why no one looked into it. Or...' She suddenly realised she didn't really know what she wanted Dean to do. What could he do? He was just a lowly constable, still choosing which department to work in. 'I need you to go in there now and take Simon Barker's statement.'

'I can't do that! Listen,' he put out a hand towards her, trying to offer reassurance, 'let me speak to my boss and see what she says. I'm sure she'll be interested. She's not like the others.'

Not like the others. What did that mean? That all the other coppers in the station would ignore a perfectly good eyewitness for a potential murder if it landed on their doorstep?

'Who is your boss?' she asked.

'I'll speak to Jen Collet. She's more switched on than the DI.'

'I want you to talk to someone in power, not some DS! You need to be knocking on the DCI's door right now.'

'Phil,' he said. 'I'm no one. If I knock on her door, she's going to tell me to sod off.'

She could feel his eyes on her. Those sad brown eyes that made her want to punch him for being so nice and good. He was like a lost angel on earth and she hated him for it.

'Don't,' she warned. His empathy was going to tip her into tears. 'I can't cry now, Dean. I'm working. Thanks for your help, if that's what it was. You can go now.'

He looked at her sadly and she turned her face away and sniffed back the tears that were trying to come.

He opened the passenger door and put a foot out, ready to leave.

'I'll call you tomorrow and let you know what happens,' he said.

She didn't respond and he clambered out with a sigh.

On the day of Clive's funeral, when mourners lined the streets dressed in outrageous costumes, clapping as the cortège passed, Phil had wished more than anything he had been there to witness the spectacle. He would have been in his element; he loved this crazy party town and its joy at dressing up for the flimsiest occasion. And everyone loved him too, which is why they put on their gladdest rags and headed out onto the streets to see him off. The drummers came, all the different troupes marching to the same beat for a change, and the Morris dancers, with their problematic historical provenance and the pirates and pagans and pretty little princesses. Drag queens and papier maché giants, mushrooms and crows. It was a sight for sore eyes, and Phil had taken great comfort in all of its silly extravagance and joy.

But once inside at the service, Phil had felt stifled by the heat of everyone's warm bodies. She was grateful for all their love and care and yet she had never felt so lonely and so overwhelmed. Their tears oppressed her. The weight of their sadness pressed into her chest. Their gentle euphemisms made her want to scream. She thought back to that moment and felt the same wave of oppression and sadness. But there was something else there, too, because now she knew for sure her father hadn't killed himself; the tall white man had. And she was going to find out who he was.

Phil walked past reception, unpopulated by Jessica or Duncan. It was still too early for the former, and the latter was... wherever he went to when he wasn't guarding the door. Phil hit the button for the lift for the last time. There would be no coming back to this strange corporate hinterland where every day felt the same and everything smelled of carpet tiles and instant coffee. This is not what humans have evolved for, she realised – spending their days under artificial lights like hydroponic salads, eating food out of plastic tubs in front of spreadsheets, working all afternoon on a PowerPoint slide deck no one would pay any attention to.

What a soul-sapping existence.

Her job at the paper might be poorly paid, she might have to spend an awful lot of time writing about who won the longest bean award at the Vale Road Allotments Open Day, but at least she got to get out and meet people. And the office was scruffy, but it felt like a human space. There was a nodding Bob Ross in the staff toilet. The walls were adorned with faded cuttings of their best reporting from days of yore when local news meant something. She didn't step out every day, blinking like a hostage victim who's forgotten what fresh air on the face feels like.

Phil thought back over everything she had learned during her week at Virtua and realised how paltry the list was. Really it amounted to nothing more than a few coincidences: someone parked on a drive nearby on the day her father was killed. Or, a few possibly irrelevant details: an HSO report that wasn't meant to exist (and which currently didn't exist thanks to Dee Dee's in-tray which apparently worked like a black hole); Simon's eyewitness account that he had seen someone tall, white and male there on the building site that day.

So what?

Lots of people were tall white males. Aldhill was lousy

with that genre of human. She could have named thirty without pausing to think.

But there was a photo.

A photo of the person who was right by the school on the day her father had died. Who was it? Ed Fielder and Andrew Templeton-Dunbar were tall, and Ed had a clear motive. Andrew maybe less so unless he was in on Gloria's cover up. Mick was tall – and sinister as hell – but why would he be involved? And yet Doug still felt like the obvious choice to Phil. Suicidal in the weeks following Clive's death – possibly after killing two people. He wasn't tall, but who knew what strange perspective was created when you looked up at a man on scaffolding? Besides, it was a long time ago. Even a mind as keen as Simon's could be corroded by time.

Somewhere in that quagmire of papers, there could well be a photo. And Phil knew exactly where she was going to start looking. She had opted to come in early, since there was a risk of bumping into Rhonda the insomniac at night. Instead, she had sat in her car and waited fruitlessly for a man with a weak understanding of how to dispose of dog poo bags before finally heading home and succumbing to a deep sleep that ended with a nightmare about being trapped in a dark cupboard while a tall man tried to push a dog in through a letter box.

Phil made a beeline for the box she thought might hold the evidence she needed: the one on the high shelf that had given her the HSO report. But a thorough search soon disappointed. The photograph wasn't there. She reached up to put the box back on its shelf and found her chair betraying her, wheeling backwards and sending her centre of gravity into disarray. As her feet were wheeled towards the centre of the room, her arms continued to reach up towards the shelf.

Perhaps if she could offload the grey box before she was too far gone, she might be able to grab the edge of the shelf and haul herself upright again.

No such luck. The chair continued its journey and Phil managed to throw the box onto the shelf before half-falling, half-jumping off onto the floor below. She fell awkwardly as the chair shot backwards, twisting her ankle slightly as she landed, which sent her sprawling down almost in slow motion, one wrist catching the bulk of her upper body in a way that she knew would hurt for weeks.

There on the floor she felt the urge to cry, but found herself laughing instead, the stress of the week catching her unaware. She rubbed her face, wondering how crazy she must look, sprawled out and laughing, and that's when she spotted it. Behind the back leg of the shelf, up against the wall, a photo. It must have fallen from the same folder when she dropped the HSO report. She shuffled forward and grabbed it, prising it from the grip of the shelf, and found herself staring at something that seemed familiar. A front path with a patch of grass to one side. A road with a row of bungalows opposite. And there, in the centre of the shot, a Virtua van blocking a driveway. Mrs Cooke's driveway.

A staple hole in the corner showed where it had been ripped from the original letter. Phil stared at the image as though it might yield an answer – tell her who the van belonged to – and it only took her a moment to realise that was exactly what it was doing. The Virtua van number plate was clearly visible. If she could find out whose van it was, she could identify who had been near St Agnes's on the day her dad died.

She slid the photo into her back pocket and headed for the door.

FRIDAY

THIRTY-ONE

Andrew stirred his coffee. He had finally decided to limit himself to one a day. Soon, he thought, there will be no vices left. He took a biscuit from the tin, an act of defiance against his monkish existence, and retreated to his armchair, cup, saucer and biscuit in one hand, and *The Times* in the other. The crossword wasn't going well so far. They seemed to get harder as the week went on. Or maybe it was just that every day was another day closer to mental atrophy. He sighed.

He only managed a couple more clues before he found his thoughts returning to the dead man (he stopped the timer on his phone eventually – probably not strictly allowed, but it was his house, after all.)

Another soul in a school building?

It didn't bear thinking about. *And* during his tenure at Virtua Services, too. He wondered what Jamie was doing right now to mitigate the problem. Probably she hadn't even turned up for work yet.

Andrew considered ringing the detective sergeant again. He should probably tell her more about his involvement with

Clive McGinty's death. He could press upon her how much of an interest Gloria had paid in Clive. He should probably confess that he had once seen the health and safety officer, Douglas Graves, having a conversation with Gloria and Ed Fielder in Gloria's office, Doug's face ashen apart from two pink bruise-like blushes on his cheeks: easily the most emotion he'd ever seen from the gruff health and safety officer. The three of them made such an unlikely trio that it had stayed with Andrew all these years. He had been surprised Gloria would stoop to meet with two builders like that.

There had been a cover up, he was certain now. The construction workers had moved in with unseemly haste to pull down the rest of the wall when Clive was removed from the cavity. No chance for anyone from the council to inspect it first. Not that the council would have said anything, Andrew was sure. He assumed that Gloria had them on the payroll somewhere along the line.

He shook his head and took a sip of coffee. What was happening to him? When did he lose his faith in Virtua? All those years of loyalty and now he realised he was coming to regard his tenure as a joke. Keeping up appearances while the rest of the leadership tried to cut costs, slash headcount, increase workloads and extract the most profit from any transaction. Everything existed in the margins at Virtua. So many of his company initiatives were really just company spin: ticking boxes to win diversity awards whilst members of the team were close to burnout.

He wished he was there with the team right now, helping his people to come to terms with the terrible news about another dead colleague. Bodies slotted into buildings like library tickets. It was too terrible to think about. He dunked a biscuit in his coffee and watched as the chocolate topping relaxed and sent a rivulet of brown into black.

Jamie would be no help at all. His people would be floundering without his guidance. Should he reach out to Rhonda? She might need his support. He would leave it until Sunday, he decided, and then he would connect – offer her a friendly ear, a walk on the sea front, a cup of coffee. Something to help her get through this difficult time.

Yes, that would be *something*. More than Jamie would do, certainly.

Satisfied, Andrew returned to twelve across: Empty gesture welcomed by endlessly large disgruntled Brit smooth talker (7).

THIRTY-TWO

The office was filling up fast but the employees Phil could see didn't know her. She took the risk, deciding she had nothing to lose, and headed straight for Jamie's filing cabinets. Jamie wasn't in yet, this being too early even on the day after a bombshell meeting with the CEO and a looming audit. If Phil looked confident enough, she hoped no one would stop to ask her why she was rifling through confidential folders. She needed to find out who used that vehicle.

'What are you racing around for, then?' said Dee Dee, wheeling herself backwards out of her cubicle and blocking Phil's path. 'It's your last day, isn't it? You're in early. Mind you, so am I – on orders of the boss. You'll note he's not arrived yet, though. Here I am, up at the crack of a sparrow's fart and where are they all? One rule for them and sod the rest of us, babes. What are you up to, then? I'd have thought you'd be hiding in the bogs looking at TikTok. Fancy a coffee?'

Phil was about to say no but then she remembered Mrs

Cooke's driveway. She followed Dee Dee into the kitchen area.

'Dee Dee, you know yesterday you told me about the 20k?'

'Yes, babes. Haven't heard anything from the blackmailer though. Maybe he got bored. I sent him an email telling him to stick it up his bum, but it bounced back.'

'You didn't say who told you to pay the money.'

'Didn't I? Well, that's probably just as well to be honest. I don't want to get in any more trouble. I'm on my final warning. And I'll be honest, Mick scares the whatsit out of me.'

'What?' said Phil, leaning in and only just resisting the urge to grip Dee Dee by the arms and squeeze her. 'Mick was the person blocking Mrs Cooke's drive?'

'Oh, I said it now. What am I like?'

'What about Doug?'

'Who?' Dee Dee said, momentarily confused. Phil realised she'd made a number of mistakes in one short sentence. Scarlett didn't know Doug. She didn't know Mrs Cooke's name either. But Dee Dee, still tangled in the yarn she was spinning, didn't seem to notice. 'No, it was definitely Mick. He claimed he wasn't even there that day so he couldn't have parked on that woman's drive, but he was – and I'll tell you how I know.'

She leaned in and Phil couldn't help leaning in too. 'Because the old dear sent a photo with her letter. There it was, clear as daylight: his van parked across her drive.'

Phil felt her heart pounding. 'Mick has a company car?'

'Yes, perk of the job. He didn't have a car when he started here and he needed something to do the investigations in.'

It took Phil a while to recalibrate her thinking. Not

Doug, not Ed; Mick. Was Mick the person who killed her father? If so, what possible motive could he have? It didn't make sense

'Have you spoken to Mick about it since, then?' Phil asked.

'I tried, hun, but after a while I gave up. He point-blank refused to speak to me about it. If you ask me he was scared. I've never seen Mick looking nervous – he's a tough ex-military type. You still wouldn't mess with him even at his age. But whenever I tried to discuss it, I swear to god he would start sweating like a dogger in a carpark. No word of a lie, I saw his hands shake.'

'Crikey,' Phil said. It was a conscious effort to sound casual, and she wondered if sounded as forced as it felt. 'Why do you think that was?'

'I reckon the boss made him do it,' said Dee Dee, crossing her arms and pulling a face of disapproval, eyebrows raised, lips pursed. 'I never blamed him for it, I just had this feeling that it wasn't his fault, you know? Call it a seventh sense if you like.'

Phil didn't have time to wonder what Dee Dee's sixth sense was, because at that moment Dee Dee's manager walked past and raised an eyebrow. Dee Dee, who had been leaning backwards against the kitchen units, stood upright.

'I best get to it, babes, before I get fired,' she said, but then a thought struck her, 'I tell you what, Scarlett. It's weird that they never fired me considering they thought it was my cock up. I mean can you imagine? A member of staff pays twenty grand for a simple complaint – the sort that normally gets a bunch of flowers and a quick letter of apology – and all they gave me was a ticking off and a written warning. Weird if you ask me.'

'Yeah, that is weird,' said Phil.
'I'd love to know why,' said Dee Dee.
So would I, thought Phil.

THIRTY-THREE

Mick climbed the steps to the third floor. It was all part of his attempt to hit ten thousand steps, an attempt he failed at every day. But no matter. Grasping the plastic-coated bannister and making his ascent gave him a sense of achievement, as though he were training for Mount Kilimanjaro one flight at a time. He liked to keep in shape. It had been a fundamental part of his identity for so many years. It was the reason the Captain turned to him for help whenever he needed it. That and the fact the boss knew he could trust him with his life.

That was why he had been given the Clive McGinty job.

At first Mick had wondered how he would live with himself – with the terrible remorse – but in the event, the guilt really didn't last all that long. He found he could slough it off like a dog shaking off pond water. It was Clive's fault after all. He should never have started a fight on scaffolding. They had stepped off the hilly bank nearby straight onto the top of the building. And Clive soon realised Mick wasn't an engineer standing in for a sick colleague. And he hadn't liked being backed into a corner and threatened. He shouldn't have tried to lash out. If he'd taken the threat like a good boy, accepted his bribe and acknowledged the power of the dirt they had on him, he would be alive and well and enjoying a wealthy retirement.

He was an idiot.

The Captain had told Mick to sort Clive out. Mick didn't ask too many questions, he just did what the boss said. Clive had seen something he shouldn't and that was information enough for Mick. Still, he had been surprised when Gloria Reynolds herself had got her hands dirty. She was the one who made sure Clive was on the St Agnes project so Mick would have access to him. The brief was fairly straightforward: get Clive under their thumb and then get him onside to cover up the dodgy wall ties. Mick knew all about the wall ties. Ed Fielder confessed to being responsible one evening after a few drinks. He'd been shifted into a desk job where he couldn't cause any more trouble. And all Clive had to do was make the best of the bad construction work and keep his mouth shut.

What they hadn't factored in was Clive spotting the faulty building ties right off the bat and threatening to blow the whistle. Talk about making things worse for yourself, Mick thought. So now there were two secrets all stored in the head of one man who didn't seem able to keep his mouth shut.

It would be simple enough to blackmail the fella, Mick reasoned. They had photos of Clive from years ago. The boss was good at acquiring dirt on employees, and this particular dirt was, it seemed, pretty easy to come by (again, Mick didn't ask questions). Mick just needed to wave the photos in his face, threaten him a little, give the bloke a scare, tell him to keep quiet and finish the building, offer him a nice bit of cash for his troubles, and then Mick could go back to his desk having earned a few extra quid himself.

Job done.

Except, in the end, it hadn't worked out like that.

With a weary sigh, Mick lifted his knee and climbed another step.

THIRTY-FOUR

Phil was back in her cupboard again. She waited for Mick to arrive, peering out through the little window in the door and watching as he entered from the stairwell and walked stiffly to his desk in the far corner. Every inch of her wanted to go out and confront him. Every cell in her body wanted to hold a box cutter to his throat and force him to confess. But she had been searching for justice for seven years. She wasn't about to spoil it all now for a moment of satisfaction. She wanted him behind bars for the rest of his life.

She had to gather all the evidence, and that meant finding the folder with Mrs Cooke's letter. It was time to go to the police. Then she would go to the paper and see what stories she could get out of it all without prejudicing a future murder trial. The journalist in her knew she had uncovered one hell of a story. The daughter in her wanted to weep for her father, sent into an unsafe building, met by some Virtua goon.

She had just located the letter when the door opened and

Rhonda came in. Phil snapped the folder shut like a child caught looking for Christmas presents.

'Working hard I see!' said the office manager.

Phil, heart pounding, knew immediately that Rhonda was checking up on her, curious what was keeping an intern so occupied on her final day. Had she seen Phil closing the folder and chucking it on the table, fright in her eyes? How long had she been at the door before she came in? Maybe she had spent a minute peering in.

'It's just that now that I've started it, it's going to really bother me leaving it unfinished,' Phil said, with a mournful smile.

'I wouldn't worry about that,' said Rhonda, eyes piercing her. 'It's going to take a lot more interns to clear this backlog.'

The office manager glanced at the folder on the table and Phil responded by moving to her desk and leaning on the edge, hoping to draw Rhonda's gaze. It worked.

'So, have you thought about applying for a permanent role here, Scarlett?'

'Um...' said Phil, looking up and to the side, as though she was really giving it some thought, 'I am definitely tempted... It seems like it's a great career for someone like me who likes working with people.'

'I'm impressed, I have to say,' said Rhonda.

'Thanks!' said Phil. She was about to humbly shrug off the compliment when Rhonda interrupted.

'Impressed that you spent a whole week doing someone else's job.'

'What?' said Phil, trying to buy herself a moment to think.

'Did you think we wouldn't find out? Scarlett's auntie used to work here. She just texted me to say she was sorry

Scarlett had let us down. As you can imagine, it led to quite a confusing exchange.'

'I–' began Phil.

'What was the plan? You take the intern stipend and she gets the reference for her CV?' Rhonda squinted at her. 'Who are you anyway?'

Phil wondered if her subconscious would save her now. Would it send a story that sounded plausible enough to fool Rhonda? Nothing came to mind, except the thud of a heightened pulse and a feeling that she might just make it if she bolted for the door. She opened her mouth and hoped inspiration would meet her there.

'Rhonda, I'm not really Scarlett Stevens,' she said. Apparently, inspiration was a no-show. 'I'm Phil McGinty... Clive McGinty's daughter. I came here to find out what really happened to my father... and, listen, I think I've figured it out.'

But Rhonda wasn't listening, and before Phil could process what was happening, Rhonda had shut her into the room. Phil heard the lock turn. She ran to the door.

'Rhonda! What are you doing? I'm not here to cause trouble. I just wanted to get some answers about what happened to my dad.'

'I'm calling security,' came the muffled reply from Rhonda as she scowled at Phil through the square of reinforced glass.

'No, Rhonda!' cried Phil, but the office manager was heading to the nearest phone. Phil could feel the floor tremble as Rhonda strode away. Or perhaps it was just her legs quivering with the realisation that she had messed up badly. She had assumed Rhonda would be on her side, a stalwart supporter for truth and order, but Rhonda was a company woman, and now she picked up the phone and dialled. Whether she was calling security or the police was anyone's guess.

Through the window Phil could see Mick walking over to see what was going on. She would have laughed at the ridiculousness of her predicament had she not spotted Rhonda pointing towards her. Phil watched as his face turned to hers, cheeks blotched with rage. She could hear the muffled sounds of Rhonda trying to persuade Mick to stop, but he pushed Rhonda aside and moved so fiercely towards Phil that Phil took a step back.

'I told you to mind your own business,' he yelled, his breath making fog patches on the glass. 'Who the hell are you?'

She should have been scared. God knows, her body was – she could feel it quivering – but the tone of his voice restored her bravery.

'I'll tell you who I am,' she yelled, grabbing the door handle and waggling it furiously, 'I'm Philippa McGinty and I know you killed my dad.'

She started bashing on the glass in the door. Mick took a step back. The sound they were making had begun attracting an audience, the nearest workers standing and craning their necks to see what the fuss was about. And now Dee Dee appeared, desperate for the gossip and yet endearingly concerned about Phil's safety.

'You alright, Scarlett?' she said, eyeing Mick warily. 'What's going on?'

'Let me out!' said Phil.

Dee Dee darted forward, elbowing Mick furiously. Rhonda called out for her to stop, but Dee Dee had already unlocked the door. Phil pushed out from the confines of the airless cupboard and lunged for Mick, who took another step back and gave an incoherent yell.

'What are you doing, Scarlett?' said Dee Dee, shocked. She grabbed Phil by the arm.

'She's not Scarlett,' said Rhonda. 'She's been lying all week long.'

'Aren't you, babes?' said Dee Dee. She looked faintly amused at the notion of anyone faking their way into a low-level internship at a small-to-medium-sized local outsourcing firm. 'Who are you then?'

Phil turned to the, by now, quite sizeable audience that had gathered to witness the drama, many of them wearing a half smile, presumably in case this turned out to be a massive wind-up.

'My name's Philippa McGinty' she said. 'I'm a reporter for the *Aldhill Observer*. I came here to see what I could find out about my dad's death.'

This got everyone's attention. Before that, people had been murmuring among themselves, trying to quietly work out what was happening. Now all ears and eyes were turned to this interloper in their midst.

'Who was your dad, then, babes?' said Dee Dee, apparently the self-designated spokesperson for the assembled crowd.

'She's a fraud and she needs to be chucked out,' shouted Mick. He spat out the words in disgust, but Phil thought she could hear a note of panic in his tone.

'His name was Clive McGinty. His body was found in the cavity wall of the St Agnes school, a Virtua Services construction.'

There was a sharp intake of breath from those of the

crowd who had worked here long enough to know who Clive McGinty was.

'Your dad killed himself,' shouted Mick, before Rhonda raised a hand to silence him.

'It's true he did, hon,' Dee Dee said. 'He wasn't meant to be there that day. You must remember the findings from the coroner?'

Her tone was gentle, as though she was trying to calm a horse in a windy field. Phil felt her anger rising.'

He didn't kill himself,' she said. 'Mick killed him.'

THIRTY-FIVE

Jen had been on her way to find Doug when the call came in from Nandini.

'Security from Virtua just rang. There's some sort of altercation going on and apparently it's to do with the case.'

'I can be there in five,' said Jen. 'Where are you?'

'Be there in ten. Also, Dean wants to talk to you. Apparently, it's important.'

'See you there,' said Jen. 'I'll talk to Dean later.'

Jen wasn't relishing a conversation with the new kid; she always got lumbered with them. It irked her. Then again, most things did these days. It might be easier to simply list the things that didn't annoy her and be done with it.

It would be a short list.

She was in trouble after yesterday. Lee hadn't been happy about her interview with Ed Fielder.

'The point was to speak to everyone calmly, try to get an ID on the victim and then pull certain people in to question later. You could have seriously cocked things up there, Jen.'

Even more annoying: he was right.

She hoped Dean didn't want advice. She couldn't bear giving advice. Plus, what did she know about anything? The only good decision she had ever made was marrying Nate, and even that had ended up costing her a broken heart and a funeral bill.

Jesus, she thought and laughed at the melodrama of her own thoughts. A woman pushing a buggy glanced at her in surprise. *This nutter is laughing to herself.* Jen could see the thought rush through the woman's mind as she hastened along, avoiding eye contact, and Jen had to smother her smile and try to regain a semblance of dignity, raising a hand to the woman in apology.

'Sorry, just remembering a...' but the woman had already walked away.

'You prat,' Jen muttered under her breath and had carried on walking, trying to look less deranged. She was only in her mid-thirties, but she increasingly heard herself speaking out loud or mouthing thoughts like someone struggling with an illness. It was like her inner monologue was trying to leak out of her. Probably in the olden days, the other villagers would be getting ready to tie her thumbs to her toes and toss her in a pond.

And then she was crying.

'Brilliant, just what I need,' she muttered, wiping away the tears. Grieving was such an inconvenience. A *process*. So much easier if she could just go to a yurt somewhere and cry for five days straight before emerging all cried out and ready to live a normal life again. Why did it have to go *on* and *on* like this? And always at the least convenient moments.

She stopped abruptly at the doors to Virtua Services.

Inside, she could see the receptionist tapping away on a keyboard hidden by the high counter.

'Get it together, Collet,' she said, pulling her jacket down and pasting on a smile. She put out a hand and pulled the door open.

THIRTY-SIX

'This is the man who killed my dad,' said Phil, pointing at Mick. She pulled Mrs Cooke's photo from her back pocket and began waving it at the assembled throng. Some of her co-workers stepped back as though she might slap them with it, but Dee Dee took a step forward and peered at the image.

'Not a great photo, is it, babes?'

She grasped it at the sides, trying to look closer, but Phil held on tight, unwilling to hand over something so precious. She thought regretfully of Doug's health and safety report, missing from Dee Dee's in-tray, and Mrs Cooke's letter, still languishing in the buff folder on the pile of boxes.

'Let me get my glasses,' said Dee Dee.

'No!' said Mick. 'This girl is a fake. We don't even know if she is who she's now claiming to be. Forget security, Rhonda, I'm ringing 999.'

'It's the photo you told me about, Dee Dee,' said Phil, keen to get Dee Dee on her team. 'Mrs Cooke's blocked driveway.'

'Mrs Cooke! That was her name!' said Dee Dee as though being reminded of an old friend. She took the photo from Phil and peered at it again before passing it to the person next to her and pointing at Mick. 'There you go, Mick. Deny it all you like, but Scarlett and I both know you were blocking that old lady's driveway.'

'Shut up Dee Dee, you silly bitch' snarled Mick before speaking into the handset. 'Police please… Yes. I'd like to report someone for identity theft and trespassing. She's here now, threatening violence.'

In that moment, watching him lean over the divider, all the anger came back to Phil in one wave of fury.

'You killed him!' she yelled.

She was tall, but he still loomed over her, lean and strong despite his age – yet something in her demeanour, or perhaps her words, caused him to take a step back.

'You killed him, I know you did,' she said.

'Hey, hey!' called Dee Dee, as though trying to break up a fight. She grabbed Phil's arms and held her back. Phil, shaking with rage and sadness, was ready to jump on him and claw the skin from his body.

'She's not wrong, Mick. It is your car,' said Ed Fielder, who had just been passed the photo.

'What?!' spluttered Mick. 'What the hell would you know, Ed?'

'You got me to pay hush money to Mrs Cooke,' said Dee Dee, still holding onto Phil. 'I got a written warning for that. You told everyone I was lying.'

'That's not all, Dee Dee,' said Phil. 'I've got an eyewitness who saw Mick at the building site just after my dad arrived.'

'I think that's enough, Ms McGinty,' said Rhonda, who was still hovering by the lift, waiting for the security guard to make an appearance. 'I suggest you tell the police. Let them handle it.'

'I didn't kill him, the wall did,' Mick said. 'Your dad fell down a wall and died. God knows what he was doing there. The site wasn't signed off. He was an idiot.'

Phil slipped from Dee Dee's grip and launched herself furiously at Mick, but he batted her away like a cat sliding keys off a table – like she weighed nothing at all – and she fell backwards onto her bottom.

'Mick!' cried Dee Dee.

'Stop it!' said Rhonda, grabbing the phone from the desk where Mick had dropped it and picking up the call to the police. 'Yes, please send someone down here as soon as possible...'

Her voice was lost as others joined in, either to berate Mick or to back him up.

'Your dad wasn't who you think he was,' said Mick as Dee Dee helped Phil up from the floor.

'What are you talking about?' said Phil, exasperated. 'Of course he was.'

'We had photos of him... why do you think he was chosen? He was just meant to finish off the work – sort it out so no one got in trouble and everyone got to keep their jobs, that was all. It wasn't much to ask was it? I don' know why he made such a fuss about it. Shouting, effing and jeffing, making a right song and dance about it all.'

'What do you mean... you had photos?' Phil felt a sudden dread.

'Nothing perverted, don't worry,' said Mick holding a hand up as if to placate her, 'just a couple of drug deals – all a long time ago, he had an afro – but enough to call his reputation as a local hero into question.'

'He wasn't a drug dealer what are you talking about?' said Phil. 'His brother died of a drug overdose, he hated drugs.'

'Funny that,' said Mick. 'I heard your dad was the one who sold him the gear in the first place.'

Phil launched herself at Mick again, but he merely grabbed her by the wrists and held them behind her back.

'Now then, I don't hit women,' he said, leaning forward to speak quietly in her ear, 'but if you do that again, I will make an exception.'

'You're lying! He didn't deal drugs,' she cried. 'You're just saying that because he was black.'

The small, slightly quizzical smile on Mick's face was all she needed to tell her she was wrong. There were photos of her dad selling drugs.

He was talking in her ear again, 'If you start mouthing off about any of this, we'll be forced to send the photos to your family and all your friends. Maybe your editor, too. It wouldn't take much to convince him that your dad was killed thanks to a botched drug deal. Addict shoved him into a wall cavity... or he got on the wrong side of his supplier...'

'Fuck you!' she shouted, trying to wrestle free from Mick's iron grip, ready to lunge at him again.

But he caught the expression and shook his head like a teacher warning a child. 'Be sensible,' he instructed. 'I can floor you in a second. It won't be pretty and neither will your face anymore.'

'You killed my dad,' she said.

Mick looked unhappy. 'I told you, I didn't kill him. The wall did.'

'And who pushed him?' she spat.

'Not me,' he said.

'Maybe we should be having this conversation down at the station,' said a voice.

Phil turned. Standing outside the lift was Detective Sergeant Jen Collet.

THIRTY-SEVEN

Jen hadn't been expecting to hear Mick making her life so easy, but there he was, giving a little speech to his co-workers about how he had been with Clive McGinty when he died. Jen was a little sad to see Clive McGinty's daughter Philippa getting caught up in this mess. She had taken a liking to the kid – hadn't needed to spend long with her to recognise that she was clever and capable. Arresting her was going to be a bit of a bummer.

'You need to get the folder out of the cupboard,' said Philippa. 'It proves Mick was at St Agnes's. And somewhere here there's the original health and safety report that proves corporate negligence.'

Nandini arrived and read them both their rights while Jen went in search of the folder. She had been wondering what possible connection Mick could have with Clive, but from what Philippa said, it was all just a mundane story of arse-covering. Now she just had to get him to confess to killing the man in the wall and she'd have the whole thing wrapped up. She thought maybe she might ask for another week off once it was all sorted. She could see mountains of pizza boxes and sobbing on the sofa in her future and the thought appealed to her.

'There's nothing there,' she told Phil when she emerged.

'What?' said Phil. 'Then someone must have taken it. You need to search everyone.'

'Let's talk about this properly down at the station,' suggested Jen.

'No!' said Phil. 'You need to find it!'

Phil wriggled to turn away from Nandini's handcuffs, but Nandini simply grasped her forcefully and got the cuffs on.

Jen sighed, feeling the dry air of the light-bleached office tickle her throat; wishing she could tumble onto her sofa and bury her head under a cushion. 'We'll talk at the station,' she said.

They were in the incident room. Petra, standing like an awkward doorman in one corner; Lee Hudson, loafing, buttocks wedged against the edge of a desk in another. Jen and Nandini updated everyone on their latest findings – Grant and Dean swivelling their chairs around to contribute.

'And this fella – Mick Tanner – was kicking off in the office when you got there, right?' said Lee.

'That's right, and the things he was saying suggest he might have been at the scene on the day of Clive's death, although sadly I don't think we can consider it any kind of confession,' said Jen. 'He claimed the wall did it.'

'And in the interview room he said nothing at all,' added Nandini. 'Thanks to the very expensive brief who slithered in and told him to keep schtum.'

'So, what evidence do we have on Mick?' said Petra.

'Not enough,' admitted Jen. 'We've got a photograph that potentially places Mick – or at least his van – near the St Agnes school site on the day of the murder. Nandini's checking if Virtua kept logs of who used the cars on particular days.'

She nodded her head towards Nandini who gave a little salute with two fingers.

'I've also spoken to Clive McGinty's daughter,' said Jen.

By now they had all heard about Phil McGinty's escapades. Jen paused. What she was going to say next could well get her into a heap of political bullshit she would rather avoid.

'She says she has a witness – Simon Barker – who was a teacher at St Agnes's the day Clive McGinty went to the site. He saw a man matching Mick's description going across onto the scaffolding after Clive.'

Petra and Lee both raised their eyebrows as the importance of this news sank in. Jen knew what they'd be thinking: why hadn't he been interviewed at the time? She carried on. *In for a penny, in for a pound.*

'Apparently, he contacted the police at the time, but no one ever got back to him and he was away when the inquest was being held.'

Lee pinched the bridge of his nose and hung his head like a man who could do without this hassle.

'I assume you're sending someone over to speak to him?' Petra said, turning her hawk-eyes to Lee.

The message wasn't lost on Jen, and she doubted anyone else missed it either: Lee was CIO on the man in the wall case, and yet everything Jen was telling them appeared to be news to him as much as it was to Petra.

'Yes, that's right,' said Lee, attempting to cover his surprise smoothly.

'We've also got Dee Dee – Deidre Dabrowski,' said Jen. She looked at Lee, wondering if he knew enough about the case to take over.

'Yes, tell the boss about Dee Dee,' said Lee, waving a hand like a benevolent emperor.

'She's Mick's colleague. She says he convinced her to pay twenty grand hush money to a woman who had her drive blocked in by his van on the day of Clive McGinty's death. She got a warning for it, so it is on her personal record.'

For the sake of diplomacy, Jen had yet to use the word 'murder' in connection with Clive McGinty, but it was only a matter of time. The top brass would just have to get over themselves – and whichever senior local dignitaries and leaders they offended would just have to get over themselves too. In fact, it would be nice to have a list of those people – the ones who were about to get really cross about this, the ones who sighed any time Clive McGinty's name was mentioned – because, she figured, they were the ones who most needed investigating themselves.

'Dee Dee sounds promising,' said Petra.

'Possibly not. Her testimony doesn't look good for Mick – but I can't see it doing us that many favours.'

Petra gave Jen a look. 'Oh?'

'She's not exactly an ideal witness. Any half-competent barrister would be able to discredit her. She's the office gossip and she's had a number of other warnings at work. We only have her word that Mick told her to pay the money.'

'And if the lawyer doesn't manage to discredit her, she'll do it herself by talking the judge's ear off or inviting the jury out for a curry,' said Nandini.

It was obvious from Nandini's tone that she liked Dee Dee very much, even if the woman wasn't likely to win any 'most credible witness' awards any time soon.

'I'm still not convinced Doug Graves is innocent in all this,' said Jen. 'Andrew may have misremembered, but he says he once sent Pennywise to Doug's address.'

'But we have nothing else on him beyond the dodgy health and safety ...' said Lee. 'Right?'

So close, thought Jen. For one brief sentence, he had almost managed to sound like he was on top of the case. He should have left off the question mark.

'Right,' she agreed. 'Seven years ago, he gave evidence that the health and safety report had not been written yet, which was why – he claimed – Clive was at fault for being on site at all that day. However, Andrew Templeton-Dunbar just signed a statement saying he saw Gloria Reynolds, the CEO, waving a signed off health and safety report written by Doug a few days before Clive went on site.'

'Can we prove that?' said Petra.

'Not yet,' said Jen, wishing Lee was the one giving the bad news. 'And then there's *another* report that Philippa McGinty claims she found. This one was a failed HSO inspection. She said it had information on it about missing wall ties.'

'Wait, what?!' said Lee, and Jen wanted to take him to one side and say, *'You do remember that you're in charge here, right?'*

Instead, she answered him. 'Yep. That's what she says. The report said the building wasn't safe. I've got a full statement from her. She said it was dated 31 July. So it's likely the original report.'

'So we've got two health and safety reports,' explained

Nandini. 'The first saying the building was a nightmare – abandon hope all ye who enter here – the second saying it was sound as houses. Both written within days of each other by the same health and safety officer.'

'Yep,' said Jen. 'Except we haven't: we can't find either report. Virtua insisted during the inquest that there hadn't even been a health and safety inspection.'

'So we've got two missing reports neither of which officially exist,' said Petra.

'And if Miss McGinty really did see the original report, someone obviously thought it was worth holding onto,' said Jen.

'Presumably some kind of leverage,' suggested Petra, and Jen was pleased to see that at least one of her senior detectives was able to follow a thought to its logical conclusion.

'Yes ma'am. Could be,' she said. 'Seems there's someone in the office blackmailing everyone. Couple of people we spoke to mentioned it. Seems like there's a culture of employees ratting out their colleagues...'

'Just not to the police,' supplied Nandini.

'And what about the HSO report for Helenswood?' asked Petra.

'Nothing so far,' said Jen. 'Though we know Ed Fielder was the site manager at Helenswood and Philippa is insisting that Fielder was also listed as the site manager in charge at St Agnes's on this missing HSO report.'

'They got pixies in there or something?' said Lee. 'Some sort of Bermuda Triangle but for paperwork?'

'Things certainly go astray at this company, don't they?' observed Petra.

Dean cleared his throat. It was so quiet that most people wouldn't have noticed, but Jen heard it. It was the sound of someone junior plucking up the courage to say something that might be important.

'Phil – I mean Philippa – McGinty mentioned that they had been sorting complaints letters to dispose of ahead of an independent audit.'

All eyes turned to him.

'And how do you know that?' said Lee and Jen wondered the same. Dean had been nowhere near Philippa as far as she knew.

'We're old friends,' said Dean, looking down in embarrassment. 'She rang me a few days ago asking if it was a criminal offence.'

'And you didn't think to mention it sooner?' said Lee.

Jen would have felt sorry for Dean if she hadn't been annoyed at him herself.

'Did you not think the news that Clive McGinty's daughter was poking her nose round Virtua Services might be something to share with the group, Dean?' Jen said incredulously.

'I didn't know she was talking about Virtua,' mumbled Dean. 'She's always up to something. It was a hypothetical question and I didn't ask for details.'

He's scared of her, Jen realised. And probably in love, poor sod. Now she did feel sorry for him.

'So we know they've been destroying things,' she said. 'McGinty also mentioned a letter from Mrs Cooke – the woman who was apparently paid 20k. But that letter was also missing when I went to look for it.'

'And what about our other victim?' said Petra, peering down her nose at Jen. 'Any more information on Pennywise? Any connection to Clive McGinty?'

Now she asks, thought Jen. How much time had they wasted trying desperately not to link these cases?

'We're still going through staff records from the various agencies that supplied labourers to Virtua,' said Nandini. 'He wasn't one of their direct employees, that's for sure.'

'And there are still some other leads to explore,' said Jen. 'Doug Graves, for one. We know that he left Virtua shortly after Clive died and rumours around the office are that he had tried to kill himself.'

'Guilty conscience?' said Lee. 'Can't see it myself.'

'Ed Fielder also has motive,' said Petra.

'Let's bring them in for questioning,' said Petra. 'If Fielder is as unhelpful this time, arrest him.'

'And then there's these two possible eyewitnesses,' said Jen.

'Yes,' said Petra. 'Shame we didn't know about those sooner.'

Dean squirmed a little and Jen turned to him suspiciously. Was that what he wanted to talk to her about? *I'm going to kill him,* she thought.

'What shall we do with Mick Tanner and the McGinty kid?' said Lee.

'I think Mr Tanner can go for now,' said Petra. 'Let's see what else we can find on him. And let's speak to the teacher and the lady with the blocked driveway. We need to establish if the two cases are indeed linked, but let us use some discretion here. I don't need to state the obvious, do I? If we missed things in the first investigation, we need to be very sure we have all our ducks in a row before the press finds out. Bad enough that Philippa McGinty has been looking into it all... Perhaps you could speak to her, Jen? I believe you have a good relationship? Maybe encourage her to keep this under her hat for the sake of her father's investigation?'

Jen wondered if Petra felt at all grubby trying to guilt a young woman into silence by using her dead father.

'Yes, I'll speak to her,' said Jen, holding Petra's gaze until the other woman nodded slightly and pretended to be busy with some nearby papers.

'I'd like to get Andrew Templeton-Dunbar in for questioning too,' Jen continued. 'I think he knows more than he's letting on. But first, let's find out if Doug and our victim were actually roomies.'

'Please never say roomies again,' said Nandini.

'I regretted it immediately,' said Jen.

'I'll come with,' said Lee.

'Great,' lied Jen.

Jen buzzed the apartment building just as her phone rang.

'Just had Ryan Sharman on the phone,' Nandini said.

'Ah yes,' said Jen, giving Lee a nod so that he knew to pay attention. 'The pale-faced man-child in the bad suit. What did he want?'

'He said he'd been talking to one of their regulars – not Babycakes – and he knew who our victim was immediately.' Jen could hear her reading off her notebook. 'Tommy "Pennywise" Pearce, a casual labourer. Said he thinks he was sleeping rough and came to the arcade, "for the company and to keep warm as much as anything". Ryan's sending an old photo from their wall of winners. I'll forward it to you. Hang on, it's just come in.'

Jen hung up and opened her emails. She located a photo

of a shaggy-haired man with a lopsided grin holding up a fan of winning tickets and showed it to Lee.

'What would he have got for those, do you reckon?' said Lee.

'Probably not much more than a bag of rubbery sweets,' Jen assessed. 'The exchange rate on Luckyland tickets is woeful.'

Lee pressed the doorbell again.

Doug answered on the third buzz, peering out with bleary eyes.

'What do you want? I'm hanging,' he said.

'Won't take a minute?' Jen said. 'Just a few questions down at the station.'

Doug took a moment to decide, leaning on the door frame with heavy regret.

'I need something to eat,' he said. 'Ask me what you want here or arrest me.'

He turned and walked into his flat leaving the door open for them to follow.

Jen glanced at Lee who shrugged and followed Doug in.

'You know your rights, Doug?' said Jen, before explaining them.

Doug grunted and began making himself a fry up in the tiny kitchen area of his living space, pulling out strips of streaky bacon with the same focused energy he brought to everything he did. Even with a hangover he couldn't help rushing, Jen realised.

'Tommy Pearce,' she said, flashing up the photo from her phone, and watching as his shoulders tensed the smallest amount, his face in shadow, unreadable. 'You used to live with him, right?'

He shrugged. 'No idea. I've lived with a lot of people.'

'I think you'd remember this one,' said Lee. 'Living here in this tiny flat, you'd be arse cheek to arse cheek most of the time.'

'I'm bad with names... and faces.' Doug shrugged again. He was moving about the workspace, buzzing from toaster to fridge to frying pan. He filled the kettle. 'Want a brew?'

'Like Lee said, I think you'll remember this particular housemate, Doug,' said Jen. 'Especially as he went missing not long after he lived with you and his dead body was found the other day down a wall cavity of a building you worked on. A building that had the wrong wall ties... Just like the St Agnes school where you also worked, and where Clive McGinty was found. The same building that you wrote two different health and safety reports for.'

Doug carried on frying bacon, turning it over with a fork as the fat sizzled. Jen watched the muscle in his jaw travel stiffly upwards.

'This housemate of yours had a Prints To Go top from the homeless shelter you worked at. The one you started working for shortly after Clive McGinty was killed.'

'You tried to top yourself around then, didn't you, Dougie?' said Lee. 'Bit out of character for you. What was it? Guilty conscience?'

'I didn't try to top myself,' said Doug, still focused on his food, his body tense with potential energy.

'Well, something put you in hospital with an overdose, Doug,' said Lee.

'Lee,' said Jen. He knew better than to pursue this without taking Doug in.

'I didn't try to kill myself,' said Doug, turning abruptly. He lifted the greasy fork like a weapon. 'He tried to kill me.'

And Lee reached over, took a slice of bacon and, grinning, ate it.

'I think perhaps we should talk about this down at the station.' said Jen.

Jen normally did the interviews.

'I do the interviews,' she said. Adding, with no small amount of churlishness. 'Plus, I arrested him.'

'We'll be able to get more out of him', said Lee with a wink, as though Jen and Nandini lacked the necessary chromosomes.

It didn't escape Jen's notice that Lee was suddenly paying an interest in the case. Talk about letting everyone else do the heavy lifting. He wasn't the only one who was paying the case more attention now it was in the press.

'Looks like you've got our man,' Petra said, although Jen wasn't sure who she was referring to. Mick or Doug?

In the event, Lee and Grant got absolutely nothing out of Doug: his very expensive solicitor made sure of that. The same suited and booted London-type had reappeared, fresh from his stint silencing Mick, to make sure the already taciturn Doug also kept his mouth shut.

'I wonder who's paying him,' said Nandini, watching the solicitor through the plastic blinds as he headed to his very smart Mercedes. 'His suit cost more than my car.'

'So,' said Jen, 'what now?'

'We need evidence,' said Lee.

Jen resisted the urge to say, 'Oh yeah, I hadn't thought of that,' and instead replied: 'We're looking through the paperwork as we speak,' and went to get a coffee.

When she returned, she was feeling a little less cross

about the loss of the Doug interview. He wouldn't have answered her questions either, so what did it matter if Lee wanted to butt in? But still, she would have liked to look him in the eye when she asked him if he had killed Clive McGinty and Tommy Pearce. She'd have liked to see that muscle pop from his jaw as he said 'No comment,' for the fortieth time. She approached Lee's desk and placed a mug down before him, grey liquid sloping side to side. A peace offering. Or, more accurately, a bribe: you stay there and drink this, and I'll do the police work.

'Andrew's coming in to give a statement,' she said. 'OK if Dean and Nandini take it?'

'Sounds good,' said Lee. 'Can't see some posh bloke doing this, can you? He'd just bury a body under his swimming pool.'

'And I'd like to have a word with Rhonda Whitford,' she said. 'We didn't get a chance to speak to her yesterday.' Jen had spotted her several times, flitting around like a moth looking for moonlight. 'She was Gloria's PA at the time. She might know how much Gloria knew about these wall ties.'

'Go for it,' said Lee. 'I've sent Grant out to pick up your friend Ed Fielder. Best you're out the way when he comes in. I get the impression he's not your biggest fan.'

'I'll be weeping into my pillow tonight,' said Jen.

Probably true, she thought with an inward sigh.

THIRTY-EIGHT

Phil arrived at Simon's breathless and flustered thanks to her earlier adventures with the law. Virtua had declined to press charges against her; evidently, pursuing the daughter of Clive McGinty through the criminal system wasn't going to be a good look for them. Better to sweep it under the carpet than add it to the company's roster of PR nightmares. She had told the police (mostly) everything she knew that might prove useful, and then Jen Collet had arrived to try to stop her going straight to her boss and telling him everything.

Angela had come to collect her from the station. She had been impressed with her daughter's life choices.

'You used a week of your holiday to intern in a cupboard so you could find out more about Clive's death?' she said. 'I couldn't be more proud.'

Her mum had squeezed her arm then, and Phil knew that under the sarcasm, she really was proud.

As it was, Phil didn't have time to call Adam Jenkins, editor. She needed to speak to her eyewitness.

She scurried up the path as quickly as she could, rapping

neatly on the front door and taking a step back in anticipation of Simon appearing. She was looking forward to seeing him: he was an oasis of calm in her weird life. But something wasn't right. She frowned. No one answered the door. No light came on in the gloomy hallway. No face appeared at the frosted glass.

She rang the doorbell this time and heard as the first few bars of classical music chimed from the speaker. The tune went on for an age, and Phil wondered – not for the first time – how they could bear to live with it day in day out.

Still no one.

Stepping back further away from the house, Phil peered up at the first floor. The house languished in late afternoon gloom, the scalding sun of the past week apparently having taken a sudden, last minute, dive for cover. She took out her phone and dialled Simon's number. It went to voicemail. She hung up before the beep and tried it again, moving up towards the living room window and cupping her hand onto the glass to peer in.

Inside, something lit up.

Simon's phone.

Wherever he was, he didn't have his phone with him. Phil felt a strange dread trickle along her spine like snow down a hoodie. She shivered. Could something have happened to them? Perhaps they had gone away and simply not told her? But Simon had texted her just a few hours ago to say he was determined to join her for their stakeout.

'They're not here, I'm afraid,' said a voice.

Phil turned to see a forty-something woman in a slouchy cardigan and Ugg boots. The neighbour. She gathered the cardigan around her to ward off the encroaching chill, and stopped en route to the recycling bin with a couple of wine bottles clutched between the fingers of her right hand.

'Oh, how strange! Simon was expecting me,' said Phil.

She made her voice as cheerful and unthreatening as possible so the woman didn't take fright at a stranger banging on her neighbour's door.

'He was rushed to hospital,' the woman said, wobbling slightly, slurring a little. 'Suspected heart attack. Debbie went with him.'

The hospital was a maze of white corridors. It took Phil quite some time to locate the right ward – and that was only after she'd stopped to enquire at the help desk manned by two cheerful elderly women volunteers clutching sandwiches. Eventually, she found him.

'How are you, Simon?' she said.

The only answer was the soft blip of the machine. Simon lay there asleep, his chest artificially inflating, the sounds of sucking and whooshing making a strange kind of music as they mingled with the rhythmic beeps from the monitor.

Phil didn't really know what to do. She touched his hand briefly but that felt strangely personal. They had not been on such easy terms – he was still her elder and better, and touching him now, as he lay there prone and helpless seemed somehow disrespectful. Yet, she didn't want him thinking he was alone.

His wife, Debbie, had taken Phil's arrival as the perfect opportunity for a quick pitstop ('I'll just pop to the lavatory and get myself a cup of tea,' she said before darting off.) So now Phil was alone with Simon, feeling a bit like a pupil seeing a teacher outside of school. They had only just met and yet she already felt as though their time together chasing a silly ghost had united them: her partner on this ridiculous manhunt. So she made a decision: she took hold of his hand and hoped he would forgive her the liberty.

She sat for a while in awkward silence – what do you say to unconscious people? – before managing a whispered, 'I promise I'll find the Poo Fiend,' which felt both ridiculous and yet somehow important, as though Simon's spirit would not be able to move on without this vital reassurance.

Debbie, bustling in with 'a few bits' from the shop, including a packet of sweets for Phil (presumably, she was under the illusion Phil was ten), sipped a coffee and told her what had happened.

'It was the strangest thing,' she said. 'He just clutched at his arm and said, "I don't feel right." And then he collapsed in a heap on the floor. Just like that!'

She said it like she was recounting a magic trick. It must be shock, thought Phil. Either that, or Debbie was really not that into Simon. Phil had barely seen her this week. She was always off at some committee meeting or working late or heading off to bed early. It seemed as though the two led separate lives. Yes, Debbie was probably bored to tears with her husband, Phil decided.

Debbie started to cry.

'Oh no, don't cry,' said Phil idiotically. She mentally kicked herself before ploughing on. 'I'm sure he'll be ok.'

Debbie nodded dumbly and wiped the tears away, trying to smile.

'Yes, I think so,' she said, as though the two of them believing it would be enough to see him through.

A dark thought belched up through the sadness: he's my only eyewitness. What if he dies? Phil shook her head a little as though hoping to evict the thought. Now was not the time to think of herself. Simon was her only witness, but witness to what? To the fact that her father had met someone on site after all. Perhaps. But it was a long time ago now. There was every chance Simon had misremembered that day. And what good did it do her, anyway? She couldn't see Mick confessing to anything. They had no other evidence, no DNA to link Mick to the crime scene. Before long, rumours would get out about Clive's past life as a dealer, and Phil would be left with even less than she had started with.

She started to wonder how best to leave without seeming callous, whilst also not lingering on past her welcome. She already felt as though she was encroaching, and visiting time was long over. She only got in by fibbing that she was Simon's daughter. Straight out of jail for identity theft and she was back at it again. Then a nurse came in and made things simple by sending her politely packing, and Phil jumped up to leave like the chair had pinched her bottom.

'I'll call in tomorrow, if that's ok?' she said, giving Debbie a small smile.

'Of course, come whenever you like,' said Debbie 'He thinks you're marvellous.'

THIRTY-NINE

Jen knocked on Rhonda's door. She had been let into the communal entrance by a young man coming into the downstairs flat. The house was a large Victorian mansion converted into separate apartments with a shared hallway and main staircase, both in a sorry state from years of neglect. There are probably Minton tiles under that carpet, thought Jen as she entered. Grandeur hidden by beige plastic. Now the floor was mainly dirt and grit, carrying a faint whiff of fox wee walked in from the front porch. When she first moved to Aldhill she had been amazed not just by the urban foxes (keen to make the world their toilet), but also by the urban badgers, who roamed the streets quite brazenly through the evenings, lumbering like drunken bowlegged cowboys along the pavements and chattering loudly outside her window at night.

'She's not in.'

Jen turned and saw a woman of indiscernible ethnicity poking her head out of the doorway of the neighbouring flat.

She was decked out with large hoop earrings and an array of rings and statement necklaces – not to mention a full face of heavy makeup and burnt umber skin.

'She's gone out,' the woman said.

'Ah shame, thanks,' said Jen, smiling.

'Anything I can help with?' said the woman, curiosity emanating from her like a perfume. The kind of woman who likes to talk, thought Jen.

'I'm Detective Sergeant Jen Collet,' she said. 'I'm trying to track down an ex-colleague of Rhonda's. I was hoping she might know something.'

'One of her boyfriends, was it?' said the woman, opening the door wider, interest clearly piqued. 'She tends to get through them.'

Jen took a second to process that and the woman continued talking. 'There's the slob, the scary one, the posh one and the boy toy. Come in if you like. I don't have to be gone for at least fifteen at a push. Want a cuppa?'

Jen realised that yes she did want a cuppa. She was also strangely curious about Rhonda's exciting-sounding roster of lovers, so far away from the life Jen had imagined for the office manager. God bless the chatty neighbour, she thought. She'd take one of them over a shrugger any day of the week.

'Lovely,' she said, and stepped into the flat.

The cup of tea looked weaker than gnat's piddle. Jen left it on the table while the neighbour – Carly – spilled the beans on her neighbour's love life. Jen had told her the year they were looking at and Carly made her best guess as to who Rhonda was seeing at the time.

'Now let's see. What did I say again?' A plump British Blue cat, wove itself briefly around Jen's legs before deciding the behaviour was beneath it. It sashayed over to the radiator and regarded her with disapproving cornflower eyes.

'I think it was the slob, the scary one, the posh one and... the boy toy?' said Jen.

'Oh yes, that's right,' agreed Carly. She looked at the cat, which began licking itself with frantic disdain, as though hoping to divest itself of all hair and skin along with the dirt. 'She's a prim madam. She's Rhonda's cat, but I let her come in during the day if she bangs her head on the door enough.'

Jen wasn't really paying attention. *Rhonda* had a rich love life? Who could have guessed?

'I never understood the appeal of a cat like that,' said Carly. 'Give me a bog-standard mog any day.'

Bog-standard mog.

Nate would probably say that was a good band name. She used to collect them for him, bring home little phrases she heard through her day for him to pass judgment on. But now she had to make her own decisions about band names. Another job he had left for her to do.

'So about the boyfriends... What about the posh one?' she said.

'I didn't really hear much about that one. A work colleague, apparently. It was an affair. Rhonda said he wouldn't leave his wife. I never met him.'

Andrew and Rhonda? Could it be?

'Did you get his name?'

'It wasn't something memorable. Was it Charles or Edward or something like that? Something normal, you know?'

'Andrew?'

'Could be. One of the princes.'

'What about the scary one?'

'Do you know, I can't remember if that was the same one as the posh one. It was years ago now. You lose track, don't you?'

She said it as though Rhonda's life was a soap opera whose plot she had lost a grip on.

'I know he was tall and strong. I only saw him once at a distance, but I could see that. He seemed a lot older than Rhonda. Could have been her dad almost. But the next one only looked about twenty-five, so she obviously wasn't too fussy. Beggars can't be choosers, I suppose. Mind you, he was a hunk. Proper muscles. She was definitely punching above her weight with that one. He didn't last long either – they never do. I think he must have had a blow to his head and finally come to his senses. Can't imagine what he thought he was playing at being with her. He could have had any woman in the local area. You could crack walnuts in those arse cheeks.'

She stared at the cat, her eyes glazed, presumably lost in a reverie in which a youthful hunk provided a constant supply of omega-3 fatty acids from his rear end.

'I mean, there's a fella who never skips leg day. He has thighs like a –'

'OK,' said Jen, interrupting before Carly subjected her to a simile. She did not want to hear what Carly thought his thighs were like. Although, judging by her hands, which were raised mid-charade, there would probably be a joint of meat involved. 'And did she ever mention an altercation at work?' she said, hoping to bring Carly's mind back from buttock walnuts and thigh similes.

'I mean, there's always some drama or other with Rhonda, isn't there?'

'Is there?'

'Well, what with her job and all. Head of human resources means dealing with a lot of angry workers.'

'Oh?'

Head of HR. She wondered if Carly had got the wrong end of the stick or if Rhonda had been liberal with the truth.

'Yes, always something going on. And that scary boyfriend of hers. He caused a *lot* of drama. I heard them shouting a few times. Luckily, it didn't last long.'

'Do you think he was violent?' Jen asked.

'Oh, I expect so, yes,' said Carly, with perfect equanimity. 'That's the impression I got. I never saw her with any bruises, mind you. But they know how to do it so you don't, don't they?'

'Don't what?'

'Don't see the bruises.'

'So you never saw any bruises on her?' said Jen, her brain beginning to spin.

'No, but that doesn't mean there weren't any. She told me he was in the navy, *before*, you know. They can be cruel, can't they? Seafaring folk.'

This was news to Jen. *Is that a thing?* Andrew had been in the navy, she remembered. Was he really the type to have affairs with his employees? His LinkedIn profile claimed he always 'put humans at the heart of everything he did'. Perhaps that was a cry for help, not a mission statement.

'What was his name, do you know?' Jen asked.

Carly took a slurp of tea. The cat came and joined her, deigning to perch on her lap, and Carly rested her cup on its fluffy back. 'They worked together,' she continued. 'That's how they met. But like I say, it didn't last. She was scared of him, I swear to god. Rhonda's a kind soul. She'll do anything for anyone. She likes things just so, and she's not too proud to do whatever it takes to get things running. She'd clean the toilets at that company if they told her it would be helpful. She's good like that. Loyal to a fault. A good egg my dad would call her.'

'But you can't remember the name of this older chap?' Jen said.

Her head was aching. Two weeks spent crying over old episodes of *House* had stolen some of her stamina, and now she was struggling to make it through a normal working day. Without thinking, she sipped her tea and was rewarded with a mouthful of something scalding, sweet and feeble all in one. She swallowed regretfully.

'No,' replied Carly. 'What was it the rope said? I'm a frayed knot.' At this, Carly laughed. Then she started coughing. A smoker's cough, perhaps, or the remnants of a chest infection.

Jen was about to stand up and thank her for her time, when Carly suddenly sat up straight – a meerkat spotting a puff adder – and the cat jumped off her lap at the indignity.

'I think it began with an M...' she said, like a medium getting a message from the other side. She slouched back down again, looking off to one side, tapping her mug with a nail. 'Or maybe an A... I can't remember now. So frustrating! It's on the tip of my–.'

Jen jumped a little as Carly shouted, 'NICK! That's it. It was Nick.'

Jen, disappointed it wasn't Andrew, was writing the name down in her notebook when Carly said, 'Or was it Mike?'

It was only after Jen had thanked her for being so helpful and had asked her to come down to the station to give a written statement, after she had begun walking towards the door to head out for some much-needed paracetamol, that Carly had shouted once more:

'MICK! It was Mick.'

FORTY

Mick climbed out of the cab. He'd barely had a chance for a shower and shit before the summons came in. He considered ignoring it, especially now the police were on to him, but he couldn't risk it. Or, more truthfully, he didn't have a choice. To ignore it was to expose himself to the whims of a maniac.

The female detective who arrested him (some makeup and a comb through the hair and she'd be halfway attractive), had been keen to let him know their interest in him hadn't ended. But once his lawyer had arrived, Mick had taken the silent option and now he was feeling surprisingly confident about the whole thing. Well, he would if he could sort out this final loose end.

One eyewitness had very conveniently had a heart attack (nothing to do with him or the boss. Not as far as he was aware, anyway. Just a piece of good luck in an otherwise cursed project). And the old lady had been encouraged to take her dogs and her caravan on a nice long trip to somewhere isolated until the fuss died down. His solicitor – one of the boss's snappy suited sharks from London – seemed sure he had nothing to worry about given the evidence they had been presented with so far. Beyond Mick's own foolish outburst in the office, it amounted to nothing much at all.

And his outburst remained an embarrassment. The girl had really got to him. Her shiny young face all screwed up in anger, anger directed entirely at him. So much sadness and fury in her that it had staggered him. She had broken his heart a little – she had reminded him of his granddaughter – and in return that had made him angry. He hadn't meant to hit her with such force, but it was her own fault for standing there accusing him of being the sort of monster who kills a young girl's father in cold blood.

He got out of the cab wearily and looked up at the building block. He double-checked the address. This was the place. An old Victorian mansion converted into bedsits. House of multi-occupancy, they called them. Shitholes, Mick called them. A gust of wind ruffled his hair. The weather was turning at last, finally remembering it was time for autumn, and although it was still warm, soon the storms would arrive and apartments near the sea front would be battered and bruised by the onslaught. Those further back, like this one, would sit in corridors of drizzle, northerly winds howling round the render. Mick was grateful for his flat up on the outskirts of town. He may not have a sea view, but he could go out his front door without a pitched battle with Storm What's-her-name.

He took another moment to collect himself. Was there anything that could prepare him for this meeting? Nothing beyond a cyanide capsule ready and waiting in one of his crowns. Too late for that now, unfortunately. He rang the bell.

FORTY-ONE

Phil watched as the dark sea crept its way to shore before sucking the stones back towards the water, a greedy child grasping at fallen piñata sweets. She'd taken a bus back into town then headed to Beachy Shed to buy a coffee and was sipping at it now as she sat on the cool pebbles. Tomorrow wasn't going to be as hot as the rest of the week. She had missed the window of sunshine and instead found only darkness.

She had a hangover. Not from drinking, but from lack of sleep and sadness. She felt jet-lagged and sick. The big moment of triumph she had hoped for had yet to arrive. She had given herself a week to try to get to the truth of her father's death, and she had done it. *Maybe*. Doubt niggled at her. Perhaps she was just suffering from the inevitable anticlimax. The police were handling it now and there would be no cathartic moment of taking Mick out into the streets and parading him before a crowd. No chopping off his head or hanging him from a rope. No lopping off his balls and feeding them to his screaming mouth.

What good would it do, anyway? Her dad was still as dead as he always was, and that was only getting worse as each day passed. There would be no coming back from it now. And really, what had she solved? Mick had murdered Clive, right? But why? This was no simple crime of passion. There hadn't been a normal argument followed by a horrible mishap. Mick had said so himself: he had been there to blackmail Clive. Presumably, Clive just needed to finish off the project like a good boy and save Virtua the trouble and expense of fixing their mistakes. But he had refused, and how she wished he hadn't. If she could change anything, it would be Clive's stubborn refusal to avoid his fate.

So he said no and Mick had silenced him. But why *kill* him? If blackmailing him didn't work, all they needed to do was find another, more corruptible builder and they could simply fire him from the project and ridicule him if he tried to blow the whistle. They already had a corrupt health and safety officer onside. They probably had people at the council on the payroll, too. Why kill Clive?

It didn't make sense.

Or maybe it just didn't make sense to *her*. She picked up a stone and tossed it halfheartedly towards the sea. Mick had mentioned photos of her father selling drugs. Hardly a huge deal, she thought. What was the worst that could happen? *Local hero falls from grace.* Sure, the papers might have fun with it, but anyone who knew Clive would have forgiven him in a heartbeat. He must have known that.

She hoped he knew that.

She replayed Mick's outburst in her mind and watched as he was led away, protesting his innocence. He seemed so determined he hadn't done it and Phil was hardly expecting him to provide a full confession, but shouldn't he at least have sounded more defensive? Instead, he seemed... irritated. Exasperated, even. Simon had seen Mick follow her dad onto the building site, and – before the police arrived and he remembered his right to remain silent – Mick admitted he was there, but he had responded to Phil's accusations with something akin to a tut. She had expected a violent, hissing denial, or else a full confession. Mick's vibe felt more like a maths teacher rolling his eyes at a latecomer.

She wondered what had happened after they had all left. Was the rest of the day a write-off for the Virtua team? All of them gathered round the kitchenette while Dee Dee told the story over and over – who had said what, who had seen what, who had done what. They were loving it, she was sure. She didn't blame them. She wondered if Jamie came in to speak to them about it all. Or maybe Gloria descended from on high to share the message herself in person. 'Dearly beloveds, we are gathered here today, to let you know that we're responsible for two dangerous schools and your co-worker might be a murderer... But on the bright side, our contract was nearly up, anyway.'

They would be doing an awful lot of firefighting, she imagined. The police would be descending on the building to find out everything they knew. She pictured Jamie clutching a cooling latte, frozen brow straining to form a crease, watching as her piles of crap were hefted into boxes and escorted from the building. She didn't envy the poor officers having to sift through that paperwork. Those few days of it had nearly driven her mad.

She pulled out her phone, a habit more than a conscious decision, and checked her messages. Dean Martin had messaged to ask if she was OK and then sent three more to asking her to call him after leaving three missed calls. Her friend EJ had sent her a series of texts wanting to know where she had vanished to. Her mother and gran had sent some silly notes to the family group, her brother had written 'idk' to a query about his evening plans. It was strange to see these reminders of a previous life, as though they belonged to someone Phil no longer knew. She had inhabited Scarlett's world for so many days that discovering her old life still existed was almost a surprise.

There was a reminder of reality thanks to an email from Adam Jenkins, editor, giving her a series of assignments for Monday morning, including a trip to a nearby beach to photograph a woman who had crowdfunded a batch of water quality test kits so she could measure sewage levels in the sea. Better than being stuck in a cupboard, she supposed.

She was still holding her phone when it started ringing.

Adam Jenkins' face popped up, all ginger beard and scruffy hair.

'So who went into the cupboard after you left it?' he said after she had filled him in on her week's adventures.

The question surprised her. She had been expecting a telling off for bringing their trade into disrepute, or criticism for getting caught. She could imagine any number of reproaches he could make for recklessness, idiocy or incompetence. Instead, he wanted to know what happened to the evidence she had uncovered and then lost. And she was amazed she hadn't been thinking about it more. Because he was right, that was the big question: who took the letter from the cupboard?

She racked her brain. Had Dee Dee gone in? She didn't think so. She thought of Dee Dee and Rhonda and Ed, all coming over after Mick had flattened her. Who had helped her up? Dee Dee, she thought. Ed had gone over to hold Mick back and prevent him from doing anything worse.

'Maybe Rhonda went in,' she said.

'Well, looks like you might need to have a word with Rhonda then, because without it, you don't have much to go on' he said. 'I'll see you on Monday, bright and early for a bollocking.'

He hung up and her email app reappeared. She was about to lock her phone when she spotted a message nestled in between a note about the latest amateur dramatic Treble theatre production and an update on fixtures for Hooe FC.

An email from Lachlan.

As usual, he'd used a burner email address, and for this one he'd picked the name "Iknowwhatyoudidthissummer," which Phil supposed was funny if you had nothing better to laugh about.

'Btw, once we have finished with J, I have returned to an old mark and acquired a little black book. Let's talk.'

She had no idea what he was going on about. Did he imagine they were now in league together, a little blackmailing duo? The intern and the sandwich boy. She had told Jen about him, of course, since he had enough information to be a useful to the prosecution. But she didn't reveal the full extent of his activities. Let Jen put two and two together. It was her job, after all.

Ah, screw it. What else did she have to do today? She stood in one fluid motion and threw her empty cup into the bin. Maybe afterwards she would try to track down Rhonda's address. She could ask the real Scarlett Stevens to ask her mum. A memory from that night in the office came back. The security guard winking, saying: 'Not got that young fella with you tonight?' At the time, Phil had just assumed it was

Rhonda's useless, stalking ex, but what had Rhonda said when they had lunch? That she and the 'sandwich boy' had a falling out. Phil assumed at the time that it was over the soggy bread. Could *Rhonda* have been this 'mark' Lachlan was talking about?

Surely not. If so, she should find a way to warn her. She messaged Scarlett.

'Weird q: does your mum have Rhonda Whitford's details. Need to speak to her for a thing. Nothing weird.'

Assuming you didn't consider warning someone their sandwich-delivery-guy-slash-lover might be trying to blackmail them was weird.

Maybe she'd do the decent thing and try to go over to Lachlan's and retrieve this little black book of Rhonda's – assuming she was the mark he was talking about. The poor woman deserved better than being humiliated by a man she bought her cheese and pickle sandwiches off.

FORTY-TWO

'Want some wine?' asked Carly.

Jen was processing the information about Rhonda and Mick but she managed a, 'No I'm fine with tea, thanks.'

'I might have one,' said Carly pulling an open bottle of white from the fridge and pouring a glass.

'So Mick was the scary one, right?' said Jen. 'What about the other ones? There was the posh one, the boy toy and… one more.'

'The slob,' said Carly taking a swig of wine. 'He was around the longest. Sorry-looking fella, five-day stubble.' She squinted like she was conjuring his image in her mind's eye. 'He had a nice arse and maybe that was enough for a while, but he couldn't seem to hold onto a job. I think he was a gambling addict.'

Jen wondered if the penny drops counted as gambling.

'Seemed to think he'd cracked the code to the machines at the arcade, or something.'

Carly boiled the kettle again, threw away Jen's cooling tea and put another bag in to make her another cup.

'What was his name? Do you remember?' said Jen.

'Sorry no.'

Jen showed her the photo of Tommy Pearce. 'Was this him?'

Carly peered at the picture and smiled. 'That's the bloke! Oh, what was his name?' She snapped her fingers and said, 'Tommy' just as Jen did.

'What happened to him after they split up, do you know?'

'He kept coming round to pester her,' said Carly, handing her the second tea. This effort was less anaemic. In fact, it was deep bronze. 'Sorry, ran out of fresh milk. Had to use the old one. Should be alright for tea.'

Jen took it with a thank-you as Carly continued. 'Rhonda picks up wrong-uns like they're going out of fashion, you know? Low self-esteem, that's what I always think. She was like fly paper. Wouldn't catch me putting up with men like that. Tommy had been loitering around an awful lot, causing a nuisance, making himself unpopular. Rhonda told me he turned up at her office a few times and made a scene. She was mortified. Rhonda's a very conscientious worker; takes her job very seriously. She would not have liked being made to look like a fool, especially in her senior position.'

'Oh yes,' said Jen. 'That.'

'But one day he stopped coming. Her new fella had convinced him to move to Brighton, apparently. Always assumed that was code for, "beat seven bells of whatsit out of him", if you know what I mean. She made a big song and dance about this other fella but then *he* vanished into the mist as well.'

'So, who was this other man?' said Jen, thinking of Andrew. 'The scary one or the posh one?'

Carly nodded, which did nothing to clarify the situation. 'Apparently, he had a bit of a temper on him – didn't like the problems Tommy was causing. That's what Rhonda said. I think she was scared of him – I used to find her crying occasionally during that time and she'd clam up about it, refuse to say anything. But if I asked if it was problems with *That Fella*, she would purse her lips and nod her head and then I knew, you see. Then I knew that he wasn't treating her right.'

'So... hang on... which one was this? You mentioned a scary one and a posh one. Was it Mick?'

'I think so, yes. But it was like a bus stop round here back then – people were queuing up to ride her. But I'm pretty sure it was Mick. She said he was ready to punch Tommy's lights out, but instead, he'd just given him a fright, you know?'

'A fright?'

'Well, he'd told him, in no uncertain terms, not to come back and to leave them alone. Rhonda said he'd said, "If I see your face round here again, you'll be toast."'

Jen felt it was unlikely he had said those exact words, given they sounded like something from a bad TV show, but she let it slide.

'And was there a fight?'

'I think he might have roughed him up a little. You know, just to make sure the message had been heard loud and clear, sort of thing. I forget now, it was such a long time ago.' She stared off into the middle distance as though recalling something that happened at the dawn of humanity. Jen began to wonder if she had fallen asleep with her eyes open when Carly turned suddenly. 'Anyway, listen, I need a shit and a shine and then I'm off out.'

Jen rose to her feet, thanking Carly for her time. 'I don't suppose you know where Rhonda is, do you?'

'Oh yes,' said Carly, a salacious grin transforming her face. 'Saw her earlier as she was heading out.'

Jen was by now convinced that Carly spent her entire time poised at the front door, ready to jump out and question Rhonda any time she came in or out.

'That boy – the one with the arse cheeks like granite – he gave her a bootie call.'

'The young one?'

'Yeah, Australian fella. She looked like the cat that got the cream when I saw her leave.'

FORTY-THREE

Phil had been about to knock when she heard voices. She had already slipped in through the front door, left on the latch by one of the tenants at some point and no doubt the reason why there were no longer any bikes in the hallway. She had time to wonder if Lachlan's electric sandwich delivery tricycle had been taken, or if he left it round at Arnie's Sarnies HQ on weekends, when she heard the first voice.

Was that Rhonda?

Phil pulled a face. She really didn't want to see the two of them together. She couldn't imagine Rhonda would be keen to see her either – not after today. She was about to walk away when she heard the other voice again.

It wasn't Lachlan.

There was no doubt about it. That wasn't a young Aussie. It was older, with flatter vowels. It took her a moment to place it, but when she did her heart started pounding.

It was Mick.

Quietly, Phil stepped back from the flat's door across the

hall and out into daylight, keen to get away in case someone came out and caught her. Mick and Rhonda together in Lachlan's bedsit? What was happening?

Phil should have just walked away but curiosity got the better of her. Her father's killer was out of jail already and hanging out at Lachlan's with Rhonda. None of it made sense.

She walked stealthily around the side of the house. Lachlan had one of the bigger rooms in the HMO, with two windows and a tiny ensuite bathroom. Phil tried the bathroom window and the sash cord lifted the bottom pane up with a gentle rattle. Whoever had put the stopper in to prevent the window opening too far hadn't done their job properly, and, with a bit of grimacing, Phil managed to thread herself through the gap, landing without too much noise on the dirty linoleum. Lifting her head, she came face to face with the toilet bowl and she held her breath until she had shuffled away from it.

She would have liked to wash her hands, but that meant risking being heard, and there was every chance she would be heard, since the door from the bathroom out into the bedsit was made of plastic and designed to concertina off to one side to maximise space. Instead, she wiped her hands on her jeans and pushed thoughts of Lachlan's stained lino from her mind. From the other room, she could hear Mick and Rhonda talking, his voiced raised in hissing anger, hers low in impatient exasperation.

Painfully, inch by inch, she slid the rickety plastic door open. In front of her, an old wooden room divider hid the bathroom door from the bedroom and created a space where Lachlan had put a clothes rail. Phil crept closer to the divider and peered through a gap in the panels.

Mick stood akimbo, staring down at the floor. Rhonda, by his side, arms folded, was looking at the same thing. Phil tried shifting positions, desperate to see the dark shadow they were both staring at. When she found the right spot, a part of her wished she hadn't. Because there on the floor was Lachlan. And Phil couldn't be sure, but it looked as though he was dead. And standing over him, Mick and Rhonda were deep into an argument.

FORTY-FOUR

Mick wasn't to blame for all this. He'd told himself that a million times. Seven years ago, at St Agnes's school, Rhonda had finished off the job properly. That's what she told Mick as the two of them had peered from the scaffolding down into the darkness of the building. Behind the half-built building, the rock face of the hillside met the scaffolding at the same level. You could step out off the cliff edge straight onto the top floor of the construction, which was how she had managed to appear, entirely uninvited, on the scaffold balcony.

'What did you do that for, you stupid bint?' he shouted.

She seemed surprised.

'I fixed it for you,' she said. 'Now everyone will be happy.'

'How is this fixing it?' he cried. 'You've killed him! We needed him.'

Even now he could remember her ridiculous face, woggling in surprise, unable to understand how he could be so ungrateful. She had followed him to the building site, like some stray dog who doesn't know it's unwanted, and now she was claiming credit for doing his job for him.

'You heard him, he was going to get the council to have the building condemned. It would have destroyed the company.'

Mick couldn't believe what he was hearing. The woman was totally insane. 'But there's a body down there. How is anyone going to sort this now? What do you want them to do? Build around him?'

He suppressed a sudden nervous giggle. It was too ridiculous.

'Oh, grow up, Mick! They were never going to sort the wall ties. The project is nearly finished.'

She was a bloody expert on everything. Even things she knew absolutely nothing about.

He couldn't help peering down into the darkness one more time to see if he could make out the body. How had it gone down that tiny space? It really did beggar belief. He listened, but there were no muffled cries for help.

'I'm going to ring the police,' he said.

'No you're not,' she said quite calmly. He looked at her and she laughed. 'What would you say? "My five-foot-nothing colleague just killed a man?" Do you think they would believe that? Or do you think they'd believe your five-foot-nothing colleague when she tells them that her ex-navy colleague went mad and pushed an innocent man off the scaffolding?' She put on a helpless voice. 'Oh officer, it was dreadful, he just went *berserk*.'

Mick clenched his fists and took a step towards her. 'You what?'

In the face of Mick's anger few people would stand firm, but she barely batted an eyelid.

'Oh, calm down, Mick. I'm not going to tell them that because you're not going to ring them. You're going to leave the way you came, I'm going to leave the way I came, and we're never going to talk about it again.'

That turned out to be a lie, of course.

It came up again a few weeks later when she needed Mick's help.

'What have you done?' he said as she led him into the bedroom, a feeling of dread washing over him. She had the same prim and officious tone she had adopted after she barrelled a surprised Clive off the scaffold, and so he had been right to be suspicious.

The body was lying at an awkward angle on her rug.

'My mother bought that from Littlewoods more than twenty years ago... It'll have to go in the bin now.' She seemed peeved.

'I told him to stop coming around,' she said when she caught Mick's horrified expression. 'What was I supposed to do? You saw how he behaved in the office the other week. He's an embarrassment.'

She'd already had a failed attempt at poisoning him, she said – painkillers in the lasagne – but Doug, his flatmate, had got to it first and spent the night in hospital.

'No one suspected anything – they assumed it was a failed suicide,' said Rhonda. 'Doug was depressed, we all knew that, and he was subletting the flat illegally to Tommy, so he didn't want that getting about. He just gave Tommy a kicking and chucked him out. I expect he assumed Tommy had tried to kill him.' She chuckled at the idea of it. 'Still, Doug's been signed off sick. I expect he'll take a nice retirement pay-off to thank him for his many years of loyal service.'

Nothing gets past her, Mick realised – not for the first time. She probably knew all about the Captain too.

She sniffed in disapproval. 'Typical. He's wet himself. That's just the sort of thing he *would* do. Can't imagine what I ever saw in him.'

And Mick didn't know where to begin forming a response. Eventually he settled on a slightly resigned, 'What are you expecting me to do about all this?'

It was only later that he realised he should have called the police that time. But something in her tone and attitude had caused him to blindly follow her instructions, and once the scales had fallen from his eyes, it was too late. He was an accessory. If she went down, she would find a way to take him with her. And anyway, it turned out it was all more planned than she let on. She had been telling her neighbour for months about her new fella, Mick. She had created quite a tissue of lies that the neighbour believed wholeheartedly. He was the jealous type. Rugged. Ex-navy. He was going to take care of her.

Mick wanted to throttle her.

She had a book where she kept everything, 'For safe-keeping.'

There was the non-disclosure agreement that Mrs Cooke had signed. The notepaper with the school's address and the time and date for the meeting with Clive in Mick's handwriting. She had that too – he knew because she mentioned it in passing one day as though it was a mild curiosity. He had understood what it meant: she had evidence he was at the scene of the murder that day.

She knew about the phone call from the office he'd made to Clive's phone. She'd been in the office. *Earwigging*, he thought with disdain. Later, she took the itemised phone bill out of finance's filing cabinet to keep on record. She told him that, too. And then there was the worst one: 'There's a second eyewitness, Mick,' she said. But she wouldn't tell him anything more than that.

She herself had taken more care when she entered the building, she told him. No one had seen her go in.

Of course they hadn't.

Mick had breathed a sigh of relief when the second witness hadn't been called, but it wouldn't be hard for Rhonda to mention it to any police officer who took her into custody. Not that he imagined they would: he could see her now, pointing a trembling finger across the room at him and pinning the blame on him. 'I came home and they were fighting over me, officer.'

No, like it or not, he was in with her now. He would have to see this through.

And so he had helped her dispose of the body.

'And then we're never speaking about this ever again,' he said. But even then he'd had the sinking feeling that she wouldn't let him go that easily, and now, standing here with the bloody woman, staring at her latest cock up, he realised she never would.

'You stupid cow,' he said.

'He knew too much,' Rhonda said and he looked at her trying to work out if she had lost her marbles.

'How did you do it?' he said, morbid curiosity getting the better of him. 'He's massive.'

Twice her height and half her age.

'Actually, don't tell me,' he said, raising a hand. He could see she was about to reveal all and he realised it would probably involve drugs and a sex game and he really didn't want to have that in his imagination.

'I just need you to help me make it look like suicide,' she said. 'And then we never have to speak again.'

That's what she'd said last time. And the time before that.

'But the police are on to me,' he spluttered, feeling a headache throb out from his temple like a molten bolt. 'This makes me an accessory, or something.'

'He found my little black book,' said Rhonda. 'I did you a favour.'

She looked at him accusingly and narrowed her eyes, 'Did you know they'd found Tommy?' she said. 'Before we were told, I mean.'

'No, I didn't bloody know,' he said.

Although he had. The Captain had summoned him, asking if he knew anything about this second body in the wall. He didn't, he said. Lied to his face, just as he had the first time. Back when Clive died he hadn't wanted to admit that Rhonda had found out about the meeting. It made him look like a fool. Better to let the boss think he had simply been too ruthless.

'I hit him and he lost his balance,' he'd told him.

And the boss had been philosophical.

'Oh well, at least it's taken care of. Probably neater this way.'

The Captain had the council and the police, and everyone else you could care to mention, in hand. Not that he needed to make many phone calls in the event. The police seemed content to cast one lazy eye over the case and put it to bed. The coroner was happy with suicide. An accident. Anything that didn't involve further inquiry. Plus, Virtua got away with the faulty wall *and* got to claim it on insurance.

'It's a shame Lachie died, but there we are,' Rhonda was saying.

'He didn't *die*. You killed him, you daft old bitch,' continued Mick. He honestly wondered if she was a psychopath or just a doddery old woman who couldn't remember accidentally murdering people.

'I'm younger than you, thank you, Mick. Young enough to pull that.'

She pointed at the floor and Mick realised with appalled fascination that in spite of the situation they were in, she was proud of her conquest.

'Sounds like he was bonking anyone with a secret. Or did you think you were special?'

She sniffed and ignored him.

'To be honest, it's a relief. Yes, he's pretty to look at, but the sex was average and after a while, listening to him drone on about sandwiches and titanium bike forks starts to get a little boring. Give me a warm bath and an episode of *Call The Midwife* any day.'

Mick goggled at her and she caught his disbelief.

'He stole my little black book, so he had to go,' she said.

Ah, the little black book. The thing that Rhonda had been holding over his head for all these years. Why hadn't he thought to break in and steal it? He supposed it was because, in spite of the work he had taken on for the Captain, he was a naturally law-abiding type. He had been well suited to the navy. Someone who followed instruction. That was how he had got into this mess in the first place.

My DNA is going to be all over the room, he realised helplessly. He sighed, and a thought came to him: *she'll kill me next.* I know too much too, don't I? She'd probably find a way to frame it as suicide and include a confession for all the other murders while she was at it. That way, she could continue running herself ragged as an office manager for the rest of her life.

The woman was a nutter.

Perhaps he should do it first. The thought surprised him a little and he glanced at her, suddenly nervous she could read his mind. But it wasn't entirely mad, was it? If he killed her, he might stand a chance of living a normal life. He just needed the little black book. Then he could see her off and frame it as some sort of murder-suicide. The black widow, killing off ex-boyfriends. He might even be able to start a rumour that she had been seeing Clive. Why not? Rhonda was constantly fibbing about her love life. She'd claimed an affair with Andrew at one point too. Poor sod. Perhaps with all her lying she had managed to conjure up an actual relationship with Lachlan. Like a twisted Mister Geppetto. Finally, a real boy for the puppetmaster.

'Where's this book then?' he said, trying to sound casual.

She gave him a sidelong glance. 'Safe.'

Bugger, he thought, because he didn't like to swear, but sometimes a swear word was what was needed.

'Did I mention there's an investigation report showing you were at Helenswood school around the time Tommy went missing?' she said. 'I booked that one in... I don't think it came to anything, though. Must have been reported in error. I expect Clive's daughter will have seen the file when she was rifling through all those boxes. I wonder if she will remember? But you needn't worry. I took it all home before the police arrived. Your secret is safe with me, Mick.'

Mick stared at her. Bugger, he thought again. Bugger it all to hell.

'Right,' said Rhonda, 'help me shift this body.'

FORTY-FIVE

Jen rang Nandini.

'I've just had a very interesting conversation,' she said.

'Me too,' said Nandini. 'Andrew Templeton-Dunbar's a dark horse.'

'Let me guess,' said Jen. 'He was having an affair with Rhonda and he killed Tommy?'

'What?' said Nandini. 'No. That's crazy... what makes you say that?' She didn't give Jen a chance to answer. 'No, he told me that Rhonda was seeing Tommy and had felt threatened by him. Tommy had turned up at the office that day to see her, which is why he sent Tommy packing.'

Jen filled her in on the conversation with Carly.

'Wait, so Andrew, Tommy *and* Mick had relationships with Rhonda?'

'And the sandwich boy, if the neighbour's to be believed, which I don't think she is,' said Jen. 'Saying it out loud I'm beginning to suspect Rhonda might be a bit of a fantasist. She told Carly she was head of HR too.'

'So Mick might have done it after all?' said Nandini. 'Killed Tommy in jealousy.'

'Or Andrew,' said Jen.

'But she wasn't sleeping with Ed. So not him?'

'Why would Andrew have killed Clive, though?'

'Why would Mick?' said Jen. 'I mean, either of them could have done it to protect the company, I suppose.'

'Cannot imagine being that loyal to *anyone*,' said Nandini cynically. 'Not even a family member. Way too much hassle.'

'Looks like we need to get Rhonda answering some questions,' said Jen. 'Can you look up the sandwich boy's address? Phil gave it to me.'

There was a muffled sound as Nandini located Jen's interview transcript.

'Lachlan Fraser, Arnie's Sarnies,' Nandini read aloud. She gave Jen the address.

'You invite Mr Templeton-Dunbar back in for a chat,' said Jen. 'We'll speak to Mick afterwards.'

She climbed into her car.

'I'll go and find Rhonda.'

FORTY-SIX

Phil watched in mute horror as Rhonda and Mick attempted to lift Lachlan's body upright. What were they *doing*? Until now, she hadn't been able to see him properly, but now she could, and the realisation hit her: *he's naked*. She watched them wrestling with his nude body and it would have been comical if it hadn't been so awful: Lachlan's perfect form being manhandled into a kneeling position as the two of them puffed and wheezed and bickered.

It took her a moment to see the other rope around his neck. No, she realised, not a rope. Or at least, not what she thought of as a rope – not a thick twine cable like the ropes that hauled in the ships down on the shingle. This was one of those plastic ropes you might use to tie a ladder down to a roof rack. Shiny blue nylon with frayed edges. Somehow that seemed worse. A tacky counterfeit of a noose. Like an afterthought.

She took out her phone and began composing a text, still watching as the pair of them tried to find somewhere to tie the rope. She glanced down to check what she had written and hit send before returning to the morbid sight. They were staging a suicide, she realised. Lachlan would be discovered, noose around his neck, naked. A sex act gone horribly wrong. And a part of her brain seemed to break away and stage a coup over the rest of her, because before she really knew what she was doing, she had stepped out and shouted, 'Leave him alone, for Christ's sake,' as though begging for clemency from torture. And that really hadn't been her intention.

FORTY-SEVEN

The girl was the last thing Mick needed.

'You!' he said, feeling suddenly light-headed. This entire situation just beggared belief. Rhonda had long ago eroded the person he believed he was, but with Phil's appearance he felt the last of his self wash away like a sandcastle. He was an old man wrestling a naked Adonis into a staged suicide. He was a helpless sap rolling a homeless man into a Littlewoods rug. He was a blackmailer staring down a wall cavity for a lost father.

He had been a good Royal Navy man. He had done his duty by his country. He had landed a decent job and lived a decent life. Yes, he had gambled a little too much. Yes, he hadn't been the best husband to his ex-wife, but he had taken care of his daughter when she asked for money – if he had it, that is – and he had been a good grandad.

This wasn't who he was.

He had only taken on a bit of extra work from the Captain to pay back those gambling debts. How was he to know it would end this way? And suddenly he wanted to reach over and knock Scarlett, or whatever her name was – *the McGinty girl* – to the ground. Not to hurt her, but to stop her being a witness to this obliteration of his identity, this travesty to his life. He opened his mouth, hoping an explanation would come. Nothing did.

'What the hell are you doing?' the girl said.

In the event, an explanation wasn't necessary. Rhonda, quick as a lizard, had darted over to the girl and belted her round the head with her handbag. The girl staggered like a marathon runner at the finishing line and Mick watched as she reached forwards, as though hoping an invisible chair might stop her fall. It didn't. She landed heavily, face pressed to the floor, not quite unconscious, but dazed enough for Rhonda to scuttle over and tie her hands behind her back.

'What the hell do you have in that bag?' said Mick.

'Looks like it's a murder-suicide,' Rhonda said, as though she was adding an item to today's agenda.

'Over my dead body,' said Mick. Rhonda shot him a look that said, 'Yes, if you like,' and carried on tying the rope around Phil's wrists.

If she kills me, thought Mick, what scene will she stage to explain it away? Probably Mick would be the villain of the piece. That was obvious. After all, he was currently the prime suspect in two murder investigations. And, of course, Phil and Lachlan would be the innocents. Two lovers brought down by a local serial killer. A psychopath of the highest order.

'Why?' he heard himself say. He was watching her fiddling about with the knots before returning to Lachlan.

She looked up at him sharply. 'What do you mean?'

'Why do you do it? What's in it for you? Do you think the company will thank you? Is that it? A promotion?'

'Oh Mick,' said Rhonda, blithely. 'I don't do this for the thanks. I do it because it's the right thing to do.'

He stared at her, waiting for her words to make sense, knowing that they never would.

'If a job's worth doing, it's worth doing properly. You were asked to fix a problem and you made such a hash of it, I had to come in to sort it for you. And then afterwards I had to clear up the loose ends too. Things have all escalated from your incompetence. So get over here and help me and once this is all cleared up we can get back to normal life.'

'Normal life?' he said, his voice rising to a shrill top note. '*Normal life?* What normal life? You've killed three people and you're about to kill a fourth. That's not normal!'

She shrugged then, as though he were talking about irrelevancies. *I can't believe I'm here* he wanted to scream. But instead, he walked over and began helping to shift the sandwich boy.

FORTY-EIGHT

She was looking through a frosted window.

For a moment, Phil wondered if she had lost her vision, that the blow had shattered her lens like a bus shelter, but then she blinked, and the tear that had been distorting her view trickled down and over the bridge of her nose, and she could see again.

She was lying on the floor, cheek abutting Lachlan's grubby carpet in an unwilling tango. She closed her eyes as the headache lodged a complaint with her consciousness. And suddenly, the headache was all consuming, as though it had been biding its time in the wings and was finally taking its moment on stage, all bright lights, and thundering tap shoes and a soprano hitting a piercing top C.

She would have wondered what was in Rhonda's handbag that could mete out such a punishing head injury if she hadn't been too distracted by the sight of Rhonda and Mick tying Lachlan's noose to the ceiling. Like many of these old houses, the HMO had once known the grandeur of Victorian decor, and some remnants remained, including the ceiling rose (now illuminated by a single dusty bare bulb) and the hook that would have held a chandelier. Mick was standing on a side table on top of a chair and the ensemble wobbled dangerously as he tried to push the rope over the hook using a pair of barbecue tongs. Tall as he was, it was still a reach, but he managed it eventually and Rhonda, very much the foreman of proceedings, looked on as though directing a play. One hand cupping her chin while the other pinched her hip.

'Now let's bring Scarlett over to the bed,' she was saying. 'If, she discovered him dead, let's have her killing herself there... Or should it be the bathroom?'

This was to be a creative collaboration, then. Phil would have liked to pipe up with her own suggestion – 'How about the plucky heroine actually runs off into the sunset, unharmed?' – but her head was still coming to terms with the tap dancing opera singer in her brain and the only noise she could currently make was a mash-up between a moan and a whimper.

'Girlfriend comes in, finds boyfriend has died in a sex act gone wrong and, heartbroken, she decides to end it all as well.' Rhonda pursed her lips, 'Well, it will have to do.'

Mick said nothing, merely looked at her with unmasked disgust and carried on trying to get the rope to stay in Lachlan's hands. It was impossible so he left it and let it hang nearby, as though Lachlan's death had set the rope free from his grip – too late to save him.

'Scarlett, I do wish you hadn't got yourself into this mess,' said Rhonda loudly, as though Phil were deaf. 'It's made the whole thing so untidy. And you should be out there living your life. Not wallowing in the past. Talk about repeating the sins of the father. He couldn't keep his nose out either, could he, and look where that got him. Everything would have been a lot simpler if you had just carried on with your nice career. It sounds like you've done well for yourself.' She sighed, her voice dropping low. 'I would have liked to have heard more about that.'

She seemed to mull something over. 'I suppose I should have paid more attention to what Clive's family was up to, come to think of it. If I had, I would have known right away that you weren't Scarlett. I didn't think the name suited you. He had a little boy too, didn't he? I shall have to keep an eye out for him. I wouldn't want another problem on my hands.'

Phil didn't answer. The opera singer had started clanging a bell now, sending out fragments of sound and vision as though her mind was stuck inside a kaleidoscope. She would give anything for a couple of paracetamol and a soft pillow. Maybe an ice pack. But Rhonda had mentioned her brother and now Phil wasn't just afraid: she was angry.

Rhonda returned to stage-managing the suicide and Phil shook herself into order. She started trying to shunt her body down towards where her phone had fallen when Rhonda had lamped her. She was inching along like a caterpillar, making steady progress, hoping to reach the phone before they noticed. She could see the screen light up as a call came in. On silent, thankfully, but not for long. If the caller tried again, her phone would override the silence and Rhonda and Mick would turn to see Phil, a toenail's width from hooking her phone with the edge of her foot. The screen went dark and Phil sent up a silent prayer that the caller would give up.

She scraped her toe against the top of the handset and watched in frustration as it slid further away. Laboriously, she began her caterpillar motion again, shunting herself as quietly as she could. If she was any kind of proper investigative journalist, she thought, she would have some kind of file or knife strapped to her inside leg that she could use to free herself. But really, who expected the editorial assistant for the *Aldhill Observer* to be captured by a psychopathic office manager and her lackey? She wiggled her way down further, feeling the grit from the carpet leaving scratches on her cheek. This time she managed to toe the phone closer to her thigh. Then she bent her knee and used the back of her foot to push it behind her towards her tied hands. Then what? No idea; no idea beyond a vague notion that perhaps she could alert the authorities before Rhonda could wrestle the phone from her grasp. She kept edging closer.

A sound distracted her and she looked over at Rhonda and Mick in alarm, trying to work out where the noise had come from. But Mick and Rhonda hadn't noticed; they were still fashioning the rig for the elaborate sex act. Given the work that was going into it, Phil had to applaud anyone who would actually go to this much trouble just to get off.

The sound came again, and this time Phil managed to locate it. DS Jen Collet was creeping along the side of the room divider towards her. Sight for sore eyes didn't begin to cover it. The detective put her finger to her lips – an unnecessary manoeuvre since Phil's brain still hadn't fully reestablished the connection with her vocal chords. She stopped worming along and tried to signal with her eyes that Jen should peek through the gap. Jen nodded, clearly already aware.

Probably not good to get caught trying to semaphore with your eyes, Phil decided. She tried to lie more casually, as though by staying extra still she could cancel out the small noises Jen was making as she edged along the divider.

'What was that?' said Rhonda, turning like a prairie dog

to an eagle call. Phil tried to cover for Jen, raising her bum up and groaning. Rhonda looked down at her. 'Sorry about all this, Scarlett. It's not ideal, I know.'

Phil's groan turned to a whimper and Rhonda stepped towards her. 'Everything alright? That was quite a bump on the head, wasn't it? You probably have a concussion, poor thing.'

Rhonda turned back to her crime scene and caught DS Jen Collet out the corner of her eye.

'You!' was all Rhonda managed before Phil, in desperation, rolled herself as hard as she could into Rhonda's legs and the office manager fell backwards, landing heavily on Phil's back.

Phil made a noise somewhere between the whine of a deflating balloon and a lost cow lowing in a field. Before she could regain her breath, Jen had a handcuff on Rhonda and was pulling her arm up behind her to fix on the other. She pressed a knee into the office manager's back to keep her down. And Phil, more than anything, wished this wasn't all happening on top of her. Oxygen suddenly seemed like an unfathomable luxury. A shadow loomed.

'Jen!' Phil managed to croak, but Mick was already behind the detective. He grabbed Jen in a bear hug and picked her from the pile on. Freed a little, Phil rolled out from under Rhonda, gasping for air as she clambered awkwardly to her feet. Rhonda lurched like a zombie towards Jen and Mick just as Jen threw her head back and smashed Mick hard in the face, his nose sending out a spray of blood before Jen elbowed him in the solar plexus. Before Rhonda could join the fray, Phil barrelled into her, sending the office manager crashing into Mick, who toppled like an oak.

A millisecond too late, Dean Martin crashed into the

room, along with a team of uniformed officers with plastic shields.

'Phil!' he shouted, racing over and helping her to her feet. Phil was dazed from her collision with Rhonda, but she staggered to her feet and Dean guided her towards the hallway. She followed but kept her head turned towards the scene, unable to tear herself away. She could see Jen being helped to her feet by a policeman while officers arrested Mick and Rhonda. Rhonda began howling.

'He made me do it,' she cried, bubbles of snot bursting from her nose. 'It was him. He forced me.'

Mick looked disgusted. 'You're a bloody psycho.'

And suddenly Phil didn't want to be anywhere near them – and she didn't want to see Lachlan's prone, naked body, kneeling like a supplicant, head face down on the rug, surrounded by this chaos. She allowed Dean to lead her from the room and out into daylight.

AFTERWARDS

FORTY-NINE

'Well done,' said Petra, her skin pulled so tight into an attempt at a smile that Jen half expected to hear a creak. They were standing in the DCI's office, Jen seated while Lee stood behind, Petra looming from across the desk despite being seated, perched on the end of her swivel chair as though afraid it might try to swallow her.

Of course, the DCI was truly irritated that Jen had created such merry hell, leaving them trying to explain to the Super why he hadn't been given more warning. Jen didn't blame her. She would have liked more warning too. She had been on her way to speak to Rhonda and Lachlan – a two for one! – when Phil's desperate text had come in.

'Rhonda's killed Lachlan. Mick's here too.'

Desperate, but still correctly punctuated, Jen noted. If she had died, Phil would have been safe in the knowledge that her final message to the world was grammatically sound. *Stupid kid.* Jen shook her head at the thought of her. But who could blame her, really? In the same situation, Jen would have done no different. After all, if the police had no plans to bring her father's killers to justice, why should she sit at home weeping?

In that moment, hands on her knees as she awaited Petra's next proclamation, she made a decision. Or, rather, she began the process of making a decision. She was going to live this life the best way she could, Nate or no Nate. And that didn't mean forgetting about him. It didn't even mean not falling to pieces any time she heard 'Witchita Lineman' on the radio, or caught sight of his ridiculously over-priced breakfast cereal on offer in the supermarket (and fought the urge to stockpile on his behalf). No, this was about a plan they had made together for the future. A plan that was currently languishing in the freezers of a Tunbridge Wells fertility clinic.

One day, she thought, she might also have a plucky young crusader, ready and willing to avenge *her* death should she ever be unlucky enough to be shoved down a cavity wall and left for dead.

'It doesn't really bear thinking about, does it?' said Petra, not for the first time. She was flicking through the photos again, peering down at the folder on her desk as though she was seeking a lost contact lens.

'No,' agreed Jen. But she had thought about it. She had thought about it a lot: seven years ago when Clive McGinty's broken body was first pulled from the wreckage, and this fortnight, when the vestiges of what had once been Tommy Pearce had tumbled out onto the school playing field like the jackpot at Luckyland. She had thought about it a lot.

'We're still not sure we're going to have enough to tie the two of them to Clive's death, unfortunately' said Petra.

'We?' said Jen, her blood turning to ice.

'Yes, the Super and I have been looking at what we have

so far, and I'm just not convinced... Without the eyewitness. He doesn't look like he'll be recovering any time soon, does he? Mrs Cooke's still missing somewhere in Wales. And who knows how long she has left, what with the shock of all this police attention... We're not sure it's enough.'

'But we have Rhonda's black book,' said Jen, utterly flummoxed.

'True, but much of it reads like the ravings of a mad woman,' said Petra. 'She never had any relationship with Andrew Templeton-Dunbar. He has alibis for nearly all the dates she claims they went on. For one of them he was in the Maldives.'

As if Jen didn't know this. 'But the phone records and the other documents? Mrs Cooke's non-disclosure agreement? The note in Mick's handwriting? The call from Mick's desk to Clive's phone?'

'I'm just not convinced any of that will stick,' said Petra, pressing her hands down on the folder. 'Clive wasn't dead when he went into the wall. There's no DNA evidence to connect them to the scene. The phone call can be explained as one colleague ringing another. And the NDA? I think you already know that won't get us anywhere.'

She was talking about Dee Dee's connection to Mrs Cooke. Nandini had discovered it. It turned out Dee Dee's cousin was Mrs Cooke's goddaughter. Dee Dee swore blind she had no idea, 'I barely speak to those cousins, they think they're better than us, and who the hell knows people's godparents? I only met my own godmother once that I can remember? Auntie Shona was an old alchy who gave me a silver bracelet and then moved to Lincolnshire, wherever that is.' Whatever her protests, it didn't look great: as a witness she'd gone from bad to terrible.

Petra was still talking. 'No, I think we are best off with the two murders for which we have clear evidence. As you know, SOCO has found some very promising fibres and stains on a rug in Rhonda's flat which might well connect her directly with Tommy Pearce's murder. And, of course, we have poor Lachlan Foster.'

'But...' began Jen, feeling suddenly desperate.

'It's enough to get them both put away, Jen. And for a very long time. I'd call that a very good job. Like I said: *Well done.*'

She would have left it there normally – would have swallowed her rage and drowned it with a glass of wine later on. But there was no Nate at home to offload it on, and she was feeling mutinous.

'This is a load of absolute bullshit and you know it,' she said.

Petra blinked like a surprised owl. 'Now, Jen,' she began.

'Jen,' said Lee at the same time, roused into life at last.

'No,' interrupted Jen, silencing them both with a glare. 'This whole thing stinks like bin day. Don't try to tell me you haven't had a call from on high about this, because I won't believe you. And don't expect me to stop looking at this case. You might be too cowardly to pursue it, but I sure as shit am not. I couldn't give a rat's fig what they think of me.'

She stormed out.

This is who I used to be, she remembered, before Nate: angry, full of fire, ready to take on all-comers. He'd mellowed her and it had felt good at the time, but now she wanted to feel what it was like to be fuelled by the fire of righteous indignation. Phil McGinty had reminded her of how good it was to really care. Telling Petra and Lee what she thought would do her no favours at all, but screw the lot of them.

Still, she thought, ruefully, her step quickening a little in embarrassment, shame about the 'rat's fig.' She'd have to work on her zingers.

'They're what?' said Nandini. Grant and Dean were listening too. Lee, almost silent throughout the meeting, had made himself scarce without mentioning Jen's outburst, muttering something about needing to update the DCI on another case before scuttling off towards whatever fox hole he hid in while the time to his retirement ticked by.

Jen pressed her fingers between her eyebrows. 'Yep. They think the CPS will reject the Clive McGinty evidence as too circumstantial.'

'But surely there's enough of it? There's enough circumstantial evidence to add up to a conviction?'

Jen shrugged. 'Apparently not.'

'This is bullshit.'

'I might have mentioned that to Petra,' said Jen.

They were wrong – clearly they were wrong – but they were also lying. The DCI had presented evidence to the Crown Prosecution Service that was weaker than this before. It wasn't about the evidence. Something political was going on.

'They just don't want to look like knobs,' said Nandini.

'Too late for that,' said Jen, still feeling rebellious.

Grant had already turned back to his desk. It didn't pay to slag off the bosses in front of an arse kisser like Grant: he'd be trotting off to tell his tale as soon as Lee emerged from his hidey hole.

This was a political decision, that was for sure, but Jen wasn't convinced it was all about saving face. Sure, it would be an embarrassment to admit they had messed up in the Clive McGinty initial investigation, but Phil McGinty was hardly going to let them sidle off whistling innocently any time anyone mentioned Clive's name. No, this felt like it was about protecting someone higher up the food chain. Jen was willing to bet there was an organ grinder behind Mick's monkey who had a lot of clout in the local area.

Thoughts of Philippa McGinty made her suddenly gloomy.

'Oh god,' she said. 'Who's going to tell Phil McGinty?'

They all looked away and Jen nodded to herself.

'Me, then.'

FIFTY

'Phil, do you ever think about having a day off?'

Dean Martin and a fellow officer had just apprehended the Phantom-Poo-Fiend-Fairy-Father-Shitmas (she really needed to settle on a name), and now he was casting a raised eyebrow in her direction, clearly amused.

'That would be nice,' she said.

It had been easy, in the end, to catch him. All those nights spent seeing nothing, she had finally borrowed a couple of security cameras off a mate on the estate and spent the evening chatting to Simon's wife Debbie in the comfort of the living room, one eye on the live feed. Debbie, having been kicked out of the hospital when visiting hours were over, was glad of the company.

'Something to keep my mind off everything,' she said.

'Yes,' agreed Phil, although she didn't elaborate. She figured Debbie didn't need to hear about her week spent investigating her father's death, nor her arrest. And she certainly didn't need to hear about how she had nearly been murdered by the same deranged office manager who had killed her dad. There was probably quite enough horror in Debbie's life right now, what with the MRIs and the treatment plan and the smell of hospital.

'I'm not sure Simon's going to be quite the same after this,' Debbie said, glancing to the sky to stop the tears.

'I'll get us some Hobnobs,' said Phil.

In the end, as the hours passed, she did tell Debbie about her week. Met with such a calmly piercing gaze, which seemed to settle on her in the silences, she found herself confessing as though Debbie had asked her outright. It was a relief to talk to someone who wasn't a police officer, or – worse – her mother, all of whom wanted to let her know how foolish she had been and how lucky she was to be alive.

Debbie had listened in placid equanimity, as though people told her that many outrageous stories all the time. She didn't interrupt – not even to exclaim at the stupidity of climbing through a window to save a dead man from murderers. Phil didn't explain the full details, she didn't think Debbie needed to know about auto-erotic asphyxiation, or the full perversion of Rhonda's plan. Nor did she think it helpful to detail how she had lain there, head throbbing, truly believing she was going to die, imagining how her family would feel being told that she had killed herself, wondering if the police would ever work out the truth.

'It sounds like you've had quite a week,' said Debbie in the end.

'Yes,' she agreed and was surprised by the fat tears that welled in her eyes.

'It must be a relief,' Debbie said, 'to know that you have found out the truth at last.'

But she hadn't. Not really. Mick must have been instructed to handle her father's death. There was still someone out there who had given the instruction. Still someone out there who knew what had happened. She realised as Rhonda and Mick were led away, that she felt very far from relieved.

They would have continued the conversation, but Phil noticed something on the camera. Two shadows passing Simon's geraniums by the front drive.

'It's him,' she hissed, recognising the tall man and the short dog. They waited, breath bated, as the pair crossed the road to the fateful rowan tree beyond. The dog squatted to do its business. They watched the man watching the dog. They watched as he placed a bag over one hand and stooped to gather the steaming mess. They watched as he deftly tied a knot in the bag and reached up to place the bag on an outstretched finger of a branch like he was pegging out laundry.

'We've got him!' said Phil. She had time, in those seconds, to register the look of sadness in Debbie's eyes and feel herself respond in kind. Simon would be gutted to miss out, she thought. But she wasn't going to let him get away this time. She grabbed her camera and raced out of the door.

She found herself going full paparazzo when she reached him, shouting for comment and barking questions as she filmed, the light from her DSLR blinding him as he raised an arm like a man witnessing an alien spacecraft. She dogged his every step as he tried to move first one way then the other, and the pair of them zigzagged along the path in an awkward waltz. Debbie, who had presumably taken a moment to call the police, emerged and loudly asked him what he thought he was playing at. Her neighbour soon joined her and began rousing others to the cause. Soon the entire street was filled with angry neighbours, all indignant, cardigans pulled around cold arms, slippers still on, PJs skimming the tarmac.

The Fiend, seemingly indignant at this molestation, retreated up the path, his little dog, trotting alongside, entirely unbothered by the crowd.

'Do you have a vendetta against someone on the estate?' Phil heard herself say. 'Do you know that Simon is in hospital right now?' As though the Fiend had been the cause of Simon's collapse. Perhaps he had, she decided. And anyway, she was not about to feel guilty about turning slightly gutter press in this moment. This man deserved nothing better.

She was following him down the dark footpath now, many of the neighbours having abandoned the chase, seemingly satisfied they had seen him off. A few remained with her, however, following more quietly now, as though waiting to hear what he had to say for himself.

It was only as they emerged out onto the trading estate carpark that Phil remembered about the doggers. The light from her camera caught the surprised faces of the voyeurs and bleached the pale bottom of the uppermost dogger inside the car. The dogger turned, a look of horror on his pale visage like a stone grotesque clinging to a cathedral.

'Goodness,' said Debbie.

Later, when the police had arrived and taken away the Poo Fiend (real name Benji Maddox) as well as a vanful of indignant doggers, Phil reflected that the night could easily have turned nasty ('No cameras' being a central tenet of the dogging credo). It was only the sight of a group of middle-aged to elderly folk in their pyjamas that had stayed their rage, sending them into shuffling embarrassment. Phil couldn't be one hundred per cent sure, but she was convinced she had heard an old lady in a quilted dressing gown cry, 'Oh, I say!' as she caught sight of the tableau.

After he'd taken her statement, Dean drove her home, his chuckles turning to seriousness as the journey progressed.

'Are you ok?' he said.

'Oh, you know me,' she replied. 'I'm always ok.'

FIFTY-ONE

There would be no story.

Phil had shouted and raged and eventually cried, but Adam Jenkins was unmoved.

'It's not my decision,' he said. 'It's out of my hands. The publisher said no, the bastards in legal said no, the sales team has said no, too. It's not going to happen Philippa, I'm sorry. That's the way things go sometimes... you can't get them all, you know? You'll get a tougher skin eventually.'

'Tougher skin?' said Phil, so angry she could feel herself trying not to reach out and throttle the little tosser. 'My dad was pushed down a wall cavity and left to die slowly and painfully to save a company's reputation, the police are refusing to charge his murderers for it, and you're telling *me* to get a tougher skin?'

Adam raised his hands in submission. 'Wrong choice of words... Look, I'm sorry about your dad, I really am. It's awful... AWFUL... but we've got no evidence, Phil. We need evidence. There's no proof about the wall ties at St Agnes because the wall was taken down to get Clive out. You admitted yourself that the original health and safety report is lost somewhere and your only witnesses are either nearly dead, missing or not speaking. If we start speculating on more victims in the case, the police will be on us faster than you can say contempt of court.'

Phil wasn't listening. She was standing with her arms folded and one foot tapping on the floor, concentration creating two furrows at her brow.

'It's someone higher up than the publisher isn't it?' she said. She looked up at Adam and realised she was onto something. 'Yeah, someone higher up. Who is it, Adam? Let me guess, one of the paper's owners has a stake in Virtua Services, am I right? Or maybe one of them plays golf with Chairman? All these old duffers play golf. They get to pick and choose what the public gets to hear about, don't they? It's just another game to them.'

Adam rolled his eyes and sighed, 'You sound like a bad action movie.'

'But it's true isn't it?'

Adam had the decency to look a little guilty. 'Look, I concede you may be onto something – don't tell anyone I said that or I'll have you writing the local listings for the next six years – but there's nothing we can do. If you had a better, tighter story, if you had a witness on record or a scrap of evidence, I could fight it. No one could stop us running it. But I'm not prepared to get sued, to risk the paper, on something we can't defend. If we're going to get into clichés, I've got mouths to feed. I'm responsible for all of you.'

Phil turned away and tried to stop the tears from flowing. It had all been a giant waste of time. There was no way to prove any of it and now her father's death would be unpunished. Mick and Rhonda would go to prison for killing

Lachlan and – assuming the police could prove it – Tommy, but the police weren't going to charge them for her dad's murder. She wasn't even convinced they were looking into the leadership team. Gloria Reynolds would continue raking in the big money without a care in the world, and Phil would go back to writing about dog shit in the local community. What a massive waste of time.

'I think I need a holiday,' she said.

'Well then, you've got another think coming,' said Adam.

'Don't give up.'

That advice came from Barry Brooker of all people. Her arch nemesis (in her mind, at least. In his mind, she suspected, there was total indifference and more pressing thoughts about scotch eggs and Megan Fox). Of course he had been given the Mick and Rhonda story, much to Phil's utter disgust ('God knows we don't need you out there being gobby, getting us fined every time you open your mouth,' said Adam), and now he was leaning back in his swivel chair, the recliner setting being challenged to its full extent. He had watched her come out of her meeting and, if he wasn't exactly lending a friendly shoulder to cry on – which was just as well giving the number of dubious stains on his shirt, coupled with his odour of pickled onion *Monster Munch* and stale sweat – nor even any real sympathy, he was at least offering some constructive feedback.

'You give in too easily,' he continued. 'Stories get killed all the time. Big boo hoos. Now you've got to decide what to do about it. If it's a good enough story, you can look at taking it somewhere else. If it's not a good enough story, you can start making it better... If you don't want it to die, you've got to make it less easy to kill. And I'll tell you this for free, the story isn't good enough.' He raised a hand as Phil began to protest. 'I'm not saying it's not a gripping tale... of course it is, I'm just saying it's got more holes than Korean sex aid. You need to start over and look at everything. You need to–'

'Please tell me you're not going to say "follow the money,"' said Phil. She groaned. 'You were, weren't you?'

Barry gave her a defensive look and continued, 'Why was your dad killed? Because someone wanted to save a few quid, right? But it was more than that; it must have been. If they'd been caught, there would have been fines, they'd have to rebuild the block, but that's pittance to them. So what's the bigger picture here? Who stands to lose so much they'd be willing to kill for it?'

Phil thought she'd answered all those questions. The building company was trying to save face, they didn't want to get caught in charge of a building that could kill children, and the obvious solution was to create a scapegoat. But that's not what had happened, was it? The wall had come tumbling down and the public was none the wiser. But there were better ways to avoid getting caught: flinging a body down there was far too labour intensive. The words stuck in her craw.

'You're right,' she managed.

'Always am,' he said and burped loudly.

FIFTY-TWO

'The local newspaper's here,' said Jaqueline as she walked out the door. She had patted Betty and told her she loved her, Andrew noticed, then shut the door without saying goodbye. He sighed and got to his feet to retrieve the paper.

A week ago, the story had been all about Rhonda and Mick's arrest for the murder of a young Australian sandwich boy (who had taken over the deliveries after Andrew had left). They were also being questioned in connection with the murder of Tommy Pearce, a local builder. There was no mention of Clive McGinty. The story had shocked him beyond measure.

They had been under his nose the entire time and he hadn't spotted anything untoward. Yes, he imagined there might be some cover-up going on, what with Gloria's interest and Clive's accident, but the idea that there were two murderers working in the company beggared belief. He had written a piece on LinkedIn about his shock – and about how it showed you could never truly know a person. The concept of 'bring your whole self to work' took on a slightly sinister hue when your co-workers were serial killers.

Now the paper was more interested in a man who had been throwing dog's mess into trees and Andrew noted with fatherly pride the name of the journalist behind the scoop. Phil McGinty.

Almost out of habit he began searching for the puzzles page, but another story caught his eye. There on page five was a photo of Jamie. Andrew read the article in some satisfaction. Jamie had resigned from her role has head of HR and Administration after Virtua Services had been referred to the ombudsman for hiding customer complaints letters from the auditors. There were noises about legal action for fraud, but Andrew doubted it would come to that. These overseers were notoriously toothless. He was surprised they had even roused themselves to issue a fine, though of course it was a paltry sum.

He roused the computer and logged on to Linkedin to see what gossip he could uncover. Mary had changed her title to 'Chief HR Officer' – good for her – and Dee Dee's boss was taking full oversight of Customer Services and Investigations. Far more sensible.

Andrew had left Jamie's bin bag on the auditor's doorstep. Like a lazy postman, he thought to himself. It amused him, despite the seriousness of the situation. He was a bad Santa, leaving a sack full of unread letters out for the auditors to find, putting Virtua Services on their naughty list. It was a present of sorts, he supposed. It was their job after all, to root out wrongdoing, to leave no letter behind. They were the heroes of complainers everywhere. How would the world function without them? He supposed he was being facetious, but he meant it too. Why shouldn't those voices be heard?

He thought of all the people who had waited to hear back, never receiving anything. He wondered how many of them had tried again; how many had given up in despair and got on with their lives. Fixed their own broken walls, glued together their damaged garden gnomes, spent an hour on the phone trying to organise a man with a van to take away the rubble from their front drive. He thought of the time he had spent – days probably, if you counted it all up – doing tedious, soul-sapping life admin: the wasted minutes spent listening to hold music; the fractious conversations to a bored minion in a call centre who didn't give a hoot; the time spent conversing with bots on company websites.

It was all designed to sap your will to live.

Just finding the time in your day to write a letter or email of complaint was an accomplishment, another thing checked off a dull to-do list between the collecting of dry cleaning and the booking of a dental appointment. But the powers-that-be hadn't even troubled themselves with a response. The older he got, the more he thought about it. We all joke about the 'hours of my life I'll never get back,' but really it was true. That time had been stolen from these individuals. He didn't mind so much about the smashed gnomes and the broken walls. It was the *time* that got his goat.

Someone had to pay.

And it was his fault, he supposed, when you thought about it. He had put Jamie into a position of power. He had asked her to stand in as customer complaints manager when Joy had retired. Of course, it had been a wildly big promotion for someone so newly arrived at the company, but he had liked her. She had clung onto the role after he left, making herself in charge of anything and everything in sight. No wonder the rest of the leadership team hadn't invited her up to their floor. They were probably afraid she'd be after their jobs next; they were probably right.

He had confessed his sins to the detectives and felt all the better for it. Jen Collet had cut him off when he claimed the deaths were his fault. 'Well, we know that isn't true,' she said. But he had pressed the point. 'Spiritually it is, and it happened on my watch.'

Rhonda and Mick.

Who would have believed it? And Rhonda a fantasist, telling the world she was in a relationship with him. The HR rules it would have contravened – *my god!* – he honestly couldn't believe it when the detective told him. *Rhonda?* He thought of her, barrelling around the office, taking on everyone's work, doing a wonderful job but treading on so many toes the whole office limped.

He didn't like to admit it, but he had been faintly insulted at the idea he would have had a relationship with someone like Rhonda. Jacqueline was a statuesque beauty. A vision in tweed. He would never stray.

Should he have noticed, he wondered? He felt he should have. He had employed Rhonda; Mick had been presented as a fait accompli by Gloria – an instruction that came from even higher up, apparently. But still, they had been his responsibility. Perhaps he could have stopped it somehow, if he had just paid more attention. He'd mentioned similar to Jacqueline, but she had simply rolled her eyes and headed off to take a bath.

Still, they were caught now. The justice system would

take care of them. And he had done what he could for the business and for his people.

'Well, Betty,' he said as the dog padded in, 'I suppose all is right with the world. Shall we wander down to the sea and get a coffee?'

FIFTY-THREE

Phil stared at her name on the front of the newspaper. It had been a few days since Jen had told her the bad news and then Adam made it worse by insisting her story about Clive would never run. Adam had given her the day off and then, when she returned, encouraged her to write up the story of the Phantom Poo Fiend and her week on the hunt.

'I'm giving it front page,' he told her when he'd finished reading it.

Phil wished she could savour the triumph a little more. She went through the motions, putting up with everyone teasing her, cracking a few bad puns herself, but really she just wanted to go home, climb under a duvet and weep.

She was meant to be interviewing someone from Simon's estate about life now that Benji Maddox had been toppled from his reign of terror, but instead she walked down to the shoreline at Bexhill and stood on the marbled clay rocks as the tide turned. She thought about everything she had been through. The stress of faking her identity, the horrors of being discovered, the near-death experience in a bedsit, and the sight of Simon, still lying in a hospital bed.

The weather was cool. Scarlett Stevens would be long gone from the beach. Her week of skiving had brought her a heap of new profile pics, sunburn and #NoRegrets. Shame Phil couldn't jump back into Scarlett's life and really live it properly this time. After all, what had she got for her efforts? A lump on her head the size of a tennis ball and flashbacks to Lachlan's lifeless body every time she closed her eyes.

'I let you down, dad,' she murmured to the waves.

She made a silent promise then. She would take Barry's advice; she wouldn't give up. She would find out the truth behind Clive's death, would tell the world. If the police weren't going to help, alone would have to do. Even if it meant tracking down everyone who knew what had happened to her dad and making sure they paid for it.

She turned from the sea and started walking back along the stones to the promenade. Angela would be waiting for her, eager to celebrate her cover story. She crossed over the road and started up the hill towards Roosevelt Court.

ACKNOWLEDGMENTS

This book could not have happened without the following excellent humans. Darika, who gave me the courage to keep going. Caroline, who read it (and said nice things) even after I'd spoiled the ending. My friend and editor, Sophie, who offered guidance, support and a selection pack of tea. I couldn't have asked for three better cheerleaders.

Philip Heys, the HSO who insists he's grumpy on-site, but is only ever cheerful as he tells me eye-popping horror stories (whether or not I want to hear them) and who, in doing so, inadvertently gave me the central idea. Thank you! Thanks also to Chris Everest, who didn't escape when I sidled over at our daughters' football matches to ask advice on how East Sussex Police works. Any mistakes in the vagaries of building regs or police procedure are entirely my own.

Kath Middleton, Catherine Santamaria, Rosie Bray and Mo Prowse for their invaluable feedback and kindness. Thanks also to my lovely Substack subscribers, who have joined me on this Top Secret Project and laughed at my jokes.

And, of course, my husband Alex Milway. Not only my partner in crime, but also the provider of amazing dinners. I love you.

JOIN ME FOR MORE
ALDHILL MYSTERIES!

There's a lot of fun to be had over on my website, so come join the Lyttle League and get all the news, stories and exclusive content.

www.kjlyttleton.com

Jen and Phil return in *A Star Is Dead* – out now.

Printed in Great Britain
by Amazon